Once Again

Tales of Destiny

Book One

M. Kari Barr

HeartString Publishing
a Division of Stone Creek Farms
P.O. Box 734
Airway Heights, WA 99022

First Edition: September 2018

Printed in the United States of America

ISBN: 13: 978-1-7321401-0-3

In Remembrance of Mama,

for the love of words

she taught me.

Contents

Mara as told in her own words

The city bus arrived. After boarding, I turned toward the window to gaze at the scene one last time. The guy I dubbed 'Mr. Sunshine' glanced up and smiled—rakishly.

Back then I practiced the art of denial. I was unlike any of my classmates. In a way, I felt ostracized. All my young life weird experiences happened to me, things no one else noticed or saw. By eight or nine I had learned to keep my mouth shut; except, of course, for talking to myself. I came to accept that others did not see glitter floating through the air, or light emanating off of people. Never mind ogres and trolls. Over the years I barely even registered seeing these things anymore.

For my eyes alone, Mr. Sunshine exuded first a golden aura followed by a purple afterglow that I found particularly enchanting. *Admit it, Sweetie, the reason photography captured you as a little girl was to prove to Mom that fairies are real,* I had thought. With fervent effort, my younger self had tried every trick I could contrive, yet I never came upon a camera or f-stop setting that could capture the authentic auras witnessed daily.

Triggered by the golden glow given off by Mr. Sunshine, a swift succession of images flashed through my mind that day—

In the garden at age three: Daddy pointing at a pair of tiny shoes beneath the ferns in the backyard. The shoes swiveled back and walked deeper into the shadowed green. Daddy chuckled and held me tight before kissing my brow and setting me down.

I re-experienced being in first grade during the third week of school: Leaving the lunchroom, a raucous clatter sounded when a lid fell off a trash can. Turning around, a scream escaped my lips as an ogre dressed in the janitor's clothes cussed and picked up the lid. The humiliation and taunting of my classmates made me sick for a week.

At Daddy's memorial service: The entire world glowed with fairy lights, but especially at the cemetery. Most of the guests emitted light, some had wings. And the air swirled with glitter and scents so sweet I would have cried because it enchanted me so. But I was already crying. Little people—I had been told by my father that they were brownies, fairies, and wind sprites—hid in the lilacs nearby. Little people that my mother said did not exist.

"They don't exist," I quoted by rote.

With a slight shake of my head to clear my mind, I dispelled the images in order to deal with the reality of work.

Aerrvin as told by Bronwyn

It wasn't as if he'd meant to sound petulant. Aerrvin couldn't have asked for a more faithful servant as found in Bronwyn MacIntash. Making a scene on the beach showed a petulance not often revealed. Most days he was his own Purple self. He loved the qualities of being a Purple Fairy; it allowed him to be more playful and carefree. In his opinion, it was better than being Yellow, like his sister.

Ah, Harmony, he thought as he lounged upon the shore, *she's the one at fault. Without her demands, I would not have yelled at Bronwyn at all.*

***

"I am not selfish! I simply want to do as I please, is that so hard to understand?"

"No, Aerrvin, I understand you. I do. It is just—hmm, you are turning one hundred and ninety years old next month, and you have yet to find a bride. Your parents are beginning to despair, and for them, that is saying something! You know how patient they are," the broad Brownie sighed but kept a steady eye on his charge.

"I know, I know! If tha' sister o' mine had waited a pint-size longer t'marry, they would not be ever fretful!" In his frustration, his Irish accent grew thick. "Aye, she be t'cause of all me woes!"

Splashing his foot in the tide pool, Aerrvin appreciated the musical sound as he witnessed the sun catching the liquid diamonds before they rejoined the small impression in the sand. Becalmed, he continued, "Just because tradition says the oldest must have a child first, doesn't mean it must be so. Does it?"

"Well, sir if I may say so, such a thing has never been done. Do you wish to break tradition, just to see what happens?"

Bronwyn had a point, so Aerrvin agreed to think upon it. The Brownie removed himself a respectful distance away. Each appeared in his natural state, being roughly six inches in height. Bronwyn climbed onto a piece of driftwood and settled down to whittle some delicate whimsy.

Situated between the two starfish in the tide pool, Aerrvin wriggled to find the most comfortable position. He visualized how he looked as his golden hair swirled in the ripples. His vanity showed on his face at the thought. Though truth be told, Bronwyn sat busily carving that very scene from the driftwood upon which he perched. The rendering would attest to the beauty of the fair prince as his hair danced in unison with the sea urchins and anemones.

The tide inched its way up each half hour, so Aerrvin dared himself to come to a decision before the pool became a part of the ocean herself. Stroking the nubby surface of the purple starfish on his right soothed his anxiety over having yelled at Bronwyn. Not only was he Aerrvin's personal servant, but the Brownie was also his royal historian and advisor. Brownies are brilliant at most any task they are given and are excellent writers. Aerrvin allowed it was quite disrespectful to lash out against him. *Here! Here!*

The truth of the matter was that Aerrvin was also partially White in his genetic make-up, causing him to cycle out of his happy-go-lucky moods from time to time. Being in a White Fairy mood meant that Aerrvin felt a need to withdraw from social contact. Sometimes he hid away for days, other times months. During these cycles, all beings learned that he was best left alone. Even so, being in a White frame of mind meant he could ponder more clearly, and make wiser decisions. It was deemed a good trait for a future King to have.

Entering The Land of Dreams within the Void, Aerrvin chose to visit long-past memories—*events, dear reader, which he chooses to keep to himself at present. Suffice it to say he pondered upon each fair maiden he had known up to this point.*

As the tide neared its highest mark, the delightful Wind Sprite, Mirri Sihee—Aerrvin's constant and invisible-to-most companion—advised, "My Lord, I do agree, tis time for you to put aside your childhood. If I could wed thee, I surely would, as well you know. But go, make a legend of your search, one worthy of the bards in olden times."

Delight warmed his soul causing a small fit of joy to bubble out. "Ha! Mirri you are the light that cheers my soul. How could I find anyone who could compare?"

Aerrvin hugged his precious companion and nodded; his chin tapped softly against her iridescently sheer shoulder. Then lying back down upon the starfish whereon they lay he continued, "But yes, you are correct: Tis time and time enough to be sure."

Mirri Sihee ran her feather soft fingers through his golden locks; breathing sweet songs of peace into his soul.

With a mental sigh, Aerrvin rose up out of the tide pool. The young Fairy Prince squared his shoulders as he prepared to upsize to full Human proportions and proclaim his willingness to comply.

In Honor of Our Queen

And for the Enlightenment

of Mankind

Bronwyn of Clan MacIntash

1

Picture Perfect

And if our dreams should go awry, what then my sweet, what then?

~ Morvayne ap Stewart

Thursday, May 7, 2009

FOR MARA, only one thing filled her life with meaning: her art. Photography consumed her imagination. With her camera, she felt she could make a difference in the world.

But it wasn't true. Nothing she did could bring him back. None of her pictures captured the proof she sought. The college student had nothing else to cling to, so she allowed her passion for photography to consume her.

Mara stood at the crossroads of life that day—unaware of the many eyes trained upon her. The destiny of that single young woman balanced upon a pin, a destiny that would affect the lives of everyone. Those watching noticed that Seattle's morning hum barely filtered into her consciousness as she walked to the corner to catch the bus. Stop and go traffic, belching exhaust from passing buses, and nearly getting run over by an angry bicyclist did nothing to sway her intense focus.

Swiping a dark curl out of her eyes, Mara spoke to herself, "Hmm, the assignment is to photograph unique images that represent nature in the city. Nature in the city—nature, natural, hmm." Unable to come to a decision for her college final, she emitted an explosive sigh of exasperation.

Mara's face brightened as she neared her bus stop in front of an old, vacant laundromat, bustling with new life. Workers were taking boxes into the building from a truck. She settled lightly on a nearby bench, seemingly enchanted by the blond in particular. Since her camera was already in her hand, Mara snapped a few shots to add to her photo journal. An annoying translucent Wind Sprite kept blocking Mara's view. Exasperated, she grabbed it around the waist and flung it aside, ignoring its protests as easily as she had ignored the bicyclist. Adjusting the zoom, Mara soon captured the object of her interest.

In the afternoon sun, an aura of gold emanated away from him for a moment. Her next sigh was vastly different from her previous one.

That was when her bus arrived. Most of her watchers followed Mara to work and later back home, once again. Yet, one alone remained, intent on knowing more about this golden boy.

May 8, 2009

"Friday," Mara said, smoothing her curls in front of the mirror. "Today, I turn in my idea for photography. And I have a calculus test. I hate math!"

Hastily, she applied a pale pink blush and a light skiff of brown eyeshadow to accentuate her lavender blue eyes. "No time for mascara, I might miss the bus," she murmured as she rushed out of her room.

Mara's housemate caught Mara mumbling, she quipped, "Talking to yourself again?" Jill rented the bedroom suite across the hall. They shared Mara's house, inherited from her beloved great aunt.

"Not any more than usual," Mara replied as the two went downstairs for breakfast. "What are we doing tonight?"

"A block party to welcome our new neighbors!" Jill shimmied down the stairs and into the kitchen.

"I am woefully ignorant of any new neighbors, but it sounds fun," Mara responded, grabbing an orange and a granola bar.

Mara's lack of enthusiasm and odd vocabulary caused Jill to roll her eyes at her younger housemate.

Offering Jill a shrug and a smile, Mara went out the door. She walked the half block to the bus stop, but she was earlier than needed, so she walked further down the street to the old laundromat on the next corner.

"Just to check on their progress," she mused. A small, twisty smile pulled at her mouth. She was lying to herself but wasn't ready to admit it. Mr. Sunshine's smile from the day before still played with vibrant color in her mind.

2

A Gentle Breeze

Then breathe my sisters, through the trees, let us sing the songs of life.

~ Mirri Sihee

Thursday, May 7, 2009

Aerrvin felt her energy as soon as she arrived outside the store. He and his cousin were carrying boxes inside. *Oh, now this girl likes me. A lot. She looks pretty sweet herself.* The upsized Fairy couldn't help wanting to catch her attention with magic. *Flipping Somersaults, what can I do?* He had his personal scent which some found attractive, of course, but he didn't have time to waft it towards her. Before he could do anything, she turned and boarded the bus.

He knew a Human could not see Fairy Light, but his vanity caused him to flash his Purple and Golden Brilliance to the world when he felt her emotions brushing against his soul.

Aside from those two mystical means for garnering attention, Aerrvin considered that the only other course of action was just that—action. Chancing boldness, he found her gaze as the bus pulled away. Her thoughts were intense, and Aerrvin couldn't help but offer his most practiced smirk.

After the bus pulled away, Aerrvin asked Gareth, "Did you see her? She's *The One.*"

Gareth, wearing his black hair in a quasi-bun, stopped to stare at his golden-haired cousin. The two looked identical, apart from hair color, and strangely enough, the pair had been born on the same day. Much like twins, they were close to inseparable. And again, like many twins, their personalities were quite different.

With eyebrows raised, and his Irish accent not yet moderated to American, Gareth asked, "Why the rush? We have yet to spend two nights in the city!"

"Then I must assume that you did not see her," Aerrvin replied. "Her stunning looks rival Athena's. But more than that, the Aeries love her. Right, I know the Aeries do not reveal themselves to you. But trust me, the Wind Sprites danced around her like a sweet flower in the meadow, even pulling at her hair. Of a truth, she cast one aside!"

Busily unpacking boxes, their companion, Jaera, rolled her eyes. Unable to hold her tongue, she said, "Crikey, Aerrvin, you must have imagined it. We all know a Human can no more control a Wind Sprite than they can sprout wings and fly. You canna' marry the first Human ta strike your fancy. Marriage is serious business."

With a shake of her head, Jaera strode away to shelve the newly unpacked items.

Very well, I will bide my time and allow things to play out as they will, Aerrvin thought.

Aerrvin beckoned Mirri Sihee with a wriggling come hither motion of his hand. Few are blessed to see Aeries, but the young Fairy Prince happened to be one such blesséd soul. Once the Wind Sprite was close enough for him to whisper to, he said, "Ask those Sprites why they like that girl so much."

Then raising his voice as Mirri flew away he called, "And learn her name—and where she lives!"

May 8, 2009

"Hey, Aerrvin, that girl you like is outside," Gareth called. "Why do you think she is *The One*?" He raised his hands gracefully for dramatic effect. Aerrvin joined Gareth at the window.

"Magic," Aerrvin replied in his rich Irish accent.

"Oh, no 'tis not fair, nor allowed," Gareth said. "Compulsion is strictly forbidden. Is that not right, Jaera?"

"Sure as my hair is red, but I doubt he used Compulsion. Did you?" With decided poise, Jaera balanced on the topmost step of a ladder, hanging chimes on hooks attached to the ceiling. She faced Aerrvin with her impish lips pursed—awaiting his reply.

"No, of course not. I am high-born and well-schooled. I used an old spell learned from my great-grandfather before he Faded, great is his memory; it makes me *aware* of someone when they think about me. I can even feel the emotions they emit. Quite useful among, say—friends and enemies." Aerrvin paused to glower at Jaera. He held no real grudge against her, but as younglings, Jaera often tried to get Aerrvin in trouble with their teachers.

"It usually only works on those in whom I have an interest, be they friend or foe, and they must be within twenty spans or so."

"Limited, but useful," Gareth said. "Will you teach me?"

"Later. Mirri says her name is Mara, and right now I sense this sweet Mara thinking pleasant thoughts about me."

The golden-haired Fairy smiled. Mara's thoughts were a touch stronger than pleasant, and Aerrvin liked the passion and hunger she projected. He picked up a wind chime and went outside to hang it on the new post installed for that very purpose. Above the post, a bronze plaque advertised the name and nature of the store.

In truth, Aerrvin could not say why he found her attention any more compelling than the girls he met at the club the night before, or the girl staring at him from the curb. The sandy-haired girl on the curb willed him to look at her. Yet she didn't garner his attention. *She wants me, and is miffed that I won't look at her,* he thought. *This dark-haired beauty has emotions bouncing all over the place.* A kind of sorrow echoed deeply, beyond his ken. *She's a puzzle I feel compelled to solve.* Suddenly Aerrvin felt a secondary stab of malice and despair aimed at him, but it was so swift and brief he could not pinpoint who projected it.

****

"*The Craftsman's Majick.* Perfect! Precisely what we need!" Mara exclaimed, raising the uninterested heads of her traveling companions for a moment. Mara rarely spoke directly to her fellow commuters, so it didn't surprise her watchers that those nearby merely glanced or nodded at her and went back to their own pursuits.

In silence for a change, she wondered, *does my angelic Mr. Sunshine work here or is he just a delivery guy?* Then to her surprise and delight, he walked out and looked sidelong at her with a secretive smile gracing his face. He proceeded to hang a wooden wind chime on a hook. A sudden puff of air blew his golden locks up off his collar and danced through the pipes, causing the chimes to sound: sweet and mellow.

"Beautiful," Mara marveled as the bus arrived.

A fresh scented sea breeze wafted towards her. With reluctance, Mara boarded and took her customary seat halfway back. Closing her eyes, she almost saw an afterimage of a tiny form dancing among the chimes. In her mind's eye, she saw the breeze lifting the angelic store clerk's hair up off his collar. Firmly shaking her head to dispel the fantastical imagery, she exhaled a musical swoon.

"Now, why didn't I take a picture?!" Mara whispered on the crowded bus. "Oh, I've got it! My final project will be about the effects of wind in the city. I'm glad I only have two classes today. I can't wait to begin!"

Her seatmate nodded absently. She'd sat with Mara before.

****

Mara captured simple images: the flag extended by the breeze, students brushing hair out of their eyes, a seagull hovering in place on a warm current of air. She went to the docks to get the wind on the water. The blustery afternoon offered spectacular shots of sails puffed out and quintessential white caps. In a parking lot, she managed to spy a particularly artful arrangement of windswept trash flung up against a chain link fence.

"Edgy—definitely edgy," she mused in satisfaction. In time, her wandering brought her back to her side of town where she once again stood in front of *The Craftsman's Majick.*

"Are you going in or not?" Mara questioned herself. "Yes, of course, I am," she answered.

Inside, the musty laundromat appeared to have undergone a magical transformation. Bright swaths of jewel-toned silk billowing down the walls offered a cheery effect. Mara felt like she had won a prize as she walked from row to row. With delight, she found photography supplies. Not many craft stores carried them, so with abandon, the photography student selected several things needed to restock her darkroom and even some she did not. Precariously balancing her items, she got in line to make her purchase. Looking ahead for Mr. Sunshine, her countenance fell.

"So he doesn't work the counter, after all," she whispered.

As she waited, she watched a tiny red-haired teen straightening the shelves. At the register, an efficient woman with sandy brown hair and warm eyes turned her attention towards Mara.

"My! What an armful," remarked the cashier. Her nametag read, "Button."

Unable to stop herself, Mara blurted, "Your name is Button?"

"Why yes it is, and a finer name I've never had."

Someone behind Mara sniggered. Blushing, Mara pulled out her debit card and completed her transaction in silence. On her way out the door she muttered, "Mm, that didn't go so well."

"What didn't go so well?" asked a decidedly smooth voice.

Feeling the humiliation crawl up her neck, Mara turned back. There he stood next to the wooden wind chimes; the wind once again fluttered Mr. Sunshine's hair as the soft melody sounded: vibrant and clear.

With a catch of her breath, she stammered, "Oh, ah—I—I think I offended your boss."

"*My* boss?" he asked with a single raised brow.

"Yes. I've never heard of anyone named Button before," Mara replied, gaining composure.

"Never you mind. Button is an old family. . ." he twisted his lips in thought before continuing with, "friend. And a sweeter lady you will never meet."

With a nod at her full arms, Aerrvin offered, "Would you like help with your packages? I do believe I am going your way."

"You are? Sure, I guess I did go overboard. I got so excited when I saw all the supplies I needed. I couldn't help myself." Mara handed over the larger of the two bags, shifted her backpack to a more comfortable position, and headed up the block. As they crossed the street in silence, Mara felt his gaze on her from time to time.

"I am somewhat afraid to tell you my name—since you go about offending people with unusual appellations . . ." he began.

Mara interjected, "Oh, no! Whatever name, my name is Mara, Mara Jamis."

". . . and I am Aerrvin ap Rosewin," he finished with a half turn, and extinguishing the impulse to bow, he flourished his free hand—without her notice. Watching to see her reaction he waited, both eyebrows raised, and a near-smile tickling his lips.

"Ah, yes, I've never heard that one before, but it suits you. You've got a slight accent. Where are you from?"

"My friends and I moved here from Ireland some time back. We have a place on the peninsula, but I wanted to try my hand as a businessman; so I opened the craft store. I am excited to see how it goes."

In shame, she covered her face with one hand; Mara did not think she could be more embarrassed. *The store belongs to him!*

"Sooo, Button works *for* you?" Mara cringed, not hearing his reply.

After turning up the sidewalk to her house, instead of fumbling for her key Mara rang the bell for Jill to open the door. Projecting calm, she turned to face Aerrvin, still sporting that slight smile on his charming face. His eyes pierced her soul. He nodded with the fluid grace of a martial artist bowing to his master and then handed Mara her bag. Her heart thundered.

As he turned away, he called back, "I'll see you tonight."

Jill opened the door and gushed, "Oh, sweet! You met the new guy down the street. Isn't he ca—ute?"

Still mortified, Mara moaned, "He's coming to the party?"

****

Jill made a big production out of her parties. Her friends across the street were often invited to set up their mondo bulky speakers on the patio. The young neighborhood never complained about noise.

As a sous chef with intentions of opening her own catering business, Jill's food never failed to delight and amaze. The only thing she allowed Mara to help with was decorating.

"I found inspiration at the craft store, Jill, I hope you don't mind. I'm hanging these gauzy curtains all around the gazebo. I want to get a few creative shots of the wind catching the curtains."

"No problem, kid. Do you want Dougie to bring his colored lights to shine on them?" Jill asked, rubbing dough from her fingers into the sink.

"Sure, that would be awesome."

At 6:00 p.m. and satisfied with her work, Mara made her way into the kitchen. The gazebo already had white Christmas lights spiraling up the columns and around the perimeter of the scrollwork below the roof. Mara's Great Aunt Lily had kept a stunning flower garden, and often hosted tea parties with her niece and grandnieces. As a result, Mara held fond memories of the gazebo and ensured that she kept the yard up to Aunt Lily's standards.

The yard was small, but lovely considering they were right in the middle of the ever-growing Seattle-Tacoma-Bellevue megalopolis. Spring in Seattle is not the best time for outdoor parties with a significant amount of success. Rain might fall at any given moment, but it had been sunny, and the temperature remained pleasant at seventy-one degrees.

The covered patio and the two oversized French doors connected the outdoors with the dining hall. The dining hall stood empty because Mara had sold the antique dining set to pay for that year's tuition. Overall the place was large enough to host thirty or so of their closest neighbors and friends, which Jill would do every week had Mara not put her foot down: two parties a month maximum.

"Okay, I'd better get cleaned up," Mara said. "How about you, Jill, are you done making all your goodies?"

"Almost, one last batch of mini quiches and then I'm done. Don't use up all the hot water!" Jill called out as Mara ran past to avoid the sponge in Jill's upraised hand.

Each reveled in using up as much hot water as they could stand; it was the one real contention between them, but even then they rarely ever ran out.

⁂

"And what is the dress standard for one of these "block" parties?" Aerrvin asked. The look of skepticism was not lost on Bronwyn as the two of them surveyed the contents of the prince's closet.

"Begging your pardon, Your Highness, it is not as though you are attending Princess Victoria's birthday party," Bronwyn replied. His nose, aimed at the ceiling, twitched. "It has been sixty years since our last excursion among Humans, and I am sorry to say, party clothes have gone downhill. You will wear no formal clothing tonight; simple jeans and a silk shirt for appearance's sake. This will have to do." Bronwyn cut short his opinion with a sniff and retrieved an outfit from the closet.

"Ah well, these jeans are not as comfortable as silk, but they do tend to grow on a body." Aerrvin's voice became muffled as he pulled on a gray muscle shirt to wear beneath his midnight blue shirt.

"Thank me little 'uns for that. Each night they wash 'em and wear 'em to soften 'em up. Next time have me wife Button make your jeans, rather than buying or acquiring them elsewise; then they will be perfect from the start!"

Aerrvin nodded in near sober agreement at his most trusted adviser. Both knew he might obey, but more than likely he would not.

"Now then, we are all set. Jaera, you look lovely as usual. What kind of shirt is that, Gareth?" Aerrvin scrutinized his cousin.

"It's flannel! Everyone wears it." He grinned. Then opening it up he proclaimed, "I even got the perfect t-shirt to go with it." Sporting a smug grin, he revealed a swamp green T-shirt with the Space Needle on it.

Aerrvin's eyebrows rose, touching the fabric he said, "Yes, it looks like flannel, but it's so thin and not made of wool. Very well then. Are you sure you do not want to come along, Bronwyn?"

"Oh, no. 'Tis quite all right with me. I'll stay home with Button and me lassies and reminisce about the time I did go to Princess Victoria's birthday party; you were mere babes then. Besides, I need young Seamus here to go and learn the trade. As I age, I will have a need to pass on the quill."

Bronwyn's middle child, Seamus, had been born one month after the prince. The two had grown up together and quite enjoyed each other's company.

"Now then, if you would shrink him to his proper five inches, and make him transparent so as not to cause the Humans alarm, Your Highness."

Bronwyn nodded as his invisible, shimmering son climbed to sit upon Aerrvin's shoulder using a hank of his hair to keep from sliding off.

Humans cannot see the shimmer unless their eyes are touched with magic. Brownies are rarely seen, even without an invisibility spell, because they are so adept at camouflage. They live in almost every home ever built. Truth be told, they would offer so much help if only people knew of their existence. Their primary task is to keep pests at bay, rats and Goblins being their foremost enemies.

"Seamus, you might need to braid a shank to make a more secure hold for yerself."

"Aye, Father." His fingers seemed to fly as he wove an intricate braid with the hair from behind Aerrvin's left ear. He finished by tying it up with a strand of gold thread.

With the ever-present Wind Sprite blowing his golden hair, Aerrvin and his companions set out to attend their first block party.

3

Of Golden Sunsets

Trailing feather-soft butterfly kisses across the sky, she paints

kaleidoscopic splendor in the heavens.

~ Aerrvin ap Rosewin

Friday, May 8, 2009

Mara's house sat in the center of the block seven houses down from the Victorian mansion Aerrvin rented. The Fairies' love of the gentle humid air of Seattle emanated from their very beings; they radiated joy. It was not raining, but clouds were forming to the west. Aerrvin knew the sunset would be fantastic. He despised missing a single one—dusk being his favorite time of day.

Cold temperatures do not affect magical beings much, but the warmth of the sun infuses bliss into the soul. The current temperature held steady at sixty-nine degrees with no wind, except around Aerrvin, who, thanks to Miree, always brought a bit of a breeze wherever he went.

14

"Jaera, I think your Fairy Dust is a little overbearing." With a slight wave of Aerrvin's hand, a breeze sent a smattering of sparkles free. "You don't need much to garner attention among college students," Aerrvin admonished as he assessed her attire.

Jaera was a five-foot, fire-haired, freckle-faced imp of a girl and could get away with wearing her regular attire: pale green leggings with a filmy, flowing short top in shades of lavender and pink accented by a green scarf around her neck. She insisted she kept her curls cut short to make them bouncy. However, most agreed it was to keep her hair from getting tangled in the brambles which she so loved to climb. The only change to her wardrobe was a pair of strappy high-heeled sandals.

Aerrvin nodded to her shoes. "How easy is it to wear those, anyway?"

"As easy as dancing." Jaera twirled to prove her statement before resuming her natural bouncy pace beside Gareth.

Approaching the front door, Aerrvin slowed to look at his timepiece. They hoped to be fashionably late, but not too late, considering they were the guests of honor.

"Ah, here we go," Aerrvin said.

"You sound nervous, my friend," Gareth said with a grin.

"Have you tried to woo a wife?" Aerrvin asked, with a pointed stare at Jaera's backside and then back to Gareth as she rang the doorbell.

"Touché," Gareth replied with a lopsided frown. He kept Jaera as an option, but like all Fairies, making up his mind was hard. Still, Jaera remained his first choice.

Jill answered the door. "Yay! You're here! I'm so glad you came. Let me introduce you . . ."

The Fairy Prince scanned the room. Aerrvin's delight with the style and décor suffused him with a gentle glow. It felt homey. Upon entering the house, one could use either of the two coat closets left and right, then the rooms opened up to either side. To the left was a study with a luxurious brown leather sofa and two matching chairs. Burgundy curtains and pillows complemented both the leather and the navy blue carpet. *Positively cozy,* thought Aerrvin. On the right and on into the main hall, which should have been a dining room, the beautiful cherry wood flooring shone as with great care.

"Brownies live here, most assuredly," he mused under his breath.

"Aye," answered Seamus in his ear.

The living room to the right soothed the senses with its soft coloring contrasting the study. Guests sat on and around the pale lavender couches; some sat on the rectangular angora rug between the wraparound sectional. With a twinge of jealous emotion, Aerrvin noted guests idly handling the tactile silk and velvet pillows. The aubergine pillows accented the sofas beautifully. The mantel stood out on the western wall as the main feature of the room, marred somewhat by the large screen TV mounted above.

In the northwest corner sat a curious chair of evident antiquity. The chair had a grand high back, suitable for royalty. The cushioned seat and back were a beautiful shade of pale yellow, tufted with lavender buttons. The desire to sit in something that delightful made Aerrvin itch! Wriggling his shoulders, he continued his quick perusal of the room.

Near the fanciful chair sat a long buffet table, placed under the front windows and piled high with tempting treats. Aerrvin ensured that Jill knew that neither he nor his friends ate red meat. In the last corner sat a pile of large red, blue and purple pillows perfect for lounging on.

Still no sight of Mara. Masking his disappointment, Aerrvin greeted his neighbors as Jill introduced him to those in the room; then she excused herself to greet more guests. With one regretful glance at the chair, Aerrvin took the proffered pillow from Gareth and joined him, along with Jaera, on the floor in front of the other guests.

"Stay seated, you just got here," said a blonde girl.

She grabbed a friend, and they sashayed to the table where they filled plates with finger foods. A short, stocky man offered to get beers for the group.

"No, thanks. Water or milk for me," Gareth replied. The tone and clarity of Gareth's voice could capture the attention of all who heard it—to say it was musical would be an understatement.

Sliding her eyes sideways toward her friend, another girl went into the kitchen to inform Jill. Meanwhile, Jaera retrieved two lemon-lime sodas for herself and Aerrvin. Soda does not affect Fairies the way alcohol affects Humans, but the carbon dioxide itself was quite addicting to Fair Ones of any kind and induced cheer nonetheless. Gareth thought it altered his voice, so he did his best to avoid carbonated drinks. On the other hand, Jaera could not seem to consume enough.

The blonde and her friend returned with three plates and sat down on the floor beside Gareth and Aerrvin. "Here you are, sorry—seems to be all fruit and bread tonight. Jill always makes amazing stuff, though," Blondie said, as she picked up a fruit kabob.

"No problem. Seems all my favorites are here," Aerrvin replied, glancing over to see Gareth brush hands with the girl bringing him ice water.

"Sorry, no milk," she said, biting her lip.

Attracting attention is never a problem for Fairies and Elves. Making friends is as easy as drinking water and dancing. The problem for Aerrvin was making a commitment at all. A pull to befriend Mara washed over him. *She might be someone I could enjoy spending nine hundred or so years with. But all the girls and half the guys in the room are thinking about me. Granted, not all are pleased; some are jealous, of course.* A smile tickled his lips for a moment. He loved how the Ware Spell let him feel the strength of a person's reaction to his presence.

Not that he needed the spell to know the effect. With focus, he could hear the blonde girl's heartbeat and quickened breath; her sense of longing tantalized him. *Maybe I should sample more freely first.*

Offering a wry smile, he asked, "What was your name? I failed to pay attention during the introductions."

With a toothy smile of her own, she replied, "Bonnie Grant. I live one house down from you, I think. You're staying in the Victorian on the corner, right?"

Jill found Mara in the backyard. "Mara, you're ridiculous! You can't hide out here all night. It's not like he's judging you for misunderstanding his status. Who would think a twenty-something guy owned the place?"

"Yeah, yeah it's just that—I don't know. He's so cute he makes me nervous."

"Fine, stay here and take your pictures. I'm going to send people out to dance; it'll give you a few people to shoot." Jill paused and then added, "Doesn't look like you're getting much wind, though."

Mara realized she was acting childish. "But I do need to get these pictures. Let's see…" Raising her voice, she called, "Hey, Dougie, can you pose for me?"

Dougie was not model material by any stretch, but his craggy face presented a wind-etched appearance. Mara assumed it was from all the sailing he did on the weekends. She posed him on the garden bench after he adjusted his sound system for the umpteenth time. The weathered fence and flowering vines in partial bloom made an excellent backdrop. Twenty minutes remained before sunset, making ideal light and shadows.

"That's perfect, Dougie. Try not to smile. Great!"

"My turn, my turn!" claimed two fellow students from college. Jill had tried more than once to get Mara to go out on the town with either one of them, but Mara always had an excuse.

"Okay, let me think," Mara answered. "Oh, and thanks, Dougie, you were perfect."

He inclined his shaggy head as he backed away before returning to the house. Mara smiled to see a glimmer of happiness in Dougie's perpetually glum appearance.

Facing the guys, she said, "I'm trying to show the effects of wind in the city. I can't take many pictures until the wind picks up."

"How about a fan?" Joe asked.

"I thought about that, but it would be cheating. The pictures will mean more to me if they are authentic."

More people spilled out of the house to dance and enjoy the evening before it got too cold. A gentle breeze picked up the curtains on the gazebo right as Mara noticed Bonnie dancing with Aerrvin.

An involuntary gasp escaped. Squinting, Mara's lip protruded as Aerrvin took both of Bonnie's hands in his and swung her about jitterbug style. She turned back to Joe and ordered, "Get a girl with long flowing hair; I need a fantastic shot before the wind dies!"

"Yes, ma'am!" Joe snapped back with a smile.

In the meantime, Mara took several shots of the curtains dancing with the music, while studiously ignoring the peripheral rainbow hues she always saw flitting around when the wind blew. The sun turned from yellow to gold, causing the entire gazebo to appear as if on fire, or made of lustrous gold.

Time ceased when Mara became engrossed in her art.

"Fantastic," she breathed.

"It is," said that familiar smooth voice. "What are you doing, by the way? I mean, why are you always taking photographs?" Aerrvin asked.

Still taking pictures, Mara replied, "I'm a photographer. My final is due soon, and I need to get these shots before the wind dies."

Joe returned with Bonnie, the only girl at the party with waist- length hair.

Smiling to herself, Mara directed them to the center of the gazebo and asked them to pretend they were slow dancing despite the hip-hop pouring from the speakers. Amazingly, the wind behaved perfectly, the curtains billowed, and Bonnie's pale blonde hair shone gold as the sun settled to orange. The gentle breeze lifted her hair higher than seemed possible; the shot was brilliant.

Mara could not contain her joy. "This is so awesomely cool!"

Hearing a chuckle, she remembered Aerrvin stood behind her. She turned to look at him and saw the most beautiful sunset ever; the clouds covered half the sky. Brilliant oranges, pinks, and purples melted into each other. Aerrvin displayed as a silhouette against the light. While he stood facing the sunset, Mara admired his shoulder-skimming hair as it flowed away from his face. Without pausing, she continued snapping pictures. When he turned to face her, she stopped.

"Oops! Sorry, couldn't help myself," Mara explained as her face warmed. Pushing herself, she asked, "Would you mind standing in the gazebo so I can get a few more pictures? I would like to go around to the other side so I can get you and the curtains in the sunset. Please?"

Looking down at her, he inclined his head with a gentle nod and replied, "Not a problem, as long as I can watch the sunset." In reality, he was trying to comprehend her, but he maintained a calm façade.

While Mara moved to the eastern side of the yard, Aerrvin walked to the center of the structure. The music became smooth and calming. Gareth and Jaera found no difficulty in joining their companion in his evening ritual, so they sat out of the way on the gazebo stairs. Aerrvin stayed in the center the entire time it took the sun to descend. With the wind billowing the curtains in and out, Mara was confident she had captured grade A photos.

*****

"Aerrvin," Seamus said in his ear, "would ye mind if I slipped down and visited with the Brownies? I am sure I can learn quite a bit about yer bride to be."

"Sure, and I'll even make you visible again. That Brownie lass under the fern there is rather fetching. For a Brownie," he amended with a mischievous twitch. "And Miree, tell your friends to cease their games in the curtains when Mara joins me."

"Aye, Love. But are ye certain she'll be joinin'?

Aerrvin shrugged.

Secretly pleased to witness Aerrvin talking to himself, Mara said, "So I'm not the only one."

Dusk settled; a pale pink glow remained, fading to purple. With a delighted laugh, Jaera grabbed Gareth and began delicately dancing about the yard. Gareth was pretty lithe himself; the form appeared to be a type of Irish jig, yet nothing Mara had ever seen.

Within minutes, they had everyone laughing and trying to copy their steps. Dougie turned on the colored lights, but after the spectacular sunset, nothing else compared. Mara took a few shots to honor the effort of putting them up and then decided to quit for the night.

Inhaling deeply, Mara spoke to Aerrvin, "Thank you. You don't need to stand there all night."

"'Tis quite all right. I can stand for hours adoring Helios."

Settling on the built-in bench, Aerrvin motioned for her to join him. The wind died down, the curtains blurred the view, softening the lights. "So, tell me about yourself." Interrupting as she started to speak, he asked, "Do you always host parties and then avoid your guests?"

Flabbergasted, she didn't know whether to be embarrassed or angry. "Well I have never—" she began, but before she could complete her sentence, Aerrvin took her hand and apologized. Her breath skipped as he stroked her hand, softly running his thumb across the back in a kind of circular fashion.

"I am sorry. That came out rude. Really, just—tell me about yourself."

Using her hands expressively, she exclaimed, "You don't come up to people and say: Tell me about yourself. What am I supposed to say? I'm in my last year of school. I work at the Safe Harbor Retirement Center four days a week. I have a mom, a step-dad, a step-brother and two half-sisters!"

She looked questioningly at him and charged, "Tell me about yourself."

His eyes sparkled as he pulled on his braid, sliding its silky softness through his fingers. Aerrvin answered, "You are right, you already know I own a craft store and come from Ireland. Ah, here's something; I have a mom, a dad, and one annoying baby sister. Not much to say. Come on; the night is young. Will you dance with me?"

❄❄❄❄

Leaving the gazebo a few songs later, Mara shivered in the evening chill. Jaera and the others were relatively calm again. Getting drunk was strictly forbidden; Mara had kicked out guests before, and some never got invited back, not that they cared.

"Oh, I forgot my camera. . . " she started and then stopped as Aerrvin held out the strap for her.

Once inside, she realized it was 9:30 already. Maybe it was a little more than a few songs later. Still, it was relatively early as far as parties go. In the living room, Jill started a game of Pictionary, and in the study, Dougie's group of friends stood around looking at videos online.

"Hey, that's my new computer, guys. Don't break it!" Mara called.

Sudden sharp hunger pangs hit Mara, having not eaten since tasting one of Jill's mini quiches right out of the oven at 5 o'clock—and she'd missed lunch altogether.

Jaera stood on the edge of the living room with a plate of fruit and pastries, "Hungry?"

"Why yes, I'm famished." Mara gratefully accepted the plate and went into the living room to watch the game. Most of the pillows were taken, so she went to her favorite chair and carefully balanced the plate on her knees. When she realized that it left Jaera and Aerrvin without a seat, she started to get up.

Gathering the free pillows, Aerrvin said, "That's perfectly okay. I enjoy sitting at the feet of pretty women."

He flashed a twisted smirk. Jaera groaned, pinned him to the ground, and tousled his hair. The display was rather intimate, causing more than one

22

raised eyebrow. Mara inhaled deeply, letting her breath out slowly. Jaera appeared quite green for a moment.

"Um, I have not had a chance to talk with you. Are you Aerrvin's little sister?"

Before she could answer, Gareth gracefully plopped between Jaera and Aerrvin and stole one of Aerrvin's pillows. "Not even close," Gareth said.

This comment set off another wrestling match, ending with Jaera on top, pummeling Gareth's chest with her tiny fists while he laughed uproariously.

"Sorry. I give, I give!" Gareth exclaimed, earning his release. He sat up to straighten his dark hair; a gentle shake and it fell silkily into place around his shoulders.

Mara was not used to such roughhousing. Her evident consternation worried Aerrvin, so he reached over to Mara's plate and took a carrot. Handing it to Jaera, he said, "No more soda."

"Yes, Father," she replied and then with a glance at Mara she piped, "No, he's not my father either. We grew up together, and Gareth is his cousin; I am Gareth's best friend, so where he goes, I go."

Gareth tugged on one of Jaera's curls. "Well said."

Meanwhile, Seamus returned, having waited behind a flower pot until acknowledged and transformed back to transparency. Once again sitting on Aerrvin's shoulder, he quickly informed Aerrvin about the darkroom in the basement.

Breathing deeply to relieve the pressure in his chest, Aerrvin felt gratitude for the tip. Jaera's antics made him feel perturbed. But his real worry was whether he was doing the right thing. On the outside, he was as smooth as could be. But inside he was a roiling mass of conflicting emotions. *If I did fall in love with her and she could not believe in magic, it would be one more heartache to add to my small collection of failed relationships. Ah, the pain!* Despite how he hated that pain, he nursed those emotions when feeling down, essentially spiraling into a bottomless abyss of self-torture. Now was not the time for such dark thoughts. He pushed aside his petty worries and watched Mara finish eating a fruit kabob. *Her lips are as luscious as that strawberry,* he thought. *How sweet and tender they must be.*

Licking his lips before addressing Mara, Aerrvin said, "We will have you over one of these days so we can get to know each other better. But for now, show me your darkroom." It was stilted, nearly a royal command; even so, he managed to refrain from 'shall and should.'

"How did you know I had a darkroom?"

"I carried your supplies this afternoon, remember?" A half-smile twitched on his expressive lips.

"Oh, yeah. I have had such a busy day! I can't remember half of it. Sure you can have a tour," she replied, inviting all three.

Jaera and Gareth declined. "No thanks," Gareth said, "I want to have a look at your computer. I need to get one myself." He fit right in with the geeks, most of Dougie's friends were dressed in flannel too.

Jaera thought Pictionary looked fun, so she went and sat on the nearest empty lap, earning sour looks from the girls sitting nearby.

The drizzle turned into an absolute downpour; Dougie and Jake came in with the sound system as Mara and Aerrvin walked past. Dougie gave her a polite nod.

❄❄❄❄

In the kitchen, Jill busied herself with tidying up. She flashed her pearly whites and gave Mara a thumbs up as Mara motioned Aerrvin down the basement stairs. Mara couldn't remember the last time she had felt so out of control. Her heart was speeding, and she kept blushing. *Probably at senior prom. Did I really think Gerry Fink was all that?*

"Not even half," Mara murmured.

"What was that?" Aerrvin asked.

24

"Oh, not even half of the basement is complete. I've been remodeling. The house was built in 1890 and has a remarkably large basement—considering its age."

Two exposed walls revealed part of the basement foundation made of river rock and mortar. The room could have been a game room, but Mara did not care for pool or ping-pong. Wires ran along the walls, where photos hung from clothespins. It was bright and clean, with two counters—used for folding clothes—and pantry shelves beneath where Jill kept extra foodstuffs.

Embarrassingly to Mara, there sat two baskets of unfinished laundry, one washed and one not. While Aerrvin studied the photos, she hastily emptied the washer and started the new load.

"Okay, so this over here is my studio and darkroom," she said as she waved to the remainder of the basement. To the left, stood the door to the darkroom. The room was 10'x10'. Even though Mara used digital, she preferred the old-fashioned way of crafting pictures.

While developer does not necessarily smell good or bad, Mara always breathed in deeply when first entering the room. She associated the odor with the magic of watching pictures emerge; it gave her a thrill every time.

Mara's excitement became infectious. She exuded her love of photography in an almost tangible way. Aerrvin enjoyed her sense of aesthetics and delight. Her pictures were remarkable. In the red glow, Aerrvin picked up one of himself and Gareth moving boxes into their store; they were each wearing khakis and t-shirts. Gareth was saying something to Aerrvin. The photo captured the prince's mischievous grin, which he practiced for fifty years to perfect.

"You take magnificent pictures," Aerrvin said, jauntily sporting that same wicked grin. "Can I have this copy?"

Caught off guard again, Mara gasped softly; Aerrvin always looked as though he were posing for a picture. *How could such a perfect being be interested in me?*

She gave her head a shake to dispel the thought and replied, "Ah, yeah, yes—sure. Please, take any of these that you want. I've got one of Jaera, which she might like too."

"Can you show me how you develop a picture?" Aerrvin turned his attention to the counter while brushing up against her with seeming casualness.

Mara forgot to be self-conscious as she efficiently taught him the process. She even laughed at his jokes instead of blushing. As they came out of the darkroom, Jill entered the laundry room with dirty tablecloths and dishtowels. "Hey you two, it's after 11:30. Not that late, but most people have left, and Jaera has fallen asleep."

Heading for the stairs, Aerrvin said, "Poor Jae, she has not slept this past fortnight. I guess it's catching up with her."

In the living room, Mara found Jaera was indeed asleep, curled up on Kevin's lap. He did not look like he was too upset about it, but when he saw them, Kevin said, "It's about time you got here. I think my arm's asleep!"

The phone rang. Wondering who would be calling so late, Mara answered. Bronwyn was on the line saying that he was in the car outside. Not that they needed a car; Bronwyn just liked to drive. Mara relayed the message.

Aerrvin bent over Jaera to wake her. Once a Fairy crashes, it takes a lot to get them lucid. "Jaera? Can you get up? Oh, never mind. Gareth you take her. I'll get the door."

Gareth relieved Kevin of his burden and held her in the crook of his arm like a wee babe. He gave Jill and then Mara a hug with the other, "Thanks for the welcome party. We had so much fun…" Turning to another neighbor, he said, "…loved the dancing."

Outside, a sleek gray car with a black top waited. The driver got out, opened the back passenger door for Gareth and Jaera, and then stood to wait for Aerrvin.

Aerrvin hugged Jill, thanking her for the party and praising her culinary skills. Then he hugged Mara and kissed her cheek. "Thank you for the delightful company."

His near purple eyes lingered on her face a moment, and she felt her cheeks grow warm. Dropping her own lavender hued gaze, she managed a muffled, "Bye," as her fingers flew to her mouth.

Then the final partygoers all said their goodbyes and left.

"Yes!" Jill screamed, "I finally did it. I knew I could find someone to interest you!"

She hugged Mara and danced her around the room.

Mara smiled in return and replied, "I guess you do know what you are doing, and it only took you three years!" With a sarcastic smirk, she hugged Jill back.

Jill went to the kitchen to ensure the oven was turned off. With a sigh, Mara straightened the pillows in both front rooms. The leftover food could wait; they would finish cleaning in the morning. Mara had a habit of ignoring how much food was left because the next day it never matched up with her memory.

"Best not to think about it."

At the top of the stairs, she called out, "Good night, Jill."

Mara yawned, closing the door to her room. She thought about her preference to be particularly neat, so as not to cause extra work for the Brownies.

"Not that I really believe in them," she said to herself as she reached for her toothbrush.

Ever since she met a Brownie, whom she named Sylvie, when Mara was three years old, she had learned to put things back in their place. And Mara always cleaned thoroughly every Saturday. She hadn't spoken with Sylvie since she was five, so of course, she didn't really think it had happened.

"Just fairytales," she told herself, pulling on a cotton nightgown. Flipping off the light, she climbed into bed.

Her window looked out on the backyard where the lights from the gazebo remained on; a soft glow shone on her windowsill. With a smile, she remembered dancing in the gentle breeze behind the curtains. Falling asleep with her eyes open, she saw a tiny figure climb into the window.

"Sylvie," she breathed as her eyes slid shut.

4

Curious Dreams

To dream and feel more alive than ever, that was the gift I'd gained—and lost.

~ Amanda Powers

Saturday, May 9, 2009

Ɑfter climbing into the car, Aerrvin reverted to his usual six-inch self.

"Bronwyn, please let me out. I want to dance a little longer."

It should be common knowledge that Fairies love to dance and sing the night away. Even in the busy city, right from the car, one could witness several groups cavorting in the rain. Jaera had been joining in that fun for the past wee bit and drinking way too much soda for her own good; she would not awaken until Sunday at the earliest. Even if he refused to admit it, Gareth was hopelessly devoted to the Green Fairy. Not that Aerrvin wanted company. Bronwyn rolled down the window, allowing Aerrvin to flit away.

Tap-tap-tapping on the bedroom window pane, Aerrvin startled Sylvie as she gently danced about dusting the window casing.

Sylvie opened it a crack and whispered, "I'm busy here. What do you want?"

"I want to come in." Aerrvin added his winning smile for leverage.

The smile did not sway Sylvie. "You were here already, the party is over and don't you be waking my person!"

Beyond him, she caught a nod from one of the guardians of the house hovering in the tree. This approval gave Sylvie permission to let him enter.

"Fine, you may sit on the bedpost. I am cleaning, and I shan't have Fairy Dust to clean up as well!"

"Feisty! Now I know why Seamus went about humming in my ear the rest of the evening."

His comment sent the fair Brownie maiden into a flurry of dusting. Aerrvin scanned the room, and it did not disappoint. "P'raps I shoulda set up an interior design comp'ny—Humans have a lot o' textiles and furnishings, which do excite me senses," he mused aloud, forgetting his diction. His fascination with texture was legendary in the Fairy world. "I dare say, this wee laddie could even improve a few things here."

His comment brought a "Humph!" from Sylvie.

Aerrvin danced a little jig when he discovered, decked out as he was, that Mara did not hate lace. He wore purple silk pants, and a spider-web silk shirt, with lace spilling down his chest as well as from the extra-long cuffs he preferred. Over this, he sported a black velvet brocade jacket with tails down to his knees, accented with a lace hankie peeking from the pocket.

Perched on the foot of her bed, the Fairy Prince admired Mara in her ruffled white nightgown, with her midnight curls cascading onto the lace-trimmed pillowcase. The room seemed to be white on white with possible pale pink touches throughout; it was hard, even with Fairy eyes, to distinguish soft colors in the dark without being right on them. So he flew about to make sure; yes, those were pink ribbons on the lacy curtains, and the satin pillows were a soft pink striped with yellow. The carpet breathed a pale yellow as well. *The coverlet has three rows of ruffles and lace!*

"Delightful! You do an excellent job here, Sylvie. The linens are so white and crisp they absolutely glow, and the other levels are quite professional."

Unseen to her eyes, Sylvie glowed for a moment, herself. "Why thank you. We do our best. Mara's family has always been very good to us."

"Tell me about her and her family." He faced Sylvie as she went to the dresser to straighten the knick-knacks and perfume bottles.

"I already told Seamus," Sylvie said.

"Sure 'n' p'raps he didn't ask the right questions. Humor me."

"And who are you to be asking me, to tell you about my Human's secrets at all?" she huffed, knocking over a perfume bottle.

Mara stirred and curled up into a ball on her side, facing the dresser. Carefully straightening the bottle, Sylvie stood with hands on hips awaiting a good reason.

Aerrvin flitted over to sit next to the Brownie on top of an old stuffed toy tiger; surprisingly soft, and it smelled—*like Mara,* he thought and inhaled deeper.

"I will tell you who I am. I am Aerrvin ap Rosewin, son of her Royal Highness the Fair Queen Laurel ap Rose herself! Moreover, I intend to have Mara as my Queen. I have been instructed to create my own Kingdom here in America, by her Highness, and I have chosen the Pacific Northwest as the center of my own Grand Council. All Fairy Rings will send a representative to me every twenty years. Does that tell you who I am?"

The fretful Brownie bowed as low as possible, and begged forgiveness, "Seamus did not tell me, Your Highness, he only said you were his master."

"Very well, continue with your duties, Sylvie, and tell me about this dear creature." He eyed Mara speculatively. She seemed to almost gleam in the pale light from the backyard.

"I am a wee thing, only fifty years old. Mara is my first assignment, you see, which I received by accidentally allowing her to see me. And then, bless me, I spoke to her." Sylvie cringed knowing what was coming.

"What? How could you do such a thing?" Then more calmly he mused, "She believes in Brownies?" With his hopes rising, he caressed Mara with his gaze. Remembering the feel of her in his arms as they danced, his fingers itched to touch her once again.

"Well, sire, yes and no," Sylvie replied as she scrambled up on top of the mirror to remove the dust. "It happened when she was a wee babe of three; she lost her Growly."

Sylvie nodded toward the tiger, where he lounged. "Her Aunt Lily and Uncle Rupert had this room; since it was their house. As it was, her bedroom was across the hall. There are two rooms over there; her parents slept in the first, and she slept in the second, at the front of the house. They were visiting—as they often did each June. Mara played all through the house, causing all kinds of messes. She mislaid her Growly, and when bedtime arrived, she howled on end. The sound irritated my ears. And—I found myself behind in my duties, you see; because she created so much extra work with all of her disorder. You must remember, Your Highness, I was very young, only twenty-nine!"

Cringing again at her confession, she continued, "I retrieved her Growly and gave it to her, telling her she needed to be more responsible. I advised her always to pick up after herself, as she was causing me extra work," Sylvie ended with a sob. By now she was kneeling before Aerrvin again. Her light brown hair fell forward, covering her shame.

"Stand up, Sylvie. I am not an Ogre. I have made plenty of mistakes as a youngling myself." Smiling to prove he was not condemning her, he begged, "Continue with the story, please."

"As you wish. A few nights later, my sweet girl lay awake when I came in to clean, and she asked me my name. I told her it was Celery. She couldn't say it right, so—she renamed me: Sylvie. And that is how I came to be her personal servant; she named me. Even though I didn't mean for it to happen, I am happy to serve her. She is a spectacular girl and—I think you might even be worthy of her," she finished with a squeak as Aerrvin threw a cotton ball at her.

"Very well, you may leave us. I will speak with you again by and by."
Aerrvin remained where he was. *Yes, this is a girl I want to know.*

❅❅❅❅

Mara awoke well rested and happy.

"What a curious dream," she whispered.

Closing her eyes, she reviewed what she could recall. Sylvie was there from her childhood fantasies. She remembered thinking of her as she went to bed. And, well obviously, Mara thought of Aerrvin. In her dream, she heard them talking, but not much of what they said. Sylvie flitted about as she always did. *She always did?* Mara questioned.

She tugged at her ear as she verbalized the dream, "Hm, so after Sylvie straightened the room, she left. Aerrvin came and sat on my pillow. In an instant, I was barely five inches tall and dancing in the air with Aerrvin, the fairy prince." Mara opened her eyes to verify reality and then closed them once again. "The dancing seemed to last till dawn, then we stopped and watched the sunrise, sitting on the rooftop of the house. Not that there was much to see, it's overcast and drizzling." She sighed, noticing how real it all appeared even as a memory.

"No, it didn't actually happen," Mara chided.

Giving her Growly a squeeze and a kiss, and then picking up a cotton ball on the floor, she went off to prepare for a new day.

"Good morning, Bright Eyes!" Jill called as Mara came into the kitchen for breakfast.

She'd slept later than usual; it was ten o'clock. Jill had cleared the buffet, having set all the trash by the door. "No telling how much the Brownies ate," she whispered. Trying to think of something else to say she shook her head before giving up. Jill hardly ever listened to what Mara mumbled anyway.

"I'm so glad you trained our neighbors to respect your home; it is always such a joy to clean up after a party." Jill handed Mara a bowl of oatmeal. "Sorry, we are still out of milk. I didn't buy any yesterday because I needed room in the

32

fridge for all the fruit. I am going out soon though. Anything you want on here?" she asked, handing Mara a paper with "Jill's To Do List" neatly printed on top.

"No, it's all good, but maybe you should get two jugs of milk instead of one."

"Ha, if you would stop leaving your uneaten midnight snacks sitting out all night, maybe it would go further."

Mara's habit of filling a plate full of cookies and pouring a large mug of milk to watch late night TV, and then leaving them on the end table annoyed her mother when she was a child. Her mother scolded her often; now Jill had taken over.

"You know, you could use a smaller mug instead of this monstrosity. Then you wouldn't waste so much," Jill said putting it away.

"But I love that mug! Just buy more milk. If we're getting low on money I can always sell another chair or something," Mara said with a shrug. It had been a mug her father used for his own midnight snacks. Mara pushed aside her emotions about losing him and focused on her love for the mug.

Jill rolled her eyes. "If only I had your money, child."

Housework was a pleasure for Mara. Only two of the rooms were carpeted: her bedroom and the study. She loved making the pile stand up, creating a more opulent look. She had fun dusting because she turned on the stereo and danced about the house causing whirls of dust motes to dance in the morning sun—when the sun decided to shine. By noon the rain stopped, and the clouds broke up. *I'll get a little sunshine, after all,* she mused. She mopped and waxed the ever-shiny cherry wood floors. By one o'clock, the house was in tip-top shape. Right when she sat to rest, the doorbell rang. She opened the door to find a broad-chested man on the porch; Mara assumed him to be the driver from the night before since the sleek gray car sat in front of her house.

"Yes?" Mara asked.

"Oh, pardon me. I am admiring your lovely home. I have an invitation for one Mara Jamis, and one Jill Beckett," he said, holding out a hand-lettered invitation.

After scanning it, she replied, "I am so sorry. I am unavailable at 10:00 tomorrow. I teach Sunday School at that time."

With a mixture of pride and dread, she awaited his response. Some people were prone to ridicule, and she was so hoping these folks from Ireland were not the type. She realized she had a severe crush.

"Very noble indeed," he replied with a warm smile and a nod. "No trouble, I have a second invite; this one is for four o'clock." The well-dressed man pulled a near identical invitation from his tweed jacket.

With an attempt to stifle her grin, she said, "We'd love to attend."

Not long after he left, Jill came home with groceries. As they put stuff away, Mara told her about the invitation for a late afternoon tea party.

"I looked through my closet, and I have nothing acceptable. Please come shopping with me!"

While driving to the mall, Mara regaled Jill with all the fun she had with her Great Aunt Lily and her cousins during their tea parties. "I miss her so much. We visited almost monthly when we moved to Bellevue. Before, it was every summer for two whole months. Then, well you know, there was the accident." She paused a moment and rejoined, "And later, Mom made me go with her—to Sequim of all places!"

Jill already knew about the tragic sailing accident, which had caused the loss of Mara's father and uncle when she was eleven years old. Two years later Lily Agnes O'Toole died, leaving her property to thirteen-year-old Mara. Her five cousins, all girls, had been jealous until the executor read the next part giving each of them $25,000. Mara received no cash, but her mother had been able to find a renter right away which, of course, was Jill. When Mara moved in at eighteen to start college, she did not mind taking the smaller suite. Jill felt at home in the spacious two rooms with its private bathroom. Besides, Mara had always wanted to sleep in Aunt Lily's feather bed. As a result, twenty-seven-year-old Jill felt no reason to dislike the young owner, and they became dear friends in an instant.

At the mall, they tried on fifty dresses and settled on three each. Jill bought another business suit, as she was sure her business opportunity was right around the corner, and she would need to go to the bank for a loan. Sure enough, on the drive home, Jill drove past the cafe which she coveted; it was on the corner next to a bus stop, with a small parking lot on the side.

"Yes!" she shouted, startling Mara. "That lousy eatery finally went out of business, and the place is up for lease," she cried and then laughed. "Mara, tell me the number. I want to call the realtor now!"

With eyes gleaming, Jill set up an appointment to meet with the realtor in the morning.

Then, noticing Mara's quietness, she asked, "What's wrong? You know this is what I've been waiting for, right?"

Mara sighed, "Yes, I do, and I am happy for you. It's just that," she paused to inhale as her chest constricted, "the place comes with an apartment above it. You will move out!" She nearly wailed the last part.

"Oh, sweetie, you are about to graduate, and you will start your own business. You are rolling in money already, and with your photography, you will make more than you ever made off of me as a renter," Jill tried to placate.

"No, that's not it," Mara keened, rising in pitch. "I don't want to be alone!" She hiccupped, and said, "I've never lived alone."

Once in the garage, Jill turned off the engine. Sitting in the dark, she took Mara's hand and said, "Listen, Mara, I've introduced you to every neighbor on the block, and half of them from all of the surrounding blocks. It's a safe neighborhood. I lived here alone for nearly five years before you joined me. Besides, it will take a month or more to renovate that dive. I'm not leaving tomorrow." Squeezing her hand, Jill got out of the car. Mara followed, wiping away a tear.

Once inside Jill said, "If you want, we can put an ad in the paper. I am sure you can always find another college student or two."

"No," Mara said, back in control and with a wavering smile. "My step-brother graduates this spring, and I think he has a football scholarship. At least, we all hope for one. Regardless, he will need a place. Mom did not want to kick you out or anything. In fact," Mara continued with a real smile, "she's ready to pay for fixing up the basement to put him down there!"

"I see," Jill replied dryly, reminding Mara of Lucille Ball at her driest.

"I suppose I can survive a few months alone. I don't think Ricky intends to move in until fall," Mara said, with apparent calm. Privately she still dreaded being on her own.

5

Shifting Winds

Fell winds that blow from heights above be strangers to my soul.

~ Brand the Bright

Sunday, May 10, 2009

At midnight, Aerrvin set out to dance the night away. Jaera continued to sleep soundly. Gareth roused enough in the nest they shared to wish Aerrvin happy dancing.

As a rule, Fairies prefer sleeping in nests of soft down or dandelion fluff. So, even when living among Humans, they preferred to shrink down and pile all together with as many others as would fit. With only the three of them, their nest was rather small. Yet, it was quite cozy since they shared it with a mama cat. She would deliver new kittens any day now, and Fairies so love Birth Days. Gareth worried about Jaera missing it, so he stayed with her to ensure she slept well. If need be, he wanted to wake her for the grand event.

The stars twinkled in the crisp night air. The moon was a waning three-quarter light, seemingly suspended by an invisible string, like an ornament with a silvery blue glow. The Fair One's nightlife was at its height. Aerrvin stopped to join a musical duo, adding his flute as they played a happy jig for three cavorting Green Fairies. Like Jaera the Green, they were emphatically the wildest Fairies one might meet. Aerrvin chuckled as he raced his way to Mara's window.

"Stop right there!" commanded a snide Orange Fairy. "Who gave you permission to be here?"

Aerrvin stopped halfway to the window and then flew up to the top of a fir tree where he saw three Orange Fairies with swords.

Swords! Weapons have not been part of Fairy attire for centuries. Arguably, not since the European Inquisitions. Aerrvin's mind buzzed as he tried to make sense of the scene.

"I did not realize this house belonged to anyone's territory."

"Oh, you're new. From the Green Isle herself, are you? Listen up, The Emerald City belongs to Lord Morvayne; he sends us out to ensure no one messes with Mara. She belongs to him, and you are best advised to go back to where you came from. Unless you want to pledge your services to him? You appear to be quite 'Bright.' He could find a use for you." The Fairy studied Aerrvin.

"Yes, I would like to meet Lord Morvayne. Does he live here?" Aerrvin gestured to the house and gazebo with a graceful sweep of his arm.

"No, he is visiting with—hmmm, friends." The Orange Fairy laughed a dry rasping excuse for mirth. "Besides, she has a ward on the house; none of our Fairies can gain access."

"Why do you need inside?" Aerrvin casually bounced on the end of a green-tipped branch, gently fluttering his holographic wings.

"That is Lord Morvayne's business. Should you feel bold enough to ask him, you may meet us at the Zoo's Fairy Ring Council on Monday night. We will introduce you to him ourselves. By the way, my name is Ozzie; this is Bud and

Jasper." He pointed first to the taller, and then to the stouter of his two companions.

Yellow and Orange Fairies banded together often, yet Aerrvin had never heard of any counsel based solely on color. He was a Purple Fairy with White traits; his sister was Yellow, also with White inherited from their Mother. Aerrvin groaned to himself; he did not like Yellow and Orange Fairies that much, mainly because of their tempers, especially when they did not get their way. Yellows were often clever at solving puzzles and wards, so he understood why Oranges liked to keep them around.

The glow around Fairies as they fly allows all who see them the ability to perceive what kind of Fairy they are, and sometimes the strength of their power. Aerrvin's royal birth gave him Silver and Gold abilities, including the capacity to mask the strength of his powers. Flashing Gold or Silver was ever in poor taste, so Aerrvin did not worry about being identified by his glow. Purple was all they saw.

Spiraling up through the air with a laugh, the prince replied, "And I go by Aerrvin. If the music is right, I will be there."

With a triple loop-de-loop, he sailed away from both Mara's house and his own. Aerrvin had never heard of a Fairy Ring Council inside the zoo. He happened to be the nearest royal, so all councils were obliged to send tributes to him yearly, and new councils were to request permission from him before forming. Exhaling his frustration, he headed for the Fairy Ring outside of Tacoma; because of their extensive library, someone there could provide insight.

"I need information on this Lord Morvayne," Aerrvin explained to the librarian, after rousing him.

"Hm, he has never made an appearance in any of the recognized councils. This news of a Fairy Ring in the zoo is news indeed!" replied the dried-up twig of a Fairy.

He must be near nineteen hundred years old! Aerrvin marveled to himself. Then, upon registering what the librarian said, he frowned.

"Now don't fret, I am aware of a Lord Morvayne, but he is not a Fairy, he is an Elf."

"An Elf? What is he doing in a Fairy Ring?"

"There will be no more answers until you learn to speak with greater respect!" sniffed the librarian. "I attended your birth, you know, and I am acquainted with your father very well. I was your great grandfather's personal musician, great is his memory. At his leaving, I chose to immigrate to the New World."

"My apologies, Balmoral, both for my rudeness and for not recognizing you. Please. Can you tell me why an Elf is controlling a Fairy Ring?" Mentally Aerrvin pinged with joy. *The Great Musician, Balmoral, is a librarian in Tacoma! Most Fair Folks thought he had Faded already.*

Smiling in approval, Balmoral replied, "No, but some ideas are flitting about in this antediluvian head of mine. Morvayne lived here," he gestured his hands to signal the land round about, "among the native tribes before the Europeans arrived. They worshiped and served him while he lived the good life. No fault there, of course. We've all experienced Humans falling all over themselves to serve us." He smiled at some ancient memory, and continued, "When this region started to grow, as Humans became more populous everywhere, Morvayne fled to the next dimension as so many others chose to do. But he left word with a band of Yellow Fairies to keep him informed of the doings of Seattle, as the city had been named. 'Tis a pity too—how they mangled the Chief's name that way. Be that as it may, Lord Morvayne said he would visit as needed."

"So," Aerrvin surmised, "these Yellows and Oranges choose to follow him by their own choice. But, that still doesn't tell me what he wants with Mara. She is Human, right? But then, why is her house warded against Yellows and Oranges?"

"Mara Jamis?" Balmoral asked. Receiving a nod, he continued, "Mara is the daughter of Brentwood Jamis, whose father is the last son of the last son of Princess Tigerlily. Princess Tigerlily, as surely you are aware, was one of the few Elven Maidens ever to choose to live life as a Human. As you know, her mother is Her Royal Highness Queen Gwennara, Queen of all The Realms. Our High Queen is in hiding as she defends herself against an unknown enemy. Mara is under observation by several factions, as she may be the final heir. The only other viable contender after Princess Arianna is a cousin, Breezy of Fairlane. The sisters of Tigerlily, namely Daffodil and Arianna, have not appeared in public for over one hundred years. Daffodil is assumed dead. Word is—Arianna, who is missing, attended Tigerlily's funeral cloaked in invisibility. But I have not substantiated it."

"That would explain the glow," said Aerrvin. Mara emitted a faint opalescence, visible only with scrutiny and one had to be close, as one would be when dancing. "So, Mara has royal Elven blood in her, and is utterly unaware?"

"Apparently."

Remorse and a twinge of shame washed over Aerrvin for not keeping up on the royal news. Yes, he had heard of Princess Tigerlily and her outlandish choice. To renounce the throne was huge enough news on its own; giving up magic and near immortality was almost unheard of among the Faire. For Mara to be so important, yet left unguarded, seemed preposterous. Too many thoughts vied for his attention. He decided to speak to Gareth about setting up sentries for Mara.

Changing the topic, the prince asked the librarian a favor, "Balmoral, if you please, it would honor me if you played at my Birth Day festival in two weeks." Then giving directions to his current home, he added, "You need to be in Human form, as I may invite my neighbors."

"I would be honored, Your Highness," replied the old musician with a graceful bow.

"Thank you." Aerrvin nodded in return. "Also, I would be most appreciative if you would do more research on what the Orange and Yellow Fairies are up to."

Taking out his flute, Aerrvin played a farewell salute worthy of the Master Musician. Balmoral nodded his approval as Aerrvin floated up. With the last note, the prince flared a brilliant silver and sped northward.

With the warm wind at his back, the flight did not take as long as the trip there. In silence, he snuggled up with the cozy mama cat and his other Nest Mates. With visions of Mara in his mind, Aerrvin promptly fell asleep.

6

Mystical Moments

What magic spells have stirred my soul? What life bestirs my heart?

~ Clay of Glennferry

May 10, 2009

Sunday morning, Mara woke up with disappointment nagging at her. Her fairy prince had not come and danced with her. "In other words, my dreams were normal," she said, flinging back her covers. "What has gotten in to you, Mara? Since when did Aerrvin become a prince? Humph! And a fairy at that!" Laughing at herself, she went to shower.

She ceded to indulgence by wearing her tea-length dress to church. "It's not that formal," she said, admiring herself and the dress in the mirror.

In truth, it didn't come close to the plain pencil skirts and blouses she wore all the time. The cream-colored lace floated airily over the pink silk underdress. The sheer cream-colored sleeves ended with the same palest of pinks in a long silk cuff, held together by little pearl buttons running up to her elbows.

"Oh, Mara, look what you forgot!" Mara surveyed her shoes. Her black heels were fine but clashed with the style. "I guess these will have to do," she said, slipping on a pair of lightly scuffed white flats. Still shaking her head, she whisked up her lesson materials and went down for breakfast.

"I'm going to miss this," Mara said to Jill, grabbing a fresh from the oven muffin and a banana before sitting down on the stool at the breakfast bar. "No more meals without thought."

". . . and preparation," Jill added. "I believe we need to speed up those cooking lessons. Besides, you can be one of my best customers." Changing the subject, she offered, "If you don't mind being early I can drop you off before I meet the realtor. I don't want to be late."

Mara timed her bus route to get her to church right on time, but she loved being a touch early. "This way I can set up my classroom beforehand," she said, heading down the hall.

Mara enjoyed teaching the 7-to-9-year-old class. Her lesson was about the travels of Paul, and as usual, she had a little craft for her students to do. She planned to teach the children how to make origami boats and then they would make sparkly glue dots on maps to show the path Paul took.

The organ music welcomed her as she entered the main chapel. To be an example to her students, Mara always sat near the front, often next to the youth pastor and his wife. The cozy old chapel glowed with golden oak throughout, made brighter yet as the sun shone in through the skylights.

As she sat, the youth pastor asked, "Somebody get married?"

"John!" Sarianne's blotchy face darkened as she smacked her husband with a soft whap. "Mara, you're beautiful today. Is there a special occasion?"

As the warmth of embarrassment rose to her cheeks, Mara explained her tea party invitation.

"Oh, it sounds awesome. You gotta tell me all about it," Sarianne whispered before facing forward as the pastor rose to address the congregation.

When they stood to sing, Mara glanced behind her and did a double take. Aerrvin, and all of his friends, she assumed, from Ireland sat in the back row. In addition to Jaera and Gareth, who smiled when they caught her eye, there stood Button arm-in-arm with Aerrvin's driver. Beside the driver stood two girls who resembled Button—only younger and slimmer—and another one of the guys Mara had seen working at the Craftsman's Majick. Seeing them together, she realized he belonged in Button's family too. Next to him stood a young woman with light brown hair who reminded Mara of someone, but Mara couldn't quite place her. She gave Mara a cheery smile too. With a final glance at Aerrvin, who arched a carefully manicured eyebrow, Mara turned around to sing.

The hymn was a favorite, *Rock of Ages*. Mara joined the congregation with her clear alto. To everyone's surprise, the voices from the back row carried throughout the chapel; the hymn became angelic. The chorister stood a little prouder, and tears slid down the organist's cheek. Mara herself experienced a lump in her throat as she tried to sing the final lines and then gave up, as most of the congregation had—to enjoy those pure, sweet voices. She was sure the baritone was Aerrvin's, and the tenor had to be Gareth.

"Heavenly magic!" Mara breathed as she sat down.

Pastor Mike gave a hearty welcome and invited the visitors to return anytime. When the sermon ended, Mara thought she'd greet Aerrvin, but the group left as fast as they could, shaking hands and excusing themselves while inching toward the door.

"Ah, well, I guess I will see them later," Mara murmured.

✤✤✤✤

After cleaning the glue off the table, Mara made her way to the exit. Sarianne caught her going out the door.

Sweeping her sandy brown hair behind an ear, she said, "Remember, tell me all about the party and the mansion. I've always wanted to go inside the O' Shea House. And if you could slip it into the conversation, ask them to join the choir!"

"Sure thing," Mara said with a hug. "I'll see you next week."

Outside, Aerrvin's sleek gray car gleamed in the diffused light; the driver motioned her to climb in while he opened the back door. Inside, Aerrvin glanced up in a leisurely manner from the small book in his hand. Butterflies danced in Mara's stomach from the intense emotion his glance created.

"Hi, I noticed you didn't drive a car and thought you would like a change from the bus." His eyes sparkled as he appraised her appearance.

Mara offered thanks and climbed in. Never in her life had she sat in such luxury. Simply happy to be there, Mara sat mutely enjoying the ride. Aerrvin appeared comfortable without talking, so they rode in silence all the way to her house. Mara climbed out and turned to find the driver also exiting the car.

"Oh, sorry I, um, I didn't think to wait. I'm not used to this sort of thing."

"Not a problem, Love." Aerrvin rested his open palm on her shoulder as the driver shut the passenger's door. "I am sorry; I have neglected to introduce you to Bronwyn, quite an old family friend. He enjoys serving and gets put out if you don't let him do his job."

"Quite right, I do love being my best self, that I do," Bronwyn replied. Then deftly so as not to startle, he returned to the driver's seat and waved, trusting Aerrvin to make excuses.

❉❉❉❉

And excuse him he did. "You need to forgive Bronwyn; he has many assignments from Button before tea time. And I have no preparations at all, so I thought I could keep you company. If you don't mind?"

He smiled slyly, knowing very well that she thought of him almost nonstop.

Aerrvin did not trust the evil Elf, nor his followers, and wanted to keep watch over Mara at all times. He did not think it possible, but he was falling for the intriguing girl who didn't seem to realize that she was not wholly who she thought she was. *Maybe it has something to do with being in Human form, this quick action business,* he thought. As a Fairy, it took him forever to decide on anything. Once, he took a week to choose what to wear to see his parents during Mid-

Winter Festival. He literally stood there naked, until he made a decision! Now, here he was aware of Mara less than a week, and his emotional attachment sent him into fits of worry, hopeless devotion, and feeling overprotective. *Is that love?*

*❋❋❋❋

Happy butterflies danced in Mara's stomach; spending the afternoon with Aerrvin seemed like a dream. As they headed up the walk, he slid his hand from her shoulder, down her arm and then lifting her hand, he rested it in the crook of his elbow. The seemingly courteous gesture sent a thrill through her. Mara remained unaware of Aerrvin's addiction to tactile sensations and his inability to resist touching the lightweight fabric of her dress sleeves.

From the foyer, Aerrvin directed her toward the study. "I have not spent any time in here yet. Shall we?"

"Sure," Mara agreed, grateful for his take-charge manner.

She never entertained on her own. Jill always instigated interaction, and before that, Mara's mother had been the one to arrange sleep-overs with friends. Boyfriends had been rare. Not that she was unattractive; guys fell all over themselves trying to get her attention. She happened to prefer things like photography, or nature and solitude. Somehow she tended to push guys away, and eventually, they stopped calling. Negotiating relationships was not her thing. *Ha, but Aerrvin has my full attention. Fates, please don't let me push him away.* Mara felt a bit guilty about begging the fates rather than pleading to God, but she wasn't sure God cared about what boyfriend she had.

"Mara, I love the feel of your house! Did you do the decorating yourself?" Aerrvin asked, brushing the rough silk curtains for the joy of it, then he opened them to peer out the window.

Looking at him from behind and with a small surprise of delight, Mara noted Aerrvin had tied his smooth golden hair back with a length of delicate black lace. *Mmm yummy,* she thought.

Breaking her reverie, she replied, "Most of the house, but not this room. This den was my Uncle Rupert's. When he died, my Aunt Lily kept it the same, even though she redid the rest of the house with the seasons. I decided to do the same. I love the warm, cozy, masculine vibe I get when I come in here. This is a picture of my dad and Uncle Rupert."

Mara waved at a wall of photos and then pointed out a larger picture showing two men standing on deck, holding up their catch. "They loved fishing on the ocean, but mostly they sailed around the Sound whenever they got together." Mara frowned, trying to shake off the weepy feeling she tended to get when thinking of her father. *Oh, Mara, don't fall apart now!*

Experiencing her melancholy, Aerrvin directed her attention to the other photos on her wall. "Are these your ancestors?"

Mara nodded as Aerrvin took a sepia-tinted photo off the wall. The photo depicted a woman who resembled Mara; only her hair was smooth, and her skin tone appeared dark, especially compared to the man she stood beside.

"You favor her. Who is she?"

Brightening at a new topic, Mara explained, "That is my great-great grandmother. We know very little about her, but her name was Tigerlily Wallace. She's from Scotland. To me, she resembles an Indian and lived here—near the Sound among them, but she was not a Native at all. The man standing next to her was not her husband either. Aunt Lily told me once that she knew a few things about him, but she never had time to tell me before—before passing on."

Aerrvin wandered back to the sofa. Smoothly, in a single motion, he removed his shoes and sat down with his knees drawn up to his chest; pausing all action to gaze raptly at Mara as if expecting a bedtime story. Mara laughed, remembering him sitting on the roof in the selfsame pose, watching the sunrise.

Mara picked up the picture from the desk and replaced it on the wall, muttering about dreams. She slipped her pair of flats off in two steps and sat in the other corner facing him, drawing her feet up to the side under her as she hugged a pillow. From her psychology class the year before, she knew it was a defensive gesture, but she felt exposed without it. His casual and open manner unhinged her in some way.

"Tell me more about your family. What were they like?" Sympathetic to her nervousness, he too took a pillow and fingered the loose fabric, enjoying the tactile nature of the silk on one side and velvet on the other.

Mara relaxed and told silly stories from her childhood.

***

"My dad even enrolled me in fencing!" she laughed. "He, of course, never had a son, so I did everything he'd wanted to do as a boy. I went hiking and camping, fishing and sailing. And of course, Aikido. I already told you about that first lesson. With college and work, the only thing I keep up is Aikido. Last year, I enrolled in fencing again, and I was better than when my Dad took me. Obviously, back then I was only ten years old."

Losing control, Mara wiped a tear away. The next thing she knew, she was in Aerrvin's arms, as he smoothed her curls away from her face, which wasn't easy because the ceiling fan came on. Unseen to Mara, and at Aerrvin's direction, the Wind Sprite—Miree Sihee—spun the blades to send a wafting breeze over Mara's flushed face.

"Shhh," he soothed. "Do you want to tell me more?"

Speaking into his cotton shirt, Mara told how her father and uncle experienced a freak sailing accident and how their bodies had never been recovered. "I was only eleven."

Mara hiccupped, mentally took hold of herself, and pushed away. "Sorry, I didn't mean to blubber all over your shirt." She excused herself to freshen up.

When she returned, Aerrvin stood in the living room inspecting the fireplace.

※ ※ ※ ※

Aerrvin had not seen the ward on Mara's house the first time he had come over since it had not prevented him from entering. Knowing what to look for, he intended to inspect each door, window, and opening to ensure that they were all still intact, and to divine how they were crafted. Perhaps he shouldn't have been surprised since the princess had lived there, but he found the wards quite complex. The corner pieces framing each window and door had well-executed ivy and holly carvings, as well as the Celtic knot drawn in Fairy Dust over the top of each carving. The doors held perfectly clear Elven kisses on each lintel. That is, perfectly clear to magical beings.

However, the most incredible thing was the maple mantelpiece. Each support holding the mantel contained a carved forest scene. Such fireplaces were so prevalent in many of the European homes he had visited over the years that Aerrvin had not noticed it at all; especially when he itched to sit in the enchanting chair! Even so, woven into the carvings were Elves, Fairies, Brownies, and Gnomes. *Enchanting.*

Of further interest to the prince was the shelf of the mantel boasting a long hand-carved chain of ivy and holly woven in Celtic knots the whole length. And the best part—the center bow of the mantel had been kissed by St. Nicholas himself.

"Why did I not see this before?" Aerrvin exclaimed softly to the invisible Brownie on his shoulder.

"Probably because you were blinded by the light in Mara's gaze," sniggered Seamus in the ear of the prince.

"What didn't you see before?" Mara asked, coming up beside Aerrvin. She extended her hand to stroke the shelf while smiling again at witnessing him talking out loud to himself.

"The other night I did not notice the mantel. It is fantastic. Who carved it?"

Mara shrugged. "All I know is that my grandfather commissioned it as a Christmas gift for Aunt Lily."

"Remarkable," he smiled in awe. "I bet you leave quite a plate of cookies for Santa." He faced her with the question in his eyes.

"Why, yes, I do!" Mara swatted him because she thought he might taunt her.

"He must surely love you," Aerrvin replied with a warm, serious glow replacing the merry twinkle in his eyes.

The ward was exceptionally powerful; the only thing it would admit was Santa himself. Aerrvin had only seen Santa's kiss twice before; his parents had received a wedding gift from the Jolly Old Elf with a blessing and a kiss, which in itself is a blessing. And Aerrvin had toured Santa's workshop in his youth. The visit included a feast with St. Nicholas and his wife, whose name is never to be mentioned, and there in her kitchen floated the brightest kiss ever left by an Elf. It hung in the air directly above her table. Smiling at the memory, Aerrvin turned to Mara.

"And the chair?"

"Sit in it," Mara's voice dropped demurely.

Stroking the carving along the top, Aerrvin tried to prolong the ecstasy he felt, but finally gave in and sat down in one fluid movement; a smile lit his face. Even disguised in his Human form, he could see his unnatural glow.

Aerrvin sprouted wings twice as wide as he was tall, they flowed from silver to white while shooting Blue Fairy Dust all over the room. The chair had granted a long-held wish which Aerrvin had never shared. He was not sure if Mara could see the wings or not.

Sylvie complained about the Dust for a week!

When a Fairy assumes Human form, their aura is hidden, even from other Fair Ones. For one very powerful, magically, a Fairy can generate wings and fly as a Human. Mind you, Fairies do not have physical wings even when small. The wings are a manifestation of power and depending on a Fairy's whim, they can have any shape or size desired. The color, on the other hand, cannot be controlled. One is either born with a color or gifted with one. Aerrvin had just been gifted with the power of a Blue Fairy.

❧❧❧❧

Mara saw the magical transformation but denied it. *You are going mad, girl.* She practiced denying what she saw on a daily basis, so without a blink, but with some degree of enthusiasm she exclaimed, "You feel it?"

"Are you making him try out your mystical chair, Mara?" Jill asked, coming in from the back door with some papers in her hand. "I swear, anytime

50

she meets someone new, she has them sit in the chair and tell her how they feel. Well, how do you feel, Aerrvin?" Jill concluded with a wink. She obviously could not see the wings.

Looking from Jill to Mara and back, he replied, "I feel like I've gone to the top of the world. This chair seems to emanate good karma. Is that what you feel, Mara?" Turning his gaze back to Mara with a satisfied glow suffusing him, he awaited her response.

Mara smiled widely and replied, "Yes, it does seem to put a spring back in my step after a tiring day. I love that chair. I've had several offers from the antique dealers when they come. The last offer was $17,000.00. It's nearly as much as all the other antiques I have sold combined."

Standing up and reaching out to Mara, Aerrvin as much as commanded her, "Never sell that chair."

Looking up into his face Mara stammered, "Ah–um, no, I won't. I am nearly done with school, and I thought I would sell some of Aunt Lily's jewelry to start my studio."

❉❉❉❉

Realizing he was far too serious, Aerrvin gave her one of his practiced smirks. He kissed her on the top of the head and said, "I buy old jewelry, so I get first dibs." Then he hid his wings once more.

"Tell me the history of this house."

He behaved as though nothing at all had occurred, in truth, he was ecstatic with his new Blue wings.

"I've heard all about this," Jill interrupted. "I'm going to get dressed for my first tea party. Be good!" she said with a waggle of her finger.

Aerrvin requested a tour of the house. In the basement, he discovered one of the wards on a window was missing. "What happened here? I don't remember this being off the other day."

Mara held up a corner piece for the window frame. "It split in two when I tried to pry it off. I want to paint the walls, and I thought it would be easier if I took the frame off."

She showed him the two pieces together and apart with a sweet little pout. Aerrvin immediately went to the window and drew a few meaningless squiggles with his finger right on the glass, rather what would seem meaningless to Mara.

"No one wash this off," he commanded to the air. Then quietly he whispered to Seamus, "Ensure the Brownie tunnels have guards."

"No need," replied Duncan, Sylvie's father. "We have doubled the patrols since Mara moved in, and all is in good order, Your Highness." Duncan stood behind a stone in the wall, so all Aerrvin saw was a glint from the harness he used in scaling walls. Mara went up the stairs shaking her head in dismay. Aerrvin soon followed, resisting the urge to reach out and take a handful of the lace swaying directly in front of his face.

It was 2:45 pm, still time to check the rest of the wards. Assuming Mara kept the jewelry in her room, Aerrvin casually linked arms with Mara and lightly stroked the silk cuff of her dress with his free hand.

Leading her to the next flight of stairs, he said, "I should like to see some of the jewelry you have for sale."

"Well, I haven't decided what I want to sell yet, or even if I will," Mara protested weakly while holding tighter to his arm as they ascended the stairs.

Mara's room was to the right. Smiling at the beauty of her room in the daylight, he left her and went to the window, appearing to gaze out while checking the wards. The lacy curtains lay over the frames, so Aerrvin asked Mirri to flutter them. While Mara went to her closet, he added his own blessing of protection by kissing the lock on the window.

"Make sure you keep the lock on your windows secure," he said opening the window and then closing and locking it.

"I do," Mara replied, returning from her large closet with a jewelry case.

"Ah! A fairy!" she cried, as the wind swirled a seedpod into the room. "Catch it, and you can make a wish," she added as she moderated her excitement. "At least, that's what we do here in America."

She blushed, causing Aerrvin to smile pleasantly in return. His violet-blue eyes sparkled in the light like jewels.

"Well, where I come from they are for sending and receiving messages. This one tells me it is time to return home," he smiled ruefully at the bit of dandelion fluff and the invisible Wind Sprite who brought it; then he placed it on the dresser. "But first, let me see what you have."

In the not-too-small chest lay a splendid collection of rings, brooches, and necklaces.

Picking up first one and then another, Aerrvin appraised each. "These are all in excellent condition, but they need to be worn to keep them in tip-top shape."

✳✳✳✳

Picking up the one Mara loved most but never wore; Aerrvin attached it around her neck before she could stop him. He said, "Never take this off. It suits you."

The necklace comprised three delicate amethyst stones of equal size set in a silver heart encrusted with diamonds to fill in the shape. The pendant hung from a delicate silver chain.

Mara became inwardly upset because the last time she wore it, she couldn't remove it for a month. She started to protest, but then sputtered to a stop, as she couldn't think of a good reason not to wear it. In truth, ever since getting it off, Mara had been afraid to even take it out of the box; but with Aerrvin here, she felt peace. Standing at her mirror, she admired the gems as they sparkled against her pale skin. She knew she wouldn't be able to remove the necklace quickly this time either.

"Would you please hold off on selling these, until I check my finances?"

53

"Yes, of course. I won't need extra cash until midsummer anyway, if then."

Thinking of past midsummer night escapades brought a wicked grin to Aerrvin's face. Taking her hand, he started to say, "That reminds me…"

"Mara Lilyana Jamis! I am shocked! What are you doing with a young man in your bedchamber?" Jill mocked, holding her hand over her heart

Mara shrugged.

Jill wore a pale blue dress with a simple handkerchief hem, topped by a plain white shrug fastened with a satin ribbon. Sporting new white sandals with a low heel, and with her short red hair spiked just so; she presented a truly lovely sight.

"Very fetching!" Aerrvin complimented.

"Ditto. You've outdone yourself as well," Jill replied, not realizing he had toned down his usual outlandish creations.

Today he wore a white peasant shirt with gathered sleeves, which Mara thought looked surprisingly like her bedspread. Looking more closely, she noted the sleeves did indeed end with a double ruffle of the very same lace as was on her bed. The shirt tied shut with a black, corded satin string. Left un-tucked, the shirt hung down to the top of his thighs. He wore slim black herringbone slacks. Mara recalled that when seen up close the fabric was actually black and a saturated purple.

She agreed it was unquestionably fancier than a stock boy in jeans and a long-sleeved pullover. Currently, he was barefooted as he wore no socks and his loafers were in the study. His feet were pure perfection. Her breathing quickened at the silly notion that feet were attractive, yet surely his were.

The phone rang, interrupting Mara's appraisal of clothing and feet.

"Hello, this is Mara. Yes, I will tell him; do you need to speak to him?" She paused to catch Aerrvin's attention, "Aerrvin, it's Jaera. She sounds excited." Mara handed him the phone and began packing up her jewelry.

"Hello," Aerrvin answered, smooth as silk.

"Yes, I did. Well, because it didn't say why, and I had something going on," he twitched his eyebrows at both girls naughtily. "Why didn't you say so?! Is the car outside or do we need to run?" Laughing, he hung up the phone, picked up Growly and gave him a kiss, and then grabbed both girls by the elbows and headed them towards the stairs. "I have a wonderful surprise I want to share with you. Can you come to my place, right now?"

Looking at each other in startlement, the girls stood at the top of the stairs as Aerrvin bounced in excitement. Finally, Jill said, "Well I'm ready. Where are your shoes, Mara?"

They arrived in two minutes at the Victorian house, known by some as the O'Shea Mansion.

7

Kittens and Tea

No sweeter music fills the air than love that soothes with gentle care.

~ Clay of Glennferry

May 10, 2009

The front entry remained the same as Mara remembered from the last time she had visited the O'Shea house with her aunt. The marble floor created a checkerboard of shiny black and matte white. The paneled walls were painted a glossy white, and above a small blue settee hung a painting of Master O'Shea with his three cats. The rest of the house had undergone a massive redo. At least, the parts Mara saw. Jaera rushed in, grabbed Aerrvin and Mara's hands, and ran them down the hall, past the kitchen, to the servant's quarters.

In a moderately-sized room, six people gathered around something in a wicker basket. Moving people aside, Jaera pulled Mara down near the basket where the main event became apparent, a cat giving birth.

"This is so exciting!" Jaera whispered. Bronwyn brought chairs for Jill and Mara.

"No thanks, I'm fine," Mara said in her own whispery voice.

She had owned a cat as a child, but one day he never came home. He seemed irreplaceable, so she never got another. But the retirement center, where she worked, had a cat named Vinegar, who loved to sit at her feet while she taught her class. *Cats are nice,* she thought.

Aerrvin pulled out a wooden flute and began to play a soothing melody in low tones. Jaera and Gareth joined in, Jaera with a silver flute and Gareth with panpipes.

Panpipes of all things! Mara thought.

Soon one kitten arrived with a sweet trill from the silver flute while the other two musicians continued playing an intricate melody and countermelody. Mara found it enchanting. Even Jill kept her quirky comments to herself. Each kitten arrived with the same sweet trill. Eventually, the weary mother cat moved to clean her kittens; all had arrived safely. The trio put away their instruments. Mara missed seeing where—entranced as she was with the wonder of God's creations. It was nearly four o'clock; the other guests would be arriving soon.

Mara took in the sight of Aerrvin, with his hair hanging limp; damp with sweat. His face glowed with joy. One lock of hair had escaped, and her hand involuntarily reached out to smooth it back.

"You're sweating," she commented. *I've never seen him sweat, not even after dancing all night.* She mentally shook her head, knowing full well she had never danced through the night with Aerrvin. *Fairies are not real.*

"I took in some of Mama Cat's pain for her." Aerrvin scratch behind the cat's ear. "After all, she has done so much for me. Haven't you, Sugar?"

With practiced denial, Mara deflected his comment from her mind. Not being sure what to say, Mara let Bronwyn lead her and Jill back to the main room; the new occupants had transformed it into a garden. The walls had shelves arranged in a stair-step pattern; various shades of blue pots of all sizes adorned the shelves, each spilling vines of ivy, ferns, or flowering plants. The carpet emanated a harmonious swamp green shade; as she thought of it, Mara heard crickets and frogs. Looking more carefully, she spied a small waterfall and pond in the corner, nearly hidden by a veritable forest of potted aspen and flowering butterfly bushes.

Jill followed Mara to the little pool. "If I wanted to own a restaurant instead of a catering business; this is how it would look," Jill said with eyes aglow.

The doorbell rang. Jill and Mara turned as Bronwyn introduced Aerrvin and his two companions to three middle-aged women accompanied by an elderly man. Button entered, followed by her two daughters, each held trays heavily laden with taste-tempting treats to challenge Jill's creations.

There were two tables, each covered with crisp white linens and blue and white salad plates and tea sets. The lighting gave the room the appearance of a shady glen. A gentle breeze stirred the air, causing flowers to nod from time to time. Mara could not help but feel like Alice in Wonderland.

They awaited introductions before sitting. Jill sat at the table with Aerrvin and the first two women to arrive, as well as their two nieces who came late.

Mara sat with Gareth and Jaera, along with the elderly Mister Garvin and his daughter Jane, who appeared to be fifty years old. The teas offered were varied, which suited Mara well, as she did not like black tea. She delighted in the honeysuckle and rosehip tisane she chose.

The triple chocolate fudge cake with mousse piping was an exact replica of one of Jill's' supposed creations, as was a delicate lace cookie that was like nothing Mara had ever seen anywhere else. Mara was too far away to ask, but she looked at Jill with a questioning stare. Jill looked near livid and shrugged her shoulders. Everyone raved about the food, especially the cake and cookies.

Aerrvin's near neighbor, Mrs. Wooster, asked who had catered, and Jane turned from Mara's table to hear the answer. With a smile to Jill, Aerrvin replied, "My own dear Button and her staff prepared this tea, but Jill is the creator of the Cinnamon Crisp and the Triple Chocolate Fudge Cake. Am I lying, Jill?"

Astounded, Jill shook her head. "Do you have business cards, Jill?" Aerrvin prompted.

Finally, her business sense kicked in as she replied, "Not on me, but I am in the process of opening up a shop on 47th street and will be changing my cards. I can give you my phone number before I leave."

All in all, it was a lovely tea party. Mara and Jill stayed later than the other guests did, as Aerrvin offered them a ride if they would wait.

❖❖❖❖

"Would you like to hold a kitten before you leave?" asked Jaera. She proceeded to make Mara hold each kitten, saying she could tell which kitty loved her best if she did. Humoring her, Mara held each one in turn. Secretly she liked one kitten the best as well, but she told herself that she had sworn off cats. So kissing the final black and white striped rat of a kitten, she sighed and rose unsteadily to her feet.

Gareth steadied her. "Princess Twinkle Toes, eh?" He laughed merrily.

"I am not used to sitting on the floor in a dress," Mara replied stiffly, due to embarrassment; Gareth was far too sweet to be angry with for any amount of time.

Aerrvin walked Jill and Mara through the kitchen before heading out. "I would like to introduce you to the rest of my—household, shall we say. You have met Button and Bronwyn already, and perhaps Seamus, their son? These two fine specimens are their daughters, Calico and Gingham." Each ducked her head in embarrassment.

That left one last woman; she appeared to be in her early thirties. Something about her caught Mara's attention, but she couldn't quite place her. Aerrvin continued his introductions, by indicating palm up toward the final— *servant?* Mara guessed.

"And this is a distant cousin of Button's from right here in the Emerald City. Imagine our surprise at finding her here. Mara, this is Juniper, and she has been such a help to us."

Mara racked her brain all the way home, as she tried to place where she had seen Juniper. She looked like an older version of the lady in the back of the church sitting next to Seamus. As she climbed out of the car, she exclaimed under her breath, "Sylvie!"

Aerrvin walked the two ladies to the door. Once on the steps, he brought from behind his back a block of wood. As Jill stepped inside, he said, "I took the liberty of having Bronwyn repair your corner piece. I'd be happy to put it in place for you."

"Sure, but how did he do it so fast? It looks like the original." Touched and quite surprised, Mara scrutinized its perfection.

Aerrvin did not reveal that Bronwyn sang the wood back together. It truly was the same piece, and with the singing, the Brownie strengthened the magical ward. Aerrvin was most anxious to put it back on the window, especially, since he had some errands to attend to, and he would not be able to visit Mara for a few days. Her safety was his utmost concern.

Once in the basement, Aerrvin revealed that Bronwyn happened to be a master craftsman with wood. "In fact, he brings most of his tools with him wherever he goes." Aerrvin deftly installed the corner piece, leaving it an inch from the wall so that Mara could still paint. He loosened the rest of the frame as well, not willing to risk her breaking another corner piece.

"There, now you can paint as sloppily as you wish," he said with a grin. "Hammer lightly to put them securely in their place when done."

"Thank you," Mara replied, demurely looking at the pendant her fingers had been fiddling with.

They arrived at that awkward moment when he should leave, and she was unsure she wanted him to. She could not ask him to view her photos; he had already seen them, and she had not yet developed the ones from the party. When she lifted her gaze, she found him directly in front of her.

Aerrvin took both of her hands in his—after untangling the chain from her left pinkie. He searched her face and eyes, and then roamed from head to toe and back again, before saying, "I have so enjoyed your company these last few days. Would it trouble you if I were to court you?" His voice was silky smooth and rich as velvet. At the same time, his thumbs never ceased to caress her hands.

To Mara the word sounded old-fashioned, her mind reeled. "Court?" she questioned. She thought she had said it in her head, but seeing his countenance waver, she quickly responded, "Not at all."

Before she could blink, he kissed her, gently cupping her face. He stopped before she was ready and asked, "You did mean yes, right?"

"Yes, I don't mind at all," Mara replied, reaching up to smooth his hair; that one stray lock still hung loosely from its queue. She kissed him in return.

After Aerrvin left, Mara changed into sweats and a t-shirt. Returning to her darkroom, she developed the next two rolls of film. She stayed up later, having no morning classes on Mondays. So it was 11:30 when Mara climbed into bed. She made and framed a close-up of Aerrvin and set it on her nightstand. It was her new favorite picture: his hair tugged to the side by the wind as the setting sun flared up behind him; creating a mere silhouette. So why it would be her favorite when she couldn't even see his face, she couldn't say.

"It's fitting," she told herself. "It embodies who he is somehow."

I could never forget his face. Closing her eyes, Mara replayed the events of the day once again. At church, his voice was angelic. His visit, letting her cry on his shirt while telling about her father. The kittens, the tea party—alone in the basement. With a sigh, she rolled over to curl up on her side, carefully keeping her eyes shut to avoid seeing Sylvie in the window. *Am I going mad?*

❃❃❃❃

Aerrvin's heart sang as he awaited Mara's bedtime. Recalling his pleasure as he held her close, even though she was so heartbroken at the loss of her father, filled him with longing—a need to ease her pain. *And my secret wish granted as I sat in the chair! I will need to research this chair. Why does she even have it? It seems like the Queen would want to keep something that powerful in her palace.* He returned his thoughts to Mara with her clear blue, near-lavender eyes, eyes that danced with joy watching the kittens being born. She never noticed him watching her as closely as he had while he played. Her joy was his. He felt ready to break forth in song as he recalled their kiss and her acceptance of his request to court her. *Tonight will be glorious!*

61

8

Fairy Rings

O, touch the sky and feel the breeze.

Now let us fly so far away, so very far away.

~ Mara Lilyana Jamis

Monday, May 11, 2009

10:00 a.m. on the dot. With regret, Mara climbed out of bed and made her way to the shower. Monday morning, never a favorite. Yet today, Mara's reason for not wanting to rise was different.

"I'd dream forever if all my dreams could be like that," she breathed, reaching for the shampoo. She went through her morning routine on automatic while her mind stayed focused on her dream.

A little after midnight, the rain began to fall. Mara found herself once again transformed into a miniature being as a silly, playful Aerrvin came and danced her through the house and up the chimney. They fluttered amongst the flowers and took sips of nectar from lilac petals. Mara didn't recall any conversation, just laughing, dancing and music. Aerrvin gently whisked Mara down the street to join a group of green and purple fairies as they played tag in Kevin and Joe's backyard. They stopped by a solitary white-winged fairy playing a charming, quiet melody on a harp, reminiscent of Mozart. Lastly, they visited the O'Shea house, splashed in the pond, and even swam with the frogs! Mara chuckled as she dried off with a fluffy white towel.

"Goodness, Mara, you are losing it. Swimming with frogs!" Retrieving clothes from her dresser, she picked up Growly and gave him a kiss. "But you know," she said to the stuffed tiger. "The best part was curling up with Mama Cat and her kittens to warm up." After getting partially dressed, she laughed hysterically at herself all the way down the stairs. Jill was at work so Mara could be as free as she wanted. In the basement, she continued her conversation with herself.

"So, Mara, either you are madly in love, or you are plain mad." She turned the dryer on to de-wrinkle the clothes left there earlier.

While waiting, she gathered photos into a plastic portfolio. The dryer buzzed; collecting her jeans, she slipped them on, then tucked in her pink scoop-neck T-shirt. She chose the shirt to showcase the necklace.

"I won't take it off," she said firmly, dropping her fingers away from the clasp.

She wanted to try but was afraid to see if it remained as stuck as it had last time. The last time she had been twelve, having snuck into Aunt Lily's room with two of her cousins to try on jewelry. Mary Lynne tried a tiara; Aunt Lily owned several from her beauty pageant days. Jaimie put on every ring she could find. Mara tried the diamond choker first and then decided to wear the beautiful purple heart-shaped pendant. "Look at me! Don't I look divine?" she'd intoned theatrically.

Aunt Lily came in and frowned while her eyes sparkled. She told them, "Young ladies need to learn to mind their manners and to stay out of other people's belongings."

She removed the crown, took the rings from Mara's cousins, and sent them away. Aunt Lily returned the jewelry to their proper places. Facing Mara, she said, "You know, you really shouldn't have been so presumptuous."

Aunt Lily unclasped the diamond choker from Mara's neck and placed it around her own. Then turning Mara around to stand beside her, they both looked into the full-length mirror. To Mara's surprise, Aunt Lily said, "This necklace is for you; please bring it back to me when you can. My will states you are to receive it." With a kiss and a pat, she sent her down to the kitchen to prepare lunch.

When Mara was finally able to get the necklace off, she was more than mournful and filled with self-pity for having ever put it on. Her cousins despised her for being the favorite—although Aunt Lily did give them each a ring at dinner and the other three cousins received a ring the next time they visited. Mara was frightened at not being able to get it off; she tried every night for a month, but the clasp simply refused to open.

"I don't want to keep it in my house," Little Mara had mumbled, as she handed it over to Aunt Lily.

To which Aunt Lily replied, "I would think not. The day will come when you will gladly wear it, and it will be glorious indeed." Looking at Mara sadly, she said, "I do wish your father was here. I want to tell you so many things! Your father left so much undone. It is not my place, and your mother will not allow me. You do remember that when you turn twenty-one, your mother may not keep it from you?"

Mara assumed she referred to a few of her father's belongings, which her mother kept in a safety deposit box. She nodded slowly, looking at the ground to hide the threatened tears; twenty-one was a long way from twelve.

That summer they moved to Sequim. Mara was no longer able to see Aunt Lily on a monthly basis. Because of all the difficulties, she did not particularly miss her cousins. But oh, how she missed her beloved aunt and was jealous of her cousins because they lived so close. They could see her weekly if they wanted; they lived right in the city and only a bus ride away.

Sighing away old memories, Mara said, "Well it's not long now, June 21st and I will be twenty-one."

After padding up the stairs in her bare feet, she sat down at the breakfast bar to eat a banana nut muffin. Once finished, Mara went to the closet, carefully placed the photos in her backpack so as not to bend the precious photo portfolio, and set out to start a new day. A day which proved to be uneventful.

⁂

Aerrvin agreed to allow Gareth and Jaera to keep watch over him as he went to visit the zoo. Thick fog made the Fairy lights in the mist enchanting, so much so that it encouraged wild games of tag. Twice, Aerrvin got tagged by apologetic Blues who thought he was one of their Nest Mates. Good-naturedly, he lost them in the fog and then snuck up on them to tag them from behind. Soon he was at the zoo. The place glowed orange and not just from the streetlights. There were other Colors as well, flitting here and there, but Orange and Yellow overwhelmed the area.

"There must be one hundred Fairies here," Aerrvin marveled.

Most Fairy Rings consisted of about fifty Fairies.

"I wonder how he wooed them over?"

There, right in the middle of the African Savannah display, was the ever-growing Ring as more Fairies joined. Aerrvin settled in on the edge of the Ring. The music began with a single drum tapping the traditional pattern, yet something about it didn't seem right. Gradually each Fairy added their personal songs with voice or instrument, weaving and harmonizing until each Fairy could not contain themselves and felt compelled to dance. Again all was part of their traditions, yet somehow Aerrvin felt out of step.

"Hey, you there. Yes, you little Purple. Who invited you here?" asked a larger than typical Yellow Fairy wearing an ornate sword.

"Ozzie invited me. Do you know him?" Aerrvin replied, gratefully leaving the dance to talk to the Yellow Fairy.

"Oh, so you're the Bright one Ozzie told us about, darting around where you need not be."

Aerrvin shrugged and waited.

65

"Fine, come with me. Let us see if the Lord will meet with you. He is busy, you know." They flew up to sit in a lilac bush to wait for the first frenzy of the dance to scatter.

Ozzie, Bud, and Jasper alighted on the branch next to them, wafting the sweet scent of the spring blossoms through the air.

"I see you decided the music was right, Aerrvin," Ozzie stated. "'Tis good, because Morvayne is interested in meeting you, and we would have had to search you out. Not my idea of a fun evening."

From their vantage point, Aerrvin witnessed the glow of the Fairy Ring diminish as those who had no requests left. The remainder would be the council and those Fairies who wished to receive something from them. The number remaining was far smaller than Aerrvin expected, especially for a Ring so large. Twenty-three Fairies remained; thirteen would be the council. Suddenly there was a snap of light, and an Orange Fairy was carried away trailing smoke. It was nearly the same for every petitioner, once a judgment was made, a pair of Yellow Fairies carted the defenseless Fairy away.

To maintain a cheery nonchalance, Aerrvin did somersaults from one cluster of flowers to another. Purples are notorious for playful silliness, so Aerrvin made sure to let his Purple qualities shine.

Not used to being in uneasy situations, Aerrvin asked somewhat tightly, "What kind of council is going on?"

Ozzie replied to the question with a nasty grin, "New and Improved!"

Put off by the non-answer, Aerrvin recalled the name of the other Fairy close to him, it being his father's. "So, your parents named you after King Jasper?"

Jasper puffed up proudly and replied, "That they did. They met him personally once."

"Is that so?" Aerrvin replied with wide-eyed innocence.

"Yes, and don't be taking that tone with me. See this sword? My father got him to part with it. See this mark? It means that King Jasper made it."

Aerrvin bent close and saw that, yes, indeed his father had made the sword; one of many which he mass-produced so the commoners could have a trinket from the King. Aerrvin again opened his eyes widely and replied, "Aye, that's a right proper sword!"

The unnamed Yellow spoke up, "All right. The council is over; we can approach."

To Aerrvin, it was a very short council, most Fairy Ring meetings included more than one dance, and most meetings were joyful. Music is often the best way to moderate spats. Furthermore, most Fairies left a dance feeling lighter and brighter. Very new and different indeed!

They flew down to the Ring. In the center stood Morvayne, very definitely an Elf. Fairies don't necessarily have pointed ears; maybe a slight pulling up, but Elves do, and there is no mistaking them for a Fairy, even when minimized.

In the order of beings, Elves rank above all other magical creatures upon the Earth (not counting Dragons); therefore, it was proper for Aerrvin to bow before Morvayne.

"So. You are the little Purple Fairy who wants to ask me a question, yes?" Morvayne said dryly.

"I don't remember my question, but Ozzie said I might be of service to you," Aerrvin said with a shrug, looking up at the taller Elf.

"Let me refresh your memory. You were flitting about a house, seemingly trying to get inside. The occupant belongs to me. You wanted to know what interest I had." Morvayne laughed harshly. "I will tell you if you are still interested, but in return, you must answer my questions as well."

"Okay, what do you want to know about me?" Aerrvin replied, fluttering his purple wings slowly so as not to appear anxious.

"Very well," Morvayne replied, "but not here. I wish to sit in comfort."

In a blink and with a slight bend of light they were suddenly in a room, which very nearly appeared to be a throne room. Aerrvin had visited the King and Queen of the Elves once and knew very well that Morvayne was not part of the royal family. Nonetheless, the chair Morvayne sat in was raised upon a crystal pedestal and the council members who accompanied him reclined on cushions of red velvet. Fragrant yellow rose petals carpeted the floor. Commanding the wind, Aerrvin gathered a pile together for a seat. Sitting down with a graceful flourish, he looked to Morvayne, awaiting his questions; while hoping Gareth and Jaera were not trying to follow.

"So tell me little fly—what brings you to the New World?"

"My parents thought I fought too much with my sister." He grinned, adding, "She's a Yellow with a strong touch of White." Rolling his eyes as though that explained everything, which in truth it did, he sat awaiting the next question.

"I see," Morvayne replied with a dry chuckle at Aerrvin's antics. "Hmm. I will have more questions by and by, but I am satisfied—for now. I will tell you my story, but you must promise to keep the information to yourself. I have brilliant plans and will not tolerate them being spoiled by a purple pipsqueak like you. Is that clear?" he asked, looking pointedly at Aerrvin's wings.

Aerrvin knew he expected an oath, so he swore, "By my Purple wings I swear; I will not reveal to a single Fairy what I learn tonight." Breaking an oath caused a Fairy to lose the power upon which they swore for a year.

Satisfied, Morvayne began, "I arrived in the New World with a group of Hold Mates in the modern year 1545. Paris became an impossible place to live. We journeyed freely among the natives of this land, enjoying peace and prosperity. Eventually, we settled in this area of the Pacific Northwest, as they call it today. Though we often roamed up and down the coast, from the land of the Inuit all the way down to the tip of Baja. It was a joyous life. They worshiped me, and over the years, the Chiefs throughout the land gave me their daughters to wife. Nevertheless, my one true love was Tigerlily." His soothing voice gained fire as he spoke, "We had nearly grown up together and were Hold Mates for four hundred years. But she refused me!"

Interrupting as though he too felt incensed, Aerrvin asked, "What reason did she give?"

"She was vague!" Morvayne spat. "She said she was searching for something or someone, and when found, she would recognize it for what is was. What kind of answer was that?" He looked around the room as though expecting a response, yet knowing he would not get one, he continued, "So, I accepted the wives offered me over the years and flaunted my fun. As the decades went by, I could see Tigerlily was sorely disappointed in me more and more. But it was her fault! Then the Europeans came to the New World in great numbers. Like locusts they cover the world. It is sickening!" Shutting his eyes in revulsion for a moment, he paused. "Sorry, young one, you are probably too young to remember the world as it was. So green and alive!"

Aerrvin nodded agreement. Humans had always populated the world in abundance. Before he could comment, Morvayne continued as before.

"So alive. In time, settlers came here—to the Emerald City. I named this region, with plans of building my own grand Empire. *They* came and began interacting with my followers. They brought their Christianity, and I began to fear, lest they decry me as a follower of the Dark One, seeking once again to take my life as they had done in Paris. My Hold Mates scattered; a few went to set up residence in the Southern Continents; some went to the Land of Dreams. I begged Tigerlily to come with me to the Land of Dreams. I know if she had done so she would have wed me." His voice became a whisper, "All things are possible in the Land of Dreams."

With a shocking roar, he continued violently, "She listened to their preaching! She believed their version of the afterlife, and she chose Humanity." Abruptly he stopped and held his face in his hands. The room became frightfully silent. Morvayne looked up realizing that all eyes were on him, though at his glance heads went down.

"She chose Humanity. I had exactly one hundred years to try to sway her. She said she loved me and wanted me to join her. Why would I give up my life just to have her as my wife for a mere one hundred and fifty years?"

Seizing the opportunity to speak during the pause, Aerrvin questioned Morvayne, "So when did Tigerlily become fully Human, and what does she have to do with this Mara, whom Ozzie said was yours?" Shifting to rest on his stomach with his face in his hands, he looked up at Morvayne as though expecting a fireside tale.

"Ah, you are clever. Ozzie tends to judge rightly." He favored Ozzie with a smile. Ozzie shifted, straightening his shoulders as he hovered near the wall of the receiving room. Only the chosen council members had pillows.

"Tigerlily finished her transition to Humanity in 1950. She died in 2001." With a shock, Aerrvin realized that Mara's beloved great Aunt Lily was her great-great-grandmother Tigerlily herself.

"Even as a Human, having once learned the secret to magic, the science of it remained available to her. She had wards set to keep me out of her home and wore powerful jewels wherever she went." Clenching his jaw, Morvayne continued softly, "She could not bend Light, Travel or Fade. She had chosen Humanity—and death was her reward."

"And Mara?" Aerrvin prompted.

In a lighter voice, Morvayne responded, "Ah, Mara is my hope for a brighter future. I have watched all of Tigerlily's descendants carefully. Her first two children died of 'natural causes.' Nature can be truly harsh," he laughed while looking meaningfully at one of his Yellow Council members. "Then, while I went to the Land of Dreams for a time, she managed to have a son. Goldenrod Jamis. He had four children: A son who died at the age of one week. Iris, still living, married a doctor and had five daughters, of which only one female could shine a flicker as a baby—the rest are as useless as any other Human. Goldenrod spawned Lily; she died at thirty, never married. And then we have his son Ironwood. Ironwood lives and is quite able to foil my plans. He is Mara's Grandfather. He has other grandchildren, also of no use to me. He is fully trained in Earth Sciences and quite aware of who Tigerlily was, namely the second daughter of the Queen of all Elves and Realms—Her Royal Highness Gwennara of the First Garden. And, of course, Tigerlily's father is the royal consort, King Brand the Bright," Morvayne paused expecting a remark.

Although Aerrvin knew Tigerlily's heritage already, it was nevertheless impressive, so with no difficulty, he swiveled upright and replied, "Truly impressive, my lord. An Elven princess in that simple house, just waiting to be awakened. And you really can't reach her?"

"No, not even when she leaves the house. A choking sensation comes over me when I get too close. In addition, more twists to the puzzle have arisen.

Bud and Jasper managed after thirty years of effort to weaken a single ward in the basement window, and it finally split. Suddenly, the next night, the ward was in place and stronger than before." Bud and Jasper hung their heads in dejection. "My efforts to reach Mara are urgent as she turns twenty-one in five weeks. On Midsummer's Day in fact."

Now, Aerrvin was truly impressed. For a Fair One, being born on any of the quarter holidays denoted true magnificence. Moreover, turning twenty-one is a significant day of birth. It is the Day of Initiation. The day when a Fair One makes their promises to serve the Light and in return permission is granted to begin training in all the powers and responsibilities the Creator provides.

"Remarkable, my lord. How can I help you?"

Morvayne smiled indulgently. Tossing his ash blond bangs to the side with a practiced snap he replied, "You, my lovely little Purple, are to find out who is aiding her. We believe she has Brownies, though we have never seen them. No one wants to divulge anything to my faithful Yellow and Orange Fairies. But look at you! You are so adorable, who could refuse to play with you?"

The praise was nothing new. Aerrvin rewarded the compliment as he always did. He gave a triple backward flip and bowed lavishly.

"I would be pleased to perform such a simple duty, sir." Aerrvin grinned with mischief in his eyes.

"Well done, well done, little Purple."

It appeared he was going to refuse to acknowledge Aerrvin with his name, even though surely Ozzie had informed him. *Just as well,* Aerrvin thought, *I don't need his evil lips speaking my name anyhow.*

"Return next Monday night and report."

In a blink and with a bend of light, Aerrvin was again in the center of the Fairy Ring. The Fairies had returned and were dancing in typical fashion, with music trilling merrily from a dozen or so pipes and flutes. Weaving in and out amongst the Fairies, Aerrvin caught sight of Jaera tumbling with a feisty Yellow tinged with Green, while Gareth looked on in bemused delight.

"Ah, there you are," Gareth sang out as he caught sight of Aerrvin. "'Tis nearly dawn. Should we find a suitable perch or head home?"

"Let us head back; we can watch the sunrise from the maple tree in the yard."

Gareth entered the fray and after several attempts removed Jaera. Jaera always appreciated a good row. Nevertheless, she smiled good-naturedly at her two companions and led the way home.

9

Searching One's Soul

To bend with the breeze takes practice, to sway in the wind brings peace.

~ Jasmine ap Weaver

May 12, 2009

Tuesday. Mara woke up troubled.

"I need to talk to someone," she said absently, "and not just myself!"

She went through her morning in a daze. She took notes in history and wrote down her assignments, but her mind wandered. At lunch, she cheered at seeing Joe sitting with Bonnie. Since they appeared to be a couple, her comfort factor increased. She liked him; it was just that he wanted a girlfriend, and she wanted a friend.

"Hey, you two. Mind if I share a table?" Mara asked.

"Hey, how ya doing? Not a problem. Plenty of room," replied Joe. Bonnie took his hand possessively and smiled tightly.

Mara noticed Joe's missing his watch. Vivid memories flashed before her as she recalled the fresh, moist earth between her toes and the scent of herbs and flowers as she hid near the golden watch with its glow-in-the-dark face. The other night Aerrvin had instigated a game of hide and seek, Mara impulsively blurted, "Your watch is under the rhododendron in your backyard. I was . . ." Realizing what she was saying she stammered, "I uh—I mean, I bet it would be since you spend your evenings out there."

As Bonnie blushed, Mara envisioned digging herself into a deeper pit. Flustered, she excused herself by "remembering" she had an appointment.

Once well out of hearing she muttered, "If I didn't have one before, I'm making one now." She canceled her craft class at work, claiming a sick day. Then she called her pastor.

*****

In Pastor Mike's office, Mara tapped her toe in a soft staccato on the floor. She was comfortable with him as her pastor, but today she called on him because he was a licensed psychologist.

"So, Mara, I understand from your call that you are feeling anxious and perhaps unhinged. Can you describe what led up to being upset enough to call on me today?" Pastor Mike was a bear-like man with a nearly neat brown beard and mustache matching his curly mop of hair.

Hesitating a moment, Mara asked, "What is the church's stand on magic, or the paranormal?"

"We don't sanction it—if that's what you mean. Are you mixed up with Wiccans?"

"No, nothing wicked. I mean I don't think it's wicked—that's why I'm confused." She paused, rubbing her forehead.

He sidestepped her ignorance about Wiccans and said, "I am not sure what it is you want to know, Mara. The church as a whole stands against practicing any of the dark arts, as they might be called."

"I mean, oh—I don't know, isn't there such a thing as good magic?" Mara averted her eyes from his and looked at the bookshelf instead. She focused on the black and red bindings, fearing his answer.

"As a matter of fact, not church policy mind, but I do believe in good works brought about by miraculous means. My doctorate focused on Mythology and Religion. I wrote my thesis on the Occult. You seem to have come to the right place." He smiled encouragingly. "If you can be more specific. I can help you better."

Even though he sounded like he might believe, it caused Mara's stomach to twist in knots. She was not sure she wanted to believe. *I don't believe in magic, I don't. Mom would kill me. No, it would kill Mom.*

"Honestly, I think I am hallucinating. Maybe my problem has to do with the anniversary of my dad's accident this Saturday."

Finally getting something he could work with, Pastor Mike asked, "Have you experienced good hallucinations this week?" When she nodded, he continued, "And what do you think they mean concerning your father?"

"I don't know. As a little girl, he always called me his Elven Princess and, as my mother said, filled my head full of silly fairy tales."

"And. . ." he coaxed, leaning back in his leather chair.

"And this week I got my first boyfriend since high school." When Pastor Mike sat there waiting, she continued, "Anyway, I've been dreaming that he comes to me in my sleep dressed like a prince—and we are fairies. We fly about the city, dancing the night away."

"Your father or the new boyfriend?" he queried.

"The boyfriend," Mara replied, blushing furiously.

"Hmmm," he responded, scribbling something in his notebook. "On the surface, you appear to be missing your father. And this new guy may be making you apprehensive. It is evident you have postponed a relationship while in college. That's not bad, mind you. But why haven't you had a long-term guy in your life?"

"Busy with school and work, I guess." Mara thought perhaps fear of losing a boyfriend like her mother lost her father might be one answer, but instead, she said, "I didn't think it had anything to do with my father, but it's possible. Maybe I didn't think I'd find someone he'd accept."

"And you think a fairy prince would be acceptable?"

She tried to hide her fear or frustration by covering her face with her hands. Her muffled voice could barely be heard as she said, "I don't know! That's why I came to you." Peeking out from behind her fingers, she asked, "Can you find me something to read about reportedly true white magic?"

"I do believe I can help you there. I am thinking of the perfect author, and he lives right here in Seattle. He is a world-renowned scholar on the subjects of mythology, mystical creatures in particular. I am not sure I will be able to get in to see him right away; he travels a lot. I will call you as soon as I get one of his books. When would you like to come back?"

Mara hummed before saying, "I feel better having someone to talk to about all this. As long as you don't think I need to be medicated or anything. Do you?" She pulled her shoulders up as if trying to ward away impending doom while tucking her head and looking up at him through her lashes.

"No, not at all. I advise you to talk it out with your new beau. I believe some of your anxiety is the uncertainty of the future. You are about to graduate and need to face the world; to make a living and all, you know?" His warm smile offered comfort. "Next time, maybe you can go into details about what you think you see, and we can puzzle them out together. Would you like to select a time now?"

Mara thought it over and decided to try Wednesday after work. "You'll be here for Youth Night already. Will that be okay?"

✳✳✳✳

76

Aerrvin's urgent business plans would take him out of town, but he wanted to see Mara before he left. He hoped that the menacing Fairies would stay away from her since he agreed to help Morvayne spy on Mara. He needed to recruit more reliable help. For the moment, he would rely on Gareth. Gareth was delicate and highly musical, but his greatest skills as a Blue Fairy were in defense and strategy. Not a commonly requested skill to be sure, but one every person of royal heritage should endeavor to keep close at hand.

Aerrvin closed his shop for the day. He enjoyed meeting people and speculating on their talents and skill with the items they bought. Really, he was ready to hire Human employees. The business had served its purpose: he had found his future wife. Now he had more important things to do—like keep her alive and free from Morvayne's clutches. He asked Button to handle the hiring and training of competent employees.

Disappointment enveloped him since Mara had not stopped in at the store.

"I need a cell phone," he concluded. Locking the door, he went in the opposite direction from home to the electronics store where he purchased four phones. "They should be suitable, and I must admit," he said quietly to Seamus perched on his shoulder, "you can be clearer than a seedpod since it is two-way communication!" Chuckling softly, he smiled at the people on the sidewalk who gave him a wide berth.

At Mara's house, he admired the manicured front yard and greenery. Jill answered the door.

"Mara is not feeling well. She has a headache and has gone to bed early," Jill said curtly.

Crestfallen, Aerrvin replied, "Could you give her my new cell number? I am going out of town on business and won't be back until Thursday. I would like her to call me."

Jill replaced her consternation with a smile. "Oh, sure! I thought you dumped her already. She came home so depressed. And she barely ate her dinner. I could hardly get her to say two words.

Concerned, but masking his emotions, he said, "Wait here a minute. I hid something around the corner." Then running to the side of the house, out of view, he grabbed a bouquet of sweet peas and lavender tied with a pink silk ribbon. Of course, he had not hidden it there; he had bent the light, creating a portal to access what he desired.

Dashing back, Mirri ruffled his hair playfully. "Would you please give these to Mara? Tell her I hope she recovers soon and I'll be dreaming of her."

****

Jill tiptoed into Mara's room, smiling in gratitude for the soft pink lamplight that helped prevent her from tripping over Mara's shoes and tossed clothes. After breathing in the fragrant blossoms one last time, she set the vase on Mara's bedside table. "Oh, you are awake; Aerrvin brought you flowers. He wishes you well and wants you to know he will be dreaming of you. How romantic of him. He also gave you his cell phone number on this note and said to let you know he will be out of town. How's your head?"

"Um, I feel a little better." Mara slid to the edge of her bed to get a sniff of the flowers. "Mmmm, heavenly."

She stood. "Sorry I was not very talkative. I know you thought I was angry with Aerrvin. It's just me, though. My dad's anniversary of—you know—is coming up and, well, that's all."

She turned on the main light so she could get a look at the bouquet. "It's beautiful. How could he know sweet peas were a favorite?" Mara asked as memories of dancing through a tangle of sweet peas flashed in her mind. Shaking her head, she said, "I think I would like some chamomile tea, and then I'm going back to bed."

"I'll make it for you. Stay here." Jill stabbed at the phone number on the slip of paper.

Mara went to her dresser to pick up her cell phone; she still had some free minutes left. "Might as well use them up."

Growly sat there too, Mara picked him up and gave him a kiss. As she did so, it caused the seedpod Aerrvin had placed there the other day to stir.

Setting Growly down, she picked up the bit of dandelion fluff and said fervently, "Help me to believe!"

She stood there twirling it in her fingers, pondering her situation. Not able to help herself she held it above her head and blew at it causing it to fly. With more cheer, she danced it around the room with puffs of air. Nearing the window, it bounced up against it.

"Ah—you would like to be free wouldn't you?" Mara opened the window, placed it in her palm, and allowed the wind to whisk it away, all the while ignoring the nearly invisible Aerie that grasped the stem and flew away with a nod.

Dusk had settled, but the evening was clear, so Mara watched the seedpod until it blew out of sight towards the east. She shut the window just as Jill returned with her tea and a plate of cookies.

"These are fresh from the oven. A new creation. You can tell me later how you liked them. Go ahead and make that call! I'm sure he's waiting. Have a good night; I will see you in the morning." She hugged Mara and kissed her cheek. "Oh! And I'm not going in to work tomorrow. I'm meeting with the renovation team." In a flurry, she was in and out.

Mara realized she was indeed hungrier than she had thought. She sat down to eat a cookie while her tea cooled. It was a soft oatmeal cookie touched with ginger and filled with a sweet raspberry filling.

"Definitely a winner, Jill."

She sipped at her tea and finished three cookies. After an explosive sigh, she said, "Mara, grow up! You want to hear his voice anyway."

With mixed emotions, she entered his number into her phone and then pushed send.

"Hello." Aerrvin's soft, rich voice came across altered, but decidedly delicious.

"Hello, it's me, Mara."

"Mara, I am so sorry you are hurting." The sincerity in his voice touched a tender spot and soothed at the same time.

"I'm better now; my headache's gone. I'm just tired. I will sleep soon. I called to thank you for the flowers. I absolutely love sweet peas…" pushing past her fear, Mara plunged ahead. "How did you know?"

❋❋❋❋

With a nonchalant shrug, forgetting she could not see him, he answered using his warm, theatrical voice, a voice he knew attracted notice, "Magic."

A memory of Mara pausing to inhale deeply every time they neared the brambly patch of sweet peas was an easy clue. But Aerrvin had never awakened an Elven princess to her true nature before and was unsure how quickly he should proceed. It seemed obvious that her grandfather believed in the true way of the world, and yet he had not revealed the truth to Mara. Perhaps it was with good reason. Aerrvin decided being coy would do.

❋❋❋❋

"Hmmm." He sounded reasonable; it was an answer anyone would give. Not proof of anything at all. "Well, it was a sweet gesture, and they smell heavenly."

"I would love to bring you fresh flowers every day, but I will be away until Thursday. They will surely last, though. Did Jill tell you that you will be in my dreams?"

"She did." Mara smiled. "I have missed seeing you already, and we haven't even known each other a whole week yet!"

"Yes, it has been rather fast," Aerrvin agreed. "But, it feels so—I don't know. I would be devastated to lose you. Please take care of yourself and—wait a minute. I've got to get this message—sorry about that. Mara, are your windows locked?"

Mara returned to the window she slid the lock and replied, "Yes, they are—now. I had been enjoying a little breeze."

80

"Listen to me, Mara, I am serious. I want you to keep your windows locked for your safety, please?"

Sensing the urgency in his voice, Mara replied, "I promise never to fall asleep with my house unsecured. Will that do?"

"Yes. Now go to sleep," Aerrvin commanded, "I will see you soon."

"All right, good night, and have a nice trip." Mara smiled ruefully at the phone.

Climbing into bed, she tried to make sense of recent events. On the one hand, she kept encouraging the fantasy to be real; she so wanted to be a part of it. On the other hand, she thought she must be cracking up. *Mom says it's not real.*

"People do not see brownies and fairies flitting around," she muttered into her pillow.

And yet, Mara mentally recalled, *Dad shared a fairy nest with me once, when we had gone for a hike in the forest. In it was a teeny-tiny hat. Mom said it was just a bird's nest, and the bird had found a doll's cap.* Mara remembered another time on the beach, her father told wondrous stories of what it was like to visit the mermaids beneath the ocean's waves. He seemed to believe it all, even though he told the stories with a twinkle in his eye.

Then again, Dad always twinkled. No wonder Mom married him so quickly. Mara could not help but narrate to herself, *Mom was a high school senior when Dad moved to San Diego. Dad was at the start of his career in oceanography. They met at Sea World and three months later, only days after graduating, they got married. Later, Dad got a job back in his hometown, and they moved to Bellevue. So, even though it seemed they had a fairytale wedding, Mom—for whatever reason—did not approve of me hearing such nonsense. To the point of forbidding—forbidding! Mom forbade Aunt Lily and Grandpa from mentioning anything remotely magical, and she threatened no visitation.* Remembering that night, a year after her father's disappearance, Mara could see her mother standing there yelling and shaking with what Mara had taken as rage. *Maybe,* Mara thought with wonder, *could it have been fear?*

❖❖❖❖

81

After hanging up, Aerrvin looked at the seedpod in his hand. It was definitely from Mara. The message was so plaintive that it made his heart ache in pity. "Help me to believe!"

There was a curious twist to the message. Occasionally, seedpods caught by Fairies carried Human wishes on them. This one had been sent on purpose to Aerrvin, by Mara, as though she already believed. And it had been sent to her father as well. With a shrug and a blessing of success added to the wish, Aerrvin returned it to the Aerie and sent it on its way. Strange things abound. Maybe it could reach her father. After all, one never knows with magic.

Aerrvin resumed his natural stature to snuggle with the kittens and prepare for sleep. He tasked Gareth with keeping Mara's perimeter safe, and Jaera chose to join him. So, the prince was alone with the family of cats.

He could sense the personalities of the kittens; the orange fluffy one was the most demanding and the white one with the black stripes was the most alert; that one loved Mara more than the others. Therefore, he was the one Aerrvin loved most. Snuggled up tight, he scratched the kitten's head and put himself into a Dream state. He preferred physically dancing all night with Mara, but he felt it was his fault that Mara was so tired. So he decided that letting her sleep more fully would improve her health. In the Dreamer's Void, Aerrvin identified Mara's Dream easily; spending time with her allowed easier access to her Light, kissing her made it stronger. He reached forward and took hold of her Dream, it expanded, and he stepped in. It was a jumbled mess, as Human Dreams often are.

One minute she was a little girl talking to her father, and another she was an awkward teen, though still breathtakingly beautiful to Aerrvin. Setting out a plate of cookies for Sylvie, she searched her carefully kept bedroom. The room was not the room in which she slept in now. It was obviously her room while living in Sequim.

"Sylvie, you can come out," she called, "I know you came with us when we moved—Sylvie?"

Sylvie never came. Then the Dream shifted to Mara in class. She sat taking notes when suddenly an Ogre entered the room, he went right to Mara and said, "Would you please come with me?" His voice was as sweet and musical as any Fairy's. But when Mara looked up, she screamed.

Aerrvin took that as his cue to interrupt the Dream. Flying in with magnificently huge silver and blue wings, he swept Mara up into his arms and flew with her out the window. Then transforming her, he gave her wings and a short, fluttering, iridescent gown with silver leggings made from spider silk lace.

She beamed radiantly at the changes and said, "Thank you. You saved me from that horrible Ogre!"

"Has he come after you before?" Aerrvin asked as they settled on a pink rose bush, mindful of the thorns.

"Yes, or something just as horrible. This is a dream, though, right? I stepped right on a thorn, and I didn't feel a thing," Mara said in amazement, having left the bush to land softly on the lawn beneath it.

"Yes, it is a Dream, but sometimes you can feel pain even here," Aerrvin cautioned. "It is important for you to be aware of where you are at all times and to guard your thoughts. What you think can come true." Then, her foot began to bleed as she thought about what the thorn should have done.

"Ow! So I can simply wish it away?" Mara asked. In a blink, her unmarred foot returned, and she found she had changed to wearing the dress she bought for the tea party, though she was still barefooted.

Smiling, she asked, "Why didn't anyone tell me this before?"

Aerrvin shrugged as she continued, "I have suffered through countless nightmares over the years, and no one ever told me I could control the dream." Looking at her dress, she switched it back to the one Aerrvin had made. With a blush, she said, "I like this one better."

Aerrvin was amazed at her masterful control; it took him months to get the clothes he wanted. "There is more to it than mere thought. Do you have a mentor?"

"No. Daddy is gone, and Mom hates and fears magic. I don't know if I am going insane." Mara reverted to her twelve-year-old self. She began to weep, so Aerrvin took her into his arms.

He held her until her sobs lessened. Then with a puff of air, he dried her tears. He tilted her face up to his, and said, "I received your message on the breeze." He searched her eyes intently. "I will be your mentor until a more suitable one can be found. Is that fine with you?"

He smiled as she reverted to her present age. She was beautiful at any age, but in that moment she was more rounded and pleasing to his eye.

"I would like that," she replied. "Someday, when I'm ready, will you tell me this is real?"

"Of course!" With a merry laugh, he led her away to enter his Dream where they danced across the continent until dawn and watched a glorious sunrise on the Atlantic.

10

Truth Revealed

Ever fair and glorious visions have filled mine eyes thus far, let not

the evil forces—turn mine eyes away.

~ Clay of Glennferry

Wednesday, May 13, 2009

The sun shone gloriously bright, enhancing the yellow walls in the kitchen. Jill was as perky as ever. "Morning, Sweet Pea," Jill said, as Mara came into the kitchen looking for breakfast.

Mara wore a sprig of the flowers as a mini corsage fastened to her white sweater set. The sweater covered the necklace, but you could still see the quarter-sized bulge of the pendant.

"What's with all the glam? Are you going to wear that necklace every day?" Jill asked, setting a plate of French toast smothered in huckleberry syrup in front of Mara.

Thankful for the excuse, Mara replied, "Aerrvin said the style suits me. He told me not to take it off." Diffidently shrugging her shoulders, she took a bite of syrupy goodness with relish.

"Wait up there, sister! I wanted you to get a boyfriend, not a slave master. You need more lessons on relationships. You do not have to do everything a guy wants just because he wants it. You are your own woman and don't you ever forget it. Got it?"

"Yes, *Mother*," Mara intoned. "I love this necklace, it's from Aunt Lily. Aerrvin gave me an excuse to wear it. Is that better?"

"Humph!" Jill snorted. "It will do. I'm not an expert on relationships, obviously, but I have more experience than you. Just so you know, you can always count on me."

"I know. So what are your ideas for colors and design?"

Enthusiastically, Jill brought out her paint chips and fabric samples. They discussed plans for her catering shop until it was time for Mara to head off for her morning classes.

After Mara's second class of the day ended, her phone buzzed. Aerrvin left a message, saying, "Call me when you can."

Mara chose a bench in the warm sunshine to return his call.

He answered on the second ring. "Hello, Mara! I am so glad you called. I have one crucial question…"

He paused as she managed to sneak in a, "Yes?"

Then continued, "I need you to tell me your one and only, absolutely true favorite color. I couldn't tell from your décor."

Puzzled, yet intrigued, Mara responded with her own questions, "What is your favorite color? And why can't I have two?"

"I might influence your answer, so I can't tell you mine yet. And one color is sufficient,"

"Hmmm. I've never made a definitive statement like this before. Are you sure we know each other well enough?"

"Most definitely," Aerrvin replied smoothly, even as his chest felt as if a boa were constricting about him, he was excited yet nervous. He was in love.

With an exasperated sigh, Mara considered aloud, "I love the crisp, clean beauty of white, but some say it's not a color. So—if I must choose it would be something cool. I love any purple from the richest jewel tone all the way down to lavender." She paused a moment and then said, "I think really, and truly, my most favorite color—would be periwinkle, kissed with gray."

It was the color of her father's eyes she realized with a shock, as well as Aerrvin's own near blue eyes. "Maybe that is a pale lavender after all. It is a hard shade to describe. You could look at your eyes to see what I mean."

"Thank you, Mara. That is perfect. I get what you mean. My guess was close. I knew it was probably in the purple family. But I couldn't determine if you preferred the softer colors over the richer ones."

Before he could babble on much further, Mara interrupted him, "Now you have to tell me yours, and why did you *need* to know?"

"I am creating a surprise for you, but it will take at least a month, maybe longer, before it is ready. Now to answer the first question, my favorite color is the deepest, richest purple you can find in nature. But, like you, I like all shades as. See? We do have things in common; a perfect match—Ack! I need to meet with a group of gentlemen who have arrived, so I must go."

They said their goodbyes as she headed toward the cafeteria; she needed a substantial lunch to see her through until her late dinner. Mara thought about what the surprise might be. "He couldn't possibly be thinking of a ring already! Could he?" she wondered as she got in line to get her usual grilled cheese sandwich and salad combo. She gave up puzzling what else it could be while grimacing at the thought of a periwinkle engagement ring.

✣✣✣✣

Aerrvin went into the office he'd secured in a local hotel to meet with a contractor. Earlier in the morning, he had looked over the property listed online; Gareth's new PC had come in handy. The land was perfect, and Aerrvin thought he had never seen a more excited and anxious person than the contractor as he negotiated a price. The beachfront property came with plenty of acreage, eight hundred acres to be exact. Most of which was forested. They settled on $2,300.00 an acre, with a bonus for expediting the sale to close within hours. The land contained a small cottage, but Aerrvin had ostentatious plans for a home to suit the fussiest princess. Not that Mara was picky, but he knew she had discriminating taste and would appreciate the visual artistry he planned for this masterpiece. He had already built two representations. The first one was an actual working model. It was not handcrafted but grown from the elements—a home fit for Fairies in their natural state, situated deep in the woods, well away from any roads or the possibility of discovery. The other was a 3D paper and plastic representation for the Human construction team.

Greeting the construction company's owner, Aerrvin nodded, waving toward his creation. "This is the model I discussed with you on the phone. I trust you printed the blueprints I sent you online?"

"Yes, we did. You have quite a fantasy project here. Our engineer is not sure that we can do parts of it the way you want." They discussed the particulars and concluded they would, "give it a shot."

Aerrvin told them straight out, "If you do not think you are the right team for the job, I can contact Hornsby Construction."

"No, no need for that. We will be happy to work with you, after all, the client is always right. Isn't that what they say?" The contractor signaled his lawyer to bring out the papers.

Aerrvin read them over in a way that a Human would have thought too brief, yet he had indeed read every word.

"I neglected to mention two key points," he grinned at their alarm. "I have a crew of fifty that I insist work with you, and I want the house done in a month or so. Not more than two. At that point, I will charge you daily late fees. Additionally, we break ground today. I had my lawyer draw up papers for you."

Aerrvin reached into his empty briefcase to retrieve papers with the exact wording, plus his added stipulations. It took the lawyer twenty minutes to approve the contract while the contractor discussed the feasibility of such an undertaking. The money eventually won them over. Who could pass up a couple million bucks, with $500,000.00 in cash? Today?

After the meeting, Aerrvin returned to his new Fairy Palace. He had already transported seventy-five Brownies from around his Home Nest in the Hoh Rainforest. This spot was closer to the ocean than the other, not that distance was difficult; being close to the waves just made him happy. The sea's constant movement and living majesty thrilled Aerrvin beyond words. He considered moving the entire Ring, but most of his Fairy companions were happy where they were, so he decided to let them be as they may. Those wishing to be closer could move into the new Fairy palace. The official Ring of Court would remain in its original place of honor.

Because of his White personality, he thought it would be good to have this place to himself, including his Nest Mates, fifty to one hundred Brownies give or take a few, and most importantly Mara. *Ah, solitude!*

It had been five hundred years since any Brownie had built a Human or Elf sized building; a palace made them ecstatic. Sadly, this was not being done with the Human's knowledge, as it had been in the past. It used to be that all God's creations worked together to make a community.

Aerrvin briefed the Brownie crew leaders on their assignments and limitations.

"As a reminder, you will begin clearing the ground as soon as I introduce you to Cline's Crew. After you have the foundation prepared, I will place the wards in each corner and angle. Then tomorrow they will pour the concrete. No need for all of you to be there for that, just the supervisors."

Aerrvin looked at the four capable Brownies, not one of whom was under six hundred years old. Each had experience building homes for both Elves and Humans and knew the spells to weave and sing for the good of all who entered. Aerrvin raised his voice a fraction to emphasize his next most important point, "What I need from you is this: Once they finish working for the day, you must come in at night and strengthen and fortify the structure. Repairing any weaknesses and beautifying sloppy work."

Aerrvin chuckled. "These Humans will be amazed at the excellent work they have done, and will forever proclaim it as the best work they ever did!" The room exploded in laughter as the Brownies joined him in his mirth.

The Humans delivered their heavy equipment and left at 6:00 p.m. By 9:00 p.m. the Brownies had the entire area graded. The outside basement wall forms sat impeccably square, except for the places on each wall that had a twenty-foot triangle jutting out precisely in the middle of each wall. The triangles had been positioned to point in the cardinal directions. The land sloped gracefully away from the structure in a perfect circumference. From above, the palace walls created a compass—with each corner of the square structure aimed at the midpoints of such a compass.

An island of land adorned the center of the structure. The prince envisioned a majestic courtyard. The exact center retained an ancient cedar, soaring to the sky. Aerrvin flew above it, judging the tree perfectly centered. He drooped down to place a pebble in each corner and angle. These were distinctive pebbles, blessed with a kiss and desire for safety, thereby creating magical wards to keep evil from bubbling up from the depths of the Earth. It may be hard to imagine, but there are some things worse than Goblins!

With the forms in place, they suddenly had no work to do. Aerrvin downsized them to their normal stature, allowing them to return to the main dining hall in his miniature palace where the kitchen crafters had prepared a feast to celebrate the groundbreaking.

✹✹✹✹

Mara arrived at the church earlier than expected. Peeking in on Sarianne supervising the teens, Mara saw they were playing team-building games. Currently, they were trying to get a teaspoon of water from one bucket to another without spilling while blindfolded. Mara smiled, recalling good times spent with her youth group when she lived in Sequim.

Sarianne noticed Mara and came right over. "They'll be at it for a while. What brings you here on a Wednesday night?" Sarianne's broad face always looked so curious; she brushed a lock of yellow hair behind her ear awaiting a reply.

"I'm feeling a little stressed, just here to talk things out with Pastor Mike," Mara replied with seeming ease. "You know, graduating and all."

Sarianne nodded as though she did. In truth, she had never gone to college, having married her husband at eighteen. She had never lived on her own but believed she could empathize with everyone, so she gave Mara a comforting hug.

"Oh, you will do great. You will have your photos in art studios all over town soon enough, and all over the world by the time you are ready to retire. I'm sure of it." Changing the subject, she asked Mara to tell her all about the tea party. By the time Mara related her experience about holding the kittens, it was eight o' clock and time to meet with Pastor Mike.

Sitting in the leather chair next to the large desk, Mara felt more peaceful than she had last time. "I think I am ready to accept whatever the verdict is. Either crazy or the fact that there is more to life than people say," Mara replied to Pastor Mike's greeting and question. His familiar bearded face and warmth comforted her.

"Okay," Pastor Mike began, "I would like to hear about what you are seeing. Is it only in your dreams?"

Mara squirmed a little in her chair. When it came to her waking world, she still felt leery of sharing. Mentally trembling, she jumped right in.

"Really it began as a child. My father told me bedtime stories since before I could talk. One time I was at my Aunt's house and I spoke to a Brownie, and she has been with me ever since. She cleans my house and eats the cookies and milk that I leave out for her. I sometimes see movement out of the corner of my eyes, but when I look, nothing is there. So—um, all my life I have been pretending that I—don't see anything," Mara bit her lip and glanced up and away several times.

She fiddled with the pendant. Thinking it might break, she tried to make herself stop; then reasoning that since it couldn't come off, she certainly couldn't break it; therefore, she could fiddle as much as she wanted. Mara allowed her hand to return to the amethyst heart as she waited for Pastor Mike to stop scribbling in his notebook.

He looked up at her. "So, this is not new. Has it changed?"

"No, it is not new. And yes, it is becoming more frequent. Let me see if I can be more clear. I pushed it away so firmly that for several years I really have not seen anything mystical, but in the past year flickers of light and flashes of hideous beings, like ogres or something have returned. And the boyfriend fairy dream is certainly new. But it seems so real!" Mara looked up with a pinched and pleading face. "Did you find anything for me to read?"

"Yes, as a matter of fact, my old professor returned from Europe last week. He graciously loaned me two books which he thinks you will find most useful." Pastor Mike opened his briefcase, took out two leather-bound books, and laid them on the table for Mara to see. "He said he can discuss any questions you might have on Saturday."

Mara stared at the books, dumbstruck. She had seen those books before. Her father had copies of them, which he kept in his study. She assumed they were stored away in the lockbox, along with her father's other things, awaiting her 21st birthday. But even more astounding to Mara was the name on the cover, which she had never noticed, as she was very young the last time she had seen them up close. The title of the brown book was *Enchanted Lives*. The green volume was entitled, *The Study of Majick*. Ironwood wrote both books.

Fearing she would never speak, Pastor Mike prodded with concern, "Mara?"

"These were written by my grandfather!" Mara exclaimed breathlessly.

Mirroring her shock, the pastor replied, "Is that so? Well yes, I guess his last name is Jamis. He always goes by Professor Ironwood, and of course, we go by first names around here too." He paused to smile. "But, why are you unaware about your grandfather's specialty in this field?"

With a rueful smile, Mara explained her mother's no talking of magic rule. "Besides, I was young when we moved away. I didn't pay attention to what Grandpa taught. He's just Grandpa, some kind of professor who is always traveling. When he is home, we have a pleasant dinner, or go see a play or some such."

"I see." Looking at his watch, he continued, "Presently, Mara, I am unable to determine your state of mind. Since you were raised to believe in the fanciful, and yet forbidden by your mother, I can tell that the situation has created a paradox for you. You may very well be splitting into two mindsets. It will take more time to determine your stability. I would like to see you again tomorrow." He paused waiting for confirmation.

Receiving her nod, he continued gently, "Mara, I am afraid we will need to find someone else to teach your class. For now. You understand, as a precaution?"

Numbly, Mara nodded, yet she was confused. "I thought you believed in white magic?"

"I have always been fascinated by it, but I have not had enough real proof for me to say that I truly believe. I want to believe. In theory, I accept it. I love Professor Ironwood and admire his research. Still, these are stories which he collects. How can we be sure that the people relaying them are of sound mind? Let me assure you, I do not think you will harm anyone or yourself. If you have any hard evidence that you could share?" Hope lit his deep brown eyes.

Mara was not sure she wanted to test the necklace with him. What if it came off after she told him it wouldn't? What would he say, or possibly worse— what if it wouldn't? She thought she was prepared for the truth, but now she felt unsure again. Shaking her head, she replied, "Maybe tomorrow."

Pastor Mike shook her hand in both of his and gave her the books. "Don't forget these. They are fascinating. Perhaps they can make things clearer. Tomorrow then?"

"Yes, thank you," Mara replied hollowly. Her slight frame seemed a mere shell of the formerly confident parishioner.

11

Remembrances

And there you were, a kindred spirit. Seeking to become one whole.

~ Ivan Andiluv

Wednesday, May 13, 2009

The bus ride home seemed to take forever. Mara was anxious to read the books and felt so grateful to finally walk in her front door. Throwing herself on the lavender sofa, she sobbed into one of her velvet pillows.

Jill came in, perplexed at the usually staid Mara.

"Sweetie! What in the world is going on? Is this still about your father?"

Mara shook her head and let forth another round of sobs. It was one thing to tell a therapist your hallucinations, quite another to tell your best friend and then possibly your boyfriend and Grandpa. How to tell her mother was unthinkable. Somehow, Mara understood her mother, Amanda, was too fragile to speak to.

Jill rubbed her back until she calmed down and breathed nearer to normal. "Let me make you some tea. I managed to get Button to give me a portion of her stash of herbs—so I can make you some chamomile with an infusion of rose and lavender. Go change and wash your face. I'll bring it up to you."

When Jill came in, she brought a fruit salad along with thick slices of homemade bread slathered with butter, and a few slices of cheese. Mara had taken a quick shower and changed into a pink nightie, which came to her knees, topped by a matching sheer robe. She felt chilly, so she had on thick white socks. She smiled gratefully, as Jill placed the food on the small table.

Hesitantly, she confessed to Jill that she was seeing a therapist for her wandering, fanciful mind.

"So, you leave the cookies and milk out on purpose?" Jill asked.

"Yes."

"And have you seen evidence that they have been eaten?"

"Yes, though I always tried to avoid seeing. That is why I am being torn apart!" Mara wailed. Seeing Jill's alarm, she controlled her voice and continued, "Things have been happening more since Aerrvin arrived. I haven't actually seen Sylvie, my Brownie, since I was five or so. But last Friday night Sylvie let Aerrvin fly into my room, and they talked about me for a while, though I was half asleep and do not remember what they said."

"Wait, wait, wait—whoa! Aerrvin can fly?" Jill had been listening calmly, but alarms began to sound louder in her mind. "He just grows wings or something?"

"He appears to be a fairy. He was only six inches tall, and he shrank me down to size too; we danced 'til dawn." Smiling at the memory, she wiped a tear from her cheek.

Gaining confidence in the telling, even though Jill was incredulous, Mara retrieved the books. Opening the book entitled *Enchanted Lives*, she said to Jill,

"Pastor Mike got these books for me. Grandpa wrote them. I didn't even know he was a specialist in Mythology and Magic, but he is! Whatever. I loved these pictures as a little girl. Sitting with Dad before bed, he would tell me a story about whatever picture I chose. But look at this one!" Mara said, excitedly pointing to a beautiful pencil drawing of an Elven Queen and her three daughters.

"Beautiful artwork," Jill said.

"It is, but that is not what I want you to see. Look at the jewelry," Mara said, eyes alight.

Not getting it, Jill asked, "I see it, but what do you . . ." then seeing Mara's necklace she said, "You think you are wearing a fairy queen's necklace?"

"Not just the necklace," Mara exclaimed running to her closet. She brought out a box of tiaras, which had belonged to Aunt Lily. "The story is that Aunt Lily earned these as a beauty queen. But this one is an exact replica of the one worn by the princess standing there." Mara pointed to the second princess.

"Do you see the resemblance?" Mara said, placing the crown on her head.

With a start, Jill acknowledged, "Yes, your necklace is on the queen, and your crown is on the princess. You have the same unruly hair as the queen and the third princess, and you share the same face as all of them."

Mara peered in the mirror. She looked every bit the Elven princess as she surveyed her appearance—until she got to the fuzzy socks.

"It doesn't prove anything, Mara. The book is written by your grandpa. He probably drew the pictures too. I'd bet he used relatives as his models. Obviously, these are family jewels owned by your family for a very long time."

Mara flopped down in her recliner and stared absently at the book. "The chair behind them is my chair downstairs. I love that chair; no wonder I feel like a princess when I sit in it."

Jill shook her head in denial. She was open-minded, but this was too far-fetched.

Mara abruptly stood up. "Jill, will you remove this necklace for me?"

Jill tried. "I can't seem to get a grip on the clasp and when I do it stays together despite how hard I try."

Mara turned with tears filling her eyes. She told Jill about the last time she wore the necklace in whispered tones.

"I can't get it off either," she concluded.

Jill flopped down on the bed. Pulling a bolster under her neck, she stared at the ceiling and then said, "Now, I have seen everything," then with a sideways tilt of her head she added, "Except a flying fairy."

Jill borrowed *The Study of Majick* and Mara continued to read the stories of magical beings by Ironwood Jamis in the collection entitled *Enchanted Lives.*

As Mara read, having started at the beginning, she could almost hear her father's voice. Apparently, he had told the stories word for word. After each story, an explanation by Ironwood described where and from whom the story had been collected, as well as his thoughts about the events of the story. By the time Mara got back to the story about the queen and her three daughters, she was growing tired but was suddenly intrigued by a part of the story she had never associated with her family before. *The second daughter is named Tigerlily!*

"I am going to have to talk to Grandpa after all." She climbed into bed, turned out the light and mumbled, "Mom's not going to like this."

❄❄❄❄

Mara sat curled up in a buttercup, having shrunk herself down to pinkie size, just to see if she could. "I am so glad Aerrvin taught me how to control my dreams!" she mused.

Without warning, a hand plucked the flower from the ground. From inside the blossom, Mara looked up at the enormous, yet beautiful, face of a stranger—wreathed with silky silvery-brown hair.

"So you awaken, do you? This is wonderful. You should invite me in to see you sometime. I would be happy to initiate you," he offered a gloriously evil smile while his eyes burned with desire.

97

He was attractive, but Mara felt uneasy. "I am sleeping," she said firmly, "I wish to be away from here."

In an instant, she was in her darkroom watching her pictures appear as if by mystical means.

"It's magic," she breathed.

"Yes," Aerrvin agreed, appearing beside her. Since it was a dream, she calmly accepted his presence.

"Do you believe in magic?" His face beamed with hope.

Mara faced him to reply, "I do when you are near." *I can be as mushy as I want in a dream, right?* She didn't even care that her nightie was so sheer.

With raised eyebrows and a crooked twitch to his lips, Aerrvin said, "As do I, but Mara, you need to accept this truth; all magic has a scientific explanation to it. I am a realist in the utmost sense. My life is more real than yours is. Watching a picture emerge in developer indeed would have been called magic in medieval times. As would electricity."

Mara frowned. "Magic is not really magic?"

"You will need to wait until later for that answer. Right now, I need to tell you more about Dreaming. Now that you have some control, you must use caution to keep unwanted beings from spying on your Dreams. The Elf you saw is named Morvayne. He is evil and wants to use you. I have not yet learned what he plans, but here is how to ward your Dreams to keep anyone from entering." Aerrvin drew a squiggle in the air with silver sparkles; it looked like a fluffy cloud with two legs.

She giggled, but copied the motions, her fingers unexpectedly trailed opalescent sparkles, which made her gasp. "I have never seen that before!"

Aerrvin smiled, "Just a part of who you are." Opening the door of the darkroom, Aerrvin said, "Come, show me your world."

12

I Do Believe . . .

Dreams within dreams capture the soul. Escape warrants more study.

~ Clay of Glennferry

Friday, May 15, 2009

Mara could almost taste the weekend. Thursday had not been much better than Wednesday, except when Mara recounted her necklace story to Pastor Mike, he tried to remove it and was stumped. He admitted it seemed to be a smidgeon of "something." She also showed him the familiar picture of Tigerlily, standing with the man who was not Mara's progenitor.

Startling Pastor Mike, she exclaimed, "This man is an Elf too!" Shadows caused distortion, but with better concentration, Mara could make out his pointy left ear. He had been in her dream the night before.

"Now you have *me* seeing things. Yes, it looks like a pointed ear, but it could be a trick of light and shadow. Mara, have you discussed your feelings about your father in relation to your new perceptions, with your boyfriend?"

"No, well maybe. I told him how sad I am that my dad is gone," Mara replied, visualizing an image of herself sobbing into Aerrvin's white shirt. "But he has been out of town since I started visiting you about all this, so I have not seen him. Unless seeing him in my sleep counts?"

Pastor Mike shrugged his shoulders and shook his head. "I can't keep calling him your boyfriend. Does he have a name you wish to share?"

"Oh, yes, sorry. I didn't mean to be secretive. You met him last Sunday, I think. He's one of the Irish guys that sat in the back row. Aerrvin ap Rosewin," she said stumbling over the name somewhat.

"Oh my! You really know how to pick 'em," Pastor Mike teased. "Going from no beau at all, until the hottest guy in town shows up. Then suddenly you have a rich, successful businessman asking you out?"

Mara ducked her head as her cheeks warmed. "Yes, it does seem fantastical, even without him being a fairy."

Pastor Mike erupted into a booming laugh. "Ah, Mara, what are we going to do with you?"

He sent her on her way without any advice at all.

✤✤✤✤

"Free at last!" Mara exclaimed after her last class. Soon she caught her bus for home.

Her mother sat waiting in the living room when Mara arrived. "Mom! I didn't expect you so early." Mara greeted her with a hug and sat down beside her. "Is Jill here?"

"Well, I love you too. And no, Jill is not here. I let myself in with my key. I took the early bus. Rick and Ricky needed both cars so I couldn't drive and—well, it doesn't matter. I have been here an hour. I put my bags in your room and cleaned up the dishes you left sitting out. Still feeding the Brownies I see," she ended with a scowl of disapproval.

Having come to terms with what she thought her mother knew and refused to acknowledge, Mara smiled through a crooked frown and shrugged a single shoulder.

Laughing softly at her daughter, Amanda sighed and said, "Mara, Mara, Mara. What am I going to do with you?"

"Not much, I hope," Mara replied, entering the kitchen to get a bite to eat. "Did you eat, Mom?" She paused and then continued as her mother followed her into the kitchen and took a seat at the breakfast counter.

"No, I ate a banana to tide me over until you got back."

Mara got out the leftover crab bisque and warmed it up in the microwave while she sliced pieces from the cute mini loaves of French bread which Jill had made for dinner the night before.

"Jill is moving out next month, so I am going to miss having all this delicious food," Mara commented as she placed their servings on the counter. "She is opening up her place soon, and it has an apartment upstairs."

"That is too bad. Jill has been a help to me; I felt you were safe with her around." Glancing at Mara, she sighed again and said, "But I guess you are all grown up now. What with graduating at the end of the month and all. Do you plan to keep working at the retirement center?"

"Probably through June," Mara replied. "But I've already started submitting portfolios at some of the local studios. Besides, I get my inheritance from Dad soon, and I can live off of it for two years if I have to."

Amanda frowned. "You could, but it would not be wise to waste it." Still frowning, she flickered her manicured fingers at the pendant Mara wore. "No point in spending it on gewgaws and fancy clothes. I remember the last time you tried being uppity, with that necklace on everywhere you went. It didn't make you popular."

"Yes, Mother, but I was a girl then. Now I am a woman. Women can wear nice things, and no one minds at all."

"I guess you are right. Just don't waste your money. Dad would have wanted you to invest it or something. It's already grown substantially since being placed in trust for you."

Then changing the subject, she said, "I noticed a few photos of a particularly good-looking man in your room. When were you planning on telling us?"

Mara took a moment to swallow her food. "I barely met him last week!" Holding her hands up in a pleading gesture she asked, "How soon am I supposed to tell you about a guy I meet?"

Her mother replied with a sniff, "The photos seem awfully intimate for having just met him."

"Mom, I'm a photographer, remember? I'm getting pretty good. If you're done, we can go downstairs, and I will show you all my stuff for my final presentation. Ready?"

Amanda swiped her bowl with her bread to get the last bits, and then followed Mara down the stairs. The smell of fresh paint hit them when they opened the basement door; Mara had painted the eastern wall a pale green the night before.

"I'm still not sure you shouldn't have been an interior designer, Mara, as much as you like doing it. But don't sidetrack me," Amanda said, as she again noticed a significant number of photos of Aerrvin.

Mara explained the inspiration of seeing the wind blow his hair, and then his living in the O'Shea Mansion and coming to Jill's block party. "The wind blew so flawlessly. Surely you can see how great they turned out? I have only known him for a week, today! It was just last Friday that I took these photos. Besides, you fell for Dad in a week, didn't you?"

Rolling her eyes, Amanda replied, "Yes, I suppose I did. But you haven't had much experience dating; you should go out more before you settle on one guy."

"Mom, it was your advice that I not date too much while I was in school. I am graduating this month! Do you want me to wait until I'm thirty to marry?"

Mara rarely raised her voice to her mother, so with embarrassment, she apologized, "Sorry, I guess I am a little defensive. I didn't think I could fall for a guy so fast myself. I can introduce you to him tonight if you would like."

"That would be lovely; besides he couldn't be a loser if he can afford to rent the O'Shea Mansion. And—" she paused to give Mara a hug. "I think your photos are stunning. I would like a copy of the gazebo on fire, myself."

❉❉❉❉

Aerrvin decided to learn to drive a modern car, so he took a few lessons from a Brownie who owned a track deep underground in a cavern lined with glittering gems. The Brownie only charged Aerrvin a blessing upon his household, so it was not a hardship on Aerrvin's tight supply of gems. Building the palace was going to be more expensive than he thought, and he had not been taxing the local Fairy populations at all. When they met for a convocation, the representatives always brought a small token sack of gems or gold, but by rights, Aerrvin could request five times the amount he was receiving.

Mirri kept pace with the car, occasionally going up ahead to feel the sensation of slipping over the hood. But she sat fiddling with his hair at the moment.

"Ah, well," Aerrvin sighed as he crossed the bridge. "I am a businessman. I will have a steady income regardless."

"Aye, my lord, ye will never be the pauper. Ye worry too much for your own good."

In truth, Aerrvin had more wealth available than half the population in the New World combined. Fairies are used to hoarding gems, and when his bag rattled so, it made him feel poor.

He considered calling Mara again to let her know he was nearly in Seattle, but then he decided to surprise her with his new car, a Dodge Viper. Aerrvin had it custom painted with an intense midnight blue, which shimmered purple when seen from a different angle. Being a used car, it was a steal at $40,000.00. The dealer in Aberdeen didn't think he would be able to sell it and was about to return it to Seattle when Aerrvin came and made his day.

The Brownies had the custom paint job and detailing done in an hour. Brownies are thorough in their work. As they finished, the crew leader said, "It was quite clean, I don't think the previous owner used it more than ten times."

Pulling up to Mara's house, Aerrvin felt a presence inside that he did not recognize. Focusing on the person, he realized that he or she thought about him with ambivalence, which heightened as he arrived. But Mara's emotions burst upon him and overshadowed the negative. Before he got to the door, she opened it and wriggled her fingers to express her desire for him to close the gap. To Aerrvin, she smelled wonderful, like lavender and rose mixed with a touch of vanilla, as well as her unique scent of sweet peas. As desired, Mirri wafted Mara's scent towards him, causing his hair to wing away from his face momentarily as he inhaled deeply. *Dreams are not nearly as good as the real thing*, he thought. Aware of the guest, he kissed Mara briefly and then allowed her to pull him into the house.

"Aerrvin, this is my mother, Amanda Powers," Mara introduced. "Mom, this is Aerrvin ap Rosewin." She had been practicing on keeping the soft v sound on the w, the way he said it, but even now she had difficulty with the oh-ah blend in Rosewin.

"Pleased to meet you," he replied. "So sorry that the occasion is not happier." Knowing she was there for the annual memorial of Mara's father, he could feel her love for her daughter's father had cooled, but a part of her still ached. Whether for her daughter's loss or her own, he could not tell.

Amanda smiled warmly. "Thank you. Mara told me about your new craft store. Have you had much experience with running a shop?"

Aerrvin talked about the joys of purchasing supplies as a first-time business proprietor while he compared the similarities of Mara and her mother. Mara was fair of skin, with raven hair that hung to her shoulders in gentle waves with a few tighter curls escaping the smoother she combed in to tame her mane. Amanda was golden-haired, with skin like honey. Her hair was pulled back in a no-nonsense ponytail that curled gently toward the nape of her neck. Her eyes were a gray-green while Mara's were a fierce periwinkle blue. He could see the appeal Mara's father would feel for Amanda, but her emotions were all a jumble. If Mara's father knew the Ware Spell, Aerrvin felt sorry for him. With a rueful smile, he realized he had missed the last comment.

"Sorry, I missed what you asked."

Mara repeated, "I said, is that a new car?"

"Yes, I bought it in Aberdeen today. I came to see if you want to go for a ride. I forgot your mother was visiting." He shrugged one shoulder and said, "I can wait until Sunday."

Amanda broke in, "No, I didn't come here to be an inconvenience. Besides, I need to go shower and get ready for dinner. Riding public transportation always makes me feel icky." She shuddered.

"Let me get my sweater," Mara said, reaching inside one of the two closets in the entryway. "Mom, we won't be long. Will you please invite Jill to join us for dinner? I have already made reservations for 7:00, and if you don't mind, may Aerrvin join us?"

"Of course, dear," she replied, and then turned her attention on Aerrvin, "Have fun and don't kill her. It looks like it could go 100 miles an hour in 60 seconds."

He smiled his most winning smile and informed, "0 to 60 in four seconds. But trust me, Mara's safety is my utmost concern, and I have been driving for a while."

In fact, Aerrvin drove the Model T when it first came out, and he had tried the Edsel. He found flying and riding the wind far more useful and thrilling, so he never tried again until that point. Bronwyn adored driving and kept both of the aforementioned cars in his private collection.

Taking Mara's arm so he could stroke the cashmere sweater, he led her to the passenger seat.

Once he was in the driver's seat, he said, "Buckle up. You wouldn't want me to be a liar, would you?"

"You can't go sixty in the city!" Mara's eyes widened as she envisioned a collision.

"No, but I can on the highway. It won't take long; I've learned my way around the city pretty well." They sat in silence while he maneuvered through the traffic.

"How did you fill your time while I have been away?" he asked at the final stoplight on their path to the highway.

"Might as well plunge right in," she said under her breath.

Aerrvin felt her emotions getting all jumbled, just like her mother's had been. She was stressed; her heart rate increased, and he could smell a light saltiness as sweat popped to the surface of her fair white skin. She glistened in an almost glittery way.

"Mara, what is it?"

"I learned that my grandfather is a respected scholar in the field of magic. My pastor gave me two of his books to read when I went to him because I thought I was going crazy." She looked over to judge his reaction, but Aerrvin kept his face pleasant as he maneuvered around a semi. "He did not know that it was my grandfather because Grandpa dropped his last name; he goes by Ironwood. Or Professor Ironwood, I guess."

"And why would Pastor Mike think you wanted to read Ironwood's books on magic? And for that matter, why didn't you ask your grandfather for them yourself?"

"Because Mother demanded that Aunt Lily and Grandpa never speak to me about it. I didn't even know Grandpa was a famous professor of anything! I just thought he liked to teach at foreign colleges and travel for the fun of it."

"I see, that explains that part. But what about the part of going to your pastor because you thought you were crazy?"

"Pastor Mike is also a psychologist. I had two questions for him: I wanted to know if he believed in magic and if he thought I was crazy because I did."

"Interesting," Aerrvin commented with a slight twitch of an eyebrow. "And what was his response?"

"Hmm, he said he wanted to believe and that he admired my grandfather, but he needed more proof."

Mara's heartbeat slowed, so Aerrvin took a plunge.

"I do believe in Fairies, I do, I do!" He smiled as he pulled over to the side of the road where it was wide enough for him to do so safely. Then he turned to face Mara. "I do." His eyes sought hers.

Mara couldn't tell whether he was serious or not. His eyes gleamed, and his lips pulled up in a quirky sort of smile.

"Mara, listen to me. Magic isn't scary, for real! It's sheer science. I promise." He looked into her eyes seriously as he tried to gauge her reaction.

"You said something like that last night." She paused to see if he thought she was indeed crazy.

"I did," he confirmed. Then seeing that a lane was clear, he seemingly froze the traffic and went from 0 to 60 in four seconds, taking their breath away. "Woohoo!" he crowed. As the traffic joined them. "What do you think of my car?

13

Wings and Wishes

Anywhen . . . back again roaming halls with me

suddenly . . . lacking time, I see

~ Clay of Glennferry

May 15, 2009

Since Aerrvin offered to drive everyone to dinner, they stopped by his house first. He showed Mara in to see the kittens while he went up to his room to change.

Jaera had two kittens on her lap, and Gareth lay on his side watching the other three try to find Mama Cat, who had gotten up to eat and go outside for a moment. Mara controlled her astonishment at Gareth's new look but failed.

Jaera laughed at Mara and said, "Gareth is always changing his looks. If he sees something new, he will try it. Right?" The upsized Green Fairy nodded at Gareth who replied with a wink.

The ends of Gareth's long black hair were now an intense blue with silver tips. His hair spiked in a crest down the middle of his head. Dressed in soft black leather with silver studs, he was quite striking. Still, Mara was glad that he was not the one for whom she had fallen. Mara took her camera out and snapped a few shots.

Shaking her head, she said, "Imagine taking him home to Mom."

Jaera laughed with a bright, tinkling flutter and Gareth joined her, provoking joy in Mara. She was grateful they were such cheerful friends, especially since she tended to blurt her thoughts out loud much too often. She considered the notion that she offended people quite a bit.

Hearing Growly mewing pitifully, she scooped him up and kissed him; he quieted and nuzzled her face. *When did I start calling him Growly?*

Mama Cat returned at the same time as Aerrvin. He kissed Growly and said to Mara, "He loves you the best, you know." Aerrvin returned the kitten to his nest of soft feather down pillows and bits of fluff. "Doesn't he, Sugar?" Stooping to Mama Cat, he gave her a good ear scratching. "I think she likes bigger hands for scratching. Can you hear how loud she purrs?" Aerrvin figured he might as well keep the flow of revelation going by artfully sneaking it into the conversation. After all, Mara's Birth Day would arrive soon, and it would be better to be prepared for it, whether her family wanted it or not.

Mara remembered being only five inches tall while trying to scratch the cat's giant head, so she said, "I don't know, I think it sounds pretty loud when we are small."

She beamed shyly at the smiles she got.

Aerrvin held out his Viper keys to Gareth and said, "DO NOT let Jaera drive." Giving her a mock frown. "Test not my seriousness, Gareth. You may drive around and enjoy yourselves, and Jaera can ride, but that is all!"

Jaera stamped her foot. "I only crashed three cars, and once it wasn't even my fault," she raved, bouncing her curls as she did so.

"I understand, Jaera, but this car is one of a kind and expensive. Give me half of your bag, and I'll get you one in pink and green," he grinned as her eyes widened. Being a hanger-on of the prince did not make her rich. Half her bag would take her decades to collect again.

Satisfied that she understood the value, Aerrvin took Mara's hand, and they went out the side door to the Mercedes in the garage. As yet unnoticed, the invisible Seamus rode in the pocket of Aerrvin's sleek suit jacket of black silk. To those with eyes to see, his shimmering form bobbed to the music he was writing in his head.

As for Mara, she was impressed that Jaera had enough money to buy two cars in her bag, which she assumed was a purse. She was beginning to doubt that she was suitable company for the likes of Aerrvin and his companions.

Bronwyn stood by the car and held the door for them.

"I'll be driving, Bronwyn, thank you. Enjoy your evening."

Bronwyn shut the rear door and opened the door to the front passenger seat for Mara. "As you wish, sir," he said sadly.

He did so love driving and had already seen Gareth receive the keys to the sports car. "May I ask where you would be going?"

"Mara's mother is in town, so we are going out to dinner. I won't be out too late; no need to fear." Aerrvin grinned mischievously, hoping to get a reaction. He failed.

Then Bronwyn gave in and pulled Aerrvin's braid teasingly. "Very well, do tell me all about it later." His comment was for both Aerrvin and Seamus.

*****

Once home, Mara quickly put on the second dress she had bought the other day. It was not a tea-length dress at all; definitely more suitable for an evening out. The cut was lower than she remembered, but it showcased the pendant beautifully. The black crepe dress with an asymmetrical hem and fluttery sleeves allowed her pale shoulders to peek through when she moved. As she descended the stairs, all eyes were on her. Jill whistled.

"Mara, that is a lovely dress," her mother said. Amanda's eyes betrayed her opinion of the deep neckline, but she kept her mouth shut. Her own dress was very figure-flattering. The deep green, long-sleeved, nylon top featured a v-cut, not unlike Mara's. The attached skirt exhibited layers of black filmy fabric which shimmered green. It was elegant, not overly fluffy. Her shoes were nicer than Mara's. Amanda had let her hair down, with one side pulled back and held in place by an emerald encrusted comb; a gift from Brentwood, which she never wore in Sequim.

Mara replied sweetly, "Thank you. You all look great too. Jill, I love your bag."

Jill had purchased a cute silver clutch to go with her strappy silver slingbacks.

"I wish our feet were the same size. I'd borrow one of your one hundred pairs," Mara said, suddenly mindful of her old shoes.

"I do not have one hundred pairs, only forty-eight!" Jill said indignantly. "Besides, you look fab, and those shoes aren't ready for Goodwill. I'll tell you when you look terrible, believe me."

Jill wore a cute red dress, cut with a halter top; the choker-like collar sparkled brightly with sequins. The perfectly swirly skirt hung in gentle folds as Jill stood to leave. Mara noticed they were all apparently waiting for her to say the word, so she did, and soon they were all buckled in and headed to Mara and her Amanda's favorite five-star restaurant.

Mara and Amanda saved their money to afford the once a year excursion. To them, it was worth the effort. The place had valet parking, which easily impressed them. But walking into the grand entry always took their breath away; it was a treat to the senses. The foyer was velvety dark, with a giant chandelier sparkling from the ceiling. A water feature burbled merrily, mixing with the live music being played off to the side. The scents were mouthwatering, inducing "mmm!" to issue from all three women.

Aerrvin cocked an eyebrow and then answered the maître d' as he questioned to which party they belonged. They were precisely on time and were taken to their table straight away. Although single chairs are more elegant and easier to sit in with a dress, Mara preferred a booth and always requested one with a view of the city.

Mara and Amanda each took a window seat, allowing Aerrvin to sit with Mara.

The mother-daughter duo ordered the same appetizer as usual; a sumptuous artichoke and seafood dip paired with crisp bread rounds. Aerrvin ordered the *Cucumber and Watercress Delight*. Jill, ever on the lookout for something new, ordered the *Sandwich Sampler* consisting of three delicate sandwich bites arranged in a row on a long narrow plate.

"Pretty," Jill said as she proceeded to gently dissect the first bite before eating. Her goal was to ascertain its ingredients in case she wanted to incorporate it into her personal menu. After sampling, Jill listed all the ingredients. Looking at Aerrvin she said, "You've got a photographic memory, right? Can you remember those for me, Aerrvin? I didn't bring a pen."

Aerrvin looked at her mildly, while thinking rapidly, *Did Mara reveal my identity?*

"Truth to tell, I am easily distracted and forgetful, but I have an assistant or two who can remind me as needed."

"Sylvie!" Jill exclaimed. "She stole my recipes and gave them to Button! I knew it was impossible for her to have created my exact masterpieces." Jill was triumphant and incensed.

Mara stared wide-eyed at Jill, and then turned to stare at Aerrvin as he answered quite calmly, "Actually it was Sylvie's mother, Juniper." A small twitch played on his lips while his eyes sparkled.

Jill began muttering about thieving brownies, sandwiches, cookies and triple fudge cake, causing alarm to rise, not only in Mara but Amanda as well.

❖❖❖❖

Amanda did not like to hear the words "Sylvie" and "Brownie" in the same conversation; it had taken Amanda nine years to get Mara to stop talking about Sylvie—Mara had been twelve years old. Amanda was sure they were talking about mutual friends, but it bothered her nevertheless, especially seeing the alarm on Mara's face. *Why does she even have a friend named Sylvie?* Amanda mourned inwardly.

❖❖❖❖

Aerrvin, noting the obvious distress coming from all three women, changed the conversation. "Should we talk about people Amanda does not know? Amanda, tell me about the first time you ate here."

Seeing Mara's relief aimed at Aerrvin caused Amanda to smile in response as she began talking about moving to Bellevue as a young bride. They had less money than Brentwood would eventually make, so they saved for a year to afford dining at the restaurant on their 2nd anniversary. Amanda regaled them with the menu, the dancing, and how glorious it was to be poor and in love.

"Your father was truly a wonderful man, Mara." Amanda smiled lovingly at her daughter just as their entrees arrived.

For dinner, Mara had crab stuffed chicken roll croquettes, with beautiful broccoli cooked to perfection. Amanda had surf and turf featuring filet mignon and rock lobster. Not that she couldn't get seafood whenever she wanted in Sequim, but she was a California beach baby and, without shame, loved ocean food. Aerrvin chose a shark steak with a garden vegetable medley, sautéed lightly by request. Jill took forever to order, finally settling on the seafood lasagna and creamed spinach. She rattled off the ingredients, as she had for the appetizers, as though someone was taking notes for her. Indeed, Seamus took care to memorize her list, along with keeping track of the other conversations.

Occasionally, the Brownie walked down Aerrvin's arm to sample the food, then returned to perch on his master's shoulder, so he could talk in his ear. "The shark is not bad, but I prefer the lobster."

Aerrvin nodded. "This is great food," he spoke as if to all.

113

A member of the waitstaff arrived with an expensive bottle of wine. "Compliments of the man at table seven," she said, pointing to a table beyond the booth where Mara sat. Aerrvin looked, and seeing who it was, gave him a wink. "Sweet," he said with a nod.

Mara could not see him from her window seat, but both Jill and Amanda could.

Jill said, "I don't know him, but I'll drink it." She gave the man a toothy smile.

Nearly on top of the other two, Amanda said, "Oh, my word! That's Morris." She nodded her thanks as he rose to greet her.

"Amanda, why it's been years! I thought you had moved to some little town, on the Strait was it not?"

Amanda replied kindly, "Yes, Sequim. We love it there. And—it has been a long time. I am here visiting my daughter, Mara." She gestured to Mara across from her.

Morris turned to greet her. "Why this surely is not little Mara?" he questioned with exaggeration. Then speaking to Mara, "My dear, what a beautiful woman you have grown into. I remember when you were a grubby little girl in pigtails." He laughed politely and then continued, "And your other guests?" His eyes swept quickly over Jill and then to Aerrvin.

Amanda affected a posh manner of speech to match the atmosphere, "This is Jill, a good friend of Mara's. We think highly of her. And this is a new acquaintance Mara has recently met. His name is Aerrvin. He's from Ireland, though lately from the peninsula. Our opinion of him is not yet formed, but if he treats her well, we may let him stay." Amanda laughed softly at her joke. Jill joined her, not sensing Mara's stiffness.

"Enjoy your wine and dinner. Perhaps, later, you would care to join me on the dance floor?"

He swept his gracious hand around the table to include them all.

"Aerrvin," he said, placing his hand upon his shoulder. "I should like to discuss Ireland with you. It has been some time since I have been there and would enjoy talking to a fellow European." As he removed his hand, it appeared that his cuff snagged on Aerrvin's hair. "Pardon me," he said, returning to his table.

In reality, he had taken Seamus. Aerrvin trusted Seamus to say the right things, so he remained as smooth as ever—though he did call a gentle breeze his way briefly.

Jill was about to speak when the server returned to open and pour the wine.

"I am sorry, but I will need to card you two," she said to Aerrvin and Mara.

"None for me. I'm twenty," Mara replied, as Aerrvin reached into his jacket for his driver's license.

After the waiter left, Amanda said, "I always thought Morris was smarmy, but he knows his wine." She sipped thoughtfully.

"I take it he is an old family friend?" Jill asked.

"A former business partner of Brentwood's, Mara's father," Amanda amended for Aerrvin's sake. "Morris was always trying to get invited to family events. I don't think he has any family here, but I would think he would have married by now." Looking at his table of scantily clad females and smartly dressed young men, she shook her head and said, "But, I guess not."

Mara spoke up, "So his name is Morris?"

"Well, that's what he goes by. Not sure if it was his first name or his last. Everyone called him Morris. He worked closely on some oceanographic research with your father. I never did hear how that turned out. . ." Amanda said vaguely, fading away from the topic.

Aerrvin added water to his wine. "I can never drink it straight. Most alcohol is poison," he said significantly to Mara.

"That's right, Mara. Your father always said the same thing. No sense getting excited about turning twenty-one. I would rather you did not become a partier. Let me and Jill throw you a big Birthday Bash to celebrate graduation and moving on. If Aerrvin has more friends who think like him, they can come too." Amanda smiled appreciatively at Aerrvin.

"Say all the right things, and you can marry her too!" Jill said, causing Mara to blush.

Realizing she was too quiet, Mara tried to think of something to say. She was simply dumbstruck to see this man who had been in her dream, as well as a person in an ancient photo on her wall, sitting in her favorite restaurant. *And he knew Dad! Did Dad know he was an enemy? I have so many questions!* She could hardly wait to talk to her grandfather.

Aerrvin knew Mara was troubled about Morvayne, but he also knew Morvayne expected Aerrvin to deliver Mara to him.

"I suppose it would be polite to take a spin on the dance floor. I had every intention of dancing with you three beautiful ladies anyhow. I can see what you think of him, having dinner with so many gorgeous young people. But hey! What are people saying about me? My ladies are far more classy and every bit as lovely, if not more," he said the last to Mara with a suggestive eyebrow twitch, causing her to giggle.

Amanda replied, "I would love to dance, Aerrvin, Rick isn't in to the social graces. Dancing especially!" Noting Mara's sour expression, Amanda said, "Mara, Morris is not an ogre! You can be polite and dance with an older man."

"That's right, Mara, nothing bad will happen," Aerrvin said, squeezing her hand under the table.

"If you say so. I am too full for dessert. I will order one later to take home," Mara said breaking her silence.

"Me too. That way I can dissect it more carefully," Jill added with a crafty chuckle.

"I'm done too," Amanda said. "Aerrvin, see if you can signal the waitress."

Aerrvin refused to let anyone else pay, but they put up such a fuss, that eventually he allowed them to pay the tip. "Feisty!" he said with a smile.

Holding out an arm for Mara and then Amanda, he said, "Sorry, Jill, I'd grow another arm if I thought it looked good."

"It's fine, as long as I get a dance."

They made a stop at the restrooms before going to the dance floor. While waiting, Seamus returned. "So how did it go?" Aerrvin asked.

"He believes that I live under Mara's gazebo and that I too have no access. You began schmoozing her, and she fell for you like a sack o' gold. You coerced me into serving you by Purple Fairy trickery. Seeing other Fair Ones about the place is rare, aside from Ironwood, who visit from time to time. I do know that there is, at least, one Brownie inside as she can be seen cleaning the windows every night. And what a sight!" Seamus sighed dramatically.

Mara found Aerrvin chuckling as she came out of the ladies' lounge.

"What's so funny?" she asked, allowing him to take her arm.

She loved the way he stroked it. For a while, she thought perhaps it was the fabric he enjoyed, but her arms were bare, and still, his hands seemed to play automatically upon her arm.

"Just laughing at something Seamus said."

Mentally shrugging, she let it pass as Jill and Amanda joined them. "All right, let's meet this 'smarmy' Morris," Mara said, linking arms with her mother.

Aerrvin reluctantly let go and escorted Jill onto the dance floor. Jill was incredibly fluid and light on her feet. "You are such a joy to dance with, Jill."

"Thanks goes to good old Mom for making me take ballet all those years. Changing the subject, I'm reading some books by Ironwood. Have you read them?"

"No, but I assume it is safe to say that Mara has let you in on her thoughts and concerns?" He relaxed, allowing his face to beam brightly, knowing that Morvayne thought him a silly Purple.

"Yes, and I find it fantastical, but there's been too much evidence presented for me to refute it. Not the least being you stealing my recipes!" Getting heated again, she thumped him on the chest.

The action caused Morvayne to chuckle as he danced with Amanda while keeping his eyes on both Aerrvin and Mara.

Smiling playfully, Aerrvin took her hand and gracefully pulled Jill into a twirl. Once together again he replied, "Juniper and Button are both Master Chefs, but since learning from Juniper the things that Juniper has learned from you, we eat more new delights than we have ever eaten before! Your business will be a definite success. Besides, it's what Brownies do; they learn from the best!" Knowing he sounded corny, Aerrvin smiled sheepishly, inciting another smack from Jill.

"I think you are the King of Schmooze," Jill said as the tune ended.

Aerrvin wanted to dance with Mara, but Morvayne would take her next, so he offered his arm to Amanda. He thought all of the music would be stately waltz material, but suddenly they went to big band music.

"Do you swing?" he asked.

Amanda grinned, "I'm the best! Do you?"

Grinning back, he said, "A little."

Mara was never very good at the two-step or any other similar dance; it was her parent's thing. She had learned but never felt graceful doing it, except with her father.

When Morvayne asked, she agreed to try. "I guess—if you don't mind my stepping on your feet."

"Nonsense, my little Buttercup, you merely follow my lead," Morvayne replied.

His dark, hazy blue eyes rarely left her face as they danced. But she trusted Aerrvin; he said no harm would come to her. She only stepped on Morvayne's foot once—hearing Aerrvin laugh she had turned to look at him. "Sorry, Morris, I did warn you."

"So you did. You must dance the next song to make it up to me," his fake pout quirked up at the corners.

Smarmy, she thought, *wherever did Mom come up with such a word? It fits.* Thinking so made Mara smile.

Morvayne smiled more broadly in return. "I need a little drink first," he commented, guiding her to his table. "Would you care for something?" he offered, holding up a bottle of wine.

"No, I don't drink."

"Ah, smart girl. Poison it is. But then, you are not quite old enough yet are you? What would your mother say? She would probably think I was trying to corrupt you," he paused to take a sip.

"Superb," he said closing his eyes as in ecstasy. "Ah, now that is a more suitable song for a reserved girl like you. Come, we should dance the night away."

Mara began to fear she would never get rescued, but on the third song, Aerrvin cut in.

"Pardon me, sir, but she did arrive with me, and I promised her an early return home."

Somewhat put out, Morvayne relinquished his hold on Mara and kissed her hand in parting. "Until next time."

Mara was so relieved that she put both arms around Aerrvin's shoulders; this caused Seamus to scramble onto the top of Aerrvin's head. Aerrvin reached up and put him in his pocket. And then, joyfully, he clasped Mara to him in a gentle, swaying, embrace. Ignoring Morvayne's chuckle at Seamus' expense, Aerrvin told Mara, "You will need to wash your hand in lemon juice and crushed mint while you whisper a chant to remove the kiss he placed upon you."

"No!" She looked at Aerrvin in horror. "There is magic in kisses?"

"Kisses are very powerful, one of the most powerful magics available. Did you never feel like kissing was magic?"

Smiling into his chest, she breathed in his scent, and answered a muffled, "Yes." Sighing, she asked, "How soon do I need to wash it off?"

"It will leave no residue if you can get it off before midnight."

"Is that true for all kisses, or is it a three-hour timeline?" Mara asked, looking into his face.

"Smart girl. You are thinking things through. It is the midnight aspect, not an hourly thing at all."

"So, if I drink lemonade and brush my teeth with a minty toothpaste, does it weaken an evening's worth of kissing?" She smiled impishly, which made Aerrvin chuckle deeply.

"Ah, Mara, I am so happy I met you."

Looking into her eyes while pulling a strand of curls through his fingers, he said, "I have not tried it, but I imagine it could work, but you still must say the words, 'be gone from me,' three times."

The song ended, and Aerrvin slowly returned to Morvayne's table. Before they were within the Elves hearing, he said, "Sorry to say, but I need to talk to Mor-Morris without you or your mother. Jill has a line waiting to dance with her. So if your mother danced with one of his pretty boys, it would help."

Mara didn't need to do anything because when she got to the table, a red-headed twenty-something asked Amanda to dance and a sandy-haired tough-looking guy asked Mara.

Aerrvin sat down and took the glass Morvayne proffered. He carefully watered it before drinking.

"A brilliant practice, Purple," Morvayne nodded approvingly. "I used to do the same before I lost Tigerlily. I believe I have built up a resistance; I could drink every day. Hah!" he barked. "I do drink every day!" Wild-eyed, he grinned his gloriously stunning smile.

Patting Aerrvin on the shoulder, he continued. "I am surprised to see such quick progress—and you are so smooth. Where is that quirky little Purple?"

Smiling brightly, Aerrvin replied, "I took acting at the Academy in Dublin. Very useful, that."

Morvayne stared at him a moment. "Yes, well the teachers are excellent there. Is Groban still lording it over the wee ones?"

On safe ground momentarily, Aerrvin relaxed and told a tale or two. Then seeing Mara returning he said, "Do you still want me to report on Monday? I don't think there is much more to add."

With a sigh, Morvayne replied, "No, I see the way things are." Then he hissed, "No kissing her though. She is mine!"

"But, my lord, forgive me for any disrespect," Aerrvin whispered hastily. "She is Human and expects it. If I stop, she will move on to another guy! Surely you see this?"

"Very well, I can undo anything your puny Fairy magic can do. Just keep her trust."

Something had been troubling Aerrvin, it suddenly came to mind again so he asked, "Morvayne, how is it that you can be near Mara? You told me that before being close caused pain."

"That was the truth. I have been coming here on this date every year since Brentwood's mishap. In disguise, sometimes as a waiter in the hopes of being able to learn what protection she wears. But lately, this year, I have been able to get closer. I think it is two-fold; her belief in reality is increasing, which weakens the protection Brentwood and Tigerlily placed upon her, based on her innocence or ignorance. And tonight, Amanda just gave me permission to invade that protective bubble, by allowing Mara to dance with me."

Broadly smiling as Amanda returned, Morvayne said, "Amanda, it has been wonderful, but I fear I have other needs to attend. Please take care." Then turning to Jill, he murmured pleasantries, making her blush.

Finally taking Mara's hand, he stroked where he had kissed her. "Mara, your father would be thoroughly proud to call you daughter. If you should ever need a comforting word, you can reach me at this number." He pressed a calling card into her hand. "I am quite aware that tomorrow is the anniversary of your dear father's disappearance. I, myself, think of him every May 16th. Such a pity. I am glad to learn that your mother saw clear to make a happy life for herself. I am sincere; I should hope you would consider me family."

He leaned in to kiss her hand again, but rightly fearing the strength of the bond would be doubled; Mara deftly removed her hand to place the card in her beaded purse hanging from the chair.

"Thank you, Morris. That is so kind," Mara smiled at him from the relatively safer distance.

As they left, Mara noted it was raining. Her mother and Jill chatted amiably in the back. They'd had a wonderful evening of good food and dancing; meanwhile, Mara felt as though she were battling for her life now, and not just her sanity. *What does he want?*

It was 10:08 p.m. They made it home early as Aerrvin promised. The three women ran to the covered porch. By the time Aerrvin sauntered up, they had the door unlocked and were going inside. "Would you like to come in for tea? We don't drink coffee, but we have a lot of tea!" Mara said hopefully.

"I am sorry, Mara, but Morvayne has created a problem, which I need to attend to. I can't tell you about it yet. Remember to wash your hand and no lemon tea before brushing your teeth," he spoke only inches from her face. His full lips thinned as he grinned his most mischievous mug.

Mara hugged him and told him she had no intention of ever getting rid of his kisses. "How powerful are *my* kisses?" she asked, offering a peck.

"Getting stronger every day." Aerrvin kissed her a sweet goodnight, leaving her wishing he could stay.

"Can you, at least, visit me—later?" Still unwilling to say right out that she believed he was a Fairy.

Aerrvin went back up the steps. "I am not sure I should go home; Morvayne probably had us followed. He may be here himself, watching us right this minute. Maybe you should call your grandfather. I will be back, Sweet Pea. I am not sure when is all." He hugged her one last time and left.

"I hate that Morris," Mara stated with heat, shocking Jill and Amanda. "He's a sickly sweet weasel!"

"Mara, what has gotten in to you?" Amanda asked in shock. "I know he's creepy, but we were in public. He could not have been indecent."

"Well, he was. I feel filthy having touched him, and he kissed me. Smarmy is right!" Mara shuddered. "Do we have any lemons left?"

Jill replied, "No, I used them up two days ago. Why?"

Mara was unable to say anything in front of her mother, but she was beginning to feel sick at the thought of not being able to wash her hand. "I don't feel well; I thought it would be refreshing to take a hot bath with some lemon and mint—you know, aromatherapy?" She hoped she did not sound as crazy as she thought. "Do we, at least, have concentrated lemon juice?"

Mara knew full well that Jill never used it, believing in fresh ingredients only.

Jill, grasping that Mara desperately needed something, said, "I'll draw you a bath and see what I have."

Mara hugged her mother goodnight; having given her room to her mother, she would be sleeping on Jill's hide-a-bed. "I'll see you in the morning, Mom."

"Okay, dear, I will be up to bed soon myself."

Mara went up to Jill's bathroom. It was bright and cheery with black and white checkered flooring and white tile on the walls. Jill had a hot pink shower curtain and pink and white striped towels. Their towels never got mixed up.

Jill had the tub nearly full of hot water when Mara came in. "So, do you want to tell me the reason for your crack up now?"

Mara had gone to the study before going up and handed Jill the photo of Tigerlily and Morvayne. "He's way more than two hundred years old, and he kissed my hand." She shuddered again and started to feel tears welling up again.

"This is getting old I know," Mara said wiping at her eyes. "Aerrvin said that there is power in kisses, and I need to wash my hand with lemon and mint while saying, 'be gone from me,' three times. At least, I think that's what he said. And I have to do it before midnight. And he said Morvayne and his friends are spying on us. AND he can't come to the house, so that means Button or Bronwyn can't either because he doesn't want Morvayne to know they are living nearby. But I can't go to the neighbors and ask for a lemon!" Mara finally stopped to take a breath.

"I do remember reading something about that in your grandpa's book. Maybe you should call him."

Sighing and gathering her wits Mara dialed the familiar though rarely used number.

He answered on the third ring. "Hello, this is Ironwood speaking."

"Hello, Grandpa, it's me, Mara,"

"And who else would be calling me Grandpa," he said in his whispery, yet musical voice.

Mara knew her cousins called him Pop Pop, which she thought was silly, but he didn't seem to mind.

When she didn't respond right off, he said, "I planned to speak to you tomorrow. How can I help you tonight?"

Unsure of how to approach the topic, she started crying and sobbed, "Morvayne kissed my hand!"

But it was so muffled Ironwood was not sure he had heard her right. Suddenly he was not whispery at all. "Pardon me?"

His tone of command straightened her resolve, yet she could only whisper, "Morvayne, the Elf, kissed my hand, and I don't have any lemons!"

"That's what I thought you said, well not about the lemons. That is only one way to remove a kiss. Do you have any vinegar?"

"Yes," she said with distaste. "Why? What do I have to do?"

"Well, it is similar to lemon and mint, but you have to wash for five minutes with vinegar and red chili pepper. Not nearly as pleasant, but it works better on weakening the next occurrence. I trust you do not intend a next time?"

"Absolutely not! But Grandpa, he's spying on me."

"I know he is, Sweet Pea. He spied on me my whole life too. Not that he found me as interesting as you. It was Tigerlily who interested him the most, but now that you are living in her place—well."

Mara interrupted, "Wait! I am in Lily's house, not Tigerlily's."

"Now, Mara I intended to tell you all of this in person, but since we are already speaking of it, my sister Lily died when she was thirty years old. She never had any children. The thing of it is, though, is that we made it appear as if it was Tigerlily who had died and Tigerlily took over being Lily. They were near identical—except for their smiles," Grandpa said, ending with a sad tone that Mara could hear.

"But enough talk, dear, I will see you tomorrow. You need to take care of your hand and know this: I have been watching out for you too. I wouldn't call it spying, but I like that whippersnapper, Aerrvin. Goodnight, call me anytime."

"Thanks, Grandpa, goodnight," Mara said, feeling relieved. "He's been watching me?"

Jill came in, "I found it, it says you can use . . ."

"Vinegar and chili powder," Mara chimed in morosely.

"I'll be right back," Jill said comfortingly.

Picking up the book, Mara read that it would most definitely irritate her hand, so with relief, she noted that the antidote for the pepper rash was rose oil hand cream. "That I have!"

14

Lessons from Grandpa

And when our wishes ascend the heights, into the darkness there

We find a friend within the light, fall not into despair.

~ Ironwood

Saturday, May 16, 2009

Aerrvin sat on a dock, watching the late-night doings of the fishermen and partiers on the water. Diving in, he found the water polluted with swirling chum, making the experience unenjoyable. So after a brief visit to the deepest parts, which were relatively calm, he exited the water. He considered staying out all night but realized that Morvayne had been watching him. He probably knew how to trace the license plate on the car, so there was no real hiding. He drove home to the O'Shea Mansion and spent the night dancing in the yard with Jaera, Gareth, and a few local Fairies who drifted by.

It was nearly dawn, when Jaera said, "Your heart isn't in it tonight, Aerrvin. Why don't you visit Mara in her Dreams before dawn?"

"I agree." Aerrvin thanked Jaera with a kiss. "Keep an eye on the heavy Orange in the willow tree, Gareth."

"Will do boss!" Gareth replied, then from the look he received, he amended, "Your Highness."

Grabbing a zither from thin air, Gareth created rock music to rival any of the bands in the Emerald City. A crowd of Fairies gathered, including a greater number of Oranges. The Orange Fairies added their discordant riffs, which set the Fairies dancing raucously, reminding Aerrvin of the Fairy Ring at the zoo.

"Distasteful," he muttered, making his way indoors.

❈❈❈❈

Mara had trouble falling asleep, what with a mildly burning hand, sleeping on Jill's fold out bed, and worrying about spies. Eventually, she covered the sheers with a sheet, which helped, and fell into a fitful sleep.

She felt a presence trying to enter her Dream, but she had drawn the little cloud-like sheep as soon as she realized she was dreaming. She could not tell how long it had been, but her dreams had been banal. It seemed to be a good time to try some of the things she had read about in the *Book of Majick*.

She tried altering her looks. It was harder than expected. With a mirror in front of her she imagined looking like a girl she envied in high school; a tall blonde with short spiky hair, but whenever Mara thought of doing something else, the image melted away.

Again, a presence tried to enter. This time, it had better success as Mara recognized Aerrvin's signature purple and silvery-blue glow. She reached her hand out to him and pulled him in.

Seeing her as a wavering blonde, Aerrvin said, "Ah, I see you are trying the Mask of Deception. Whatever made you think of that?"

127

Reverting to her natural beauty, Mara replied, "I read about Transforming. I wanted to give it try. You do these things in real life too?"

"Yes, but it takes some of us years to master, and you must be diligent. Not many Fairies are single-minded enough to bother with it. We prefer the lighter side of life, you know—dancing, singing, the arts. Elves, on the other hand, can be severely focused and will stay on task until they master it. I can guide you, but I would like to understand for what purpose? You are far more beautiful than the blonde you created."

Blushing, Mara replied, "I don't want to look like her. I took the first girl who came to mind. Could I hide my identity in front of Morvayne? Or more importantly, can he hide in front of me? Or Grandpa?"

"With practice, yes to all of those questions. I am positive that Morvayne has mastered the skills; he *must* be over eight hundred and fifty years old. Tigerlily trained Ironwood, so he is most likely proficient too. Part of the deception is hiding our power; magical eyes can see our glow. Mara," Aerrvin said, taking both of her hands in his, causing her to face him, "your power is awakening. It does two things: One, you can see more than you have ever seen before, like seeing me gain my Blue wings. I know you saw that. It was so bright. I thought surely Jill could see it!"

Mara smiled at the memory. "I was still in denial, but it was magnificent. Is that chair a power source of some sort?"

Aerrvin considered before answering, pulling the silk ribbon that hung from the neck of Mara's nightgown through his fingers. "It must be a gift from the High Queen Gwennara to her daughter, Tigerlily." Forestalling another question he inserted, "Ask Ironwood. But, yes, the chair is most assuredly connected to the Crystal Throne upon which Her Royal Highness sits—I do not know how, but it is a Receptacle and Transmitter of Power."

Mara noticed the emphasis on the important words. Her long-lashed eyes widened. "Impressive. No wonder the antique dealer, who is most likely a flunky of Morvayne's, wants it so much. He offers every six months to buy it. Do you think the dealer was him? Morvayne?"

"No, you said the dealer had been in your house. Morvayne cannot enter your home even if invited. There are powerful spells woven and placed throughout your house. They keep Morvayne out specifically, and all Yellow and Orange Fairies. His underlings who are not Yellow or Orange Fairies can enter if the openings are left undone, like your windows or doors, IF they have been invited in before. That is why my friends and I can enter, as well as Ironwood and your other family members. Do any of your cousins have any mystical powers?" Aerrvin asked unexpectedly.

"No. Aunt Lily frequently said that I was gifted, but she was never specific. I assumed she meant above my cousins, so I doubt they had any power. I think my cousin Mary Lynne has a flicker. She claimed she could feel something while sitting in my chair. Well, it was Lily's then, but, hmmm. . ." Mara shrugged.

"In any case," Aerrvin continued. "The second effect of becoming more aware of your powers is that we with eyes to see can see how Bright you are. And believe me, you are getting Brighter every day!"

Aerrvin eyed her up and down appreciatively, admiring her opalescent skin glowing as brightly as any stone of that variety; the rainbow sparkles were minute but glorious.

Mara's nightgown had come undone at the neck where Aerrvin had been playing with her ribbon. Pulling the silk from his fingers, she redid the bow with a reproving look. "So you are saying I need to hide my power more than my appearance?"

Aerrvin fashioned a cozy pile of fresh rose petals mixed with downy feathers. Using his wings, he fluttered up a wee bit and plopped down into the pile with the classic grace of a Fairy, bouncing three times before settling on his side. He offered a sideways nod and a raised eyebrow by way of invitation. Mara had not yet tried fashioning wings, she trusted in Aerrvin's power when they flew through the night. So she walked casually to the pile and climbed on top, trying not to cause the feathers to fly about the room. Aerrvin burst out laughing at her.

"What?"

"Mara, Mara, you need more lessons than I can even imagine. Let Ironwood teach you about Masking and Transforming. I need to teach you how to have Fun!" Aerrvin then taught her how to plop on a pile of feathers with never a care until dawn.

✻✻✻✻

Mara awoke with her hair in a wild mess and her blankets twisted and falling off the bed.

Jill startled at the sight as she entered the room. With sympathy, she asked, "Rough night?"

Grinning, Mara jumped out of bed and hugged Jill. "Actually, once I got to sleep it was delightful!" Mara went across the hall to her room. Being that Amanda was an early riser, Mara was sure she was out already. Joyfully she kissed her stuffed Growly, found her clean clothes, and went to her own bathroom to shower. By the time she got out, she could smell the scent of blueberry muffins wafting up the stairs.

"Morning, Mom." Mara surprised her mother with a cheerful hug and kiss.

Amanda expected Mara's usual glum attitude on her father's day of memorial. Surprised, Amanda smiled in return. "Maybe I should have encouraged you to get a boyfriend sooner!" Amanda picked up her half-eaten muffin to spread honey butter on it. "Jill is still putting out her best creations. These are better than anything you can get in town."

"Yeah," Mara replied, aiming a pout at Jill. "That is why I am going to miss her so much when she abandons me."

"Mara! Jill has a right to pursue her dreams as much as the next girl."

Eyes still sparkling, Mara replied, "I'm teasing. She said she would let me pay half price anytime, and I get three-day-old stuff for free."

"I don't remember that offer!" Jill spluttered, "But, it sounds reasonable." Turning to Amanda, she said, "What I offered was friendship for life and an open invitation to visit whenever she wanted."

Amanda patted Jill's hand. "Ah, Jill you are like the big sister Mara never had. Of course, I would have been twelve when I had you." All three women broke out in laughter. They continued their breakfast and morning chores with light talk of future plans.

Mara's mother intended to try homeschooling her two young half-sisters. "Since Ricky is going to be in college and the electronics store is stable—we have a reliable manager now—we thought we'd do some traveling before we get too old to enjoy it. Besides, Rick will want to come for every single one of Ricky's games, so we'd need to take the girls out of school all the time if I wanted to attend as well. I thought too, maybe you could become a 'favorite big sister' to the girls if they saw you more often."

Amanda smiled at Mara as they folded the laundry. It was a sore point for them; Mara did not want to set up her photography studio in Sequim, and they did not see each other very often, or rather, as often as Amanda wanted. She continued, "You know, treat them the way Aunt Lily treated you. Becky is almost old enough. I am thinking of letting her stay with you for a while this summer. What do you say?"

A jolt of fear and wonder bolted up Mara's spine to think her mother would trust them to her care. "Sure, it would be fun. I am quitting my job at Safe Haven, so be sure to send her over before I find a new job."

As they finished up, it was nearly noon. "Grandpa will be here soon. We'd better get dressed," Amanda said.

Ironwood arrived at 12:30 sharp, as he always did. The tradition was such that they meant to be at the memorial at precisely 1:43 p.m. That was the last time Brentwood had spoken to Amanda. He had called from his boat before it capsized. Ironwood hugged Amanda warmly, and she returned the gesture. Her fear of his filling Mara's head with magic had diminished with time as she saw what a responsible young woman her daughter had become. Moreover, he was truly a warm and gentle man.

Upon seeing Mara, Ironwood said, "Why, Mara, you are simply glowing!"

Mara blushed lightly. "And you are looking extra bright and chipper yourself."

Amanda, not understanding the exchange, added, "Mara has a new beau. You should check him out and give your approval. Make him sweat. My dad was totally hard on Brentwood. Yet, Brentwood persevered. And he appreciated the concerns my dad displayed; after all, I was so young."

Walking the two women to the door, Ironwood asked, "So, Mara, you think you have found a keeper, have you?"

"Yes, I feel like I am in a fairytale. But I do believe he may be a perfect match."

They stopped by the florist to collect the pre-ordered memorial wreath and bouquets of flowers. Since Aunt Lily died, they incorporated visiting her grave, as well as other family members. One visit a year was enough.

Nearing the cemetery, the mood grew solemn. Mara missed her father more than ever. Understanding that he had so much more to teach her than she could have suspected, caused her sorrow to well up into spasms of sobs and silent tears. Walking along the graveled path, Amanda held Mara's hand until they arrived at the white marble statue of Brentwood.

Ironwood was a sculptor as well as a professor and had created the near likeness in the purest white marble he could find. It had taken him the entire first year of Brentwood's absence to sculpt it. The base bothered Amanda, but she accepted it, as it was a part of who Brentwood was. Carved on the base were sailing ships, Water Sprites, Mermaids, dolphins, sharks, and whales. Brentwood loved the ocean more than anything, not counting his family. Everyone who knew him found it a fitting tribute. Amanda shook out the hankies she brought and handed one to Mara. The contrast of Mara's happy morning with her current terrible sorrow troubled Amanda. Yet, she too felt more pain than she had thought to feel. The previous year she barely shed a single tear. On this occasion, looking at the beautiful statue filled Amanda with a deep sadness which she did not wish to express in front of the others, so she excused herself.

"Mara, honey, I will be waiting in the car."

Silently, unable to say more, she nodded to Ironwood and made her way to Aunt Lily's grave and Uncle Rupert's memorial where she placed her flowers. Then Amanda went to sit in the car alone.

Mara wept the entire time. Finally hearing the car door shut she fell into her Grandpa's arms and whispered, "Morvayne did this."

"Yes, he did."

Feeling her Grandpa's strength, she quelled her feelings of loss as she battled with anger instead. Sensing her stiffness, Ironwood soothed her shoulders with gentle strokes from his firm hands.

"Mara, I hope you don't harbor any anger for me. I was forbidden from speaking to you," Ironwood began.

"No, Grandpa, I'm not angry with you." She backed out of his arms and sat down on the nearby bench. "I understand Mother's fears too. As you know, I went to see Pastor Mike. I thought I was going crazy." Mara smiled a bittersweet smile and wiped her face with her hankie. "I am livid with what Morvayne has done and is doing. What can I do to get him to leave me alone?" She paused a moment and said, "This is real, right? I'm not in some delusional dream in a mental hospital am I?"

She looked searchingly at her grandpa's old but smooth face and his nearly always twinkly eyes. At that moment, they were like steel.

"Mara, you truly are a remarkable youngling; that is the term they give to young Elven beings. And— yes, this is entirely real. I visit colonies of Elves and Fairy Rings, even more so in the past ten years, and none of them are as Bright as you. Your first lesson is to mask your Brightness. I will visit each evening, or you may come to my house if you would prefer, to give additional lessons."

"But I want revenge!" she spat, blinking back more tears.

"I do too. That is part of my research. I will tell you my thoughts and plans regarding that, but first things first. We mustn't detain your mother too long. You need to locate the center of your power by closing your eyes and focusing on the Light. Close your eyes. Find the Light, do you see it?"

"No, I just see colors and shapes swirling."

"That is the Light. Focus on it; it will brighten. Gather it all together. Do you have it?"

Seeing her smile, he continued, "Good, so wad it up as though you could see yourself compacting it smaller and smaller. And put it in your pocket."

Mara opened her eyes with a blink. "That's it? How can I tell that I did it?"

Smiling at her, Ironwood said, "Yes, that's it. I can tell because you are no longer a sparkling, rainbow of a girl. When I first met you at the door, you were so Bright you nearly knocked my socks off! But now you look like any ordinary girl. Even Morvayne could not find you, not by your Light at any rate. You can tell that you succeeded by learning to see your own Light. So, here is your second lesson. Close your eyes, take out the package of light and shake it loose. Can you see the Light?"

"Yes, it is like a rainbow, well not in order, but all these colors are dancing about." She smiled in wonder.

"Okay, open your eyes," he commanded. "Look at your hands; focus on seeing the Light."

"I see it!" she squeaked, amazed. "I glow like Aerrvin did when he sat in my chair!"

"You let him sit in the chair?!" Ironwood sputtered, shaking her out of her reverie.

"No one said he couldn't," Mara replied accusingly.

"No, I guess not. So he glowed, did he? What else happened?"

"He grew these huge silver and blue wings that shot blue sparks all over the room." Mara allowed herself to remember without fear. "It was incredible and so difficult to pretend that I saw nothing out of the ordinary." Her animation made Ironwood smile.

"Amazing indeed!" Ironwood replied. "What happened to him is not normal for a Fairy either. He must have been just as surprised and sore tried with keeping his amazement hidden."

"So what happened to him, if it was not normal?" Mara asked.

"He was granted a secret wish."

"He wished for giant blue wings?"

"No, I think we should ask him, but I suspect he is of Royal Blood. That would be what the Silver indicates; he must have desired to be a Blue Fairy deep down or to gain those attributes. Each color has different qualities—but don't get me started on a lecture, or we will never get to lunch. Stuff your light away. Let's go visit the others."

He led Mara to his own dear wife's grave where they left a remembrance bouquet. She died shortly after Brentwood's accident. Mara's memories of her were sentimental. Then they laid flowers for Aunt Lily and Uncle Rupert.

"So this is really Tigerlily?" Mara questioned. "Then where is your sister?"

Lily's grave rested behind the lilac bush next to one marked Jacques Jamis. "Tigerlily's first husband, right?"

"Yes—*My Grandpapa,*" Ironwood replied, smiling at long-lost memories. "Very well, let's see about lunch. Shall we?" He offered his arm to his sweet granddaughter, feeling a sense of increased dignity knowing one day she would be his Queen.

15

Deluge in All

Ever-present mist enshrouded thoughts ~ impaled upon my heart

shades of you linger ~ breath of meaning remains as soft memories

capture moments ~ and steal time

~ Amanda Powers

May 16, 2009

Amanda experienced a good cry in the car and hoped she looked reasonably recovered when they returned. But she begged off lunch, as she felt exhausted and thought a nap would do her good.

"Sorry for the trouble, Dad," she said as Ironwood dropped her off at Mara's house. "I hope you didn't have reservations?"

"No trouble. No, I want to try a new bistro downtown. It should be easy getting a table."

They left in Ironwood's car and spent lunch remembering Brentwood with fun stories of misdeeds from Grandpa and bedtime story memories for Mara, as well as vacations, hikes, and punishments.

Mara said, "I never understood why Dad got so mad at me for picking all the daffodils around the house when I was eight. But he was nearly disgusted with me! He was so mad." She shook her head in dismay. "Did it have anything to do with magic?"

"Daffodils? No, nothing magical in and of themselves. He planted them the first year that he moved into the house, as a gift for your mother. I suppose it was that you had destroyed the landscape." Mara's Grandpa laughed at the thought, and she joined in with a rueful laugh of her own.

Instead of driving straight home, they went to Ironwood Estates. "Grandpa, why don't you use your last name?" Mara asked as they drove beneath the sign.

"Well, the real surname was James, and Jacques changed it. He was Native American from his mother, and he was proud of being French. At least his father said he was part French. Anyhow, Jacques thought Jamis sounded French, so he changed the name. It's not a real name, and I like to deal with reality. I know it is in truth my name, but—well, you understand. I guess it's simply a quirk. I did pass it along after all. Though . . ." he trailed off and parked the car in the large circular drive in front of his house.

"Another question: Why do you live here in this great big old house? Don't you get lonely?" Mara asked, imagining how hard it must be to keep such a large estate clean.

"Lonely? Hah! Never. Two weeks ago I would have told you that I have my studies to keep me busy, and I travel often."

With a bounce back in his step and a twinkle in his eye, he opened the door and said, "But now I can let you in on a little secret. I got married to a sweet Elf five years back, and she brought half of her family and servants with her."

Greeting them at the door stood an elegant woman with honey-colored hair swept up into an intricate bun. Mara saw Brownies out of the corner of her eyes flitting in every direction.

"Mara, I would like to introduce you to Lorelei ap Corwin, my wife. Lorelei this is my greatest treasure in all the world, Mara Lilyana Jamis."

Reaching out gracefully, she pulled Mara into a motherly hug.

"Mara," she fairly sang, "Ironwood has filled my head with pictures of you for years; it is so wonderful to meet at last."

Being that close, Mara could definitely see her pointed ears. The only other Elf she had ever met was Morvayne, so she felt herself grasping at what to say.

"Um— it is a surprise, but I welcome you into the family."

"I am honored," the Elven maid curtsied.

Ironwood sensed their unease, so he called the Brownies back into the room. "Come on in all of you rapscallions; I would like you to meet my granddaughter."

Fifteen Brownies scampered, danced or scurried into the entry hall. Well, one trudged. Ironwood introduced each by name and they, in turn, bowed to Mara and ran off to hide again. "Lorelei's family members are almost all even shyer than she is, so I will introduce you to them later. Not all of them are here currently," Ironwood explained.

"We have been working on Lorelei's social skills and willingness to transform her ears so that we can go to a concert together. Haven't we dear?" He smiled gently at the motherly Elf.

"Yes, dear one, I did take a stroll down the lane last Tuesday without running off when a neighbor stopped to say hello." She looked up proudly and then ducked her head at Ironwood's praise.

"Yes, fantastic progress indeed. You may return to what you were doing if you would like to, Lorelei, or you may bring your needlework into my study while I help Mara learn her duties."

"Thank you, I was in the middle of watching a chrysalis. I should like to return."

"Very well, I will see you later, and you can tell me all about it." Ironwood kissed her goodbye and led Mara into his study.

The study was a full library with three freestanding rows of bookshelves nine feet long each, not to mention two walls filled floor-to-ceiling with books. Along the outside eastern wall sat a large fireplace flanked by two cozy suede chairs; off to the side was a large desk with two monitors for the computer, as well as an additional laptop. Mara had not known her Grandpa was so computer savvy.

Seeing her eyebrows rise, Ironwood chuckled. "I have many students who are taking my online course. It's very convenient. I can go where I wish and still teach and grade and offer support. Besides, one of Lorelei's cousins has become utterly fascinated with the electronic age. He has nearly taken over my class, answering questions and clarifying misunderstandings. Truly wonderful."

"I guess it's more convenient than seedpods?" Mara half guessed.

"Ah, that Purple Fairy has been telling you much more than I expected!" Ironwood replied. "Actually, seedpods will always have their place. A cell phone allows more clarity, obviously, with two-way communication, but both parties have to have their phones, and they must be charged. Yes, it is a hassle. E-mail can be precise, but if it is urgent then maybe it's not so hot. Who knows when someone will look at his or her mail? With a seedpod, you can infuse it with your message, admittedly short, but it will keep trying until the message gets through. Remarkably wondrous!" He gestured for Mara to sit in front of the fire, which sprang to life with the sweep of his hand.

"Um, Aerrvin didn't tell me about them, that was a guess. He received one once and then left me with the seedpod. Later I made a wish and sent it out the window and watched the wind take it toward his house."

"Yes, that is how we do it. The wind took the message to the one you wanted to receive it, or if it was a general wish, then any Fairy or Elf could catch it and answer as they saw fit." Ironwood nodded thoughtfully at Mara as he considered what to share.

"So, where do we begin? It seems that there is so much to learn," Mara asked despairingly.

Laughing away her worries, Ironwood replied, "Why at the beginning, of course!"

Chagrinned, Mara nodded. "Okay, what is the beginning?"

Ironwood told Mara about the start of all creation on this planet. Introducing the story of Adam and Eve as told by the Fair Ones. "So you see, magical beings are part of the whole plan. They began under the care of Man in the Garden, and when the Fall of Man occurred, that responsibility remained, as did all other commands he had received. Of course Man, in his fallen state, found the powers of the magical beasts at times something to be feared, and at other times something that caused jealousy. This antagonism is why it is such a challenge for me to ferret out the truth of a myth. Men's fears have exaggerated and distorted the facts.

"Now there was a point I skipped over in the narrative—let me think—ah, yes. When all creatures lived in the Garden, or the First Garden as the Elves refer to it, peace was had among all beings. As the beasts and creatures left, they consulted among their kind and voted as a council whether they would serve Good or Evil; those who chose evil are those we now associate with being wild beasts. They did not wish to be tamed by Man. Among the magical, we have Ogres, Trolls, and Kraken to name a few. Those who chose the Light were all gentle creatures, even those who have volunteered to be used by Man. Those listed among the Fair Ones would be Fairies, Elves, Brownies, Gnomes, Sprites, Dryads and Mermaids and so on. At this late date, there has been intermarriage among all species, so we have a wider variety of unclassified beings with a mix of powers and looks."

Mara took a chance to interrupt the lecture. "Then, why is Morvayne so wicked?"

Ironwood bobbed his head. "Good question. All creatures still have a will of their own and may choose to be as evil as they want, or life in the middle as Nyads and Dragons do; they will serve either side as it suits the individual. I am friends with a very fine Ogre who lives right here in Washington. In Aberdeen, actually."

"Really?" Mara asked, "Good ogres and real live dragons?"

"Yes, really. But let us not get ahead of ourselves. Morvayne chose poorly—out of frustration and loss. He loved Tigerlily. When she chose salvation, a new eternal life in another dimension was not a choice he could accept. You see, the Fair Ones can, in essence, live nearly forever, if they were to spend all their time in the Land of Dreams. Some propose that Fading will put one in a state like Paradise—prepared for the magical. It takes faith to Fade. Just as it took Tigerlily faith to give up her Elven power to become Human. But she had deep faith and died in peace with a bright hope in her future life."

Tears filled Mara's eyes. "That was another fear I had. I did not want to give up my faith to allow myself to become who I really am. So, what do you intend to do, Grandpa? I mean, are you more Human or Elf?"

"That is going in another direction again; at present, I am evenly balanced. If I choose, I can take the final steps through a ceremony and become a fully powerful Elf. Let me say this, the old stories of changelings have some truth to them. Fair Ones have difficulty producing offspring, and they have found inter-marriage strengthens their abilities to have children, and it also strengthens their powers. Humans, in particular, can create spectacularly Bright Fair Ones."

Suddenly, Ironwood glowed as bright as Aerrvin had while sitting on the chair in Mara's living room. With magical eyes, it would not be considered blinding, but the thought comes to mind. Mara saw details with greater clarity since awakening; she could see Ironwood radiating an opalescence similar to what she saw in her mind's eye.

Laughing at her wonder, Ironwood lowered his Brightness to a gentle hum, had it been a sound. "You should have seen my father, Goldenrod. He was nearly as Brilliant as you. He chose Humanity like his mother, believing they could meet on the other side. I believe Fading will allow the same visitation rights, so I lean towards becoming a full Elf. I mean, I am an Elf, but I have never lived as one, nor have I taken the oath. Besides, I feel responsible for you, and my bride. I would be gone in twenty years were I to maintain a hold on my Humanity. It takes nearly a hundred years of training for you to be considered an adult among the Fair Ones. That is if you were so inclined to choose such a course," he paused, his eyes asking the question.

"Oh, Grandpa, I can't decide! This is too new," Mara said, surprised at such an enormous decision before her.

"I know. I didn't mean to have you make a choice today. I only want you to know that the question is there, and it is yours alone to answer." Rising out of his chair he took her hand, "Well, that is enough to make your head explode; time to return you to your mother."

✳✳✳✳

Mara returned home just as dinner came out of the oven.

"Amanda, Jill, I am sorry for taking so long with Mara. We stopped by my place for a while," Ironwood apologized.

Amanda's jaw tightened a fraction as she considered what that might mean.

Jill answered first, "No problem. I am used to Mara not being here for my culinary delights. She is always coming in late." Jill smirked at Mara, eyes sparkling. "Are you joining us, Ironwood?"

"No, no. I have papers to read and correct before classes tomorrow. Thank you. I would like for you to cater Mara's birthday. If you would allow me to host it, Amanda?"

"Well, the size is much better than here." Amanda waved towards the backyard. "And the price is better than a hotel ballroom. Unless she would like to have it on the beach in Sequim?" Amanda replied, nodding her head at Mara.

Mara shook her head emphatically against Sequim. "No thanks, Mom. Thank you, Grandpa. That would be lovely."

After seeing Ironwood out, the three women sat down at the kitchen bar to eat.

"Mara, you really should get a dining set of some sort. You can't expect to feed people like your grandfather standing up," Amanda reproved.

"Yes, Mother. I am glad your nap improved your health."

142

Amanda replied with a flick at Mara's curls, "In truth, I feel much better."

"I talked to Rick, and he will be here by 10:00 tonight. So we need to make beds for the girls on your couches. They will be pretty tired by then. We will leave tomorrow around noon. I want the girls to get enough sleep before school on Monday. Oh! How I look forward to homeschooling; no more set schedules!"

Mara replied, "You know, my Pastor's wife home schools. You should come to church with me in the morning to meet her. I am sure she has plenty of advice."

"I'd love to," Amanda said, relieved to learn Mara still attended church. If Mara kept her faith in religion, Amanda believed there would be no room for pretend magic in her daughter's life.

16

Little Blessings

The moon ~ her tones ~ soft and pure

add magic to the air

~ Gareth ap Rosewin

Sunday, May 17, 2009

As Mara got ready for bed, she remembered that spies encircled her house.

To Jill, she said, "I forgot to ask Grandpa how to check the safety spells." Squinching her eyes, she discerned a small glow coming from the corner bull's eyes on the window frame in Jill's room. "Of course, Aerrvin checked, and he says I'm safe. Still, I like to have a little control, you know?"

Mara went from window to window in the suite.

Jill acknowledged, "Yes, it is a bit unnerving to learn that an entire unseen universe is lurking in all the world around us."

"That's an understatement," Mara replied. "Grandpa said I'm undergoing an awakening. Evidently, my abilities will increase. Right now, I think I can see all the spells on everything. They are a kind of sparkly—no, a glowy essence, I guess—on each corner above the windows. I'll be right back. I want to see what else there is to see!" Mara stepped out to the landing, checked the window there, and soon headed downstairs.

A gentle glow rested above each window. Additionally, a faint silver gleam hovered on each lock. On top of each door, gleamed a spot she had always assumed was the woodwork catching the light, the soft golden glow made her think of Aunt Lily.

In the basement, surprise enveloped Mara when she witnessed the silver scribble Aerrvin had drawn on the window earlier. Furthermore, the broken corner piece shone brighter than the others.

"Must be because it's newly made," she mused.

Remembering she had one more opening, she went to the fireplace. On tiptoe, so as not to wake her sisters, she stopped in front of the mantel and stared in amazement as though she had never seen it in her life. The entire fireplace was a carving masterpiece, a gift from Ironwood to Lily. *Tigerlily*, Mara reminded herself. As a young girl, Mara had spent hours daydreaming in front of it as she admired the woodland scene, with fairies and Santa's helpers hidden in the trees. With her eyes fully open to magical things, Mara could see that at the very center of the mantel sat a snowflake—glowing richly, shifting from silver to a snowy, sparkling blue iridescence while thoughts, actual pictures, of Santa flowed through her mind.

"He's real!" she breathed.

"Who's real?" seven-year-old Becky asked.

Startled, Mara regained her composure and said, "Santa Claus."

"Duh, why are you walking around in the dark?" Becky asked, sitting up on her makeshift bed.

"Well, I didn't want to wake you up, and I wasn't sleepy yet."

Then Sarah said, "I'm not tired either." She rolled off the couch with a soft thump.

Mara realized it was probably her fault for waking them, so she said, "Okay, don't tell Mom, but we can drink some cocoa with cookies, and then you have to go back to sleep."

Softly giggling, they crept into the kitchen where Mara made three cups of cocoa in the microwave and retrieved a plateful of Jill's sugar cookies, cut into tulips and butterflies.

As they finished their treats, they all froze when they heard someone coming down the stairs. The girls screamed as Rick jumped into the kitchen shouting, "Caught ya!" Then they all burst out laughing.

Becky said, "Sorry, Dad, we couldn't sleep."

Mara shrugged her shoulders. "Guess the party's over girls. Go brush your teeth. We wouldn't want cavities—would we?"

Rick grabbed two cookies for himself with a smile and shooed the girls up the stairs. Mara noted the levels in the cups and with a smile took two extra cookies from the cookie jar and put them on the plate. With a sigh and a last glance at Santa's mark on the mantel, she took herself to bed.

❄❄❄❄

On Saturday Aerrvin had stayed away from Mara because she was busy with her family memorial. He spent the day six inches tall, lolling around with the kittens and swimming with the frogs and fish; Jaera had added quite a few remarkable koi who loved being tickled.

When not thinking of Mara, Aerrvin thought about his upcoming Birth Day. "What do you think Jaera, Gareth? Should I host my party here or back home in the woods with the Fairy Ring?"

Jaera answered first, "I think you should do it here."

Aerrvin questioned her opinion, "If I do it here—either I can't invite the local council, or I do and announce my identity. Morvayne will realize that I deceived him. Is that wise?"

Gareth joined in, "Morvayne will learn, sooner or later. Unless you want to celebrate your 190th Birth Day with just us?" Gareth motioned to the cats in the nest. His freshly washed hair hung in silky threads to his shoulders, the tips were still silver and blue fading into his natural black. Dressed in silver leggings and a white vest gave him a striking air. Cozily, the Blue Fairy snuggled up against Mama Cat, luxuriating in the sensual nature of her fur.

Still wet from swimming with the fish, Aerrvin looked on jealously at Gareth snuggled up in all that fur. But he generously allowed Mama Cat to use her rough tongue to clean him up. She was thirsty and didn't want to stir her kittens as they enjoyed a late night snack.

146

With a merry laugh, Aerrvin said to Jaera, "Why don't you get her some water; I don't think I've got enough on me to satisfy."

Jaera complied, allowing Aerrvin to cozy up between Fluffball and Growly.

Speaking to Gareth, Aerrvin said, "I'll sleep on it and tell you later." In an instant, he drifted off to Neverland.

❖❖❖❖

Mara felt her eyes widen as she gasped at the sight upon arriving in Mama Cat's nest; it contained three near-naked Fairies. She grew tired of waiting for Aerrvin, so she decided to search for his Dream. When Mara entered the Void by mere thought, it surprised her, but not nearly as much as it stunned the others when they learned she had done it on her own. Once in the Void, looking up at the swirling heavens, Mara found she could identify the owners of a few of the star-like sparks—family members, Jill, even George from the retirement center. At last, she recognized Aerrvin's Dream. With a stretch of her hand toward it, she drew near enough to step inside.

Jaera, clothed in a tiny pink toga curled behind Gareth in his silver leggings. Aerrvin stirred and woke up with a smile. His hair looked as though it had been licked by a giant cat. Mara laughed, realizing where they were. His muscled body flexed as he stood to greet Mara. Aerrvin gathered that his white silk swimming trunks were a bit too revealing for Mara, he unconsciously turned them into sleek white leggings which still showed off his well-muscled calves. Sensing she still thought he revealed too much skin, he added a sleeveless tunic, belted with an intensely dark purple sash.

"Mara, what are you doing in my Dream?" Aerrvin questioned, taking her hand in his.

"I got tired of waiting."

She explained the technique, and he confirmed he did it the same way. Still flushed from coming upon him unaware, she said, "Sorry about not announcing my intent. Is there some way to do that?"

147

"Not really. When you peek in on a Dream, you see whatever there is to see. We Fairies rarely feel shame, certainly not concerning our nakedness. The Creator made us, and He gave us our own commandments, rules, and expectations. Wearing a lot of clothes was not one of them!" He grinned suggestively, to make her blush deeper. Because she had not hidden her power, it made the blush turn into a shower of rainbow sparkles which fell and gathered on the ground.

Mara's eyes remained downcast, unable to look at Aerrvin as another bout of blushing surged through her. With amazement, she breathed, "What is it?"

"'Tis called Fairy Dust, even when made by Elves. We collect, sell, or trade it. I imagine yours is quite valuable," Aerrvin replied, directing it all together on a wisp of a breeze and depositing it into a crystal vial. Handing the vial to her, he said, "You need to learn to accept a little more nudity. I am having my 190th Birth Day party this Friday night; I would be disappointed if you could not attend."

Mara garbled a response—too much information at once. Suddenly a gentle breeze fanned her face, scattering another round of Fairy Dust at her feet. Unsure of which topic to tackle first, she stuttered, "You—you are having an orgy on your 190th Birth Day, one hundred—one hundred and ninety years old? Really?"

Aerrvin scooped Mara up, flew her to the waterfall, and stuck her underneath it.

Spluttering, she shrieked, "That's cold! I thought it was warmer before. Wasn't it?"

"Heh, heh," Aerrvin chuckled, "Hey, it's my Dream. I wanted to cool you off."

He conspicuously leered at her soaking P. J.'s. The sporty blue and white baseball top and blue shorts had not looked all that great dry, and being wet did not help. Not her best look.

Mara swiftly thought of herself in the pretty, white cotton nightgown she had worn the other night with the long silky ribbons. "Don't look at me that way Aerrvin ap Rosewin! All right, maybe I deserved it. I know you will not be having orgies. Grandpa spent time with me today—explaining the First Garden. Generally, we consider the Fair Ones to be in a state of innocence. Is that right?"

With a languorously insolent shrug, he responded, "In a manner of speaking. We are far and away closer to nature than Humans, and we are not subject to rules of modesty. We wear clothes because we love them, not to cover our God-given glory. We are innocent, but not without knowledge. We too were commanded to be fruitful and multiply. It helps that Fair Ones usually present themselves in their prime. It might offend anyone's senses to spy a fat, old Elf sunning on the beach!"

Mara ignored his discriminatory remark; her mind was elsewhere. She became increasingly aware of Aerrvin as he moved nearer— to once again begin pulling on her ribbons. *Did I wear this gown on purpose?* Removing his hands from the ribbons, she left the gown open; it only revealed the necklace after all. Looking into his impish face, she kissed him. At her request, they spent the rest of the night dancing over the ocean.

❄❄❄❄

On Sunday morning, arriving at church minutes before the scheduled hour, Mara and her mother snuck in to the last row, right next to Aerrvin's entourage. Aerrvin embraced Mara, leaving his hand resting on her shoulder— eliciting a loud response from little Sarah.

"Mama, Mara has a boyfriend!" spoken just as the organist stopped playing.

Mara felt all eyes turn and bore the humiliation with a smile at Sarah. Looking down, she realized she was sitting in a near puddle of Fairy Dust. This time, it was real, not Dream Dust. Jaera sighed, and Gareth tried to covertly manipulate the Dust his way. He did not have Aerrvin's skill of moving the air at a simple command. With a silent chuckle, Aerrvin collected the Fairy Dust into three separate piles and filled three invisible vials. Then the vials floated to Jaera, Gareth, and himself. Mara thought she almost saw wings. Aerrvin tucked his vial inside his suit jacket and winked at Mara. Amanda sat stiffly as though she too could see it all herself.

149

"Mom, are you all right?" Mara asked as they stood to sing.

"Yes, dear, it's been a long weekend, I guess."

The singing was, once again, a delight. Sitting with the group of exquisite voices made it all the more enchanting. Trusting that they were here by Divine command enhanced Mara's worship even more as she allowed the music to touch her soul. Evidently, speaking with Mara had affected Pastor Mike; his sermon was on spiritual gifts given to mankind, and how they are to be used to build up the kingdom and fight against evil wherever found.

Refreshed by the sermon and the music, Amanda said, "You have a remarkable pastor, Mara. I loved what he had to say."

"Yes, I like him. Aunt Lily liked him too. He's been here for thirteen years," Mara responded with a nod.

Aerrvin did not plan to stay for Sunday school, so Mara quickly introduced him to her little sisters. "Aerrvin, these are my sisters—Becky and Sarah. Girls—this is my friend, Aerrvin, and this is Jaera and Gareth. More friends!" The Brownies had already slipped out.

Sarah, who was six years old, said, "Did you kiss Mara?" Her comment caused the older Becky to giggle along with Jaera and Gareth; children's laughter is particularly infectious.

Aerrvin naturally began pulling her silky blonde ponytail through his fingers, as he said, "Yes, are you jealous?"

Sarah shook her head, and Becky said, "Then that means you have to marry her!" Looking at her mother, she said, "Right, Mom?"

"Sorry, Aerrvin," Amanda apologized. "Little girls have silly notions."

"Sounds good to me." He grinned, first at Amanda and then at Mara, raising his eyebrows suggestively. Then grabbing Gareth and Jaera, one on each arm, he made his goodbyes and left, leaving both Mara and Amanda with mouths agape.

Mara recovered first. "Uh-hm. Let me show the girls to their classes, and then I will introduce you to the pastor's wife."

While talking to the pastor's wife outside his office, Pastor Mike asked to speak to Mara privately.

"I wanted to touch base with you. How did your day go yesterday? You seem well today."

With a smile, Mara responded, "Yesterday was better than any other memorial day I have ever had for Dad. I appreciate you for your time this past week. Grandpa has helped too. Talking with him has calmed my fears concerning my faith. I've learned that all God's creatures have a place in the world, not all are good, and not all are bad. Like everyone else; we all have to choose for ourselves," Mara replied in the longest response Pastor Mike had ever gotten from her.

"Mara! I am pleased to see you making such a remarkable turnaround! It is wonderful that you are feeling better. Have you also discussed these things with Aerrvin?"

"I have. We feel compatible. I hope to keep him around forever! I don't think I could find a better person for a companion." Holding up her hand to forestall his comment she continued, "I know I barely know him. I will wait one year before getting married—if I can help it." The last comment raised the pastor's brow.

"No, not like that. I mean, I may need to go away with him for my protection. I have learned that this Morvayne guy is intent on causing me harm. He goes by Morris. My mom and I met him at the Grandview Hotel dining room on Friday night. He was a colleague of my dad's. Anyway, I had to dance with him to be polite; and let me tell you, he gives me the creeps. So if I have to marry Aerrvin for my protection, I guess I will suffer through it," she ended with a smirk, and then a small blush at her boldness, spilling sparkles everywhere. *The Brownies are going to have a fit cleaning it up. Though they rarely barter with Dust themselves. At least, they could sell it if they wanted to,* Mara thought, dropping more Dust as she stood to leave.

"Do call the police if needed. And anytime you need to talk, I will be here," Pastor Mike said sincerely.

"Thanks, I appreciate it. Okay, let's see what Mom has learned from your wife."

When they got to Mara's house, they found Aerrvin sitting on the porch. It was not raining, but the wind was brisk.

"Aerrvin, why are you sitting out here? Jill would have let you in," Mara said as soon as they stopped.

"I enjoy the breeze; besides I haven't been here long. I came to invite you and your family to lunch if you have the time. Sorry, nothing formal."

Mara wanted to accept but deferred to her Mother. "Mom, what do you think, do you have time?"

"Let me ask Rick; he might be in the middle of a ball game if I know him." Going inside they saw Rick was indeed watching a game on the giant screen TV he had given to Mara the year before, for this very purpose. Finally catching his attention between plays, Amanda said, "Rick, this is Mara's friend, Aerrvin."

"Hey," he replied.

"Aerrvin has invited us to lunch, do you think we will have time?" Amanda asked, wisely not asking if he would like to.

"Yeah, if he has a large screen television. It's almost half-time. How far is it?"

"Down the block," Aerrvin replied. "And I think you will be satisfied with the screen."

Rick talked electronics with Aerrvin as the rest of the family went up to change.

17

Supper at the Mansion

My love for your sweetness enchanted that day

Your love for all beauty shall ever hold sway

~ Aerrvin ap Rosewin

May 17, 2009

Mara knocked on Jill's inner bedroom door. "Knock! Knock! Jill, are you home?" she asked as she opened the door.

Jill looked up from the bed, "Yeah, I'm here. I'm just reading these books of yours. They're pretty fascinating—your grandpa has a gifted writing style. Did you want me to make you some lunch?"

"Jill, that's not the only thing you are good for. Besides you've been teaching me to prepare meals on Sundays. Remember? But that's not what I want either —"

"What? Already!" Jill interrupted.

"Aerrvin invited us to lunch," Mara answered, then looking critically at Jill, she added, "At the mansion. You might want to change." Mara left to do the same.

Mara recognized that Aerrvin liked soft or silky fabric, so eschewing her tweed jacket, she chose the cashmere sweater set her mother had given her.

"Nothing like killing two birds with one stone," Mara quipped. Pulling jeans from the basket of clothes on the floor, she quickly slipped them on and padded down the stairs in her bare feet. She sat on the sofa; her mother would take a while to get the girls ready.

Turning to her stepfather, Mara said, "So Rick, Mom says you guys want to do a little traveling. Where will you go first?"

"Well, we have a toss-up between Africa and Australia. Ever been to either of them?" he asked Aerrvin, almost hoping to belittle him.

"I have sensitive skin, much of Africa is too dry. I would like to give it a go sometime, maybe during the rainy season. Though I have been to Australia. Along the river is very nice. Like I said dry, hot weather does not agree with me, so I did not explore the Outback itself." Aerrvin left out his extended trip to India and parts of the Middle East.

Rick wasn't sure whether to sneer at Aerrvin's sissy skin or to be impressed that he had been to Australia. So instead he said, "I better hurry up The Girls."

Soon they were loaded into the minivan, except for Jill, who opted to drive her own car, not wanting to try climbing into the back seat in the short skirt she wore. It had been twelve years since Amanda's visit to the O'Shea Mansion, so she was excited to see the interior. The front entrance set the girls to oohing and aahing while Rick whistled.

Amanda was amazed at the transformation. "Did you do the renovation yourself, or was it like this when you moved in?" she asked.

"We made most of the changes ourselves," Aerrvin replied.

Entering the garden room, the girls ran to the waterfall where Jaera sat tickling the fish. After assuring Amanda that she would watch the girls, Amanda allowed Aerrvin to give a full tour of the house sans the Servants Quarters where Mara assumed everyone else was hiding—at least those not in the kitchen, from which delicious smells were wafting. The rest of the main floor had a library equal to Ironwood's, and a music conservatory where they found Gareth playing the piano along with Seamus and Sylvie, who were playing woodwinds. Mara was startled but said nothing. They merely nodded as they continued playing. Amanda blinked and swiftly turned away. Next, came the formal dining room with seating for twenty. But who was counting chairs? And the grand finale, as far as Rick was concerned, was a game room in the basement with a viewing room opening off the far wall.

The game room contained billiards, ping-pong, and gaming tables for cards or other board games. A low shelf decorated with more of the ivy and flowering vines contained a variety of such games. Also, along the opposite wall sat a massive sound system. Upon seeing it, Jill and Mara looked at each other and said, "Dougie."

Aerrvin smiled in response. "Yes, Gareth and Dougie have taken on well with each other. We have this gaming system as well." Aerrvin pointed towards the final room.

In the screening room, Rick sank into a seat and exclaimed, "I have died and gone to Heaven!" The screen was half the size of a commercial movie theater screen. The video setup was hooked up to a gaming system, obviously Dougie's idea. Rick fiddled with buttons in the captain's chair and sighed when he managed to find the football game.

"You can go on and see the rest of the house dear, other people's bedrooms don't interest me much." With a wink, he turned his attention to the game as it was about to resume.

Upstairs, the landing and halls showed few changes as far as rearranging walls; it had the same Victorian feel and old-fashioned wallpapers as on the main floor.

"We didn't feel the need to change these rooms extensively. After all, who wants to spend much time up here when there is so much to do downstairs?" Aerrvin's smooth tone drew nods of agreement.

The upstairs was divided into four quadrants with each suite done in a unique theme. The first was a man's man kind of style: lots of leather with touches of animal print pillows. The first room they entered was like a receiving room, with the two bedrooms in the back sharing a bathroom between them. The other suites had the same layout. The sumptuous beds were tall, massive affairs.

The next suite was in shades of green, delicate, yet earthy. "Oh, this must be Jaera's suite!" Jill exclaimed, touching one of the moss colored throws. The couch was a pale celery, laden with ten different kinds of green pillows in varying fabrics. One of the bedrooms replicated the feel of a shady glen, and the other presented that of the ocean.

Aerrvin felt the need to offer a warning at the next suite. "These rooms are Gareth's."

The three women were pleasantly surprised to see an eclectic assortment of antiques, charmingly arranged with high tech silver and steel. Most notable were the antique children's toys. "Gareth found most of these up in the attic; they reminded him of happy childhood experiences."

One bedroom was styled in an ultra-modern punk/grunge motif featuring black leather and hot pink, with touches of silver, navy, and chocolate. Instead of a four-poster which all of the other rooms so far had contained, the bed rested on a platform with two stair steps surrounding it on three sides. The stairs were padded black leather with pink neon lights beneath, creating a night light in the stairs. The silver-studded black velvet headboard extended as high as the bed was long. The carpet and curtains were chocolate brown. The room felt complete with the modern set of armless velvet chairs in navy with hot pink pillows on them, one in the shape of a butterfly, the other a set of lips. The wall art displayed varying musical instruments and two stunning pictures of Jaera, one in which she almost appeared to have wings.

Mara and Jill spoke at the same time. Jill said, "Now this is more like it, this is hot!"

Mara asked, "Did Gareth take these photos?" She stepped closer for a better view.

"Yes, he has been into photography almost since the invention of film!" Aerrvin replied with obvious gusto. "By now you should know; if it involves technology, he likes it."

Amanda stifled her first thoughts and said to Mara, "I'm glad you chose the calmer of the two."

Even though Amanda meant it for Mara's ears only, Aerrvin cautioned, "Ah, but you have yet to see my rooms. But first Gareth's alter ego."

The second room was in shades of blue, from blue-greens to nearly violet. It was quite dark, but it exuded a comforting, calm atmosphere. Even the ceiling was painted the sweetest robin's egg blue. As with all the other rooms, a wide variety of textures were featured. The blue room included a mink coverlet dyed a midnight blue. Aerrvin's fingers caressed the cover as he spoke. Mara kept thinking she wouldn't be surprised if he picked it up and stroked his face with it as he did with the kittens. Seeing her smile, Aerrvin ceased and led them to the final suite of rooms.

"Wait," Jill said, "try to guess Aerrvin's color scheme." Her wide brown eyes became calculating.

Amanda stopped and considered. She had only seen him in three outfits: His classy suit for dinner, in black. His deep blue Sunday suit with which he wore a purple tie, and at the moment he wore fashionably faded blue jeans and a thin, oatmeal colored, long-sleeved rib-knit pullover, similar to what he was wearing when she first met him. His golden hair flowed away from his face. "Well, I haven't known him very long," Amanda ventured, "but I would say it is understated and classy, maybe black and white."

Jill said, "I would guess he would have lots of jewel tones."

Everyone turned to Mara waiting for her guess. "I would say lots of white, lots of silk and lots of lace." Mara smiled right into Aerrvin's face as he returned his own quirky upturned smirk.

Amanda tsked, "Mara, Mara."

Opening the door was like entering a Fairy Wonderland, drawing gasps of appreciation, swelling Aerrvin's sinful pride to near bursting. The walls featured a high gloss, brilliant white finish, with contrasting off-white layered moldings attached to ceilings and floors. Nearly fifty mirrors in varying states of antiquity gleamed, framed in either silver or gold—if they were framed at all. Some were so old one could barely see an image in them. The windows opened to the west to capture the sun as it settled. On a perfect day, the rays would reflect off the mirrors, bathing the room in brilliant gold, fading to purple as the sun took its course.

Balloon shades, made of the most delicate lace imaginable, topped each of the three windows. Mara gave the walls a closer inspection; the walls appeared to be covered with the same intricate lace as the shades, creating a reflective quality as one moved about the room. The lace emitted a mild shimmer, almost like pearls. Crystals hung below the shades, casting rainbows as they twisted in the breeze. There were two white leather love seats with a silver tea table set between them. On each loveseat, sat lavender and plum colored pillows in the plushest, most touchable fabrics Aerrvin could procure.

"Wait, how do you get the sun to shine into your windows when it isn't even noon yet?" Mara asked, before thinking maybe it was magic.

As she pulled a face, Aerrvin chuckled, taking her hand he pulled her to the window. Five steps down sat a balcony upon which he had mirrors slanted at an angle to catch the early sun. "Magic," he replied smartly.

Amanda and Jill had followed for a look out the window.

"Brilliant! I love magic when it has science to back it up!" Amanda smiled at the clever solution. "Looks like your guess was right, Mara. He must have told you about it already, or else you have been in here before?"

"No, Mara has never been upstairs; earlier I took her to the Servants Quarters, and the kitchen," Aerrvin responded. Remembering the birth of the kittens always brought tender smiles. Even Jill smiled.

"Must have been fun; you are all grinning like a bunch of fools," Amanda mocked.

"We went back there to see a cat give birth to kittens. They are so sweet. Are their eyes open yet?" Mara asked, turning away from her mother towards Aerrvin.

"No, not for a few more days yet. They are only seven days old today. We should see the rest of my rooms and go eat before Button gets too fretful."

The next room held an impossibly delicate bed suspended from the air by chains so fine you would not believe them strong enough to support the bed. Sheer lace hung over the silver silk sheets, dropping down below the edge; backlit by a pale purple light fastened under the bed. A spinning chandelier danced rainbows around the room in a hypnotic slow-motion sequence, first spinning right and then left at a very slow speed, stopping between direction changes for a minute, before continuing its dance. Of course, the free hanging crystals continued to sway when the device was at its pause, thus creating a never-ending dance of color in the room.

Aerrvin jumped on the bed to prove it was safe. "See? It is secure—come on, try it! It's like nothing you have ever felt before."

Jill jumped on and chose a satin and silk pillow to prop her head up. "He's right, you gotta try this. Come on, it's a king size I'm sure."

Amanda jumped up beside Jill, and Mara jumped up beside Aerrvin, using his shoulder as a pillow. The bed swayed, the lights swayed, and Mara felt herself drifting away.

"Good thing I don't get seasick. Are you sure this is a good thing to do?" Mara asked.

"Not, if you don't invite everyone else!" Jaera said, entering the room with Becky and Sarah. She picked up each girl, tossing them up next to Amanda, and then jumped on at the foot lying face up, enjoying the dancing sensation for a moment. "Oh, I was sent to announce lunch is ready."

With a nudge to Mara, Aerrvin got up and helped Jill off the bed. "One last room to see and then we can eat."

The last room was gold and royal purple with a nod to royal red and blue in the drapes. The sumptuous carpet was in the deep purple that Aerrvin loved so well. A golden metallic wallpaper flocked with a dark gold fleur-de-lis pattern running upright, created stripes.

"I guessed close enough!" Mara exulted.

"Me too!" Jill chimed. "Are you guys sure you don't want a design studio instead of a craft shop? You have such exquisite taste! I would love to hire you to help design my catering shop."

"We'd love to!" Jaera responded, without getting her companions opinions.

Sarah thought they were testing beds, so she took a running jump and landed in the middle of the smaller queen sized bed, messing up the deep purple coverlet; revealing a white fur-covered mattress.

"You have fur for sheets? Now that is the ultimate in luxury!" Jill said, then changing topics she added, "Let's see what recipes you've stolen lately."

They ate lunch in the game room. Jaera and Gareth sat with Becky and Sarah while Aerrvin, Mara, Jill, and Amanda sat at the table near the viewing room so Rick could sit with them and still see the game.

Button and Calico placed the plates from large serving platters. Gingham delivered strawberry lemonade.

"Rick, Honey, lunch is served," Amanda called.

"I'm coming," he called, backing away from the screen. Finally able to peel his eyes away, he noticed the food. "Hey, this looks great!" Lunch consisted of a sub sandwich, made with turkey, provolone, and all the trimmings with fresh fruit salad artfully arranged on the side, and light homemade potato chips complementing the meal.

Jill admitted, "Okay, it looks like you didn't steal anything this time, but do you think Button will tell me what is in the vinaigrette?"

Aerrvin replied, "Jill, you are one smart cookie. I bet you could solve it on your own."

Button returned with a plate of seconds, along with a cruse of the vinaigrette. Jill studied the contents and then tasted it, making guesses until Button nodded with a final grin.

"There you go, lassie; we knew you had it in you. Here's a tip, they use it at the new Bistro on 22nd Avenue," Button informed. With a final look at the plates to ensure all was well, she said, "I will return shortly with dessert."

"Dessert!" everyone at the little girls' table said in unison.

"There's none for you if you don't eat your lunch," Amanda chided.

Mara spoke up, "So Aerrvin, you said your birthday was coming up. How old will you be?"

"Guess," he said, first to his table and then beseechingly to the other, "How old should I be?"

"I know, I know," Becky said with a giggle. "One hundred and ninety-three."

"Close, but not quite that old," he grinned at her and then winked at Mara.

"I think you have one of those ageless faces," Amanda said. "I mean, you could be anywhere from eighteen to thirty years old! Rick, what's your guess?"

"What?" he asked, turning back toward the table. "Oh, well judging from his set-up here I'd have to go with older, say twenty-eight?"

Aerrvin smiled. "Jill, I'll give you a clue: Gareth's Birth Day is the same day as mine, as well as the year. Jaera is the same age, but she's six months younger."

Jill looked at them all thoughtfully. "You're all so accomplished, but yet so youthful. I'm going to have to say twenty-four, based on Jaera; no way is she older than twenty-five."

Jaera piped up, "Your turn Mara! How old are we?"

Mara knew their age, but Aerrvin didn't give her a hint as to what age he wished to represent, and now he wanted an age from her. Looking around her, she finally cleared her throat and said, "Well—I never intended to get involved with an older man, so I hope you are twenty-five-ish?"

Aerrvin turned to Gareth. "Gareth? Do you wish to have the honor?" He was at a loss as to what age he should be and tried to pawn it off on his friends.

"Not me either." Jaera laughed merrily at Aerrvin's discomfort.

To any Human onlooker, the young man looked suave and cool, lounging comfortably at the table. But Mara noticed reflective sparkles of purple and blue emerging on his skin, swiftly whisked away by a subtle breeze. *So dreamy*, Mara thought as she realized she had never really seen him sweat, and this was the closest she was going to get. Not able to contain herself, she joined Jaera with a giggle of her own. That decided Aerrvin.

"All right, if you must know, we are thirty," Aerrvin replied with a twinkle in his eye.

"What! He is lying!" Jaera pointed to Sarah, "I would no more be thirty than that babe is."

Aerrvin raised his voice musically, "Jaera, I gave you a chance to proclaim your age. Would you object if I said, we were indeed twenty-four going on twenty-five years of age?"

Gareth joined the conversation to forestall Jaera from another round; in fact, their equivalent age would be near nineteen Human years, but that would appear far too young for their present situation.

Ever the tactician, Gareth said, "Best to admit to it now, nearly a quarter of a century." He placed a calming hand on Jaera's shoulder. "I imagine the party we host will be the biggest thing this neighborhood has seen in two hundred years!"

Mara approved of the age with a nod. "It's a good age. Why didn't you tell me it was Gareth's birthday too? It would have been rude for me to come and not bring a gift for him."

Aerrvin replied with a rueful twist. "Gareth is a little put out that his Birth Day is not on a holiday. It is good luck to arrive on a holiday you know."

Jaera responded, trying to cheer Gareth up, "Ah, but you were born on the same day as Aerrvin. How much more luck do you need?"

Everyone laughed at the comment, thinking it was a jab at Aerrvin's pride. In reality, it was almost as impressive as being born on a holiday. For Gareth, it ensured a lifelong friendship and commitment to Aerrvin. Still, sometimes he didn't see it that way.

"Hmm, must mean Jaera was born on a holiday," Amanda interjected. "Were you born on Christmas?"

Jaera pointed her delicate finger to the tip of her pointy little nose with a flourish.

All eyes turned to Rick when he suddenly said, "Couldn't be very lucky if Santa didn't keep you. You must have been too tall." He chuckled at his joke, drawing smiles from everyone else.

"As a matter of fact, I did visit Santa's workshop, with Aerrvin and a few others. It was a school field trip, and poor Gareth was sick. He has never gotten over it," she patted his hand comfortingly.

He certainly looked downcast. But he brightened as the girls began asking questions and Jaera filled them in on all the wonders of the workshop. Talking about Santa always cheers the soul. Mara noticed Amanda looked a little stiff as Jaera began spinning fantastic stories, but a look from Rick loosened her shoulders if not her jaw. Rick was a big believer in Santa; every year he dressed up for the girls and visited them before bed, eating the cookies, and drinking the milk before tucking them in. Mara had always snuck out of bed after he had gone to his room—to set out a new plate and glass of milk for the *real* Santa.

"In any case, I wouldn't want to be one of Santa's helpers, because the Elves were a little snooty. Not allowing me to touch their tools for goodness sake! It is not as if I could have broken anything. But let me tell you a secret. The best gifts to get are made by Santa himself; they are always handcrafted and one of a kind. If you really want a present from Santa, don't ask for an Easy Bake

Oven or a doll from the store. Those kinds of things can come from any of Santa's helpers."

Jaera looked up to see both parents looking at her. She smiled amiably, not realizing the pressure they now felt to find or create a handcrafted gift.

"Thanks a lot, Jaera," Rick said good-naturedly. "Since you seem to know Santa so well, maybe you could send him our way a little early so we can learn a few tricks of the trade."

"Hah! I've only met him twice; Aerrvin or Mara would have better luck getting him to leave the North Pole early."

Amanda was done with make-believe. "All right enough of that; it's not even summer yet. Did Button say something about dessert?"

At the mention of her name, Button appeared carrying a tray with a variety of treats from which to choose, namely a pear cobbler with caramel sauce, a chocolate cheesecake topped with sugared raspberries, and soft gingersnaps served with a mango sorbet.

Aerrvin took the sorbet, and when no one else from his table took one, he reached for another. Rick chose the cobbler and shared with Amanda, who wanted the cheesecake. Jill agreed to take the cobbler if Mara would take the cheesecake; she secretly wanted to taste all three as Aerrvin surmised, so he shared his second bowl too.

The other table took two of everything and shared it all, putting all the plates in the center of the table. The little girls were laughing at silly things Gareth said—flirting as only little girls can.

Before they left, Becky begged Mara to take her picture with her new best friends.

"Sorry, sweetie, I left my camera at home," Mara replied sadly. "I didn't even think of bringing it."

Gareth overheard and offered the use of his, which he seemingly grabbed from a buffet around the corner.

"Thanks, Gareth."

Mara gratefully accepted the camera; then she posed them in front of the waterfall. They were so sweet, hugging Jaera and Gareth. In the last shot, Sarah gave Gareth a kiss on the cheek, and Jaera's eyes flashed with jealousy, but only long enough to be caught on film. In an instant, the Green Fairy was kissing each girl goodbye and giving Amanda and Rick hugs as well.

"Thanks so much for the tour," Amanda told Aerrvin. "The house is very different from the way it was the last time I was here; I am surprised they let you change it so much. Lunch was super. I think you may have my approval as a future son-in-law. We *will* have to see what Ironwood has to say, though." She hinted at ferocity.

Rick added, "If I have a vote, I say go for it. You both have a lot going for you, and you can't go wrong marrying a businessman."

He smiled at Amanda self-importantly, so she rewarded him with a kiss. "That's right, dear."

While the rest of the family loaded up, Mara thanked Aerrvin.

"It was wonderful! I do believe my family approves of the young entrepreneur and his companions. I would like to revisit sometime. Why do you have so many rooms when you sleep with the cats?"

"The house came with the rooms. What can I say? Oh, you probably mean; why did we get such a giant place for three people? We knew we would want to party, and this place was available. Don't you think it was a good thing?" Aerrvin made an unconvincing pout.

"Yes, of course, it was. Do you guys ever use your rooms?" She asked noting her family waiting for her.

"Yes, when we want to meditate. I think right now your family is waiting. Call me when they leave, and I will be at your door in a flash." So saying, he kissed her hair and walked her to the minivan. "It was nice to meet all of you, and please, drive safely." He slid the door shut and danced a little jig back to the foyer.

Ten minutes later Rick loaded the suitcases into the minivan while Mara hugged everyone one last time.

"Bye. Love you," Mara said to Becky and Sarah.

Amanda reminded Mara she would be back for graduation and her big birthday party. "If you want, you can go ahead and let Grandpa and Jill arrange everything. I'll just come and have a good time."

"No, Mom, you can talk to Jill and discuss the food. Grandpa will do the decorating, and I will send out the invitations. Okay?" Mara smiled encouragingly; one never wants their mother being a martyr.

"Fine, sounds fair. See you in a few weeks then. You will be there for Ricky's graduation, right?"

"Yeah, I mean to. Bye!"

18

Permissions

Diaphanous spirits in dreams we greet

Infused as one ~ we connect for life

~ Mara Lilyana Jamis

May 17, 2009

Mara's grandfather arrived at the same time as Aerrvin. Mara introduced the men formally and then invited them into her study. Her grandfather took the recliner. Mara and Aerrvin sat together. Jill made herself scarce by retiring to her room.

For whatever reason, it seemed to feel like an interview. Aerrvin sparkled for the second time. Fairy Dust gathered in drifts about them as they sat on the couch, the more Aerrvin thought about it, the more he glistened. Mara felt tense beside him, but because of his Ware Spell, Aerrvin knew she was filled with mirth. Ironwood was a mask as hard as his name implied. Somehow, the spell could not penetrate into Ironwood. Reason dawned, as he concluded that Ironwood maintained a counterspell. Respect bloomed, and the Fairy Prince regained his composure. These thoughts ran through Aerrvin all in a matter of seconds as they sat down on the soft leather seats. Mara removed her shoes, and curled up next to him, waiting to hear her grandfather's questions.

Ironwood looked at each of them sternly and said, "Am I to understand that you wish to court Mara, or is this some fairytale fun you are having?"

Mara's eyes widened at the directness, but she remained silent, allowing Aerrvin to prove his case before the judge.

"I have asked for the honor of courting Mara. I was unaware of her having a male relative for me to have asked first, sir," Aerrvin replied. Then with rich satisfaction, he continued, "Mara agreed, and I have maintained a respectful distance, meeting her in her Dreams or mine for dancing and instruction. I am sorry if I woke her before you were ready, but she kept seeing and doing more every time I met with her. She amazes me."

He looked her in the eyes, which she dropped before he could cause her to blush. She felt a need to control any puddle of sparks by not allowing them to start.

"I see. Is this what you want, Mara? Before you answer, you need to understand the importance of your situation," Ironwood said.

"Like what? He's a Fairy, and I have Elven blood. I thought you said mixing races made us stronger?"

"It does. No, I am not speaking of prejudice. I am speaking specifically about your present situation, and Aerrvin's to a small degree. Tigerlily is the daughter of Her Royal Highness Queen Gwennara of the First Garden, along with Brand the Bright, of course. Right?"

"Yes, so I come from royalty, but she was the second daughter. It's nice but—what?" Mara shrugged.

"Not just nice. You have responsibilities. Tigerlily's oldest sister, Daffodil, became *removed* from the world ten years ago, and her younger sister, Arianna, is essentially missing. Neither of them had any heirs. Arianna has a changeling daughter whom she raised. But she is not a true Elf, let alone of royal blood; therefore she is not in line to succeed the Queen. Had there never been a daughter of power born of Tigerlily's line, I would have been forced to become the First King of the Elves of the First Garden. Unless I choose Humanity, in which case the Empire would cease to exist. Or more likely, war would ensue as different factions would fight for control. But we have you now; you are our one last hope."

Aerrvin felt a chill down his spine. "Morvayne said words very similar, about her being his last hope." Bringing a breeze to gather his Dust, he produced a crystal vial and filled it half full.

"Sylvie is still complaining about the Dust in the living room," he explained, since he did not often clean up his own Dust.

Ironwood nodded and continued, "I have a concern, Aerrvin. I like you, and I see you are keeping a watch out for Mara, but why have you met secretly with Morvayne?"

Aerrvin described his visit to Balmoral and the Fairy Ring at the zoo. "I could not say anything sooner because Morvayne made me promise by my Purple wings, and the time was not right. I hoped to learn a bit more about his plans while he thought I was on his side. But I am ready to reveal my true self to the entire region. Morvayne wants me to deliver Mara to him, and I have no intention of letting him near her again."

"What does it mean to swear by your wings?" Mara asked.

"If a Fairy fails to keep an oath made on their powers, they lose their power for a year," Aerrvin replied.

"But I wouldn't want you to do that, Aerrvin. By telling us have you lost your power?"

Aerrvin smiled impishly, and said, "Twice no. I said something like, 'I swear by my Purple wings that I will not tell a single Fairy.' Neither of you is a Fairy, and if you were there is more than one of you, so I am not telling a single Fairy!"

"Clever boy," Ironwood said with a chuckle, "but there is more. Am I correct?" Ironwood lifted the vial of Dust, which sparkled silver, blue and purple.

Aerrvin said, "Yes, of course. I have allowed each of you to see more of my power than Morvayne. He only saw the Purple as far as I am aware."

"Interesting," Ironwood stated. "I guessed the Silver and Blue manifested because you sat upon the Throne of Desire." He nodded toward the room across the hall. "But you say you had Silver and White already."

"Yes, quite true," Aerrvin answered. "The Blue was truly a heart's desire, simply because growing up, I admired Gareth so." Aerrvin allowed his Blue power free for a moment of splendor.

Basking in the beauty, Ironwood said, "As you may know, the study of Fairies, in particular, has been my life's work. I have not yet met The Queen Rose, but surely you are related. Are you perhaps a cousin?"

Aerrvin took the vial from Ironwood's hand and shook it, causing each tint to collect in layers according to color. The layers went from weakest power to strongest. Starting with Purple on the bottom followed by Blue, White, Silver and there sitting on top—a brilliant Gold.

"Queen Laurel ap Rose and King Jasper ap Rosewin are my parents. I am an heir to the Rose Crown of Ireland, after my sister, of course. My parents sent me to America to make it my own."

Ironwood looked puzzled. "I knew that the Queen's oldest son was named Aerrvin, of course, but I never even considered that he, you—would leave Ireland. Many people name their children after royalty. I have not heard of you being in the country. Have you been using a different name?"

Aerrvin replied ruefully, "Ah, my friends often call me Ae. The Fairies have been tight-lipped, evidently, for they surely know my name and that I have been here for quite some time. I admit I have been lax in my efforts to round up a kingdom of followers. We Fairies enjoy our freedom, and the New World seems to make the desire stronger. I have required a meeting in the Seat of my Kingdom at my Grand Fairy Council once every forty years. Soon to be twenty."

Ironwood nodded, "Yes, I was in Europe during the last one, and when I returned and learned of a new royal line in the Americas I was disappointed for years! I thought it was someone other than Aerrvin ap Rosewin." Turning to Mara, he said, "You have been quiet, Mara. What do you think? Is this something you categorically wish to be involved in?"

Smiling at the two men whom she loved most in all the world Mara said, "I don't think I have a choice! I love you both and could never leave you to fight evil alone."

"Then, it's settled. Would you like to set a date?"

"What, a date for marriage? Already? I thought you were seeing if he was worth dating?"

"Oh, he's worth dating, but we were seeing if he was worth being allowed to court you. Anyone worth courting is worth marrying, and you just proclaimed your love for him. You love him and want to marry someone else?" Ironwood ended with a twinkle in his eye and a smile tickling his stern mouth.

Mara was speechless, opening and closing her mouth like a landed fish.

Aerrvin came to her rescue. "We would like to discuss matters privately before we announce a date, my lord."

Chuckling, Ironwood stood and shook Aerrvin's hand and hugged Mara. "This calls for a drink," he proclaimed.

"But I thought alcohol was poison? Dad always said so. What do we drink in celebration, soda pop?" Mara held her head at an angle as she did when perplexed.

"Ah, something better." Going to the desk, Ironwood opened a secret compartment behind the decorative front and removed a wee bottle and three wee wine glasses. In a blink, the three were sized to match the bottle and glasses. Sitting under the desk with the glow of their power offering a magical, mystical aura, Ironwood opened a bottle of Rose Elixir and poured a portion into each glass.

It smelled heavenly. Eyes alight, Mara sipped it. "It's not alcohol!"

"No, it isn't, it is the elixir produced from the roses tended by your intended's very family," Ironwood replied.

"You'll not taste finer in all the world," Aerrvin said, thoroughly enjoying it as much as Mara and Ironwood. "I am bringing in a shipment for my Birth Day, as expected."

Mara filled Ironwood in concerning Aerrvin's age and upcoming party. Ironwood responded by saying, "I always thought you were a whippersnapper."

As they sat enjoying a scandalous second glass of elixir, they heard Jill enter the room. "Hey, any—Where'd they go?" They heard the front door open and then close. "Must have taken a walk, their cars are still here." She grumbled her way to the kitchen.

Ensuring they were not going to hit their heads they were soon back to their normal size. Ironwood returned the half consumed bottle and magically cleaned glasses to the secret compartment. Then they went to the front door, opened and shut it, simulating a return.

"Oh, there you are, I never heard you go out. It's nearly dinner time. I'm not too hungry, but I was thinking of egg drop soup. Any takers?" Jill asked.

Ironwood made excuses, "Not tonight. I still have more work ahead of me, but I understand you will be the head chef for Mara's Birthday Bash. If you would like, I can show you around my kitchen soon and get you acquainted with my staff?"

"Oh, I would love to, maybe Tuesday?" Jill replied excitedly. She had heard descriptions of Ironwood's estate, and this was her first chance at getting to see it. If it was anything like the O'Shea Mansion, she knew it would be awesome.

Mara agreed to a small bowl of soup; she had eaten more dessert than she should have at Aerrvin's. Aerrvin chose to stay as he had nothing better to do. Jill enjoyed their company as she prepared the simple dish.

"You two seem especially cozy, did something noteworthy occur?" Jill asked, eyeing Aerrvin's arms wrapped around Mara's waist as he stood behind her, nuzzling his face in her hair or neck from time to time while Mara returned his affection by reaching up to stroke his silky golden hair, apparently with no shame at such open affection.

"Grandpa approved Aerrvin as a noteworthy suitor, and since we obviously want each other, he said we should set a date," Mara giggled.

"What? But—I guess—well, you have to name your first child after me since I brought you together," Jill ended lamely.

"Perhaps. I tend to think we were drawn to each other. That first day at the bus stop, in front of my store, I was smitten and would have pursued regardless," Aerrvin replied silkily. This time, Mara spilled a shower of sparkles that went cascading to the floor.

Laughing, he said. "I think I'm going to enjoy finding ways to make Mara blush; she does it so prettily."

After the light dinner, Aerrvin and Mara excused themselves to go for a ride in his car.

"Don't wait up for me. No telling when we will get back. We've got a lot to talk about. Please remember to *not* lock the bolt," Mara instructed.

"Yes, dear, but now I'm feeling like a big sister again. Be safe." Then turning to point at Aerrvin, she said, "I'm happy for both of you, but remember; she's a good little Christian girl so respect her. I mean it. I don't care if you are a fairy prince come to fly her away to Neverland. If you break her heart, I will find a way to convince a troll to eat you for supper!" Jill got fired up quickly. With a smile to soften the outburst she added, "Probably with one of my gourmet sauces."

Aerrvin and Mara each hugged Jill and promised to be good.

Once in the car, Aerrvin said with a crooked smile, "How good do we want to be?"

"The best! What are you talking about?"

Directly in front of the car, Mara saw a light as though it bent around an unseen corner. Suddenly the car was on a long empty stretch of road. The terrain was mostly flat, and she could see mountains in the distance.

"Where are we? Is this real?"

"It's real. I popped us to Nevada. This stretch of road is almost always empty."

Pressing the pedal to the floor they were soon screaming down the road until Mara thought she was going to lose her voice—at least, she was screaming; he was laughing like a maniac. Eventually, he pulled off the road and drove down a dirt track which looked out over a canyon. Dusk had settled; the last of the sun faded while they ate dinner.

"We missed the sunset, but I thought we could watch the moonrise."

Getting out of the car, Mara immediately felt the warm, dry desert air. "Oh, this feels so good after all that wet spring air." Aerrvin opened his trunk and retrieved a blanket and pillows from inside. "Were those really in there?" Mara questioned, taking one of the pillows he handed her.

"Truth to tell, they were. I do have experience with planning a date from time to time."

"Do you? Being you are so long-lived, tell me about your dating history."

Aerrvin walked to the edge of the ravine and set the pillows on the blanket he had spread out. The pair lay down, looking up into the brilliant stars.

"Oh!" Mara breathed. "I haven't seen the stars this bright since the last time I went camping on the beach near Mom's place."

"No, you can't see them like this in the city," Aerrvin replied. He continued talking softly, telling about his past girlfriends. His first crush was Jaera, but she was too wild for anyone to tame back then. Besides, everyone could see that Gareth and Jaera were meant to be together, even if they were not ready to admit it. He explained that mostly Fairies prefer to tease and play.

"So in truth, the only times I have in reality had a girlfriend was when I visited among the Humans. I think deep down I knew that the one for me would be Human."

Mirri Sihee yanked his hair before flying away. Aerrvin winced but remained mute on that relationship. He shifted his gaze from the stars to face Mara, then lying on his side, he drew his finger down her profile, stopping at the pendant that lay on her chest. She smiled briefly at the thrill but continued to examine the night sky.

Aerrvin went on, "My first serious girlfriend was an English schoolgirl who was on holiday in France. We met to dance on the beach. My skills were not so well refined back then, so I was only able to enter her Dream once."

"How old were you?" Mara asked.

"I was thirty years old," Aerrvin replied. "Really 'tis young, tis like Becky's age to you. Remarkable, really, that I was able to be in her Dreams at all, and that I was able to go on holiday myself without a chaperone. So maybe not really like Becky. Fairies mature at the same rate as Humans up to the age of sixteen; then we slow dramatically. I guess it was more like letting a teenager vacation alone."

"Hah! Letting a teen out alone is nearly like letting a little child out. The amount of common sense is the same. I don't see much improvement on the campus at college. Go on, tell me about the next one."

"Well that was a holiday, so I went back to the Academy and continued my studies. My final year I elected to study Sea Life, so I went to live and study in a Mermaid colony off the coast of Greece. I fell head over heels for my instructor. She teased back."

Aerrvin smiled at the memories, then seeing Mara's raised eyebrows he smoothed his face, leaving only a crooked grin. "Mermaids are quite flirtatious, as you might have read, but she told me she did not prefer two-legged creatures. So I finished my studies and returned home to Ireland. By then my sister had been born, and my parents had their hands full teaching her to be respectful. She is a White and Yellow Fairy and quite willful. My White powers had manifested, causing me to spend quite a bit of time alone Dreaming or studying texture. Occasionally, I visited with Gareth and Jaera, but they had their own studies which interested them, so for about twenty years, I did nothing much. My parents assigned Bronwyn as my personal assistant to teach me my Royal Duties, and just—be there for me. We decided to tour throughout Europe, to see the larger world, and to get away from my sister." He rolled his eyes.

"Surely she's not that bad?" Mara chided.

"Wait until you meet her. She may come to my Birth Day party along with my parents; they have not yet responded. But one day I will take you home, and you will certainly see," he chuckled. "Okay, she has improved with age and marriage. I must admit, she pushed me into seeking you out. I have her to thank for that."

"So she cares for you enough to want to see you married. That's sweet," Mara replied.

Aerrvin fell flat on his back and convulsed with laughter, causing Mara to sit up and stare.

The quarter moon had risen and did not offer much illumination, but Mara could see tears coursing down his face as he laughed so hard.

"No," he finally gasped, "she may care for me, but it is her own desires which concern her." He sat up to face Mara, crossing his legs he pulled her close. "My sister wishes to have a child," he said, as though that meant something.

Mara held her hands out in a gesture meaning, "so?"

Aerrvin elaborated, "In my family, it is a tradition for the oldest to have the first child. She is anxiously awaiting my announcement of an heir so that she can continue with her own plans. How do you feel about children anyway?" His fingers inched up to caress the cashmere sleeve of her sweater.

Mara swatted his hand away, "Is that why you are pursuing me, to get your sister off your back?" Mara did not know why she was offended, but she was tired of hearing about past loves. *Maybe one should not inquire too deeply about such things.* She stood up and walked a little ways beyond the blanket, not wanting Aerrvin to see her tears.

❄❄❄❄

Talk about Yellows, Aerrvin thought, not understanding her sudden state of sorrow. "Mara, sweet Mara, what is the matter?" He followed after and wrapped his arms around her. The desert air had cooled, and he felt goosebumps on Mara's forearms. He plucked a shawl from the air and settled it around her shoulders; she dried her tears on his shirt.

Mara's mind was a jumble of emotions, but finally, one thought jumped forward. "You haven't said that you love me." She spoke into his shirt, relishing in the strength of his firm muscles as he clasped her to him. Breathing in his fresh, clean scent, she realized he smelled like the ocean.

Aerrvin let her go and pulled her face up to look at his. Taking in every detail of her refined opalescent features, her wide long-lashed eyes, her perfect straight nose, her full lips—still pouting. His heart swelled with emotions as he said, "Mara, I did not mean to hurt you. I was trying to stage the perfect moment and find the perfect way to say how I felt. Red Fairies have a way with words and poetry. I have no skill in that arena."

Mara stopped pouting, her mouth parted in anticipation, he thought—when instead she stamped her foot and said, "Get on with it already!" A gleam of joy and true anticipation in her eyes met his.

✢✢✢✢

Suddenly, Aerrvin opened his entire self to her, revealing his full Glory. His wings were not as huge as they had been when he received the Blue Power, but they were brighter as they shone the purest white Mara had ever seen with purple and blue coalescing with silver along the edges, shooting Fairy Dust in every direction. Most amazing of all, he was encompassed in a halo of golden light. *My Mr. Sunshine.* Mara's eyes shut momentarily as past visions danced in her head.

"I love you with all the power of my eternal soul and offer you my Light and Glory to do with as your heart desires." Calming his Brightness, he enfolded her in his arms, kissed her for an eternity and then asked, as he flew her into the air above the canyon, "Mara Lilyana Jamis, will you marry me?"

She kissed him in return just as passionately and responded in a breathy whisper, "Yes, of course, I will."

177

Aerrvin danced her down to the river in the bottom of the ravine, skimming their toes delicately in the water and then swooped her back up into the air, then catching a rollercoaster of air, he landed her softly upon the blanket. Looking down she realized he had changed her clothes to a shimmering sheer gown of long white and lavender petals which fluttered in the wind—and she was barefooted, yet as exhilarated as she was, she no longer felt cold. Aerrvin wore flowing white pants, fastened at the ankles genie style by an embroidered band of silver and blue, with an intricately embroidered tunic to match.

"I'm going to have to learn how you do that," Mara said, smiling wickedly while pushing Aerrvin down onto his pillow. "But not tonight."

19

Rekindling

Such clarity of vision ~ such precision of soul

to see and be seen as the ones that we are

~ Mara Lilyana Jamis

Monday, May 18, 2009

Mara awoke before Jill left for work.

"You came home earlier than I thought you would," Jill said, heading out the door dressed in her white chef's coat, hat in hand.

Mara replied brightly, "True, but I remembered that I still have my math to do, and I need to proofread my English paper. Aerrvin brought me home by 11:30, so I'd be able to get up bright and early."

"Good girl, we wouldn't want your grades to slip. Well, I'd better get; we don't want Dev mad at me either! Have a nice day."

"Sure will. Bye."

Jill's coffee cake, made with peaches and blackberries, sat on the stovetop. *To be served with clotted cream,* Mara assumed. She went to the fridge to confirm her guess when she saw Sylvie scamper behind the fridge.

"Sylvie, come out. You don't need to hide from me anymore. I think I am fully awake. At least I know who I am anyway. Please, Sylvie?"

With seeming reluctance, Sylvie came out and bowed with a faint flourish. "I am most sorry for not serving you better throughout your young life. Please accept my humble apology." She remained bowed.

Mara realized she needed to release her from her stance. "Sylvie, of course, I do! Stand up, do not scrape so low before me. I have always loved you. I am so sorry I stopped believing in you." Mara brushed a tear from her cheek.

"Now do not be crying. You should know that crying is the one thing I cannot abide," Sylvie said, wiping her own face surreptitiously. "Don't fret over it, dear. It is the way of the Human world. Your mother herself did believe once."

"Yes, my mother is a mystery to be unraveled another day. Did Jill buy any cream?" Mara asked, opening the fridge and finding it. "Great! This should be wonderful." She heated a slice in the microwave, and then smothered it with the perfectly sweetened cream and sat down to enjoy.

Meanwhile, Sylvie climbed up to sit on the covered butter dish.

Sylvie hesitated, but then boldly continued, "My lady—ummm. Your welfare is my greatest concern, and I think it best if you know that Morvayne is trying harder than ever to get inside the walls of this home. He found the Brownie entrances, and he has some ugly Orange and Yellow Fairies working on them with new spells that are weakening them. My father thinks it will be only a matter of months before they have broken through." She paused, cringing pitifully waiting for a reply.

"Sylvie, stop cowering. You are quite competent." Mara spoke succinctly, but not without compassion.

"Yes, my lady."

"Much better. I knew Morvayne was trying to get in but did not know this bit about finding and weakening the entrances. I guess this means I will have to move. But what about my brother? Will anything happen to him if I let him move in?"

"Not likely. If Morvayne sees that you have left for good, he will follow to where you have gone. Your brother should be as safe as he is in Sequim. It will be safer for my family members who wish to stay with this house. Not all Brownies serve the individual Human as I do. Most are territorial. My parents for one, do not wish to leave," Sylvie squeaked and then hastily added, "Pardon me, I called you Human when I know you have awakened to your royal heritage. You do intend to defend the Crystal Throne and stand against evil, yes? That was Tigerlily's fondest dream for you."

"No offense taken, Sylvie. I still consider myself Human, and I do intend to fight against evil. I have not yet decided how far I want to go with becoming a full Elf, but I think I will have to go all the way to save the throne, so never mind what I said. You should know by now I think out loud."

Mara paused to rinse her dish, nearly leaving it in the sink. Seeing Sylvie's disapproving glance, she removed it from the sink, placed it in the dishwasher, and then wiped the sink, gaining a nod.

"Yes, Sylvie, I intend to honor the Crystal Throne and defend it against anything or anyone who dares to overthrow it. I understand that Queen Gwennara is in hiding. I hope Grandpa can find her before Morvayne does."

Mara went to the closet to get her backpack. She had not even opened it since bringing it home. She found her thumb drive with her English assignment on it and took out her Math book as well. Seeing the front of the desk in the study, where the secret compartment was, made her smile at the memory.

Sylvie had followed, so Mara asked, "Sylvie, what is in Rose Elixir anyway, and what does it do?"

"Yes, I missed the occasion, but I heard about it; congratulations, my lady. If Ironwood approves, surely I can as well. The Fairies who serve the Rose

Crown collect the dew each morning from the roses in their gardens all through the spring and summer. They also induce the nectar to rise each evening and add it to the vials collected. Then they distill it, bottle it and allow it to age. It is delightful at any age that I have ever tried, though I have only had it five times myself. Once a decade is all we can afford, my lady," she added with a curtsy.

"And what does it do? What are its properties?"

"It induces joy, but not by affecting the chemicals in your body the way alcohol does," Sylvie taught. "It heightens the senses, allowing one to experience the world with more clarity and peace. It calms your thoughts, allowing you to think more clearly, so you can focus more precisely. When in this state you can enjoy your senses of touch, taste, smell, and hearing to a fuller degree. Which is why it is reserved for celebrations."

"Oh, Sylvie you explained that so well. No wonder I recall last night's events with such clarity. They must have been etched into my soul with precision. Is that what it does as well?" Mara inquired.

"Exactly. I am delighted that you are swiftly learning about your heritage. Nearly as quick as your father, bless his soul," Sylvie said. Then adding maternally, "Not so with your math skills, you best get to your studies, as I must finish up mine own duties and be off to bed."

"Thanks, Sylvie." An overwhelming sense of love for her childhood companion enveloped Mara, but no words came to mind.

Putting off math to the last minute, Mara proofread her essay, which took an hour as she decided to add a few paragraphs and change her conclusion. Stretching, she stood and went to get a glass of juice. Walking through the house with her newly awakened sight, she marveled at the power which guarded and kept her safe. With her glass in hand, she went back to stare at the mantel.

Jaera explained that Santa's kiss was an ever-changing crystalline snowflake and that he had left one for his wife hanging in the air above her table. Mara had no doubt that Jaera told a true tale. Mara placed her glass on the mantel and gently touched the blessing, as Aerrvin had explained kisses could be. Upon her touch, it flared softly. Afraid she had activated it somehow, she called Sylvie for advice while watching it closely.

"Sylvie, I touched Santa's blessing, and it brightened and then went back to normal. Did I do anything to it?"

"Probably not. What were you thinking about when you did it?" Sylvie asked.

"Santa—and how wonderful he is."

"Well, now he will know what you were thinking. No harm in that. Now if you had touched it while wishing for something, he would judge whether it was a worthy wish and grant it, or not, as he is wont to do."

Mara sat down in her special chair. "Oh, that is marvelous!"

She started to say more, but suddenly she was suffused with energy and her necklace heated up near to burning, yet caused no pain. Then the pendant opened in half as a locket would, only there was no clasp. Mara looked down and saw a tiny golden key inside, she pinched it between her forefinger and thumb and held it before her face in wonder. While in this state of shock, she then saw words float across the air as though written in neon lights; these were the words: "You now have the Key."

"I now have the key?" Mara asked, "Sylvie, what is this? Have you ever seen such a thing before?"

Sylvie answered with circular logic, "It is a key. I have seen them, they are for opening things which are locked."

"No, I mean what is it meant to unlock? Did Aunt Lily ever tell you about this key?"

"No, she did not talk about keys. It must be important. For it to be revealed to you, it must mean you are meant to use it," Sylvie reasoned.

"Did you see the words floating in the air?" Mara asked.

"No," Sylvie replied quickly, "but I can see the Power welling up in you. You had best get out of the chair and fold up your energy and put it in your pocket else when you go outside, every evil fiend will spy you and flock to tell Morvayne."

Mara had been intent on the key and only now noticed that she was filled with more energy than ever. Like Aerrvin had said before, she felt as though she could go for a month or more without sleep.

"Delightful!" She smiled as she replaced the key and shut the locket. Then leaving the Chair of Desire, as Ironwood had named it, she focused on the rainbow-hued light and wadded it up as her grandpa had taught and put it in her pocket. Smiling proudly, she asked Sylvie, "Did I get it all?"

Smiling in response, Sylvie replied, "That you did."

Giddy with Power, Mara danced about the room. She had never felt so alive.

"I think I am fully awake, I don't think I could be more wide awake if I tried! I don't think I should sit in the chair for a while, though, and I need to ask Grandpa about the rules for its use. Strange that it never affected me like that before. It must have something to do with my belief. I do believe in Fairies! I do! I do!" Laughing, she said goodnight to Sylvie and danced her way back to the study.

"Oh wait, my juice!" Mara retrieved her juice and hurriedly started doing her math assignment.

She then took a full hour to bathe and eat her lunch. All her photos were already in the lab, so once dressed she put her work back in her pack and went to catch the bus in front of the Craftsman's Majick.

Being early, she went inside to say hello to whoever was working. "Hi, Aerrvin, I'm surprised to see you here. I dropped in to say hi to Jaera. She is usually here in the mornings, of course. I guess it is nearly noon, though. How's things?" She paused to breathe.

Aerrvin smiled broadly, "Sleep well, did you? I don't think I have ever seen you this energetic." Pulling her close, he whispered in her ear, "Must have been the company you kept last night."

She kissed him lightly and replied. "Actually, I sat in *The* chair not realizing it would be different now that I'm 'awake.' I'm like a baby on caffeine.

Oops! There's my bus, see ya!" Mara dashed out the door, garnering stares from everyone.

At school even getting a B on last week's math test didn't upset her. Mara enjoyed the sun on her walk from the main building to her photo lab. She noticed an increased number of looks from the students on campus, she assumed it was the smile on her face making her approachable.

Try as she might, she couldn't keep from smiling, so she just said, "Hi" when a guy approached and kept walking.

"It's a magnificent day isn't it," said a beautiful voice from behind.

Turning, Mara confirmed that it belonged to the one she feared it would.

"Morris," she said, quickening her pace. "What brings you on campus?"

"A consultation with one of the professors about a business project," he replied musically, looking her up and down as he matched her pace. "I see you are getting a lot of male attention, perhaps if I walked with you…"

Mara cut him off, "No need. I can handle my affairs quite well. I was only polite the other night because of Mother. I am not interested in a relationship of any kind with you."

Having noticed that she had rid her skin of his kiss completely, he spat, "I might have known your grandfather would be back in town. I see he is still protecting you from me." Taking her arm, he caused her to stop walking. "Mara, listen to me! Whatever he has told you could not possibly be true. I mean you no harm! I have a marvelous…"

"Hey, Mara. Do you have time to show me your photos?"

Relief flooded Mara as she turned to see Gareth and Seamus.

"You said anytime, but if you are busy —," Gareth said casually, barely acknowledging Morris holding her arm.

Mara moved away from the loathed hand and replied hastily, "No! No problem at all, Gareth. Now would be perfect."

With an oily smile, Morvayne said, "I will speak to you later. Please have a care. I would hate for anything to happen to you." Having looked at everyone as he spoke, it was hard to know to whom he was speaking, perhaps all of them.

With relief, Mara went inside the lab, flanked on either side by Seamus and Gareth.

"How did you? Oh, never mind. How long have you been tailing me?"

Seamus said, "We've been attending you for six days now."

"Not in your house mind, only when you go out," Gareth added.

Mara did not like the feeling of unseen eyes watching her, but shaking it off she said, "I guess I'd better get used to it, this is part of my life now, eh?"

"Aye," Seamus agreed with a smile. "I'll stand by the door."

"So, Mara, I really would like to see your pics. I have not been inside with you, only Seamus has done that," Gareth said, his sincere blue eyes open and friendly.

"Sure, come with me. How did Seamus get in here without notice?" Mara wondered out loud.

Gareth laughed, catching the attention of students passing by. Quietly, so as not to be heard he said, "We put him back to size, then we used an invisibility cloak on him. Works great for hiding among Humans. Elves and other Fair Folk can see his glittering outline as 'Morris' did at the restaurant."

"Seamus was at the restaurant?'

"Yes, and 'Morris' questioned him too. Calm down, no need to excite the neighbors. Seamus convinced him that he is working with Aerrvin, to lure you out; to be delivered to him sometime next week. 'Morris' is not alarmed by seeing us with you, he thinks you are in our control," Gareth finished whispering. Raising his voice to its musical norm, he said, "So, show me your stuff."

Mara led Gareth over to a bin in which the framed photos were kept upright at an angle making it easy to flip through for viewing. All eyes were on them—if done in quick, stolen glances—so Mara tried to appear casual, but she was bad at it.

"Loosen up, Mara. I am just a friend looking at your art. You have friends, don't you?"

"Not as far as these people know," she said miserably. "I'm pretty quiet here. They are probably in shock."

Gareth laughed as though she had told the silliest joke. Then he directed her attention to a photo. "Mara, I am not sure this is the best setting for this picture. Do you mind?" She shook her head, and he brought it back to her workstation. Taking it out of the frame, he said the color was all wrong. "Look what happens when you use this shade of blue versus this one," he laid a darker matte over the pale one she had chosen. She looked as he flipped between them and she considered, cocking her head one way and the next.

"Well, I was going for a dismal mood, with the trash and I'm going to set it with these as well, she collected two others along with one not matted at all. Gareth smiled at the photo of Dougie.

"Yes, I see what you were trying to do, so maybe this charcoal would be better."

They spent the rest of the hour discussing the pros and cons of laying them out in certain ways and even involved others who became interested in the discussion.

She had a few pictures of Gareth in his Mohawk punk wannabe get up, though they did not show any wind. "Hey, when did you take this one?" he asked as they cleared off the table.

Mara smiled. "Oh, that was right before you went out in Aerrvin's car; you know me I always have my camera, or almost always. You can have this copy if you'd like. I have one of you and Jaera too somewhere—oh, here it is." It included the kittens.

"Thanks, they are lovely. I have the perfect place for them." Gareth said, hugging her. "Let me speak with Seamus; then I will walk you to the cafeteria."

Mara's nearest classmate spoke up once she thought he was out of earshot.

"Where do you find these hot guys? Does he change his hair color often? I thought he was blond." She nodded toward some of the other photos.

Mara smiled, and said, "No, they are two different guys. Gareth does like changing his style a lot, though."

Smiling at her brazenness, she linked arms with Gareth and Seamus and let them escort her to a late lunch, which would count as her dinner since she had to work late that night. After lunch, her math class was two hours long and surprising to her, she understood the teacher clearly the first time through.

Bronwyn came with the car and drove Mara directly to work after a short stop to change her escort from Gareth to Aerrvin. "You don't mind my coming to work with you, do you?" Aerrvin inquired.

"No, of course not." While she had him alone, she took the time to tell him about the key revealed in her locket. "So while you are using your lovely creative mind to ponder the universe, please spare a minute to solve this one too." She smiled winningly at him, so he kissed her and caressed her hand as they rode to work.

Mara introduced Aerrvin to her class and noticed George was absent. "Where is George today?"

She learned he had been moved to the other wing. The wing she worked in was for those who were still mobile and had sound enough minds to interact with one another.

"Why, what happened?" she asked breathlessly, as her face paled.

"He stopped feeling well, and wouldn't get up, then he went into a coma, so they moved him," Berta said.

Mara taught her class, but her heart wasn't in it, she appreciated Aerrvin's help. They made wind chimes from supplies she had bought at his shop; she especially liked the small tinkling ones, but the elderly students said they couldn't hear them, so they chose the larger ones. The project could be finished in one session, so everyone left happy, except Mara.

"I guess George was special to you?" Aerrvin asked as he helped put the supplies back in the closet.

"I like them all, but yes, he was especially playful. I saw his Dream the other night when I came to yours. I would like to see if I can find it again. Is it safe to visit a mind in a coma?" Mara asked with concern.

"Yes, with assistance. But it would work better if I met him in person first. I'm coming too." They checked at the wing office and found his room. It was clean and clinical, not at all like the other wing where the patrons still had dignity and personality in their rooms.

Mara gasped upon entering and not at the sight of seeing a frail old man. It was George, but he glowed ever so faintly. A tiny, near invisible Fairy sat on his pillow—weeping in time with the beeps of the machinery so as not to be heard. Glancing a question at Aerrvin, she went forward and asked the Fairy straight out who she was.

The Fairy startled at being seen, but then saw a faint glow from Aerrvin as he filtered a bit of light to let her see it was safe to speak among friends. "I know you, Mara; you work here giving George joy. I did not know you could see me; you never let on before."

"I don't recall noticing you, but I have been blocking my vision for ages. Aerrvin here has awakened me, and I know who I am." Mara emulated Aerrvin by letting a small gleam leak through her own shield. But she was not as skilled, and a burst of light escaped before she got it under control.

"Sorry." Mara blushed, scattering Dust as she did so. "I have only been at this for a few days. What happened to George and who is he?"

"Please sit," said the little Blue Fairy. "George is my son. My name is Estelle. Hmm, okay, he was a changeling. We found him as a babe, abandoned in the woods near my home some one hundred years ago. We raised him, but he never felt like he fit in. Oh, he tried and tried, but eventually, he said he needed to make his own way in the world and left.

"He lived with us sixty years. I tried to keep track of his doings, but in time, he lost me. I think it was when he went off to help in one of those Human wars they keep having. I finally found him five years ago. He seemed to have lived a good life, he had married, but no children, though he loves them so.

"He refused to *see* me for the first three years, but these last two he has not only recognized me as his mother, but he accepts that he is a Fairy, and he wants to Fade. Why would he do that? I do not understand." She went back to sobbing.

Aerrvin said, "He does not seem to realize that he must be in Fairy form before he Fades, perhaps he has forgotten more than you think. Maybe he means he wishes to live in the Land of Dreams. Mara told me that she saw his Dream the other night. Have you tried contacting him yourself?"

"No," Estelle sobbed, "I am not gifted with the ability."

"Oh." Aerrvin was a little shocked; it was a basic ability, being rare when a Fairy could not learn it. "Estelle, do you mind if we tried, Mara and I?"

"Please do!"

Aerrvin instructed Mara in how to go into a dreamlike state while awake and then put himself there as well, meeting Mara in the Void. "Now, can you make out his Dream?"

Aerrvin thought he knew but, since he did not have a relationship with George, he wanted Mara's opinion as well.

"Yes, that one belongs George," she said confirming Aerrvin's guess.

"All right, you lead the way. I'll be right here with you."

Peeking in, Mara saw George just sitting in a gray mist. "George, what are you doing?" Mara asked, not expecting such dismal thoughts. She brought her glow with her, casting rainbows as she gestured.

"Mara? What are you doing here? I'm in my Dreamworld, but I seem to have gotten lost somehow, so I sat down to rest."

"I came to see what you were up to. I met your mother, and she is very worried. Tell me, where are you trying to go? Maybe I can help." Mara so wanted to be of service to him, even if it meant helping him pass on.

"I left Mother and Father because I thought I belonged with my own kind. I enjoyed getting a job and being responsible for my wife's welfare and happiness. Then she died, and I wandered around a bit—but I found I had no real reason for living. I moved back to Seattle thinking maybe my memories of a young Fairy life were true, but I could find no trace of it. So I moved into this retirement center while I was still fairly young. I was 70 years old according to my military records. I never knew how old I really was. I've lived here 20 years. I've had fun making the others happy; that's my thing. Well, Mother showed up, and I started thinking I was losing my mind." Mara nodded in understanding and George nodded again.

George continued, "But I noticed a lot of the others saw her too. Not workers, of course. So I started talking to her, and now here I am." He looked at her as though she should understand.

Mara said, "George, I still don't get it. You believe, but what is it you want to do? Do you wish to return to the woods, or to Fade away to the other side? Or do you want to visit a Dream of your own making? I think those are your only options, but a choice needs to be made soon because your body is dying."

George looked at her, tears streamed down her face in sparkling rivulets. "Mara are you really here? Who is that behind you?"

Mara smiled blearily as Aerrvin dried her face with a breeze. "This is my fiancé, Aerrvin. We want to help you."

"If all this is truly real, I would like to go to the woods with my mother and then visit the Land of Dreams for an extended reprieve, then I will decide whether I am ready to Fade for good. I feel like I have been Fading from reality for a very long time. Can you really help?" He looked at each of them and then at the blue sky as the mist floated away.

Mara turned to Aerrvin. "Now that we know what he wants, how do we help?"

"This is easy to solve. George, you put yourself in the coma you are in. All you have to do is wake up and allow the doctors to nourish you properly, as well as your mother. She will feed you specific foods. Then you can check out of the retirement center. I analyzed your body, and you are as fit as anybody can be. Your mother can direct you home, and you can live or Fade on your own timeline." Aerrvin brightened the Dreamscape further to give George hope and then left.

Mara hugged George and spoke softly in his ear, "Goodbye, for now, hope to see you soon!"

Mara and Aerrvin came out of their trance-like states and explained his situation to George's mother. "Oh, thank you, sir, my lady!" She curtsied daintily. "You have saved my joy. I surely do know the foods he will need. Let me retrieve them now." She slipped through a crack of light and was gone.

"How long will it take?" Mara asked.

Aerrvin shrugged. "It all depends on George."

❧❧❧❧

Mara had typed up a two weeks' notice letter earlier. She decided it was as good a time as ever to turn it in. Karen was not currently working, but Mara would see her tomorrow. She hoped it would not be the worst two weeks of her life. Walking out to the waiting car with Aerrvin, she doubted it.

20
The Power Within

I'd climb the highest reaches, I'd plumb the greatest depth

Upon the sandy beaches, I'd track you step by step

~ Clay of Glennferry

Monday, May 18, 2009

Despite having been a long day, Mara's energy continued to buzz within her. After another history lesson with her grandfather, she made her way home. For no real reason, she did not feel like sharing her newfound strength with Jill, so she went to bed as usual. The newly attached thick drapes on her windows helped prevent getting the creeps from whatever was lurking out there. When a light pinging on the glass caught her attention, she approached with trepidation. With relief, she saw Aerrvin fluttering, but then doubt filled her.

"How can I tell it's you?"

He flared Silver followed by Gold. Having learned those colors were rare, only for true nobles, she rushed to let him enter.

"Clever, Mara, I am sorry that I forgot to call you first. I didn't mean to frighten you. I did not think you would be able to sleep after receiving so much light, so I came to spend the night."

He maintained his six inches, doing a backward flip and he landed on her little Growly. "Oh, Mara this reminds me, the kitten's eyes are open."

"Wonderful. But are you going to stay small?"

"Yes. I thought you could use some lessons on bending light. If you want a hug without crushing me, you need to want to be small too."

Aerrvin taught Mara the method of focusing her attention on the center of her personal Light while thinking about her desired size, or any other desire. Mara understood it was similar to what she did in her Dreams. Unlike her Dreams, which shifted at the slightest thought, this took more concentration. Aerrvin made her practice it for an hour until she could do it at his command.

"Okay," Aerrvin said, "prepare me a meal, on the spot, hurry!"

As quick as a wink she had a bowl of cereal and a glass of orange juice on a tray. Aerrvin burst out laughing, his voice rich and pleasant.

"What? I never claimed to be a chef. This is what I know how to make," Mara explained.

Aerrvin sent it away and in its place were pastries filled with cream cheese, a sumptuous fruit salad, an ornate glass bowl of shrimp in melted butter, along with delicate crab cakes.

He instructed, "You do not need to know *how* to make it to have it. You just need to want it." Creating a miniature table with two tiny chairs, he set the tray down and motioned for Mara to join him.

"Now you get the drinks," he challenged.

After only a slight hesitation, Mara smiled as a half-empty bottle of Rose Elixir appeared with identical crystal wine glasses like the ones she had drunk from on Sunday evening. Aerrvin nodded approval.

"How does it work? Is someone missing their pastries now? I mean, is this the actual bottle or did I recreate it from my memory?"

"Excellent questions, Mara," Aerrvin said opening the bottle. "Taste."

Mara smelled it first. The scent infused her with its heavenly aroma. She tasted it; it tasted divine. "It seems to be the same. What am I missing?"

"The sensory effects will not occur. It is a synthetic made from your desire; so it will not have the same outcome as the real thing. Now, with the food, it contains half the calories with twice the nutrients, but, hey how do you think we keep so fit and trim?"

He laughed, the sparkle in his eye enchanted, but Mara doggedly remained on point.

"Okay, so what is the science behind it? Can I comprehend it, or will I need to attend your Academy to get it?" Mara asked.

Aerrvin plopped a shrimp in his mouth and chewed before answering. "Probably both. Not all Fairies go to the Academy, or stay very long if they do; ten years of training is not unheard of, it gives most Fairies the basics. It is not that we are less intelligent, most of us simply don't care."

Aerrvin perceived Mara still wanted a better explanation, so he began, "Have you heard about this string theory which is bandied about now among Humans?"

"Yes, I took a science class last year; we discussed the theory."

"Good, the Humans are on the right track, it will take a while, but maybe some Fair Ones are helping them. Anyway, Newton and Einstein had our help as well. So, the concept is that there is something smaller than atoms, yes? These strings vibrate and, based on the vibrations, something comes into being." He closed his eyes a moment and continued, "It is brilliantly beautiful; all things are created by Music and Light. The pertinent questions are, 'Who is conducting the orchestra and where does the light come from?'" Aerrvin paused to allow Mara to consider.

"It must be the Supreme Being." Mara paused to think. "And scriptures say He is the source of truth and light." Her eyes widened, "This is His Power?" Her glow grew brighter, lightly illuminating the dresser top.

Aerrvin smiled with delight at her wonder. "Yes, it is as simple as that. We use the Light to cause music, and the thing we desire can be found, made, or created. To make fully loaded caloric food requires us to expend far more energy and concentration than most Fair Ones can sustain at one time. There is no need, so no one works on increasing their strength in that direction." He paused a moment to eat a grape and said, "We could create fake money, but we are honest at heart and collect our gems and minerals the same as any other being, through mining. Although, some of us do have the ability to sing the gems, and precious metals right to the surface." He grinned, "Not me. I tax my subjects."

Mara sat and pondered awhile as Aerrvin ate his salad in companionable silence.

Finally, she asked, "So what is the difference between making something and creating something; aren't they the same thing?"

"To make something is to fashion something which has been in existence before. To create something is to fashion something new and unique. Jill attempts to create new things, but it is hard to do when most culinary morsels have been made countless times. Brownies have access to recipes from the beginning of time on this earth. Jill will have to tax her creative genius to best a Brownie. There are Universal Laws in place along with gravity and the like, which we are constrained to take into account. But from time to time, a Fair One manages to create something which has never been before.

"All Mankind are God's chosen people. He means for them to be exalted to live with Him. Elves and Fairies are a step down. He desires that we along with the rest of His creations reach our full potential and the only way to do that is to seek after the Light. Once Humans as a whole begin to believe in the One True God, they will surpass anything we could ever hope to be able to do. I think that is why Tigerlily chose to become Human."

Mara's face crumpled again. "I don't think I have cried as much in my life as I have this month!" she squeaked breathlessly. Thinking of Tigerlily's faith strengthened Mara's resolve further. Deeply inhaling, she squared her shoulders and said, "I can do this. I can be the best that I have been created to be." She paused momentarily and then continued, "I will fight against evil, namely Morvayne, and I will serve the Light."

With that, she revealed all that she had become to Aerrvin, knocking him off his chair. He stared from his kneeling position as Mara's tiny form glowed with enough power to light every corner of the room. Mara heard a squeak come from behind the curtain. She lowered her Light and asked Sylvie to join her and Aerrvin. The little Brownie hastened to kneel before her, mimicking Aerrvin. Mara was dumbfounded at their response.

"I am sorry. I did not mean to frighten you. I only meant to share my Light as you did, Aerrvin. Sylvie, both of you, stand up! You are making me nervous!" Mara tittered.

They stood, but Sylvie kept her head lowered; Aerrvin flourished another bow. "Never have I been in the presence of one so Bright, my lady."

Mara wadded up all the light and stuck it in her imaginary pocket. "Stop it! Both of you. It's just me, look at me!" They looked but were not able to keep the wonder out of their eyes. Aerrvin offered his hand to Sylvie to calm her.

"My lady," Sylvie whispered, "I should like to be about my duties—if you please." Once again bowing her head as she awaited dismissal.

Mara understood the Brownie's discomfort, so she agreed, and watched the sweet Brownie scurry out of the room through a tiny door Mara had never noticed before.

Mara turned to Aerrvin and walked towards him. Taking his hand, she said, "Let's be Human-sized," as she pulled him off the dresser. They landed with a soft whisper on the ground. "So tell me what just happened."

Aerrvin swallowed painfully and pulled her towards the bed to sit. "Never has a Fair One burned so Brightly when they were that small. I can only guess that an attack on the Crystal Throne has succeeded. The Transfer of Power has occurred."

"What does that mean?" Mara asked.

"You are not only the heir-apparent but the new Queen-in-Waiting. You will not be the actual Queen until after your 21st Birth Day when you must pledge to serve the Light. After that, you will be prepared for a Ceremony of Coronation. Surely a gathering notice is on its way!"

"But I so wanted to meet her. I thought finally I had a female relative to discuss all this with. Do I at least have any distant cousins? Anyone?" Mara's full lip quivered in a pout as she flung herself back across her bed.

Aerrvin collected some pillows to prop their heads and gathered her in his arms. They lay crosswise on the bed, with Mara curled into a ball inside Aerrvin's protective embrace. Aerrvin thought it would be more comfortable to be lengthwise, but here she was, so he grimaced and brushed the thought aside.

"Mara, I am here for you. Besides, Ironwood must know of some relatives for you to talk to." Changing his mind, he repositioned her on her bed and then re-joined her, grateful to be able to stretch his legs.

She turned to face him with a soft smile, her eyes searched to see if he had removed the reverence from his face. Contented, she shut her eyes.

Aerrvin stroked her hair and murmured, "You may feel like your physical energy is high enough that you do not need to sleep for months, Mara, but you need rest for your mind. Go to sleep. I will watch over you." He hummed a simple lullaby. Mara snuggled closer to feel the rumble and marveled that he could mute the sound so softly, as she easily drifted away.

✤✤✤✤

Aerrvin added a few Celtic lullabies, after copying a lullaby he had heard Mara singing under her breath while she worked. He marveled anew at her softly radiant skin. Even if she thought she had hidden all of her power, she could never hide that opalescent glow from close-up.

He reviewed the events leading up to meeting her. It hardly seemed like chance: All the paths in life he chose to take led to meeting and becoming engaged to the Future Queen of all the Mystical World. Yes, choices made led to this singular consequence.

Oh, poor Mara, he thought, *you are a mere babe! I thought I was young, but now I see—What? Who are you kidding?* He stifled a chuckle so as not to disturb her. *I too am young. I have no idea how to get us out of this mess. I will need to consult with Ironwood, though he is younger than I. Perhaps then some of my old Masters. This little key is intriguing. But it is not related to the Transfer of Power.*

He hated missing the sunrise, so he drifted off to sleep, meeting Mara in her Dream. They flew up to the top of a mountain peak to view the sun as it rose and then down into the valley see it anew.

✷✷✷✷

Mara awoke to breakfast in bed: a bowl of cereal and orange juice. Aerrvin's eyes twinkled as he smirked. "Good morning sleepy-head. I made you breakfast."

Smiling back with a twitch of her brows she said, "Half the calories, I hope?"

"Naturally. Mara, do you mind if I stand in as your bodyguard today?"

Aerrvin asked as though she might refuse him.

"No, of course not. But I'm going to be considered fast or worse by my classmates."

"How's that?" Aerrvin asked. "I mean what does 'fast' mean? I have been among Humans a time or two, but I have not encountered that one."

Mara smiled indulgently, "Yay! I never get to be the teacher, and it's about time, thank you. Let's see, it means that people will think poorly of me for switching between boyfriends quickly. They think that Gareth is my new guy and maybe Seamus. Of course, yesterday guys were eyeing me all day. I got two phone numbers and three invitations to go out. Not counting Morvayne's."

"Precisely why I wish to attend you. Fairy Dust is highly potent, and yours is particularly so. I can charge a very high price for my collection so far. Jaera and Gareth are going to have a field day bargaining at the next fair. I imagine they will be able to leave with anything they want. Mara, you are a— what is the word they use? Ah! Mara, you are a cash cow!"

199

"What?" she screamed, throwing a pillow at him as she jumped from the bed. "You just called me a cow?"

Laughing richly he fended her off as she beat him with a pillow. Jill opened the door to see the bed made, but cereal had been spilled on it, and Mara stood there beating a laughing Aerrvin.

"I don't want to know." She started to leave, but then said, "Wait, yes I do. My curiosity gets the best of me. Aerrvin, what are you doing here so early, and why is she screaming about being called a cow?"

Mara stopped whacking her pillow and fell on top of him as he tumbled backward. "Turns out," Mara replied as she regained her breath, "that as I accept my Elven heritage, my Powers grow stronger, and evidently the Fairy Dust I produce when I sweat is very powerful stuff; so Aerrvin called me a cash cow." She thumped him for good measure.

Aerrvin grinned and said innocently, "And I came to give her breakfast in bed."

Jill looked at the mess again and said, "Huh! Will wonders never cease? I suppose you thought Toasties was a good breakfast?"

Aerrvin and Mara both looked abashed but then burst out laughing at their first private joke.

Mara said, "I think I will take a shower. If you don't mind Jill, you can take Aerrvin down and teach him what I like for breakfast."

"Okay, but you better get that coverlet in the laundry, you don't want the milk to dry on it," Jill responded, pulling Aerrvin out the door.

As Mara went to clean up the bed, the mess disappeared. No food left, just an empty bowl, a spoon, and glass sitting neatly on the tray. With a smile, she hurriedly showered and dressed, not even bothering with blush. She didn't want to keep Aerrvin waiting. She felt as giddy as a schoolgirl but didn't care.

Aerrvin smiled appreciatively as she came in sparkling clean, with her wet hair twisting up into ringlets as it dried.

"Jill showed me how to make French toast with the right touch of vanilla and cinnamon. Would you like blackberry or maple pecan syrup?"

"One of each, please. I am famished. That cereal did not seem to have much substance to it." Mara sat down at the bar to eat.

Jill finished up her plate. "Hate to eat and run, but I've got a living to make, unlike some around here. Hey, is there any way to make Fairy Dust profitable for us lowly Humans?" Jill chuckled and went out the back door without waiting for an answer.

Aerrvin replied anyway, "Honestly, yes. When you dust it on people, they are more attractive, and things tend to go their way. Give her a gentle dusting, and she might find that she is able to get her remodeling contractors to work a little faster and to find better deals for her. Fairies sometimes use it to gain attention, well, all right," he amended when Mara arched her brows at him, "we always use it. But I am sure you would have found me irresistible without it. I do not use much. Mostly my own with a touch of Gareth's and my father's in a mix I like to keep for special occasions. I will shut up now."

He ended his discourse by sitting down to eat a small plate of French toast smothered in the fresh blackberry sauce, topped off with the leftover clotted cream.

"Mmmm," he said, "nothing like berries and cream."

Mara finished her breakfast and started cleaning up after herself, "Jill isn't usually this messy! Oh, sorry, I guess it was you helping her. Do you never actually prepare food yourself?"

"No, not unless you count foraging in the woods. I can always find the sweetest berries, and nuts seem to fall on my head whenever I think of them," he concluded by looking up as though a few would descend at any minute.

"Hm, well I'm not so great myself. It is a good thing you have Button, or we would be eating poorly all the days of our life." She finished with the counter and started to load the dishwasher.

"I like that part—all the days of our life." Aerrvin pulled her to him and kissed her soundly. If you would like to keep your reputation less sullied, I can change my appearance."

Suddenly, he looked like Gareth except he kept his own lavender eyes. His hair spiked in a seven-pointed crest. He tried to kiss Mara again, but she squirmed away.

"No, thank you. I like him and all, but this is too weird for me. Go get yourself cleaned up and looking decent. I will suffer through whatever. It's not like I have many friends there that I hang with anyway."

When Mara finished with the dishes and judged that she had not left too big of a mess for Sylvie, she turned to look for Aerrvin. She found him at the mantel staring at Santa's kiss, dressed in faded blue jeans, which were just a touch ragged at the hem, and a tight light blue t-shirt. He wore a thin leather headband to keep his hair out of his eyes, a look more in line with the 1960s, but not too unusual on campus in the Emerald City. She appreciated the broadness of his shoulders as they contrasted with his narrow waist, creating a perfect V-shaped silhouette. His jeans were not overly baggy which she appreciated even more; she really hated that whole saggy pants, in-a-shambles look.

"What do you think it means?" Mara asked as she came into the room and stood to stare at the ever-changing wonder.

"Not sure. Another thing to remember to ask Ironwood about. What time is school?"

Mara looked at the clock with a start, "Oh, I should catch the bus now!"

She grabbed her backpack and headed out the door. Seeing Aerrvin's sleek car parked in front, she slowed and waited for Aerrvin as he shut the door. "I guess I will be early rather than late. It takes the bus forty minutes to get there, but driving takes only fifteen."

Mara saw a flickering presence and then watched as a tiny figure climbed up Aerrvin's body and then stopped to sit on his shoulder. "Oh, that must be Seamus. He's been out here all night?"

Aerrvin nodded his head slightly, but said, "I don't know. Seamus, where have you been hiding?"

Mara stepped closer so she could hear, and she noticed Aerrvin's hair getting tied into the sexy little braid he liked to wear. Little bells dinged as she realized it was a safety strap for Seamus.

Seamus spoke as he braided, "I secured the perimeter, and then I spent the night inside as did you, my lord."

Aerrvin grinned wickedly, "Ah you little devil!" Then to Mara he explained, "Seamus finds Sylvie highly attractive," he ended with an "Ow!" as his braid snapped tightly.

"Oh, I never thought about Sylvie's private life. So I never considered whether she was married with children or not. I don't suppose her married status impacts her ability to — um, do what she does. I guess."

Before Aerrvin could reply, Seamus said, "Not in the least, Your Highness."

The title did not sit well, and Mara felt disinclined to be overly flirtatious with a Brownie sitting on Aerrvin's shoulder, so she talked about math, surprising herself that she was suddenly getting it. The school day went smoothly, no more visits from Morvayne and the approaches had ceased, even if the looks had increased. She was apparently taken, and she couldn't have been happier.

Work went by quickly with Aerrvin's help, and surprisingly Karen understood Mara's need to leave pending graduation. It so happened that she already had two applicants, which she would interview on Thursday, putting Mara's mind at ease. On the way out, they checked on George. The nurse said he had indeed come out of his coma, but he had a bad cold, almost pneumonia. So no visitors until he recovered.

❧❧❧❧

Thursday, May 21, 2009

Wednesday and Thursday began much the same. With Aerrvin by her side, Mara enjoyed school and work—often with Aerrvin hidden in her hair.

Arriving at Mara's home, they discovered Jill had double booked herself. Jill wanted Aerrvin's advice on what to do with her place. She had also agreed to meet with Ironwood's staff, both things she really wanted to do.

Aerrvin solved her problem by offering to drive Jaera down to look at the shop. They promised to take notes on their ideas. Then they would come over later to get her input and approval.

"Thanks, Aerrvin, that would be a big help," Jill acknowledged while taking the shop key off of her key ring. "Okay, Mara, direct me to Ironwood's mansion."

❉❉❉❉

Jill was doubly impressed with Ironwood Estates. "Mara, you never told me you came from this kind of money!" she whispered as she came out of the bathroom.

Mara replied in her softest voice. "It's not my money. He didn't give me any of it. Probably Mom's fault too."

Going back to the main room where Ironwood waited, they admired the sculptures lining the broad hall. "Ironwood, you have many lovely pieces of artwork," Jill offered. "Do you collect from a particular artist?"

Ironwood smiled graciously. "To tell the truth, most of it is my own. Occasionally I will find a piece in Europe that I like in particular and buy, but usually, I photograph them and make my own versions. In most cases, though, I let the stone or wood, as the case may be, speak to me. It speaks, and my hands follow. The results are what you see."

"I am impressed, Ironwood. Do you ever sell them?" Jill said brightly and then quietly, "Talk about a cash cow," she whispered at Mara.

"Oh, not very often," he answered. "If there were a need, I suppose I could. Well, come along. I will introduce you to the kitchen staff."

The kitchen was nicer than the restaurant Jill was currently working in. It had three prep stations, five ovens, and two stoves along the outside wall to allow for easy venting. It had a wonderfully long counter for laying out the courses as they were completed. The pantry was as big as Mara's kitchen, and the walk-in refrigerator was amazing. Before setting out to see how they did things, they had a look at the dining room. There was a narrow butler's pantry to separate the dining room from the noise of the kitchen. Upon leaving the pantry, they were to the right of a long walnut table which was, amazingly, longer than Aerrvin's had been; it seated twenty-six. The main entrance into the room was right at the center of the table, coming at it broadside so one would need to look left and right to see the entire scene. Directly across from the main dining entrance were three sets of French doors, which lead out to three terraced patios overlooking a carefully manicured lawn and several gardens.

"I see why Amanda did not argue over your offer, Ironwood. This a perfect place for social gatherings."

Ironwood nodded amiably.

Returning to the kitchen, Jill went about learning how well they could follow her lead. Ironwood suggested she have them prepare a meal for ten, with the menu being her choice. "We will leave you to your work," Ironwood said. "I will be talking to Mara in my study; send Delia when it is nearly ready. We will eat in the green dining hall."

Mara noticed that all of the staff bowed their heads as they passed, *Wow, they really respect Grandpa*. Once in the study, she learned something else. The study was filled with Brownies, Elves and a smattering of Fairies. It seemed over thirty individuals crowded the library. They all bowed as she entered and did not rise. Mara looked to Ironwood and to her surprise, he bowed as well.

Still bowed, he handed her a handwritten note on delicate onion paper. "News arrived this afternoon."

Mara thought she knew what it would say. Before reading, she begged, "Grandpa, all of you, please stand up."

Despite having been pre-warned, she needed a chair. Ironwood had anticipated, and a Brownie had one beneath her as she went into a near collapse. "Is this true? I mean is it from a reliable source?"

Mara waved the note, mindful of not tearing it. The note was from Her Royal Highness Queen Gwennara. It said:

My Dearest Ironwood,

I write you a message in my most direst of circumstances. As you know, I have been in hiding so as to evade an enemy assailant attacking our family. I can now name the assailant. He caused the loss of two of my daughters because he had been spurned by a third. You know of whom I speak. I have been taken hostage and am even now buried deep beneath the sea. Which sea I know not. My powers have been drained. With the last of my spark, I sent my Authority and the Rights and the Power to Rule from the Crystal Throne to your sweet youngling, Mara. I know not if she will be able to free me, or those who reside with me in the depths of this dark and lonely existence. I am compelled to include that - she has the key - though I know not what it means.

You may trust this message and the messenger.

Your loving 4th Generation Grandmother, Gwennara.

Ironwood spoke gently in answer to Mara's query, "Yes, Sweetness. May I introduce the messenger?"

Mara nodded. Ironwood, in turn, nodded to the group. They parted and before her stood a man who tore her heart in two with joy and sorrow equally. She leaped from her seat and ran to him throwing her arms around him. He was a near image of her father, and yet she knew immediately who he was—Brand the Bright, her very own progenitor, the former King and Consort to Queen Gwennara.

Finding the strength to speak Mara whispered, "I never knew you were a Fairy."

Hugging her tightly and then standing her straight and at arm's length, he said, "I never knew you were so Bright."

Mara looked about and at herself and realized she had lost complete control. Those in the room were again all bowed lower, if possible, than they had been the first time. Still, her Brightness blinded them with awe, not harshness. Lowering her own eyes, she apologized and wadded up her power. She tore it into fourths and put a piece in different pockets. She didn't know if that would help or not, but it seemed a neat trick. Smiling with self-confidence, she excused the Brownies and asked those who wished to help her solve the puzzle, to stay.

Apparently, Ironwood knew how many would be of help as he had ten chairs set out in the study and there were ten who remained, including Mara, Ironwood, and Brand.

A kitchen staffer arrived to inform them that dinner would be served in ten minutes in the green dining room unless they wished to postpone. Ironwood told her to proceed, they would be in shortly.

All eyes were on Mara. Clearing her throat, she thanked them for staying. "Before we go further, I would like to be introduced, please?"

Ironwood stood with precise grace and introduced his newest family members.

"Mara, you have met my wife, Lorelei. To her left is her sister Rowan. Next, to her is my dear friend and assistant Johann and his wife, Sasha. Their two sons are great assistants in my research, twins are very rare indeed among Fairies, this is Berry and Bright. It's okay to smile, Mara," he said seeing her mouth twitch. "Remember, they are Fairies. They gain joy from giving others delight." The twins smiled infectiously, and everyone smiled in response. "And last, but not least by any measure, my Ogre friend from Aberdeen; his name is Morthe."

Mara's eyebrows raised, but she nodded welcome. His image wavered somewhat, or rather it appeared the air in front of him glimmered as though she should be able to see something other than what she saw.

"Thank you, Grandpa. Hello, everyone. Morthe, are you wearing a glamor? I'm afraid your disguise hurts my eyes. Will your looks offend me that much?"

Morthe laughed a deep rich bass, like rocks tumbling from a cliff in the distances. "Ironwood did not wish to shock you immediately, as he knew you were to receive the others shortly. Shocks I mean. I commend you on your sturdy comportment. I understand you were only recently awakened. Truly amazing. I do not believe I am so hideous, but I will need to resume the Mask when we go to dine as I am famished and must begin grazing, or I will become truly horrifying." His sing-songy words were not as lyrical as most Ogres, but he did his best.

Garnering nervous titters from the others, Mara gathered that there was some truth to his statement. He removed the glamor and revealed a face far less scary than any Hollywood had created. Not horrifying just different. He had normal flesh-toned skin, though much browner than normally found among people in the Northwest; his head and shoulders were far more broad. His head was as wide as two football helmets together, capped in thick shaggy black hair, and his shoulders were as wide as the largest player ever seen with his shoulder pads still on. Mara wondered how he could fit in the chair. His hands were long and spindly, ending with dark brown fingernails. His nose was broad and flat, and he wore a wide smile on his impossibly wide mouth. His eyes were a deep dark brown with dark lashes, reminding Mara of a horse. His clothes were the same as the glamor had portrayed, which explained why the waves were most noticeable on his face.

Mara smiled to assure him she was not horrified. "Thank you, Morthe, that's much better."

Mara relayed her experience in the Chair of Desire, especially including the key and the neon message. "That's all it said 'You now have the key.' It might help us release Gwennara from wherever she might be."

Mara paused as a Brownie once again signaled at the door. Morthe resumed his disguise, and the Fairies and Elves hid their power. The Elves masked their ears with greater skill than Morthe, Mara observed.

They found their places where name tags had already been placed. Mara was really beginning to admire Brownies. Grandpa sat on one end, and she sat on the other. She looked up and smiled at him, stifling a pang of melancholy as she saw Brand sitting next to her grandfather, looking like her father at any family dinner in days long gone. Mara could not tell if she was seated at the head or the foot, though it hardly mattered to her.

Rowan sat to her right and to her left sat Johann. The first course was a light spinach salad served with strawberries and a smattering of bacon in the dressing. Morthe asked for larger servings. The next course he received double portions; it was a hearty vegetable soup served with oyster crackers, very homey and quite delicious. The main course delighted everyone except Morthe; he preferred red meat, but considering in whose company he was, he merely harrumphed.

It was a seafood trio consisting of a bowl of oysters, three large battered prawns, and a tower of scallops. Morthe started eating his oysters shell-and-all but seeing everyone else delicately picking the meat out, he harrumphed again and did as they did. "Lots of calcium in the shells you know," Morthe said to no one in particular.

As they waited for dessert, the talk turned to the research Ironwood had been doing over the past ten years. Mara held her shock in but shocked she was when she learned that Ironwood believed her father might still live. She always referred to the event as a disappearance just as he did, but she had no one to speak to, so she had kept her belief to herself. Now she gathered that it was her grandfather's belief in Brentwood's capture, which caused the rift between her mother and her father's family. *Grandpa must have tried to convince Mom when Mom threatened him with losing all contact. "No more talk of magic," Mom had hissed. Gosh, her rage had frightened me!*

"But Grandpa, what were you trying to convince Mother to accept, and why did it make her so terribly angry?" Mara asked hoping to verify her guess.

21

An Epiphany

Mostly now I wish to weep, like the gentle rain on a summer's eve,

cleansing and sweet . . . and oh, so welcome . . .

~ Tigerlily ap Wallace

May 21, 2009

Just as Mara hoped to get some answers, Jill arrived to present her grand finale: individual chocolate cobblers served with a berry compote topped artfully with fresh whipped cream.

As the two assistants served the guests, Jill complemented Ironwood's staff, "Ironwood, your kitchen is a dream come true, and your staff members are amazing to work with. If I had a few staffers like them my business would be a piece of cake to run."

"Thank you, Jill. I too appreciate how efficient they are. Your skill is superb as well. We have enjoyed this feast for the senses, truly a delight. Thank you." Ironwood nodded in dismissal.

Jill flashed a pleased face to Mara and departed.

Ironwood began, "Now where were we? Ah, yes. You wished to know why your mother became so angry that she moved you away and denied us the right to teach you about your heritage. Correct?"

Without waiting for her answer, he continued, "That is a long story, but I shall condense it if I can. You know that your mother is adopted."

Mara nodded, wondering what that had to do with anything, but kept silent.

"As near as we have been able to tell, she was abandoned at a church in Southern California, again something you have known. What you do not know, and your father discerned upon meeting her, is that she has a spark of magic in her. In fact, we believe she is a partial changeling sent away from her Fairy Ring as a baby, most likely because she was too weak. They must have felt Humans could raise her better. We believe she is a Water Sprite, backed up by her being a water baby by nature."

Seeing Mara about to speak, he raised his hand to signal her to wait and continued, "When your father met her at seventeen, she acknowledged her limited ability to 'see.' She began to believe in the truth and fell madly in love with Brentwood, your father. He may have gone a little heavy on the Fairy Dust, but she loved him fully. He thought she needed the boost—that it would strengthen her spark. But, alas, her spark really is quite weak. As you grew, she began to deny reality and eventually spoke out against any of us filling your head with tales of magical things.

"Brentwood had told her of attempts to snatch you, and it frightened her. She would hear no more of it. Then tragically your father disappeared, sending her over the edge. We love your mother and held no grudge against her when she took you away and hold none now."

Johann and Rowan each patted Mara in comfort as a sob escaped. "You mean to tell me I am barely Human at all?! I have been living this dreary life all this time, and I never knew? Is everyone in the world part Faire?"

Mara's voice had risen, and she realized she was spraying the room with sparks as she lashed her hands about in frustration; with satisfaction, she saw that her Light had indeed spilled from only one pocket.

Calming herself quickly, she added, "Sorry for the outburst, but I would like to know what percentage of magic is really out there?" She waved at the walls, to convey the wide world beyond.

Brand smiled warmly and offered an answer, "Truth be told, Mara, the Fair Ones, as I know you have been instructed, have been in this world as long as Humans have. It is only a matter of time, say three thousand years, and an entire population of compatible beings would all be related. The only ones, as far as I know, to have not had mixed relations are Trolls, Dryads and possibly Nyads. As we now approach seven thousand years upon this Earth, it is likely that all of the Fair Ones have some Human blood in them, and certainly, all Humans have some portion of our Magic in theirs."

Mara slumped back in her chair. "Huh! It makes sense when you say it like that. What does that do for peoples' hope in the afterlife?"

Surprised that she would dare to speak, Mara turned her attention to Lorelei, who replied, "Obviously, we do not know the Creator's Design, but we accept that it is part of the Pattern. We have a theory that He will judge based upon the degree of Light within each soul and the depth of one's desire to serve the Light. Therefore, it matters not if you are Human or Faire as long as you choose to seek the Truth. Then again, if you seek to be exalted, you must choose Humanity as Tigerlily did." Lorelei lowered her eyes, as she realized she had spoken boldly before such an august gathering.

Mara took a few bites of her dessert. Taking in all of the information at once was beginning to crowd her brain.

"So, I'm just a baby, evidently. What am I supposed to do?" She looked helplessly around the table and received compassionate looks and smiles in return.

Ironwood responded, "Education always comes first. You are to finish your studies and get your degree. On your birthday—and are you aware the Faire separate it with a capital B for Birth and a capital D for Day?" Mara shook her head as her grandfather continued, "Anyway, we will have a grand celebration with all your Human friends and family. Of course, many of us will be in attendance as well. Lorelei is willing to let me announce our marriage, not the year, of course."

He stopped to smile at his wife. Lorelei blushed prettily, sending minute pink sparkles into her lap.

"Let me back up a bit. Midsummer's Night is traditionally the beginning of Midsummer's Day and starts the night before not the night of. It would be appropriate for you to make your Vows to serve the Light at midnight rather than waiting because it would be more potent. That is the moment of your birth into this world and a most powerful Holiday indeed. So, I would be pleased to offer my rose garden for the ceremony, unless you had plans for gathering elsewhere?"

Mara shrugged. "May I ask Aerrvin's opinion? He might have made plans for me."

"No problem at all," Ironwood responded, chuckling. "A fiancé would want to be involved in such an auspicious occasion, especially on this particular holiday!" Everyone chuckled heartily at that, except Mara as she racked her weary brain trying to remember what she had read about Midsummer's Eve.

Brand the Bright added with reverence, "Truly, my lady, you must have been touched by the Source of Light to have been born at that precise time on that precise holiday. I foretell that you shall reign with such Glory and Justice as has never been seen before, including Gwennara's glorious nine hundred years of service to the Crystal Throne." As he spoke, his countenance glowed near to filling the room and then blinked out as he came to an end of speaking.

Everyone began murmuring to one another. Rowan said to Mara, "That was a Foretelling, my lady. That means it will come true." The slim Elven maiden bowed her head, lowering her eyes as she did so.

Mara finished her dessert as Morthe ate a third. She felt mentally drained, so sliding back her seat she announced, "Grandpa, I am thankful for this lovely evening, but I fear I am exhausted. Forgive me if I must leave so soon."

She stood, and everyone at the table stood. Morthe dropped his spoon noisily in his haste.

"Of course, Mara. A truly exhausting day I am sure. Let me send for your Attendants," Ironwood said.

She had not known she had attendants. Dazed, Mara watched as Gareth and six others flew in. They were downsized Elves, as discerned by their pointed ears and lack of wings.

"Mara, these Elves were assigned to you at your birth, a gift from Tigerlily. It is time you met them again." Ironwood introduced three females, Hannah, Jasmine, and Daisy. Then he named the three males, Clay, Elwood, and Ivan.

Questions popped up, but Mara was too drained to form them into coherent words, so she merely nodded, receiving miniature bows with beautiful dainty flourishes. In a blink, they winked out. With great effort, she was able to discern their full-sized forms but dismissed them as her body forced her into a faint.

Mara came to in the garage as Jill turned off the engine. Still groggy, Mara waited until strong arms came and carried her to bed and tucked her tightly under the covers. Jill murmured something to whomever it was, then came and offered a cool cloth. "Here, hon, this should soothe you. Would you like some aspirin?"

Mara was truly spent but sat up enough to have a drink of water and refuse the medicine. She decided her clothes were too restrictive, so she went to the bathroom and changed into the clean nightshirt Jill found for her. Aerrvin was the only other person there. With relief, she scanned the room to be sure she was alone and lay back down.

"I need sleep. Can you stay?" Mara whispered wearily.

Nodding at Jill, he turned to Mara and said, "I will not leave you until I know you are safe." He sat down on the edge of the bed.

Jill pondered and then said, "All right then, I am going to bolt the doors, so don't leave in the night, Aerrvin. We don't want anyone coming in to steal us blind. Would you like a spare blanket?"

"No," Aerrvin said, absently toying with the ruffle of the coverlet. "You keep this house warmer than I am used to. I am fine, thanks. I will keep watch over Mara; she is simply exhausted." He glanced at her slack face. "She will be fine in the morning; rest easy, Jill."

"Okay, but if her breathing gets erratic or something, try to wake her. I don't want her—Oh, I don't know, just keep an eye on her. 'Night, Honey," Jill said softly before shutting the door.

Mara recognized the tune Aerrvin began humming as one her father always sang before tucking her in and giving her a final kiss. "Do you know the words?" she asked.

He did, so he began, "Sleep my child, and peace attend thee, all through the night . . ."

Mara wanted to hear the whole song, so she forced herself to keep her eyes open as Aerrvin sang the lullaby. His own eyes were locked on hers. She thrilled to hear his rich tenor voice easily climb the scale to reach the high notes and then drop to sing with velvet softness the soothing lows. Aerrvin began the song again moving to lie beside her; he caressed her eyes shut, kissed her gently once, and then continued softly—switching to humming as her breathing indicated sleep.

Friday, May 22, 2009

During the night, Aerrvin had returned to his own six inches. When Mara awoke to the sunlight peeking in through the heavy drapes, she started at the tiny form nestled up under her neck.

"Aerrvin, I could have squashed you! Why did you revert anyway?" Mara questioned breathily, trying to keep her tone down so as not to disturb Jill.

Aerrvin kissed her behind the ear, causing her to wonder if she had washed well yesterday while simultaneously quelling the shiver it sent down her spine.

"Your charms overcame me, and I could not help myself," he said into her ear. Then he kissed her lobe and flew around to kiss her nose, and teased her by flying a smidgeon out of reach as she tried to swat him. "Some thanks I get for watching over you."

"Oh, you'll get your thanks all right," Mara said, reaching for some cotton balls to throw at him.

Jill tapped on the door, and before she entered, Aerrvin resumed his full six-foot stature. Jill saw him standing by the window as Mara threw a cotton ball, hitting him in the face.

"I take it you will have a wonderful marriage if this is how you are going to start your mornings," Jill said dryly. "Mara, you seem refreshed. How do you feel? Are you ready to eat? We still have muffins in the freezer which I can defrost, not as good as fresh, but I had to freeze them because I did not want them to get stale. Well?"

"I am famished!" Mara exclaimed, "I think I will need bacon and eggs too. And probably some of the tea you got from Button."

Jill stopped and stared at Mara, narrowing her eyes she looked at Aerrvin and then back to Mara.

"You're not pregnant are you?" Jill queried seriously.

Mara screamed, "Jill! How could you even say such a thing? I am quite filled with virtue. And besides, we only set eyes on each other two weeks ago!"

Jill eyed her again as she stood in front of her bed in the flimsy short nightshirt. "Well then stop running around half-dressed, or you won't stay virtuous for long," Jill snapped.

Aerrvin chuckled as he led Jill out of the room, calming her quick temper. "Trust me, Mara is completely safe with me. Come on, teach me how to scramble eggs."

After Jill went to work, Mara retrieved the two books written by Ironwood. "There is something on the edge of my mind that I am trying to remember," she explained. "Here it is!" She pointed to a picture with three Elves lounging in a shady glen." I knew I recognized some of those Elves. This one is Hannah, this one is—don't tell me —Jasmine, and this one is Elwood. Does he always wear a sword? And by the way, did you know about them too?"

Aerrvin waffled his head from side to side. "Yes and no. I never recognized them as Attendants. I only saw them from time to time flying through the night, like hundreds of others. It is not as though they were posted sentries standing at your doors. I assigned Gareth to ensure your safety last week, and he noticed a pattern and alerted me. He met with them two nights ago and learned the truth and informed me. Hannah is cute; I danced with her last week while Elwood and Clay played a happy little jig, lots of fun," he chuckled.

Mara huffed a prolonged sigh, "Humans do not like their intended to discuss fun with other girls."

Aerrvin stifled his smile and replied, "Fairies don't like it too much either, but it sure is fun!" Smirking wickedly he quickly clasped her wrists together to prevent her from slapping him. With his other hand, he hugged her to him and kissed her neck, ending with a bite on her earlobe.

He had released her wrists, so she hugged him and allowed him to nuzzle his face in her hair momentarily.

Suddenly he stepped back and said, "I don't like this shirt. Would you mind changing?"

Mara considered. His face had taken on a puppy dog look so she replied, "Come to my closet and destroy everything you cannot stand, and then fill it with your heart's desire."

Joyfully he flew up the stairs, literally, expending the energy heedlessly. This truly was a dream come true for Aerrvin. He considered destroying everything without looking, as he had so many things he would like to add, but he reconsidered, assuming rightly that she would be offended at such haste. Mara rushed into the room behind him amazed at his alacrity.

"Do I really dress so poorly?"

Aerrvin looked at her up and down twice before replying, "You could be wearing a paper sack and still be stunning. It is just that—you recall I studied textiles, yes? I have a very sensitive sense of touch and—well, coarse fabrics rub me the wrong way. It's not you sweetie, it's me."

So it was that it surprised Mara when Aerrvin kept the nubby tweed jacket and incinerated the synthetic silk blouses. Most t-shirts went, as well as all her Sunday skirts. Her shoes went, and for that, she was grateful. He kept the three new dresses she had bought: The cream-colored tea party dress, the dancing dress she wore on Saturday and a decent sweater dress in a rich plum knit, which she bought to wear on Sundays. She had not seen her closet so clean since moving in. It did need vacuuming. Shocking Mara, the carpet was suddenly freshly vacuumed, including the telltale lines.

"Did I do that or did you read my mind?" Mara asked.

"I guess it was you, Sweet Pea," Aerrvin replied proudly. "You are so talented, with training you will be out of this world fantastic. But you will need to guard your thoughts if these things are happening at the merest thought, without your conscious demand. Normally, babes learns this trick within their first ten years of life so as not to cause harm when the full Light is granted upon them. We should have thought to teach you this lesson sooner."

"What do I need to do?" Mara asked, with no doubt that if he said it could be done then, it could be.

"Okay, close your eyes and see yourself in your mind's eye. Do you understand?"

"Yes, I learned this with Grandpa, when I learned to wad up my light and stick in my pocket."

"You wad up your light?"

"Yes, it's what Grandpa told me to do when I was blasting him with it last Saturday at the cemetery. Why? What do you do with it?" Mara asked opening her eyes again.

"Everyone has their own technique, but I have never heard that one. I separate mine by colors, of course. Not something you need to do, seeing as how Elves generally only have the rainbow pearls. Nevertheless, after I have them separated by color, I place them in boxes with locks. Then they go carefully into my closet in the same order you saw in the vial of Fairy Dust, weakest to strongest. With two locks on the silver and three locks on the Gold. In this way, I am sure that I am not offending anyone by flaunting my power by accident. Then if I lose momentary control, only the Purple escapes. Does this make sense?" Aerrvin asked.

"Yes, it does. Last night I tore my power into four wads and stuffed them into different pockets; I hoped that only one would escape. Is it the same concept?" she asked, proud of her own genius.

Aerrvin was horrified at the treatment she gave her Power and Light, but he chuckled heartily and said, "Yes, that is the same thing exactly! You should add zippers on your pockets—and perhaps divide one small portion to put in a fifth pocket. That fifth pocket will be the one you want to use on an everyday basis. So, close your eyes and complete those steps."

"Okay, done! I even folded the small portion neatly like a hankie and placed it carefully in a chest pocket," she added shyly, understanding that he was appalled at her wadding technique.

"Perfect, Sweet Pea. Now, this is what my mother told me: Imagine a neighbor girl wants to come to play. Can you see a little Fairy?" Mara nodded. "Good, now whenever you have a thought to have anything at all happen, this little neighbor has to knock and ask permission. If permission is not granted the action cannot take place." Aerrvin paused to give her time to reason through what he just said. "Okay, now open your eyes; conjure up a glass of lemonade," Aerrvin requested.

Mara imagined the glass in her hand, but before she could feel it, the little Fairy asked her for lemonade. In her mind's eye, Mara nodded permission;

suddenly she had a glass, sweating cool beads of perspiration down its sides. Beaming, she handed it to Aerrvin who drank it thirstily, leaving her a sip.

Aerrvin questioned her on what had happened and tested her several more times with increasingly harder demands, the final one being to dump water on his head.

"But I don't want to dump water on your head. It will ruin the carpet, and we need to leave for school soon," Mara temporized.

In truth, she could not make herself do a task she did not wish to do, which was part of the test. Suddenly she was drenched with lake water including a crappie which went flopping about on the closet floor. Now she wanted revenge, yet she was still unable to do it. Concentrating harder, she found the Fairy in her mind and demanded that she grant the water drenching. The Fairy complied. Mara sent a deluge over Aerrvin so large that it finished soaking what Aerrvin had missed. And it was glacier water, so it sent her shrieking from the closet.

Aerrvin chased her down and twirled her around the room. "Tell me, did you chase the Fairy and make a demand?"

"I did, but you didn't tell me I could do that," Mara replied straightening Aerrvin's hair out of his eyes.

"I know. My mother didn't tell me either; it took me five years to figure it out." He hugged her proudly and then said, "Mara, you are such a pig, clean up this mess!"

In a blink, she had the closet and their clothes dry and vacuumed, as well as making her hair dry and having it straightened silky smooth.

"Ah, now there you go again, messing with nature. Mara, I prefer your hair in curls," Aerrvin complained.

"I know you do, Aerrvin, but a girl has a right to her own style. Today I want it smooth and silky. If you don't like it, you can lump it."

"You have some very interesting colloquialisms, Mara," Aerrvin said. "I guess we ran out of time to recreate your wardrobe. Let me redo your attire and then we can go."

"Very well, but I get to style you."

Mara put Aerrvin in khakis and a gray ribbed muscle shirt with a collared blue plaid over the top, left unbuttoned of course. "Very scholarly," she said with a grin, adding sandals.

Mara went to the full-length mirror to survey Aerrvin's—sense of humor, she decided, not style.

She was pleasantly dressed in a peasant skirt of the softest white cotton she had ever felt, complete with a matching top embroidered in a Spanish style: tiny pink rosebuds linked together around the yoke of the blouse by a chain of green leaves. A soft pink-netted shawl was tied loosely around her hips with the knot to one side. She was also wearing very comfortable white sandals.

Shaking her head, she said, "Oh, Aerrvin, it's beautiful," she twirled in front of the mirror, "but I would feel silly wearing this to school, please put this in my closet. I do want to wear it, but not to school." Suddenly she was standing there in her tank top and undies. And just as suddenly, she was in a nice pair of jeans and a t-shirt.

Aerrvin shrugged as Mara glared. "You said to put it in the closet!" he explained in his defense. "Seriously, Mara I do not like you in t-shirts." He put her in a gray ribbed tank top edged in lace and layered it with a second one in pink, topping it off with a blue plaid shirt to match his, although the plaid was smaller.

"Very cute." Mara smiled. "Now let's go."

❄❄❄❄

Since being made aware of her escorts, Mara noticed more flickers at the edge of her sight all morning. By lunchtime, she had had it. "Okay enough! Please materialize and have lunch with me. I have a few questions."

Before they arrived, she heard Seamus say to Aerrvin, "Does she mean me too?" Aerrvin shrugged as he winked at Mara.

"Might as well," she said. "Looks like I'm going to have a party."

221

The six Elves came from around the corner, one of them carrying a picnic pack. "We can eat across the street in the pavilion next to the gardens," Daisy offered. Her auburn hair reminded Mara of Jill.

Daisy and Hannah took more food out of the pack than it could possibly hold. All of the foods were Mara's favorites. Including Sprite. "Are you sure this is okay? I remember what happened to Jaera."

"In moderation, Mara," Elwood replied, popping a can open for himself. "So what did you want to discuss, my lady?" He amended after the glares from everyone else, including Aerrvin.

"I prefer Mara over my lady." She glared at everyone in her own turn, especially Aerrvin. "I want to know the details of your duty. You were charged to guard me as an infant? Were you in my house then? Do you come in now?"

Clay answered for the group, "We were your constant companions until the age of three. Then we were asked to maintain our watch from a distance. Your mother did not want interference in raising you. Since then we have kept watch in whatever home you have lived in. But since you were three, we have never entered a single dwelling place in which you have lived."

Hannah's soothing, melodic voice surprised Mara as she said, "I have attended school with you every year of your life. Sometimes I had so many questions to ask; it drove me crazy!" She paused to laugh. "Usually, only one of us stays nearby when you are out in public, while the rest maintain a watch on your home. We also take turns sleeping. But since your rise in status Brand the Bright requested that more of us be constant companions, and he now has others watching your home. None besides Brownies have ever entered your home. Rest assured you are not being spied upon inside. By us."

Seamus added, "Sylvie has told me no other Brownie is allowed in your bedroom. She takes great pride in serving you herself."

Mara smiled, "She does a wonderful job too. Thank you for speaking with me, all of you. I was beginning to feel like I had bugs crawling on me every time I thought of being spied on. Please continue as you must, but stop and say, 'Hi,' from time to time so I won't feel so creeped out."

They laughed and agreed, finishing the meal with happy chatter. Hannah asked if she could remain in her present form to go with Mara and Aerrvin to her photo lab. Hannah had wanted to offer her own two cents worth of advice for the display, "since forever!" Mara felt an immediate kinship and agreed.

22

Jill and Sylvie

There is comfort in knowing that others are aware

Comfort in feeling a friend's tender care.

~ Dougie of Clan Byrne

Friday, May 22, 2009

Jill loved the ideas for the storefront. Gareth thought she wanted something classy, but with an edge. So he suggested a black, white, and silver theme offering tips on switching out pops of neon color with the seasons.

"So imagine this," Gareth said, his musical voice painting the scene vividly for Jill and the others. "Your customer walks in off the street entrance. The first thing they see is an open and inviting floor in polished white and gray-streaked marble, checked with black silver-flecked tiles. To the right, they can browse a display case of sample foods, like wedding cakes and desserts, which by the way, can also be seen from the large picture window by passersby on the

224

street. Inside, they will come to a small seating area where you will have three or four tables set up, like an elegant dining room, a place where potential customers can look over your sample menus or write their own based on your offerings. Also, they can sample bites of this and that."

The imagery entranced Jill, so he continued.

"I envision high shine here, black mirrored walls, maybe with a chandelier above the tables. Deep plush silver carpeting but no, never mind, too much rain. Customers would destroy the carpet too fast. I know, black leather flooring, pre-scarred so that neither you nor the customers will mind when their heels scratch the surface. The tables should be delicate, lacy silver with the same black leather bound within its banded edge. Beyond the dining display or rather to the north of it, you will have your refrigerated display cases. This time, I'm thinking in polished nickel plating. It will run the entire width of the store cafeteria style, so customers can browse before they buy. Ending, of course, with the checkout station.

"On this side, you will want a full showcase window for seasonal displays." Gareth motioned toward the western storefront. He continued for a while and ended with, "Sound good so far?"

Jill exploded in happiness, hugging Gareth. "I love it! That is exactly what I want." Then she paused, looking at Mara, "Now if only I had a cash cow. I don't think it's in my budget. Is there a cheaper alternative?"

Gareth looked aghast, "Hey, I'll help a friend get her business up and running. I have contacts. I can call on them to find things to fit within your budget. If you have to, go with less, but always go with quality."

Having waited patiently, Jaera was able to get a word in, "Hey, Jill, could not get upstairs to the apartment because it was locked. Do you have the key on you?"

Once they got a tour, Jaera begged to do the bedrooms, "Please, please, please! I am so thoroughly bored and would love the challenge. No cost to you, just let me do it."

Shocked, Jill said, "All right, go for it!" Mara gave Aerrvin a secretive smile. She had indeed dusted Jill's underclothes drawer with her Fairy Dust. Just to see.

❧❧❧❧

Mara stayed up all night reading the last stories from the book *Enchanted Lives*, with the tiny Aerrvin tangled in her hair, sleeping cozily next to her neck. Mara thought she could get used to a little guy being in her hair, except when she had the urge to brush her hair back over her shoulder. He was sleeping soundly, so after nearly knocking him off, she gently patted his backside; he nuzzled closer. She hadn't noticed that he had lost most of his clothes in his sleep, as tightly wrapped and tangled in her hair as he was.

I really should have been reading the other book, she mused, *as it's more instructive.* But she enjoyed the stories much better. As dawn loomed, she remembered that Aerrvin's Birth Day was the next day.

"What do you give to someone who can make whatever he wants? If he can't make it, he can buy it."

"Excuse me, my lady, were you asking me?" Sylvie asked as she dusted the headboard.

"What? Oh—no, well maybe. Hang tight, let's go out in the hall." Mara carefully untangled the tiny form. With a "tsk," she realized he was in his smallclothes. She tucked him into her bed with Growly. He hugged the toy to his chest.

"He must have had too much soda yesterday," Mara said.

In the hall, she sat down on the steps and asked Sylvie what kind of gift she was supposed to give to a Fairy Prince.

"Well, that's one of those things that takes months to decide. Hm, the last time I went to a prince's Birth Day was—never. So let's see, someone important I always give…"

226

"Something shiny!" Mara exclaimed, realizing that the shiny collection she kept in a carved wooden box (which she had received from her grandpa) were indeed gifts from Sylvie.

"Yes," Sylvie smiled, pleased to be recognized at last. Mara dug the box out of her sock drawer and went back out to the landing. Sylvie polished them regularly, so she had no need to look closely. But Mara had not looked through it since Christmas, when she had found a curious silver button in the shape of a daisy, right outside the bathroom door at her mother's house. No one claimed it, so she added it to her shiny collection. It became a tradition for Mara to look for something shiny on her birthday and Christmas; now she knew why.

"Thank you, Sylvie! I love them all. Hmmm—I guess I don't know him well enough yet," Mara sighed.

"Nonsense, Mara, use your noggin! What thrills him beyond any other thing which you have seen?" Sylvie demanded, forgetting to be meek.

Mara thought out loud, "He loves dancing, and sunrises and sunsets. He loves light in all its facets. The wind, I think he loves the wind. I can't give him those things! He loves his nest with Mama Cat, my hair, my skin. Oh! He has told me repeatedly, he loves anything tactile. He loves texture, but not cheap fabric." Pursing her lips thoughtfully, she continued, "Okay, I have one and half days to think. Thank you, Sylvie."

Since Mara was up first, she decided to make waffles, and she didn't need any help. Jill came down before Aerrvin.

"Oh, I thought you were Aerrvin. Did he go home? I looked in your room, and no one was in there," Jill said, setting the syrups on the counter.

"No, he should be up there. I tucked him into my bed with Growly…" then she stopped mid-sentence. She had finally accepted the truth, but she was not sure if Jill was simply playing along.

"Jill, you do believe in Fairies, right?"

"Aw, Mara, I don't know. Ya know? I know you can't get the necklace off, and I can see that Aerrvin and his family of friends seem to 'magically' have whatever they want. But—are you telling me that he's six inches tall, asleep in your bed? Right now?"

Mara replied sadly, not sure how hard to press, "Well, he was when I left him."

"I was what?" Aerrvin asked, fully dressed in khaki shorts, with a soft V-neck cashmere sweater, in deepest purple. His golden hair was pulled back and tied with a black silk string.

"Oh, yeah—that was a nice trick, leaving a guy hugging a toy when he thought he was cuddled up with a tiger," Aerrvin said, suggestively raising his brows. "I woke up with fuzz in my mouth," he grimaced.

Jill laughed, relieved at not having to admit yes or no. "So Mara, this smells yummy! What made you get up so early?" Jill asked as she spread butter on her waffles.

"I couldn't sleep, so I read the rest of *Enchanted Lives* and then decided to let Aerrvin sleep in my bed. So I came down and started breakfast."

"You two don't sleep at the same time do you?" Jill asked warily.

"Not generally, but he's only been guarding me this week. And we don't need much sleep anyway," Mara replied, cutting her waffles into bite-sized pieces.

"We don't, huh? Then what was up with that passing out business?" Jill huffed.

"Jill? Do you really, really want to know or not? Because I can tell you, but you have to be able to accept the truth."

Jill looked at Aerrvin and then back at Mara. "Can you make my dreams come true?"

Mara smiled. "I think I can." Adding a hysterical giggle, she went on to explain who all the people at Ironwood Estates were, including Brand the Bright. Mara ended with the note from Gwennara. "So, now all we need to do is find her locked up somewhere in the bottom of the sea," Mara concluded, as though it were a common event.

"I can see how that could be an exhausting day," Jill agreed. "Can you open the locket now?"

Mara shrugged her shoulders, "I was afraid to find out. But with you two watching, maybe it will be okay." Mara fiddled with the pendant, but there was no latch. Aerrvin reminded her about asking.

So Mara closed her eyes and had the imaginary Fairy ask to open the locket, to which Mara's inner self then nodded. With a click, the locket popped open revealing a tiny golden key.

"Ooh!" Jill said, "So delicate. I'm starting to believe. You'd better lock it up; you wouldn't want to lose it. So what else d'ya got? Aerrvin, she says you are a fairy prince. Do you agree, or are you taking advantage of my girl as she loses her mind?"

Aerrvin looked at her puzzled. "I thought you already met with some of my Brownies and were all upset with Sylvie's mother for collecting your recipes."

"I met with your kitchen staff, and I admit they share a lot of similarities with Ironwood's staff. I've watched Mara's left out cookies and milk lately, and the level is lower, and the cookies are usually gone. But, maybe we have mice?" She smiled, knowing that was plain wrong. "Okay, let me meet Sylvie. Then I will believe."

"Sylvie is very timid, so you cannot scream at her. Do you promise?" Mara asked.

Jill locked her lips, threw away the key symbolically, and then folded her hands in her lap.

"Sylvie," Mara commanded, "please come here."

"Yes, my lady. Do you think this is wise?" Sylvie said from the cookie rack shelf. She had been listening and was prepared, but she nevertheless doubted the wisdom of it.

Jill said, "How did you . . . ?"

As she turned her head to where she thought the voice had been thrown, there, standing in the open cupboard, stood the sweet little Brownie with her soft, brown hair done up in a bun, in a cream-colored dress tied at the waist by a brown apron.

"She's so tiny!" Jill breathed. "You really shine these floors and keep the windows so bright?"

"Not me alone, my family helps," Sylvie responded as she flushed pink.

"Okay, okay, I get it," Jill said. "So this means that this Morris/Morvayne guy is positively trying to get in here? And there are truly evil little orange and yellow fairies trying to break the spells that are keeping us safe. Right?"

Mara nodded, knowing something was coming. And it did.

"What the heck are you still hanging around here for?" Jill yelled, "Are you insane? You need to go somewhere!" She stopped but looked about in a panic. Sylvie ran away. Aerrvin stood, casually watching with a half-smile; curious to see how Mara would handle Jill.

"For now, I am safe. Grandpa said I am to continue school and graduate. Things will get totally hectic on my Birth Day, but until then everything should be okay. I think. Aerrvin do you have anything to add?" Mara asked, getting upset at his lack of help.

"You are doing well," he smiled, casually looking as though he were at a photo shoot. "I guess the only thing I would add is the bit about needing to move out before they break the wards on the Brownie tunnels."

Turning to Jill, Aerrvin explained, "Morvayne has taught some stronger magic to the Yellow and Orange Fairies; they figure they will have broken through in about three weeks."

Jill began to hyperventilate.

"Jill!" Mara commanded, releasing her Power from her imaginary breast pocket. "They do not want you and will stop trying to get in when I leave. We will both be leaving because Sylvie's family does not wish to leave. They are devoted to this house no matter who lives in it. Listen! I mean it, when I leave they will stop, and they will not follow you. It is only me they are after."

"How can you be so calm?" Jill wondered.

Mara replied gently, "Because I believe, and Grandpa believes. And Aerrvin believes—in me—if they say it is so, then surely it must be so."

"But my place won't be ready to move into that fast," Jill complained.

"Yes, it will," Aerrvin assured her, "We will help you." With a wink at Mara, he walked to the door and opened it just as the doorbell sounded.

"Bronwyn, what is it? You could have called," Aerrvin stated politely.

The Brownie replied, "I prefer the personal touch as you well know. Your shipment of Rose Elixir has been received, along with They who brought it. Namely your parents, your sister, and her husband. When shall I tell them you will be available?"

Aerrvin threw a panicked look to Mara and then recovered quickly. "Tell them I will receive them in my private quarters. I will be ready shortly."

His clothing transformed to a royal blue velvet doublet, over lavender leggings, complete with silver shoes. The shoes came to an upward curling point with tiny silver bells which tinkled as he walked towards Mara. His hair lifted in the breeze, wafting his sudden burst of Fairy Dust through his hair and past him to the floor.

"Trailing clouds of Glory," Mara breathed as he closed in on her. He wore an intricately wrought silver crown with a single pink gold rose in the center. Her already wide eyes opened in wonder, her lips parted in awe.

"As you heard, I must attend my parents' arrival. If I am delayed, please continue on to school without me. Hannah is outside the back door. You can ask her to accompany you in my place, or I can send Gareth."

He paused expectantly. Noticing her awe, he sported an arrogant smile; he did know how grand he looked after all. "Mara, you need to learn to accept my considerable charm. While I revel in your adoration, I need to know if you will be okay without me. Mara?"

Snapping out of her wonder, she finally comprehended his words. "You revel in my adoration? I'll show you adoration!" Mara unleashed two of her pockets of Light as she carefully unfolded the breast pocket hankie of Light and drenched herself in glory, all in her mind's eye.

Within seconds, she was bathed in opalescent light radiating outward, touching Jill, collapsed on the couch. Jill could not see the Light and glorious sparkling Fairy Dust, but its effects were nevertheless felt. With precision, Mara had copied a gown worn by Tigerlily in one of the beautiful line drawings in Ironwood's book, *Enchanted Lives*. Unknown to Mara, it was delicately woven silver thread twined with spider web silk. It draped luxuriously and puddled on the floor around her feet, the sleeves were woven in a wider, lacy pattern, allowing her opalescence to shine through, yet they too hung lavishly below her fingertips, ending in long points which tinkled from the tiny bells attached as fringe.

Her fury was spent nearly as quickly as it had arrived. Looking down at Bronwyn and Aerrvin, each bowing humbly to the floor, she felt shame, causing showers of sparkles to go cascading to the floor. Hastening to lock up all the Light, she forgot her resolve to treat it with respect, as Aerrvin preferred. She wadded it all up and put it away zipping the pockets shut firmly, then placing a straightjacket on her imaginary self.

"Oh, Aerrvin, stand up! What has gotten in to me? I never used to be so moody. Please. Bronwyn, you too, accept my apology. I will keep better control of myself, I promise."

Aerrvin was humbled, but not truly abashed. "Mara, my future Queen, you are my heart's desire. I glory in your presence, and you make me look good." He took her hand. "I am thrilled beyond reason that you would accept me as worthy of *your* presence."

He brushed her face with his gentle breeze, then cleaned up the room. Collecting both of their Dust as one and placing it into a crystal vial, he handed it to her. "Please, forgive my arrogance and accept this vial in apology."

Mara learned later that only those who are in tune with each other, in peace, could allow their Fairy Dust to mingle. If either carried a grudge, their Dust would have fled the bottle.

"Of course, Aerrvin. It was just a flash of emotion. I do marvel at your beauty, and I am the luckiest girl in the world."

Bells tinkled silvery soft as she threw her arms around him. They exchanged a magical kiss, leaving each other glowing. That is until they looked at each other and drew in the Light to hide it from spying eyes. They had bound themselves to each other more tightly than Morvayne could ever hope to achieve by kissing her hand. If Fair Ones allowed every kiss they ever received to stay upon the surface, they would glow brighter than the sun at midday.

Somewhere along the way, Mara learned the trick of absorbing wanted kisses into her being. Morvayne's kiss was unwanted. Therefore, it had sat upon the skin. Without physically removing it, it would have settled into her. Morvayne's hope was to saturate her with his kisses, thereby making her his.

Bronwyn awaited a pause in their kissing to interrupt, "Excuse me, Your Highness, but I must return and inform your Family of your instructions. But before I go may I offer some advice?"

Both nodded, still clinging to each other.

"Mara, Elves are quite calm and stoic by nature, yet they tend to become jealous if someone seems to be more glorious than they. This is why the most glorious ones do not often congregate all in one place; the rivalry would be too dangerous.

"Additionally, the Elves chosen as servants to the Royal Family are not often affected by this jealousy. They rightly assume they were chosen for their superiority. Just look at your Attendants to see what I mean.

"Fairies, on the other hand, are affected with this malady to a lesser degree, but enough of it exists certainly between Aerrvin and his sister Harmony to have caused his parents to separate them—by an ocean no less!

"Bowing before you is no chore; truly you are magnificent in your Glory and Power, and breathtaking in your beauty. Aerrvin certainly has the 'luck o' the Irish' upon him to have been positioned to find and receive your pledge of love. I should have kept my eyes lowered, but being a Chronicler of his life; I had all the rights to watch, so watch I did. Still, I beg your forgiveness."

"Thank you, Bronwyn. No, I was unaware of the jealousy. Well, I did read of some squabbles, but the stories did not play up the cause. And of course, I forgive you. I accept that I am never truly alone and am always being watched—

still a little creepy but accepted." She shrugged her shoulders and stuck her tongue out in a decidedly unroyal fashion.

Aerrvin created a window by bending the light, allowing Bronwyn to return directly. "Thank you, Bronwyn. Go along then; I will be in my rooms anon."

❧❧❧❧

Bronwyn stepped around the corner of light, arriving in the entry hall of the O'Shea Mansion. He proceeded to inform Queen Laurel and King Jasper of Aerrvin's desire to meet them in his rooms.

They were happily refreshing themselves in the waterfall and finished up before assuming Human proportions. The self-assured old Brownie led them to their son's quarters, hoping Aerrvin would be on time, for once.

23

Gifts

Whispers of beauty embrace my soul

from you, I feel connected to we

~ Mara Lilyana Jamis

May 22, 2009

Aerrvin left after Mara assured him that she did not need Gareth, as Hannah would do fine.

"As you wish," he replied, crinkling his eyes merrily." I will catch up with you when I can."

"Okay, but don't hurry. I am sure it has been awhile since you have seen your family. I don't mind really," Mara said sincerely, still holding his waist lightly with one hand as she walked a few steps towards the door, stopping when she remembered Aerrvin could walk through a bend of light.

"Only ten years," Aerrvin replied, "not time enough to forget Harmony's wedding fiasco." He grinned wickedly; before taking a step around the corner of light, leaving Mara's arm empty. Remembering Jill, she turned towards the couch, while changing her clothes back to jeans and a tank top.

"Oh, Jill, I am so sorry. Are you ill?" Jill did not look too chipper as she sat on the couch in a daze.

She replied, "I'm just peachy, considering." She waved her hands at the room, suggesting everything.

"I think I am going to call in sick. There is no way I won't chop my fingers off if I go today."

She called in and then said, "I think I will start packing."

"Jill, wait! You can wait until Tuesday. I am sure Jaera can have your rooms cleaned and decorated by then. I need help finding something to wear." Mara led Jill up to her closet.

"Where did all your clothes go?"

"Aerrvin did not like them, so I let him destroy them. I think he burned them up on the spot, so hot it left no trace. Anyway, they were gone in a flash whatever he did. Then we ran out of time; he was going to fashion new clothes for me, but we never got back to it. I have t-shirts in my dresser, but he doesn't want me to wear them; they offend the senses." Mara tried to mimic his accent but failed.

"Mara, I saw you fashion yourself a grand dress, just make something up and wear it!" Jill said, her voice rising as she went along. "Besides, I have told you before not to bow down to any man's wishes. Be your own woman." She role modeled defiance with hands on her hips and her chin in the air.

Mara laughed. "Ah, Jill. I am not meek for Aerrvin's sake or demands. I *want* to please him. He is a very tactile individual, and rough fabrics really do rub him the wrong way. All the synthetics were the first to go." She laughed again remembering. "He has a delightful sense of style too. I just need something to wear to school that's stylin' and comfy. You know my style sense is lacking. I need advice."

Mara created a few outfits from ads in magazines she had looked at; a few looked hilarious and just plain wrong. Eventually, Jill suggested a simple cotton blouse with bell sleeves, topped with a close-fitting vest which she had seen in the mall the other day.

"Perfect," they said in unison. Mara owned hardly any shoes, so she made comfy slip-on's as well. They went downstairs, Mara grabbed her backpack, and then went to the back door.

"Can you drive me to school, Jill? I'll be late if I take the bus," Mara asked as she opened the back door.

"Sure," Jill said. "I'm just going to my shop to make sure the contractors work as hard as they should. What are you looking for?" Jill asked, watching Mara search the yard.

"Oh, I wanted to see if I could spot my escorts, but I can't. They excel at hiding." Then raising her voice slightly, she said, "Hannah, would you go to class with me as a companion?"

Hannah appeared in miniature from behind the flowerpot on the porch. "I would love to."

Taking on her full size, they saw she wore what appeared to be a full body suit, which was opaque and sheer, depending on the light and her movements. It shimmered delicately. Like an oil slick; rainbow colors swirled and sparkled tantalizingly, only to disappear when one tried to get a closer look. Hannah wore a miniskirt, which appeared to be an upside-down thistle, but when Mara touched it, she found it to be incredibly soft.

"What is this?" she asked, gesturing to both the skirt and the suit.

Hannah laughed, her tone was beautiful and soothing. "I fashioned this skirt after my Family Crest and Sigil, which is the thistle, of course. But as for this," she brushed her hand lightly down her arm creating movement. "This is a long story, so we should be going so as not to be late." She headed to the car, and the others (both seen and unseen) trailed after.

Hannah morphed her skirt into hip huggers and caused her bow and quiver of arrows to disappear altogether, which Mara had barely noticed since she was so entranced by the swirls. She did notice that Hannah kept her belted knife.

Once on the road, Hannah began, "Very well, this is a suit of armor acquired by courage and skill. It is elastic. Here, feel." Hannah held her arm forward for both Jill and Mara to feel. It felt like they were touching her bare flesh, yet not. It was incredibly softer, smoother, and cooler—in a refreshing way like mint. Taking her hand away, Mara felt a slight oily-powdery residue on her fingers, again not unpleasant.

"Oh, what a delightful fabric! What is it? I think Aerrvin would love it. I want some for his Birth Day gift. What kind of skill do you need to acquire it?" Mara was enthusiastic about discovering the perfect gift to give Aerrvin.

Hannah held her hand up. "Slow down my—Mara, this fabric is not fabric at all. It is truly armor, as soft as it is. It can prevent this," Hannah suddenly stuck her hand forward and slid her knife across her wrist, causing Jill to swerve as she lost control for a moment. "Or this," and she stabbed herself softly in the chest.

"It cannot be pierced, although when attacked with force, I can still get bruised. But it has restorative properties associated with wearing it, so I can take a pretty good beating and survive."

She offered her gracious, gleaming smile, looking every bit the delicate lady, at great odds with her statements of brutality. She reminded Mara of Daryl Hannah's character from the mermaid movie.

"I understand you want some, but let me continue my explanations. It is very like a living thing, and once attained cannot be taken off longer than twenty-four hours. If left longer than that, it sickens and turns brittle, crumbling beneath your fingers. Crushed into a powder it has other uses, but I prefer this one, as it keeps me alive and free to protect my family and the Crystal Throne."

Mara was not sure she wanted Aerrvin wearing it forever. She recalled his chest after swimming, with water droplets rolling down his tight, well-muscled frame.

"Shame to be covered all the time," Mara murmured, as she looked in the visor mirror at Hannah to relieve her neck.

Hannah replied, "It adjusts at will. I can turn it into a bracelet."

She held her bare arm forward with just a few thin strips swirling around her wrist, not unlike a friendship bracelet. Mara kept her eyes forward, not daring to see if Hannah had given herself another top as yet, somehow she doubted it.

"Or it can just be a shirt or underwear," she replied. "I wear it as a catsuit most days since it feels like my skin and fits like a glove; only better. I can wear anything I wish."

Then Mara did turn to see: Hannah sported a celery green lace tank layered over a baby tee, both stopped above her belly button, revealing a taut white tummy and no hint of the armor.

"Awesome! Okay, tell me how you got it," Mara said as they pulled into the parking lot. Jill wanted to hear too, so she parked the car instead of dropping them off.

"As you wish. I come from a family of warriors. It is tradition to seek a Quest of some danger to prove one's worthiness to serve the Crystal Throne. I chose to visit the cave of Meriel, a Sea Dragon, who lives in a range of caves off the coast of Italy. No one had seen her for one hundred years, as she had built a nest to give birth to her young, and had not yet resumed her hunts in the depths of the sea. The danger was that she was a young mother and would not want anyone coming in to speak with her for fear one would take her hatchlings. Before that, she had been quite social and entertained Fair Ones often. The second danger of course being, she had not eaten a properly fresh meal in the wild. A Dragon sits thirty years on the nest, waiting for her clutch to hatch; she usually lays eight or so eggs; only half ever succeed to fruition. Then she raises them another one hundred years before she allows them to search out their own caves.

So Meriel's drakes were about seventy when I made my Quest. A very dangerous age, as they are beginning to become ravenous and chase anything which moves, especially if it is smaller than they are. But, it is the age when she must begin taking them out to sea; so she could not have been too angry with me for introducing them to the outside world. I arrived in the morning, swam down to the opening, and entered her secluded beach, climbing to the ledge. On the ledge, I called the formal Salute to Dragons and waited for her response. Fortunately for me, she was becoming bored and lonely, so she did not eat me; she decided to grant my request for a shed of her children's hide. That is if I could solve her riddle."

Mara interrupted, "So, it's dragon skin?"

Hannah smiled and nodded her head, then changed the subject. "It is nearly time for your class. I will tell you the rest later. Sorry, Jill." The fair Elf patted Jill's shoulder as she got out of the car.

Mara only had the two classes, and now that math had become comprehensible she sped through the test in half the time and met up with Hannah, who sat outside in the hall. They went to the photo lab early, and since no one else was there, Hannah continued to tell Mara how she solved the Dragon's Riddle.

"Honestly, the riddle was easy. I knew I would be able to solve her riddle before I even went there because she always uses the same ones and everyone in my family knows them. The tricky part is this: She has a ten-point system for granting a request. One point for each: If you are granted permission to speak; if you solve the riddle; and if you smell good. Two points if you make her laugh, as well as two points for being an Elf. Oh, I forgot, it is one point for being any other magical being, Fairies included. Two points for bringing an acceptable gift (hint, she likes jewels) and finally, she gives a point for anything she wants. For me, it was my graceful beauty and skill with my bow. I went with hopes of being granted permission to display my talent. As a result, she allowed me to wait for her young to finish shedding. Fortunately, they were in the process when I arrived. The sheds must be harvested within fourteen days. In the caves with Dragon breath all around they tend to last a little longer. Also, the younger the Dragon, the more supple and durable the skin is. If you were able to secure a Dragon shed from her drakes right now, they would last a week without having to be worn because her newest Dragonlets are only forty years old. Of course, getting them very young has only been tried five times; only one was successful, and he was a Fairy, very lucky," Hannah concluded as she arranged Mara's pictures on the table.

"Who was the successful seeker?" Mara asked.

"Thought you would never ask," Hannah emitted a delicate and soft tumbling cadence of laughter that made Mara feel joy as well.

"Wait, don't tell me it was Aerrvin! I couldn't stand it," Mara cried frantically.

"No, not that Fairy, but he was a Fairy, nonetheless. One that you have met—it was Brand the Bright; he did it to prove himself worthy of Gwennara. She would have accepted him without it, but it won her parents over, which *was* more important, by the way. A Royal had never married a Fairy at that point"

"Sweet! Can you take me there today? I need his present by tonight. Can I get it in a few hours? I don't have much time; Aerrvin will probably want me to meet his parents for dinner. Well?" Mara looked pleadingly at Hannah.

"I am not sure it is wise. What if she wants you to stay and wait like I had to? It took two days for the Dragonlets to finish shedding." Hannah looked doubtful, then brightened.

"Very well, we can go for it, you are the future Queen, so she can't eat you. We may as well try. But let us set up your display first."

They walked to the display wall assigned to Mara. In a blink, Hannah created a backdrop of weathered paper in a collage of newspapers, and wrappers from a variety of foods, interspersed with notebook paper and handmade paper. Mara was surprised; it wasn't what she would have thought to do. But she chose to keep it, deciding she was in a hurry, so she arranged the photos in her mind's eye and commanded it to be. The little Fairy asked, but Mara had forgotten about putting the straight jacket on herself; when she nodded her head, nothing happened. She loosened the imaginary jacket, and in an instant, the first portion of her display was done. "All done, can we go?"

Hannah informed the others where they were going. Seamus was Aerrvin's assigned escort for the day, so he relayed a message to Gareth with instructions not to tell. Soon Mara and her six Attendants, plus Seamus, went around a bend of light, into the warm blue sky over the deepest blue waters Mara had ever seen.

24

Tales of Dragons

And never a tale was ever told, but that they mentioned Dragons.

~ Chaslain

May 22, 2009

They morphed their clothes into swimwear and sliced into the water. Mara was an excellent swimmer. Her parents had taken her swimming since she was an infant.

They dove down and down. Mara marveled that she did not need air as yet. They swam through a cave and came up into the light of a secluded lagoon, very small, only the size of half a football field. The beach itself was smaller than Mara would have thought, and then the ledge was up forty feet. Rather than climb, she flew up and sat on the edge.

"So—do I go in alone, or will she allow more? Will she make each of us answer a different question or riddle, or can the visit be counted as one since I am the one requesting?"

Daisy answered, "I believe three is her limit; if she feels so inclined, she will grant three requests and only requires the answer to one riddle, but she will want her points to total thirty."

"Hmmm," Mara pondered. "I think I will take Seamus. I doubt she has ever met a Brownie before. I think if Hannah went again she might refuse. What do you guys think?" Mara turned to the group.

Hannah agreed she should not go again. They debated whether another female should go, or if two males would be better. After a short debate, it was still up to Mara to decide. Finally, she chose Clay, not really for any particular reason, except he seemed to yearn to be chosen. His companions clapped him on the shoulder with good wishes.

Mara felt an inexplicable attraction to the pale Elf with translucent skin and nearly white hair, hair which hung down to his shoulder blades, falling in feathery points. He was so quiet. He reminded her of Dougie in a way.

Mara asked, "Ummm—Clay, are you certain you know the answer to the riddles? I mean, whoo!" She breathed deeply to calm her nerves. "I don't want to miss out on a great opportunity."

Looking at her kindly he replied, "Yes, Mara, I assure you; I have heard every riddle she has ever asked a visitor before."

Laying a hand softly upon her shoulder, Mara felt a kind of sincerity and calm wash over her.

Clay taught Mara and Seamus the Salute to Dragons, and then all three chanted it together:

Dragons High and Dragons Low

Give to me what I should know

Give me lessons by your Light

Grant to me your knowledge Bright

Give me lessons by your Light

Give to me what I should know

Dragons High and Dragons Low

As soon as they finished, a low rasping rumble issued forth from the cave's interior. Eventually, Mara began to hear words in the rasping.

"Who would dare to arrive at my cave when I have young to attend?" breathed the raspy head as it snaked out to view the visitors. Before Mara could gather her wits enough to speak, Meriel continued, "And why so many?"

"I—I—come to ask a favor, Meriel, and I wish to bring these two companions with me. Will you grant us permission to enter?" Mara released her hankie of Light, she did not want to be rude, but she wanted to prove she was as she claimed, a seeker of Light and knowledge.

Meriel considered, still looking at the others who stayed on the beach. "I remember that one." She flicked her tongue and breathed, "Hannah Thistlewite," causing the Elf to look up and salute.

"If she is a friend, I will grant you entrance. Move slowly; my young are impetuous. That is one point for each of you plus two points each for the Elves for a total of seven. You, I do not recognize. You have Light and Power, but I have not met your kind up close. Speak up—introduce yourself," Meriel hissed.

"My name is Seamus MacIntash, and I am a Brownie. My family is honored to serve the Rose Crown. I am a special servant to Aerrvin ap Rosewin and a Chronicler in training." Seamus bowed with a beautiful flourish.

"Delightful!" Meriel issued from deep within her throat. "You shall tell me a story in a moment. Two points for leaving your tiny underground burrow. That is nine points. And you Elf-man, tell me about yourself. What ties you to this company?"

Meriel was not particularly large compared to stories Mara had read about Dragons. Meriel was about the size of three elephants combined; nose to tail she measured twenty-five feet or so. Her tail was long and snake-like, and her neck was equally sinuous. Balancing her diamond-like head delicately; it caught the rays of light from the openings in the cavern above. Her eyes were faceted like emeralds and just as richly hued. Being that she was a Sea Dragon, she was not built for flying. Her clawed hands and feet were webbed, yet she did have wings which Mara later learned were capable of allowing Meriel to glide down off of her ledge. A few flaps were all she needed to get back to the lip of the cave.

Clay bowed before beginning his introduction. His classic looks, remarkable grace and carriage spoke of years of service to the Crystal Throne.

"My name is Clay of the Glennferry Harbor Elven Council; I claim no family. I have been in the service of The Crystal Throne all the days of my adult life. We no longer number our years in the old way, so I am nine hundred years old in Human years. Princess Tigerlily tasked me, along with my five companions, to be Attendants for her great-great-granddaughter, Mara."

Indicating Mara with a graceful sweep of his hand he said, "This babe was born twenty-one years ago come this Midsummer's Night. I am here because she wishes to receive a gift from you. Being in your presence grants me my desire," Clay concluded with another sincere bow.

"Truly remarkable, I am honored to be in your presence Clay of Glennferry."

Meriel's three young Dragons had been napping, but the conversation woke them up. Sidling up beside their mother, they sat and peered at each of the guests, politely keeping quiet. The green one chewed on her nails until her mother swatted her.

"Now, are you this 'Mara' which Clay spoke of serving?"

Mara nodded and curtsied passably, thanks to ballet. Realizing she was still in her swimming suit, she blushed, scattering sparkles everywhere. Seeing them fall sent another round of sparkles which went flying through the cave as a breeze fluttered in and about the cavity.

Clay's eyes sparkled merrily because Aeries are often visible in the presence of Dragons, they were deliberately causing a stir. Mara was so transfixed on her Dust and the ensuing action, she failed to notice the Aeries at all.

The wafting Dust caused an explosion of movement as the three young Dragons were suddenly laughing and chasing the sparks, knocking each other over and spilling a small horde of Dragon playthings around the cavern floor. They were so cute to watch, reminding Mara of kittens at play. If she had not been afraid of getting run over or causing them to be punished by their mother, Mara would have delighted in it more. As it was, Mara sought protection under the neck of Meriel. Being so close to the Dragon, Mara felt, before she heard, the chuckle erupt from the so-very-long throat.

"Oh, my," Meriel sighed after a good long chuckle. "They have not gotten into antics like that for years.

"Thank you, Mara. Five points for making me laugh, two from me and one each from my brood. That is fifteen total points; I gave a point to Clay for his exquisite bow. Now, Mara, I see you truly are a babe. What brings you here and not yet sworn?"

Having put away her hankie of inner Light, she was plain Mara, she hoped. She replied, "I have recently become engaged to Aerrvin ap Rosewin and tonight at midnight is his Birth Day. He will be one hundred and ninety years old. I could not think of what to give a Fairy Prince. Sylvie, my Brownie, told me it takes up to six months to come up with a good idea, but I only met Aerrvin three weeks ago, or less rather. So, um, I don't really know him that well and have not had six months to think. When I saw Hannah's marvelous armor, I thought Aerrvin would love it. He has a delicate sense of touch. I hope to give him something that shows I understand him. You know?"

The Dragon nodded thoughtfully. Mara continued, "The only other thing I thought of was something from my shiny collection, but I did not think he loved shiny as much as soft. Besides, Sylvie gave me most of my shiny things." Mara felt herself rambling, so she shut up.

Meriel sighed, "So you have a shiny collection as well, do you? Did you bring me something for *my* shiny collection?"

Mara started, "Oh dear, I forgot. I have something in mind, but I don't know how to make that beam of light everyone walks around to get somewhere. Clay, can you help me?"

He bowed to the Dragon, "With your permission, Meriel?"

Meriel answered hastily, "Yes, please. I would love to see what she has to share."

Clay said, "Mara, for now, you do not need to learn Traveling. You can reach your desired object using your power and desire. Open yourself to your power. Not all!" he added hastily. "Just enough to reach your desired object—and call it forth."

Mara opened two pockets and thought about one of the rings in her jewelry box which she intended to sell. This one was particularly large, and to Mara, gaudy. It had a very large garnet set in an ornate silver scroll, probably for a man and certainly shiny. She did not think the Dragon would be interested in bottle caps, foil wrappers or buttons; they were her personal gifts of love, she did not wish to give them away. After a moments' thought, she had the ring in her hand.

A startled look from Clay gave her pause, but just barely as his eyes only widened momentarily, and he kept his thoughts to himself. Mara offered it to Meriel.

"If it pleases you, I would love to offer this in exchange for a desire of my heart."

The Dragon purred, making Mara jump. "Ooooh! I love it, four points for beauty. That makes nineteen if you were still counting," she purred again, taking it with her delicate, though large claws.

"Beautiful. Do you have more like this?" Meriel asked craftily, putting Mara on notice.

"I have a few things given to me by Tigerlily," Mara answered with a shrug, earning a half-lidded contemplating stare from Meriel.

Turning her attention to Seamus, the Sea Dragon said, "First I will give you a riddle, any one of you may answer it. Then I should be pleased to hear a tale about the Fairy Prince. Here is the riddle—This thing I say—I demand from you: Tell me, oh tell me the answer true. This thing you can keep forever and a day, yet only after giving it away. What is it?"

Mara thought she recognized the riddle, but the words were different; it was throwing her off. She was grateful that Clay knew them all. She turned to him as he turned to her.

"This is a new one, Mara, let me ponder on it," he spoke calmly as his eyes gained fire.

The statement shocked Mara into thinking harder, trying to remember the riddles she had learned from her father.

Seamus began his tale, "This tale is from the life of Aerrvin ap Rosewin, son of Her Royal Highness Queen Laurel ap Rose and Her King Consort, Jasper ap Rosewin. Beginning at the age of thirty, he was permitted, from time to time, to go off on his own to explore the whole wide world before us. Aerrvin loves the ocean almost as much as he loves his Nest Mates. On this particular adventure, he left his beloved Nest Mates, their names being Gareth ap Rosewin and Jaera the Green. He flew straight to the White Cliffs of Dover. He had been there before on a class field trip and resented not getting to stay longer.

"First, he flew to the top of a cliff and surveyed the deep green sea. Being very patient, he stayed up on top exploring tiny openings and fissures. In time, the sun began her nightly ritual. Aerrvin has a deep love and admiration for the sun, especially at dawn and dusk when it paints the sky in glory.

"With full dark upon the beach, he dove straight off the cliffs, allowing gravity to take him in a free fall to the smashing waves below. He will tell you to this day it was a smashing time! He truly felt exhilarated. Yet he only did it once. Once within the water, he was battered against the rocks, and he needed to use his full power to swim free of the turbulence. Coming to the surface, he whooped with joy because of the thrill of it all. Then he dove down and explored the ocean floor. Obviously, he was not down very deep, close as he was to the beach. He reveled in the colors of the starfish—yes, he shone his own light brightly to view the colors at night—yet even more joyous to him was their texture. He flitted with the fish and crawled with the crabs. He came up on the beach and explored the tide pools. Finally, he decided to see what it was like to cuddle with a oyster. Finding a suitably large oyster, he climbed inside the shell, and then to his surprise and delight it closed on him. Ensuring he designed a suitable breathing apparatus for himself, he cozied up, reveling in the soft moistness of the muscle and went to sleep."

Mara interrupted, shocked at Aerrvin's adventure, "Are you telling a true tale, Seamus? Honestly, he enjoyed being trapped in a oyster shell?" Mara stuck her tongue out in an exaggerated gagging gesture.

Seamus smiled, and the others in the room chuckled. The Dragon and her young filled the cave with deep vibrations.

Seamus continued, "Eventually, he awakened, not knowing at first how long he had slept. As you well know, Fair Ones can sleep for months. And months it had been indeed. The oyster was shut; he had slept through her repeated openings and shutting. Now he wanted out; he was bored and wished to leave. But alas, it would not open. He was young and had not yet learned the Art of Traveling. His Chronicler, my dearest Da, Bronwyn, had located him and placed the oyster up on the beach. Yet he loathed to destroy the creature to free Aerrvin, so he sat and waited. And the wait was three more days. Now normally that is a blink of time for us, but—when a Fairy is tired of a thing, three days is like an eternity."

Meriel rumbled in mirth and agreement.

The Brownie's voice filled with a storyteller's emotion, "Aerrvin was frantic. He wiggled and prodded, but nothing would budge. The oyster refused to open. On the third day, Aerrvin decided to compose a song. Having the ability to send for small items, he retrieved his wooden pan pipes, and this is the song he played." Seamus produced his own pipes and played a plaintive tune, which evoked a longing desire for freedom and home.

When the tune ended, all was hushed. The Dragonlets even had tears sparkling down their cheeks, yet they sat motionless waiting to hear the conclusion.

"Aerrvin was spent and thought to sleep again—when, slowly the light of dawn leaked in upon the opening shell. Barely containing his joy he sat idly caressing the viscous oyster in thanks for sharing her space with him. When she was fully open, he reached forth and carefully removed the black pearl she had been growing. He thanked her with a kiss and hugged the joyful Bronwyn! Aerrvin never again chose to sleep with the oysters, but it is a fond memory for him to this very day."

Seamus concluded with a bow, every bit as formal as his first, blushing at the soft hoots of approval from the Dragons, mother included.

"Very well told, Seamus! Very well indeed. Being cooped up can become tedious without a doubt. It is near enough time for these young ones to go swimming in the lagoon. But I have decades to go before I can once again explore the wide, wide oceans anew. Three points for such an enchanting tale. That is twenty-two points total. Can you answer the Riddle?"

Mara became so engrossed in the story that she forgot to be thinking of an answer.

"No, not yet," she replied glumly, looking to see if the others had an answer. They did not.

"Very well. Clay do you have a talent you wish to share?"

"I have many talents," he nodded gracefully. "Yet, I have been trying to think of that which would be most valuable for your young ones to know."

"Very thoughtful of you, Clay. Hannah did the same by teaching my first brood the dangers of an arrow. Although our hide is impervious to slashes and stabs, we do have a weak spot which can be reached with skill. Would you be willing to teach my young ones of this danger?"

Clay bowed in compliance and presented a display of skill with a spear, frightening the young ones into huddling near their mother, beneath her wings. The eye of a Dragon is their weakness. They can close the protective membrane over their eyes, but it is not able to remain in effect for more than five minutes. At that point, they become vulnerable for three seconds. Using a spear of light, Clay was able to pierce Meriel's eye. Had it been a true spear, she could have died. Then he explained how he timed her blinks, and recognized facial clues to know when to throw. Although frightening, it was a valuable lesson for the young ones to learn.

"I must tell you, my little friends, there are none faster than I, and you have no reason to fear an Elf, myself least of all." Bowing, he concluded his lesson.

Meriel whispered a musical, whispery compliment, "What a precious lesson for my Dragonlets to learn, thank you. I never thought today would be so filled with joy. Three points for you, Clay of Glennferry.

Turning her attention to Mara, she raised her voice to its normal raspy nature. "Mara, you are young. I fear your talents must not be developed. What do you think to do to gain the remaining points needed to allow me to grant your heart's desire? I will accept more from your shiny collection, but I cannot give you more points for them. You must have something else to offer?"

Mara questioned Meriel, "What about scent, don't we smell good enough?"

Meriel huffed once, "Clay smells sweet, Seamus smells earthy, and you smell heavenly, but you bring a Human taint, which I am sorry to say offends the senses slightly, sorry no points there."

Had anyone been focused on Clay they would have noted his heart rate quickened for a few beats at the slight Meriel proffered towards the future queen. His anger was not because she was to be queen, but because Mara's scent was indescribably perfect to him. But having years of experience he quickly calmed his rage and lifted his eyes calmly, to assess Mara's response.

She made a moue and asked, "How long have we been here?" I do not want to miss dinner with my future in-laws, it would make me look bad."

Clay replied smoothly, "Two hours. It is 1:30 p.m."

In desperation, Mara turned to the Dragon and asked, "Could you please repeat the riddle? I should like to hear it once more before I make a guess."

"Very well, but you must answer it now to gain a point. This thing I say, I demand from you, tell me, oh tell me the answer true: This thing you can keep forever and a day, yet only after giving it away. What is it?"

Mara murmured, "You can keep this, only after giving it away. I've got it! Your word. You can only keep your word or promise after you have given it to someone. Right?"

"Yes, that is twenty-six points, for your troupe. You need thirty to gain your desire. The others have given all that they can. I have two questions for you: Have you given your word and kept it? And—how much Light do you have? Clay directed you earlier not to use all of your Light, the amount I saw appeared to be all a youngling like you could hold. I should like to see all that you have. If it pleases me, I will grant you your desire."

Mara was hesitant to reveal her Light but willingly answered the first query. "I made a promise to serve the Light and fight against evil. I will always keep that promise."

The Dragon lifted her head and scoffed, "Young one, that is a promise you make on your twenty-first Birth Day, which is still a month away. Whatever in the world would prompt you to make a promise like that?"

"I made that promise when I pledged my love to Aerrvin ap Rosewin. He awoke me to my true nature. Before he arrived, I had been in the dark as though asleep. I have found that an evil force wishes to see me used for his own purposes, namely Morvayne of the Emerald City, as he likes to be called."

"Yes, I know of him. He wishes to take over the seas as well. Why should he wish you harm? He was a Hold Mate of your great-great-grandmother. Why does she allow such mischief?"

Mara related Tigerlily's transformation to Humanity, causing Morvayne's hatred. Quickly telling about her father's disappearance and the suspected link, Mara tried keeping her emotions under control, but the mention of hope in finding her father still alive caused her voice to waver.

Meriel broke in on Mara's explanation, "I see you had good cause to have made such a promise, but surely, Ironwood and the Crystal Throne have spoken with you about your youth? This is not a Quest for the weak; leave it to Gwennara and Brand. They are capable servants of the Light. One day you will make a fine Queen, of that I am sure . . ."

Mara removed all the constraints on her Light and found she had clothed herself once again in the lace dress of Tigerlily's. Distractedly, she mused about whether it was associated with the power. It seemed to want to be a part of the glory when Mara called it forth. *Very well, so be it,* she mentally shrugged.

Mara was herself in awe of the effect the Light had upon the Cave of Meriel. It exploded from the walls and reverberated ever so softly as it bounced off the previously hidden silver and gold flecks bound within the stone walls. The hide of each Dragon shone gloriously; oily rainbows swam upon the surface of their skin.

Mara realized that, once again, all heads were bowed, and the Dragonlets had their eyes shut tight. Meriel bowed to the ground, her eyes hooded.

Tucking away two pockets worth of Light, Mara replied, "Gwennara's daughters are all dead or missing. The Queen herself has been kidnapped and may be in the same place as my father. At least I hope so. She transferred her Power to me moments before she was trapped, wherever that may be, and sent word through Brand letting me know what happened."

Noticing none had moved, she commanded, "Please, rise. I am a babe and have yet to be crowned. I have learned enough to know that all of this is out of order. I should have had time to learn my craft and meet my fore-bearers, but that is not to be. Please believe me, I am bound by my word every bit as much as if I had given it on the day of my twenty-first birth. Meriel?"

Meriel raised her head. Clay and Seamus recovered, though they kept their heads lowered as they stood. "My lady, I had no knowledge of these events. Perhaps I should encourage visitors a little more often. I pledge to serve you and the Crystal Throne as long as you serve the Light. Please, take as many sheds as you would like. They will surely be of use as you search the depths of the sea. None will dare harm you when they see what you wear."

She was referring to Kraken, Merpeople, and other Sea Dragons; they would see the skins and know they were a gift from Meriel. Each Dragon family had their own coloring, recognizable by each clan. "If I had it to do over, knowing who my visitor was, I would have granted you eight points from the start. Forgive me. Seamus, have you an additional desire?"

Bowing slightly, careful not to bow lower than he had for Mara, he replied, "Yes, my Lady Dragon. I desire a ring to offer to my sweet intended. If you have something simple, she prefers clean and shiny." He smiled at his pun.

"Very well, Gwendyll, please find the perfect ring for Seamus," Meriel instructed her only daughter. Then she continued, "Clay, are you sure you desire nothing further?"

Clay had been awaiting the question and already knew his request, it was not his first desire, but it was more important now. Putting aside his true wish he stated, "I desire that when the need arises, you allow the ring Mara gave you to be used as intended."

Mara recalled Aerrvin's counsel not to sell anything until he had a chance to look them over. With a grimace, she thought: *Well, why didn't he tell me they were worth more than money?*

Meriel replied huskily, "Wise you are, Clay. Wise as befits one of your age. Do not hold it against me for accepting a gift as valuable as this from an innocent. I will surely allow the one who has great need, to use it. I will safeguard it with my life. Perhaps it would be wise to allow me to guard all your treasures, Mara?"

Mara smiled her thanks to the Dragon. "I may need to access them quickly. Maybe closer is better. But thank you, I will always count you as a true friend."

Turning to Clay and Seamus, she directed them to collect the three sheds piled in the corner. Upon touching them, they shrunk to the size they desired. "Oh, I forgot, I guess I can carry them myself." Taking their supple smoothness in her hands, they instantly formed themselves into gloves and a bracelet.

"Thank you, Meriel. May I hug you and your little ones?"

Being granted permission, Mara hugged each precious Dragon and kissed them for good measure on the top of their long snouts. Walking out to the ledge, Mara thought of one last thanks she could offer.

"Meriel, I have not learned how this is done, but I would like to leave a blessing on your home. May the Light always shine upon you and yours, and all those who enter in peace."

With a blush, she sprinkled sparkles everywhere and then, returning to her cute blue swimming suit, she glided down to the beach to greet her waiting party.

25

Of Queens and Princesses

You are the voice that gives song to the wind

and the essence within the spray from the sea

~ Aerrvin ap Rosewin

May 22, 2009

Aerrvin had become attuned to Mara's presence, both because of his Ware Spell and having pledged his love to her; each acted to strengthen the other—along with the kisses they absorbed. Therefore, when she stepped across the ocean, he felt the sudden loss. Aerrvin and his mother sat discussing his plans for the party when he felt an urgent need to run out to find Mara, thinking perhaps Morvayne had taken her. But before he could make excuses, Gareth entered with a bow and explained how Mara convinced Hannah to help her get Aerrvin's Birth Day gift. Filled with relief, he sank back down into the sofa.

"Forgive me, Mother, I felt her leave, and it frightened me," Aerrvin admitted.

Laurel smiled indulgently at her only son. "Sweetling, I am so pleased you have found your soul's desire at last. I am so looking forward to meeting her. I have brought the ring you desire to give her as you announce your engagement. I am sure she will adore it."

She held up a lavender box lined with deep purple velvet. Inside were two rings; the engagement ring was white gold; fashioned to look like a rose twisted about the finger, with a pale translucent lavender diamond set in the center. Upon closer inspection, Aerrvin made out the floating rose inside the diamond. The rose emanated a deeper lavender blushed with pink, the gem shone brilliantly with the cuts of the diamond radiating away from the rose, creating an exquisite star-like effect.

"Precisely as ordered, Mother! You always do beautiful work, but this must be the most stunning yet. Thank you!" He hugged and kissed her joyfully as only a Purple Fairy can. In truth, she had already designed and created the settings in anticipation of her son's engagement. She merely needed to craft the gem when Aerrvin made his request.

Aerrvin continued explaining the party celebrations as he envisioned it. Not that everything always had to go his way, but he certainly liked things better when they did. He considered telling them about his new blue wings but decided the revelation would be 'more grand' to reveal it to the entire gathering. Furthermore, he planned to invite Mara to announce her pending ascension to the Crystal Throne. This too he chose not to tell beforehand.

Giddy with excitement, especially since he was only allowing his Purple traits to shine, the prince literally pinged off the walls. His mother, Queen Laurel, tried to ignore him as she took out her knitting. After her second sigh, Aerrvin conceded—he had too much energy so he simply must go swimming in the pool.

Jaera and Harmony were already there, along with Harmony's husband, Culain. They were their own miniature selves, so Aerrvin took great delight in disturbing the water as he maintained his large stature and took a running leap. They were of course barely clothed, reminding him that Mara might be too shocked at the midnight celebration. The dinner party would end at 11:00, at which point the Fair Ones already in attendance (each agreed to be polite for the Human) would then feel free to don the fantastic, or go as free as nature made them.

"Mara is somewhat conservative, so I would appreciate if you could try to be reserved at the 'Midnight Madness,' if you will." He tried to talk sweetly, but however kindly he said a thing, Harmony always found a way to get uptight.

"Why would you bother marrying a Human-Elfling if she didn't care to bend with the wind?" Harmony asked, spraying water into Aerrvin's face.

Before answering, he shrunk down to size since swimming to the bottom of the pool when it was farther away made for greater fun.

"Because she is more than she appears and I love her!" he exclaimed, "I simply would like for you to have a little respect, Harmony, Culain, can you try?"

Culain wore his bright orangey-red hair long, even though it curled in large puffs around his head. Aerrvin would have magically altered his hair structure had he been born with such hair, but Harmony considered it cute and liked to put flowers in it. Right now, his hair hung down to his shoulders in a dripping mass of tangles.

Culain would never tan, even if he spent years as a Human in South America. His spindly frame glowed as white as ivory, and he wore not a stitch, aside from a vague puff of mist for a swimming suit so he might pass as clothed, but Aerrvin was hoping for real fabric. Even for a Fairy, Culain was ridiculously pitiful. *And to think he will be King one day!* Aerrvin mentally expressed gratitude that his parents sent him to the Americas; finding Mara was only one reason.

Culain finally said, "'Tis your party, Aerrvin. I am sure we can accommodate you. As family, it would be a pleasure to help ease Mara into her new life. How long did you say she has been awake?"

"Hm, I think she has always been aware, but she was in denial. She fed her Brownies every night, even when she was a little girl she would sneak out of bed at midnight to do so." Aerrvin chuckled at the thought and then sobered as he remembered the shaking twelve-year-old girl in her Dream. "After meeting me, she came around daily until—boom—she was wide awake!" Aerrvin used Miree to splash the water with a gust, causing Harmony and Jaera to squeal. "It has been about two full weeks that I have been affecting her, one week totally alive and she is glorious. Believe me, you will love her."

❖❖❖❖

Harmony doubted Aerrvin's certainty. She did not like Fairies who were prettier or smarter, and she rarely hung out with Elves. She knew of Aerrvin's concern with aesthetics, so she did not doubt his fiancé was beautiful, but she doubted she could be very wise. *Aerrvin is Purple after all; how smart of a girl could he attract with that? Of course, he has White to balance his antics, but being White is not much help in attracting a mate. When we shine White we want to be left alone,* Harmony thought, making allowances for her own quirks as a White Fairy.

It is not right to use Silver and Gold to attract, Harmony mused. *Although, most Royals cannot help letting a little Silver slip from time to time.* Harmony smiled as she paddled about the pool on her back. She remembered using her Silver on Culain that first time; he nearly melted in awe. Her Yellow could get out of control, so she felt compelled to mix in Silver to keep herself from going overboard. *Yes, Aerrvin must have used his Silver too.* Swimming back to Aerrvin, she kissed him on the top of his head and promised to be full of propriety.

❖❖❖❖

Mara returned home by 3:30. After convincing Hannah to give her a quick flyover of the countryside —after all, it was her first visit to Italy. Her return seemed fortuitous because Aerrvin called within a minute of closing her bedroom door. "Hello," Mara answered breathlessly, having run up the stairs.

"Hello yourself. That was a long shopping trip. I hope you found what you were looking for."

"I did! It was so exciting, I can't wait to give it to you and tell you all about my adventure! Did you get your parents and sister all settled in?"

"After a fashion, Harmony and her husband have agreed to be nice and respectful. We shall see how long they last. Mother would like to meet you for dinner at 6:00 tonight. Does that work?"

259

"Aerrvin, why would you even need to ask? Of course, it would. Only— you forgot to fill my closet…"

Aerrvin hung up. Then Mara heard a tapping at her window where she found a mini-Aerrvin fluttering at the glass. Opening it, she laughed, "Aerrvin, why not just arrive inside my room?"

The light around him rippled, and Aerrvin became his full man-sized self. "I cannot arrive inside a person's home, it is forbidden, and in poor taste. Even if you gave permission, the wards on your home prevent it. Someone inside must invite me in." Closing in on her, he kissed her soundly and then became all business. "Now, about your wardrobe. That top is passable, but really you can do much better than that."

Mara breathed a mental sigh of relief, knowing that she had had enough time to deposit two of the Dragon sheds into her sock drawer. She wore the third, which she intended to keep. But she realized Aerrvin was probably going to start dressing her, so she shrunk it down to a slim belt. Surely, he would not dare to undress her again, once was rude enough. *Okay, it was funny,* she thought. With a smile, Mara returned her attention to Aerrvin's chatter.

"Let's start with tops then. With your fair skin and dark hair, you can go with nearly any color, but I would stay away from bright yellow, it's just not you. Try this."

Instantly Mara found herself wearing a cute red top with short puffed sleeves and a fitted waist defining her narrowness.

"I like it, Aerrvin, very cute," Mara responded. He made one in five different colors for her.

She looked in her closet and found she had more sweaters, all of them decidedly soft. She noticed she had baby tees and a few other t-shirts, which he found acceptable. She started to tell him she kept those in her dresser, but stopped short, remembering she did not want him going through her drawers as well. *Wouldn't want him finding his present now would we, Mara?*

Aerrvin dressed her in several styles of pants, slacks, and jeans until he settled on the ones he liked; placing them in the closet, including several shorts and leggings.

"Now. At long last, we get to the good stuff," Aerrvin smiled mischievously. "For tonight, we are meeting as Humans and Elves, more or less, so you need something simple and understated. We will eat in the formal dining hall, along with a few dignitaries my parents have invited, including Ironwood and his wife." Aerrvin had foregone the idea of having his neighbors at the dinner.

Mara thought she might burst out in sparkling showers, but she managed to maintain her cool. "Sounds wonderful. How about silver? I have always wanted a silver dress." Mara chose one in her mind's eye. She stood in front of the mirror in a sleek silver gown. A halter top clasped it to her body, revealing her smooth white shoulders and highlighting her slimness as it rippled smoothly to the floor.

"I like it, Mara, it is lovely. But I prefer being able to see the necklace," Aerrvin soothed as he transformed it from a halter style to a strappy dress with a square-necked front, which then became a sweetheart neckline with slightly wider straps trimmed with crystals.

"Perfect, you look stunning. But not for tonight. You are meeting the Fairy Queen for the first time, and it would not do to outshine her." He stopped to stare. "…and, Mara, you outshine everyone."

Mara magically replaced the dress with a robe as she placed the gown in her closet. "Then when can I wear that dress? It is truly stunning. I love it!"

"Your Birth Day would be perfect, Mara," Aerrvin replied as he stroked her shoulders. "Nice robe."

It made Mara smile to learn that not everything had to be silky smooth, she had donned a fluffy pink terry cloth robe, which she had seen at the mall and could never afford. Her own shabby robes were cotton and polyester. As Mara went to stroke the fluffy softness of the sleeves, it vanished. She found herself adorned in a striking red gown, nearly the same cut as the silver. This dress had a little more fullness to it which gathered into a slight bustle in the back.

Aerrvin sighed, "Still too magnificent. Mara, you look beautiful in red. How come you never wear it?"

"I don't know; it is such a bold color, ya know? I don't like drawing attention to myself too much. It does set off my skin and hair. It reminds me of Snow White and Rose Red, have you read those tales?" Mara smiled at the thought.

"I have read the old versions. I do not know how they have been changed over the years, but believe me, they have nothing on you. I have met them." He sniffed disdainfully.

Ignoring her shocked expression, he modified the dress to a deep plum, which played up the amethysts on the locket. "Yes, this will do." He smiled, adding a velvet cape for her to wear against the night's chill. It was a clear day, and no precipitation was expected, but the fog would settle in the wee hours of dawn. "I will send Bronwyn to pick you up at 5:45. Invite Sylvie to help you with your hair. I prefer it down, but it would elongate your neck and make you appear taller if you wore it up."

Aerrvin took her into his arms and sat in the chair she had in one corner of the room. Idly wrapping a curl around his finger, he sighed. Pulling her closer, he whispered in her ear, "I hate being away, but I still have some decorating to do before the big party tonight. I will see you soon, and no more popping across the ocean without me!" He chucked her chin and stood up, setting her down on her feet, "Oh, I forgot shoes. Get Jill's opinion. Fairies often go without, so I am not much help there; perhaps I will study up one day." Aerrvin drew a line of Light, kissed her longingly, and left through the portal.

Mara looked at the clock, it was 4:30. "Oh work! I completely forgot. I'd better call; Karen is not going to like this."

Mara called anxiously, only to learn that Karen had hired one of the applicants on the spot during her interview. She intended for Mara to train her, but if Mara wanted to, she could consider yesterday her last day. Mara was not sure how she felt about being replaced. A sudden emptiness filled her.

"Well, it had to be done, and I was covered; that is what counts."

Letting her mild jealousy go, she took a refreshing shower. She was learning that while one can instantly do or create many things with the Light, it was far more satisfying actually doing them. Take showering for one. She could become instantly clean, but the relaxation from the pounding water would have been missing. She spent the entire thirty minutes it takes to use up the hot water. Feeling the water cool, she reluctantly turned it off. Belatedly, she hoped Jill did not suddenly need a shower. She had forty-five minutes until her ride would arrive.

Mara had only had her hair done professionally once, and that was for her senior prom. Getting all the tangles out she sighed and decided to go for it.

"Sylvie? Are you here? Aerrvin seems to think you can do my hair. Would you like to try?"

Sylvie came into the bathroom, dressed in a pale yellow dress with an attached white apron, it buttoned on at the chest, and down to the waist, the apron had two large pockets. "Why yes, my lady, I have wanted to do your hair since I first laid eyes on you!"

Mara realized she had not learned the trick of enlarging a five-inch being. "Oh, Sylvie, I guess you can't do it with you being so small."

"Nonsense," Sylvie replied. "I can do anything. Just sit and make yourself comfy."

Mara sat in Aunt Lily's lovely wrought iron stool, padded with a white tufted cushion, placed in front of the low counter before the mirror. Mara watched as Sylvie expertly wove crystal butterfly beads into tiny braids which she then swept up to the crown of her head, arranging the long wavy hair into a masterpiece of loose curls, causing them to appear as if they were spilling from the braided well. Sylvie left a few loose tendrils at her nape as well as just below her temples down to her ears.

Mara hardly ever put her hair up, even in a ponytail, so it was a mild shock when she saw a slight upward pull to her ears, they were more pronounced than they had been the last time she had noticed. Her ears had always been delicate—narrowing as they rose, generating teasing at her expense as a little girl. She reached up to feel them, they still felt the same, truly they were barely altered at all, but those few centimeters made all the difference.

"I look—I look like Tigerlily in Grandpa's drawings." Mara recognized the hairstyle now.

Sylvie beamed, "Aye, my own mother, Juniper, created this style for her. And you have finally grown your ears. Truly beautiful." Sylvie kissed the top of Mara's ear before climbing down to stand on the counter.

"Now makeup is a frippery, but a small amount of shadow and liner in deep plum would go well with your dress. You flush nicely on your own, and your lips have a delightful tone, so a clear gloss is all you need, in my opinion, my lady," Sylvie added remembering to bow.

"I do have plum eyeliner as you surely know. Thank you, Sylvie. I hear Jill in the kitchen. Would you tell her I need her opinion?"

By the time Jill arrived, Mara had her eyes done and was just applying the lip-gloss; she chose one with sparkles.

"Mara! You look stunning. Who did your hair?" Jill stood staring from the doorway.

"Sylvie, she is a master stylist. Who knew? My ride will be here in thirty minutes, but I wanted to show you the Dragon sheds I got."

"You mean you managed to convince her to let you have *them,* more than one? That is amazing. You will have to tell me the whole story when you have time."

Mara removed her robe and showed Jill her full body armor.

"It's like Hannah's, only this one came from the only daughter of Meriel; her name is Gwendyll." It shone with delicate sparks of light, like tiny glitter, in addition to the oily swirls that the male Dragons produced.

"Mara, it's stunning, let me feel." Jill brushed her hand down Mara's arm. "What does it feel like on? It is so soft."

Mara moved to view it in her full-length mirror, she had not yet seen it on herself. It was striking; nearly the same tone as her own skin, she looked as though she had shifting tattoos covering her entire body.

"It feels like nothing at all—like I am standing in my own skin, yet I guess it feels—let me think." She ran her hands up and down her body. "It is extra soft to the touch; but I guess I can feel it as I move as well, it gives a kind of energy and heightened awareness. Oh, no! Will that make Aerrvin too sensitive? He might not be able to touch anything if it makes him too aware!"

"Mara, you are overreacting. I think he will love it, especially if you give him yourself wrapped up in it."

"Oh, this one is for me," Mara said going to her dresser. She pulled out one more and handed it to Jill. I am giving this one to Aerrvin, and I guess I will give the last one to Grandpa, he will need it for when he starts searching under the sea." Mara thought that it was much like a scuba diving suit, though infinitely more comfortable and lovely.

Sliding it on her wrist, Jill asked, "I wonder, does it work for humans?" Suddenly her arm was covered in a bakers mitt made of Dragon skin. Laughing in delight, Jill said, "Amazing, I guess it does!"

Mara went to her box of gift-wrapping supplies, and chose a tiny box to place the bracelet into, then retrieving it from Jill, she wrapped it in gold foil and tied it up with a vibrant blue silk ribbon.

"There, now I need to get dressed. Jill, I do not have any shoes, could you suggest the right ones for this dress?" Mara asked as she pulled it on.

Jill zipped it up for her and considered. "One would think you were visiting the Queen! Mara this is beautiful. But get rid of the swirling arms, you don't want to ruin your surprise."

Mara reduced the armor to undergarments as she had forgotten to retrieve any since donning her robe from the shower.

"Convenient," she murmured, and then to answer Jill, she exclaimed, "I *am* visiting a queen, have you forgotten? Aerrvin is a prince; his mother is Queen of all the Fairies in the world!" Then sitting down trembling she whispered, "I'm about to meet the Queen of the Fairies!" She sat there holding her face in her hands.

"Now, I will have none of this nonsense. As your human friend, I can tell you I have full confidence in you. I know it is hard to remember, but you are the future Queen of the Elves; you rank higher. I read it in Ironwood's books, so it must be true. Now stand up so I can see what shoes will be best."

They tried three pairs before settling on three-inch silver pumps, with straps wrapping around the ankle twice. The doorbell rang. Jill ran down to answer it, giving Mara time to collect herself. Calmly, she arranged the velvet cloak and picked up the gift. She did not have practice in super high heels, but she felt an added sense of balance and grace as she nearly floated down the stairs.

"Goodbye, Jill, and thanks. Don't wait up; we will be partying until dawn."

Tears filled Jill's eyes, "Oh, it is like sending you off to the prom. This is so special, let me take a picture!" Jill went to the study and grabbed one of Mara's cameras. "Come, stand in front of the fireplace! I wish Aerrvin were here."

Mara complied and posed for Jill, not at all confident that any would be in focus, Jill's photo skills could use some improvements.

"Thanks, Jill, I will have some pictures taken by Gareth," Mara said, taking the camera with her.

Mara composed herself as she rode the short distance to Aerrvin's front drive. It was still daytime, but Mara noticed tiny Christmas lights twining through the foliage in preparation for the celebration which would begin at dark and continue into the following evening.

Another car pulled away, so Mara took her time exiting the car to give the previous guest space to be welcomed. Bronwyn walked her to the front door and opened it. Aerrvin stood there in the foyer waiting for her arrival. It appeared she was last to arrive, was that planned? She didn't know.

With Aerrvin guiding her around the garden room, she relaxed and greeted each guest confidently. She knew more than half of the guests already. Gareth, Jaera, and Ironwood with Lorelei, of course. But Morthe and Dougie of all people were there! As were four of her six Attendants. In time, the four people she did not recognize were introduced to her by Aerrvin.

"Mara, this is a distinguished guest of mine, Balmoral ap Drew, the finest musician in all the realms; he is spending his retirement as a librarian in Tacoma." Aerrvin nodded a respectful bow.

Balmoral in return nodded a slightly deeper bow to Mara as he took her hand. "I am so pleased to meet you, child, it has been an honor for me to edit your stories as they are sent in to me."

This caught Mara off guard. "What stories—oh, you mean I have a Chronicler too?"

Balmoral nodded, and Aerrvin's eyes sparkled. "How many more beings are trailing? Have I no privacy?" She nearly shouted, but she saw the looks and calmed down before the others closed in to hear her complaints.

Aerrvin soothed her arm, removing her hand from Balmoral's. "Get used to it Mara, it is part of being Royal. You have experience ignoring them all these years, now use that skill, bring it back except keep the belief. You have accommodated to Sylvie being at your beck and call. True?" Aerrvin gentled her with his silky, rich voice.

"True," Mara replied. "Sorry, Balmoral, that was rude of me. I should love to hear your music. You will be playing tonight won't you?" Mara asked, taking Balmoral's hand back. She thought he was such a dear looking old man.

Balmoral's eyes twinkled with delight. "Yes, of course, I never get invited anywhere unless I agree to play!" He chuckled, with Aerrvin and Mara joining in— if slightly delayed.

"Balmoral you are always welcome in my home," Aerrvin added after their mirth subsided. "Ah, I see my parents are about to enter. Come this way, Mara."

A chime sounded, beckoning guests to turn to the far entrance.

Bronwyn intoned: "We are pleased to announce, Her Royal Highness, Princess Harmony ap Rose, heir to the Rose Crown and her beloved Culain, future Consort to the Crown. They entered and walked to the left, towards the waterfall where a display of cushioned chairs sat arranged in a half circle on a short dais.

Mara assumed they were for the musicians when she first saw them. She bowed as did all the guests. Not a deep bow, but humbly respectful, she copied Aerrvin.

Bronwyn continued, "Her Royal Highness, Laurel ap Rose of the Rose Crown; King Jasper ap Rosewin, Consort to the Crown; and our beloved Brand the Bright."

There were whispers among some of the other guests and miniature spectators, which Mara just noticed at that point, peeking from the foliage. Mara supposed they were not expecting him. Indeed, she found herself surprised as well.

Evidently, he was on equal footing, being a King in exile of a sort. Nevertheless, King, he was. Had he been with his Queen he would have been placed above the Fairies altogether.

Aerrvin took Mara's elbow and guided her gracefully slow towards the dais. "Mara, I am sorry I did not have time to introduce you to the remaining guests, it will have to wait. I will introduce you to Brand first, though I know you have met. I do not wish them to know your full identity just yet. I want them to approve of you as you. You understand, do you not?" He sounded sincerely worried. A tiny crinkle of pinched worry formed between his brows.

Mara felt compassion for his nerves and determined to win them over on her own merit. "Of course, I do. I must say you look fantastic. I have not had the chance to tell you."

Aerrvin beamed just a bit brighter. He had chosen silk tuxedo slacks with a deep purple slash down the pant leg, extra-long, so they puddled appropriately at his feet. He wore a silk shirt, in deepest plum, unbuttoned up top so she could see the pulse of his heart in the hollow of his neck. The sleeves were full, and the cuffs folded back in points, held together with large diamond and silver cufflinks. He wore a large ring on his right hand, which Mara had never seen him wear before. His hair had been smoothed back into a sleek queue, tied with a jaunty silver string bearing silver bells on the tips, barely heard above the hum of the room in its silence. Mara realized that all eyes were on her.

"Your Highness, may I present my intended, Mara Lilyana Jamis."

Mara had been so intent on meeting the parents that she forgot she had not seen Brand since the night she fainted. Being this close, she once again shook with recognition as she saw her father's face, deftly drying her tears with her will, she bowed low giving herself time to recuperate.

"Your Highness, it is my greatest pleasure to be in your presence."

☘☘☘☘

Harmony controlled her smirk at Mara's fawning. She knew it was not her fault, she had never met Royalty before. The girl had truthfully honored Brand with her deep bow, as was fitting for the King. They had just learned of his tragic news and had sworn to offer their help in recovering the Queen.

Though, Brand said she had already transferred her power to their great-great-great-granddaughter, thereby making him no longer the King. It would be complete when they crowned the Heir to the Crystal Throne on the next quarter Holiday. Harmony gave Mara points for beauty and style; she actually looked like Brand's daughters. *No wonder he replied as he did.*

☘☘☘☘

Brand responded, "Thank you, my daughter. The pleasure is mine."

Mara needed to release a pocket of Light, in addition to her hankie, in order to quell her shaking. She hoped it was not rude, but she thought it better to shine than to tremble. Appearing weak was not acceptable. Rising gracefully, she turned her attention to Laurel. Aerrvin introduced her, and Mara again bowed, though not so deeply, yet deeper than she had when Harmony made her entrance.

This bowing thing is tricky, she thought. Then smoothly, in her whispery voice, she proclaimed, "Your Highness, it is a pleasure to be sure. Now I see where Aerrvin received his good looks." She smiled gently as she received a delighted laugh in return.

Addressing Aerrvin, the Queen said, "Aerrvin, you told me she had no experience at court! She's a natural." Then turning to Mara, she said, "You will need to sit close to me at dinner, Mara, you are such a delight."

Once again, she bowed after introductions to Jasper. He sported a decidedly mischievous look, much like Aerrvin's at his worst.

Mara said, "It is my pleasure to meet you, sir."

269

"Please call me Jasper, 'tis my name." He smiled merrily, causing a laugh to escape Mara's control.

"We are getting a little long here, so let me introduce Harmony, my sister, and her husband Culain," Aerrvin continued, deftly slighting them.

Mara smiled as warmly as she could. "Harmony, I am pleased to meet you. I look forward to getting to know you, and you as well, Culain. She bowed to the air between them, rather than twice, hoping she was not insulting them.

Taking her elbow, Aerrvin explained to his family, "Now, if you will excuse us, I have not introduced Mara to the rest of my guests."

The last three were Fairies, instead of Elves, the proportion of Elves to Fairies was rather Elf heavy before the royal party had arrived. Now Mara saw it was mostly even except for Dougie and Morthe. As they were walking toward the cluster of Fairies, Mara asked, "What is Dougie doing here? He seems to know Grandpa!"

"Ah, that is a story for him to tell. Rest assured he is not shocked by any of this." Aerrvin waggled his finger at her as he looked her in the eyes. "Mara, I am pleased to introduce you to my former teacher, Master Groban. He would never miss my Birth Day, would you, sir?"

Master Groban bowed, "Never, as long as you serve the famed Rose Elixir." He grinned. Taking Mara's hand, he said, "I can see why he would give up his wild and wily ways. You are a fit companion, my dear. I hope you have patience. He can try the stoutest soul." He laughed, patting Aerrvin on the back, turning him so he could introduce Mara to the two other Fairies standing there.

Two beautiful girls; Mara found their beauty striking, but then pulled back some of her awe as she realized they wore extra Fairy Dust. Somehow, she was able to resist its draw when she realized it was there. Aerrvin introduced them as Seanna and Talitha.

"Two old friends who would never miss a party of mine, they have lived in the Hoh Rain Forest with me these past several years." He smiled playfully at them, and they kissed him in unison on each cheek. Then turned and did the same for Mara.

"You are lovely, Mara, we can't wait to get to know you," Seanna said.

Talitha added, "Yes, and we can't wait to tell all on Aerrvin." They tittered and went off to meet up with Harmony.

Aerrvin turned to Mara, "Well, that is everyone. Actually, all of my Fairy Ring from the Forest is here, they simply were not invited to dinner. I invited all the Rings throughout the Pacific Northwest. So as the night progresses, we will have guests in and out, as it suits them. Tonight will be grand!"

Mara smiled warmly at Aerrvin, "If I were a Fairy I would probably have been White; I would have hidden in that little alcove behind the waterfall."

Aerrvin responded in kind, ". . . and I would have sat with you."

26

Glory

spiraling inward ~ pathways familiar

beyond the dark abyss

deeper I roam

finding my home ~ my magical fairy tale bliss

~ Mara Lilyana Jamis

May 22, 2009

Dinner was superb as expected. Queen Laurel sat at the head with Aerrvin to her right and Mara to her left. Next to Mara sat Harmony with Culain beside her. Across from them next to Aerrvin sat Jasper, then Ironwood and next to him was Lorelei. Mara did not pay attention to who else sat where, except she noticed Dougie sat on the end with Brand the Bright, who was sitting at the foot of the table. Reminding herself that she needed to get his story, she put the thought aside as she got pulled into the conversation around her.

"So tell me, Mara, what are you studying at your college?" Harmony asked.

"Photography. I graduate June fifth, so I am nearly done," Mara replied. "Woo! Hoo!" she added not too loudly, yet gaining raised eyebrows from those close enough to hear and eyewinks from Aerrvin and Jasper simultaneously. She blushed, her first of the evening—spilling sparkles all over her lovely dress. She decided to ignore them and let them lie as they would.

"What were your favorite subjects of study, Harmony?" Mara asked, having no idea what subjects were taught at the Academy.

Harmony brushed her hair behind her shoulder, scattering small sparkles as she did so.

"I preferred philosophy and still seek it out, actually. Also, I like gardening; it soothes me." Harmony always gave those answers, as she found it impressed people if they saw her as well rounded. She was ever the diplomat, trying to curry favor, rather than trying to help two sides meet in the middle. She did indeed mean to rule as an autocrat, but she was sure they would find her fair and pleasant. It pleased her too that she would rule over Aerrvin one day. It rankled that it seemed her parents favored him, always allowing him to flit about at will, doing as he pleased. Meanwhile, she had to have a strict watch kept over her, with so many rules of court to follow. Harmony patted Culain's hand absently.

Mara kept the conversation going by asking, "Really, which philosophy has the most adherents?"

This was going to be less boring than Harmony thought. She doubted the youngling would be able to grasp the concepts so she would go easy on her as she explained them, but she felt it should provide some distraction against the mundane.

"A favorite among those in the classes I attended was the idea of no afterlife for animals. Actually, it was evenly split; that is why it was so hotly contested. Proponents say that since animals cannot reason and speak as we do, then surely they have no spirit to be returned to anyplace at all."

Mara was aghast at such a thought, "That is pure nonsense! Of course, animals have spirits! Surely, you could not agree with such a nonsensical thought? Aerrvin, what is your stand on this philosophy?" Mara could not imagine anyone at this table willing to accept such an absurd idea.

Aerrvin took his time to swallow and wash down his food with a sip of his apricot nectar. Looking serious for a change, while still wildly attractive he said, "I have always asserted that I should agree with whoever is in charge of the conversation." Cracking a smile, he gained a slap on the back from his chortling father.

Mara threw him a sharp glance while she smiled anyway and continued, "Then you shall have to agree with me. I certainly do *not* believe that animals do *not* have spirits. A spirit is what animates the body. It is far too simple a concept for big thinkers to grasp I know, but there you have it. For any being to live, it must be infused with a spirit. That spirit cannot come from thin air, it comes from somewhere; therefore, when it leaves its inanimate body it must return to Him who made it, and if He doesn't want them back, then they still have an afterlife because a spirit cannot cease to exist. It simply is and cannot be unmade!" Mara realized that her voice had risen somewhat, and everyone was looking at her.

"Well, can you refute it?" Mara concluded.

Laurel applauded, and the rest followed her example, Mara could not tell if it was in agreement or merely good form to do as the Queen did. Yet her grandpa beamed at her, as did Aerrvin; she would count it as an argument well presented.

Harmony replied, "No, I do not refute it. Clearly, that was succinctly well said. Two points for you." Harmony was pleasantly surprised and not afraid to give praise when it was rightly earned.

Button arrived and confidently presented the dessert, brought in on four trays, she describe the tasty confection being placed before them. "I trust you have enjoyed your dinner. To complete the meal, I present a sweet berry tart, lightly sprinkled with sugar served with crème fraiche. If you would like we have additional berry sauce for you to apply on the side. Please, enjoy."

Laurel wished to know more about Mara's background as Aerrvin had not discussed much with her. "Mara, do you have any siblings?"

"Yes, I have a step-brother and two half-sisters. They live in a small town on the peninsula," Mara replied.

"Does your father live out there too?" Jasper asked.

"No, my father was in a sailing accident in the Sound and has never been seen since. I was eleven when it happened; my Mother moved to Sequim shortly after that." Mara was still touchy about that subject, but unless someone wore a Ware Spell, they would not know how deeply it troubled her. Aerrvin for one knew and tried to steer the conversation elsewhere.

"Mara has a roommate who is an excellent cook; she has been teaching me how to make breakfast."

Harmony and Culain both broke out in laughter. Harmony said airily, "Oh, Aerrvin. That is the last thing I would have thought you would wish to learn. To what purpose? Do you plan to send Button away?"

Mara could not tolerate the belittling of Aerrvin. "He does it because it pleases me." She smiled at him, thinking of their private joke. Receiving his knowing look in return, she continued, "Do you not do a thing, however, trivial, solely to please Culain?"

Harmony glowed a little brighter. Laurel intervened before she could answer, or perhaps to prevent her first response. "I have. Mara, let me tell you a secret, which is not so secret. Jasper loves anything sharp. He collects knives and spears as well as thorns, splinters, and nails. Every Christmas I give him a new and unique pokey. It makes him happy, which gives me the ultimate satisfaction."

She patted Aerrvin's hand, and Aerrvin patted his father's hand, in effect passing it on. Mara noted it with a slight twitch of her brow. She thought it was sweet and smiled softly. Looking up and noticing Ironwood smiling at her made her feel wonderful. *Life is good.* She turned to hear Harmony's response.

Harmony was still glowing, Mara noted that she did indeed have a slight yellow cast to her sparks. Rather than shooting out and away the way she had seen Aerrvin's do from his wings, Harmony's sparks were spiraling out of her hair and fingertips and then fizzling. It was very dramatic and quirky; Mara could not help but smile.

Harmony was very well aware of the effect her spitting sparks had on people, so she ignored them, pretending that she was not firing off in every direction. "Now that you mention it, I do have a trivial thing I do for Culain, which makes him happy. I design his clothes. Though usually, we prefer the less-is-more approach." She shot a mildly malicious grin at Aerrvin.

Despite the rivalry between the siblings Mara could not help but recognize the similarities between them, as Aerrvin obviously loved to dress Mara. And they sought any occasion to belittle the other. Certainly not something Mara was used to, but she could tell they also loved each other in their own way.

Jasper decided to get Ironwood into the conversation. "So, Ironwood, I understand you are newly married, what do you do for your lovely new bride?"

"Well," he scratched the top of his nose lightly before thinking of something, "I guess I do not have any wacky ideas. I give her flowers and—well, I allowed her family to move into my big old house!" He turned and smiled sweetly at Lorelei, gaining a blush in return.

Mara realized that making Fair Ones blush was a game. She was not sure how she felt about that yet. She thought it might be fun to get Gareth to blush. *But how?*

Aerrvin felt Mara thinking mischievous thoughts, and it intrigued him. Noting that everyone had finished, besides Morthe, he invited them to join him in the gardens to view the sunset.

❋❋❋❋

Mara found Ironwood and Aerrvin both waiting to walk with her to the garden.

Ironwood hugged her and told her how proud he was of her, "You handled the delicate dance of family politics remarkably well, Mara. One would think you had been raised in a family of ten. Aerrvin, I am so pleased to be here. I am honored. I have tried for years to gain an audience with your mother, but it never seemed to work out. She is every bit as delightful as has been reported."

They spoke companionably as they made their way to a perfect vantage point for viewing.

When Mara saw the setting sun, she remembered her camera and her promise to get pictures. "Aerrvin, do you think they would mind if I took pictures, or do I need to ask first?"

"You should ask first."

"Okay, but catch Gareth, I told Jill I would have him take our picture."

Two female Fairies flocked Gareth as well as one of Mara's attendants, Jasmine. He was setting out an electric guitar and explaining that he had written a song for Aerrvin's present. Jaera was off on the other side of the Garden, flirting with Clay, who had not been at the dinner at all. Mara surmised that he had been outside keeping the garden clear of Orange and Yellow Fairies.

Suddenly she realized that Morvayne would have heard of Aerrvin's party since invitations were sent everywhere. He would know that he had been tricked. Mara felt panic rising as she began imagining what he might do.

"Mara, what is it?" Aerrvin scanned the yard and saw nothing amiss. "Mara, sweetness, look— nothing will happen tonight. You are worried about Morvayne, yes?" He held her to him, calming her trembling knees. "I took a calculated risk and concluded that he will be terrifically angry, but will not be able to make a move for tonight. I promise you are safe. We are surrounded by the strongest and the Brightest." He paused and smiled confidently, "As well as a massive bubble of protection over the entire property. No one with malicious intent can even get in the yard. Come, let's get our pictures taken before the sun sets too low."

After obliging Mara and Aerrvin, Gareth allowed the ephemeral young maidens to follow him as he went about taking pictures of guests who were willing to have him do so. Balmoral began to play as the sun settled in golden magnificence. Standing from the center of the garden on a terraced hill, allowing a higher perch, Mara could now see all the little Fairies gathering for the real party as they sat among the trees and hid in the cool greens of the garden.

Right before the sun went below the horizon, Aerrvin called for everyone's attention. Mara saw that glasses had been set out on banquet tables and bottles of Rose Elixir were being poured. A whole table filled with the tiny bottles and glasses were tended by Calico and Gingham in their natural five-inch state. Two trays were prepared for Mara and Aerrvin's upsized guests.

"As you know, I love sunsets as much as I love myself." Everyone chuckled at his ability to speak the truth. "I wish to add a third love into my life," Aerrvin took Mara's hand and kneeling gracefully before her, he asked her publicly to marry him. "Mara, I had hoped to propose to you like this from the moment you spoke to me." Taking the ring from his pocket, he said, "Mara, I would be honored if you would consent to be my wife. Will you?"

Mara should have known this was coming, but she was caught unaware after all. The ring was not hard to see, as the dark of dusk had not yet occurred. There were hardly any clouds at all in the sky, which still held a deep blue in the east, fading to a white gold before it met with the fiery blaze of the sun. Mara saw that the ring was made to represent a rose wrapping around her finger, and the stone was larger than any she would have ever thought to wear. Yet looking at it on her long slender finger, she could only see perfection. After only a small hesitation, she hugged him and whispered softly, "Of course, I will."

Aerrvin announced for all to hear, "She said, yes!"

Cheers and congratulations were offered, as the music began anew and the Rose Elixir was distributed. Dancing ensued, and Mara allowed herself to be floated around the garden in the graceful arms of Aerrvin. After an appropriate interlude, others began cutting in to offer congratulations.

Jasper danced as smoothly as Aerrvin and barely looked older, perhaps thirty. "I am pleased with Aerrvin's choice in a bride; it has been quite some time since we have mixed our family with non-Fairies. Our pride caused us to think it unnecessary, as we sought only the most beautiful. But you prove that we can incorporate beauty with strength of character. I wish to offer a blessing on your future children: May they have your beauty and Light all the days of their lives."

Jasper then kissed Mara on the top of her head, making her feel truly loved and accepted.

"Thank you, Jasper; how kind of you to offer."

Jasper was perplexed, "Mara, you are so well poised for one who has been newly awakened. I have met other Human half-breeds if you will, and they took forever to accept the new ways being opened before them. How have you been able to cope?"

Mara knew Aerrvin wanted to keep her status secret, but she could not see why. She waffled on what she should say. "Hmm, my life has probably not been as ordinary as other—what did you say, 'half-breeds'? That is archaic, sorry. Anyway, I realize Aerrvin did not introduce my grandfather to you as such, but he is here tonight and has been a strength to me." Mara paused.

Jasper took the opportunity to interject, "Truly, your grandfather is here? Who is he, was he at dinner?"

Mara smiled at his interest. "Yes, my grandfather is Ironwood. He has not been around much as he travels with his studies. Of course, I did not know what his studies were. As my birthday is approaching, he planned to begin the process of awakening me. But Aerrvin beat him to it." Mara smiled.

"But why were you asleep? Why were you kept in the dark, if your grandfather knows who he is; why is it you did not?" Jasper danced near the pool; Mara could see all the lights dancing off the water as it rippled in the breeze.

"It really is complicated, but the short story is that my father knew, but when he disappeared my mother threatened Grandpa with never being able to see me if he could not stop speaking of magical things. So I had been in a gentle training up to age eleven, but after that, my mother pressured me to deny any truth I witnessed." Mara paused as Jasper spun her in a graceful twirl, then she asked, "I think Aerrvin told me that he told you about Sylvie; did he?"

"He said you still feed your Brownies. Is she a Brownie? I don't recognize the name."

"Yes, when I was three I could not say Celery, so I renamed her Sylvie. She has been with me ever since."

"I should expect so!" Jasper laughed. "Didn't your father explain to you about renaming Brownies? No? He should have told you that Sylvie would serve you for life, then you might have retained more alertness when he departed."

Mara was thankful that Jasper did not assume that her father was dead. As with Aerrvin, she did not know that Jasper used a Ware Spell. Therefore, he felt her gratitude and was touched anew by her grace.

"It must be hard growing into adulthood without your father. I am glad that Ironwood is here to help you. I sense more magic in you than I did him. Now, my dear, I know genetics can leave some children entirely without the spark, but I am gifted at sensing one's bloodlines. Mara, you have Water Sprite in you, but Ironwood does not. Is it from his first wife perhaps?"

"Oh my! You are full of surprises. Aerrvin should have known not to try to keep secrets!" Mara laughed delicately while blushing lightly, sparkles cascaded in a spiral as Jasper whisked her towards the garden once more. "Grandpa believes my mother is a Water Sprite, but she is weak and was left for Humans to raise; she was found on the steps of a church in California and shortly after that adopted. My father was an oceanographer when he met her, and they married within three months of having met. So yes, I guess I have more Faire blood than Human, in fact, if I have my genealogy right; I am a complete half Water Sprite, a very strong strain of Elf, and I even have a 1/32nd portion of a very solid Fairy. So really, I am barely Human at all!" Mara concluded with a theatrical sigh.

Jasper beamed down at Mara as the song ended. "Thank you, m' dear, for the delightful conversation. I look forward to speaking with Ironwood. He has suddenly become far more intriguing." He raised his eyebrows with a waggle reminding Mara of Aerrvin.

Where has he gone?

Mara caught sight of Aerrvin as he spun Jasmine off towards the pool. Then she saw Dougie as he was messing with his sound system, evidently set up for Gareth's song. She lifted her dress and swiftly caught up with him before he went inside.

"Dougie, wait up," Mara called. He stopped and smiled at her with a bob as she neared. "So . . . Aerrvin says you have an interesting story to tell. You don't seem surprised to see me here. So fess up, what's your story?"

Nodding slightly before he began, Mara realized he always did that. *He's been bowing to me all along!*

"Let's sit." Dougie led her to a wicker lounge set near the pool. "I am, as a matter of fact, a Brownie."

"No!" Mara breathed.

"True!" Dougie breathed in return, taking his normal tone he continued, "As you may or may not know when a Brownie is Transformed he can only be returned to normal by the one who transformed him. I have been a college student these past ten years because he who transformed me is lost."

Mara blinked tears away as the truth became apparent.

"Mara, I am your father's . . . Brentwood's personal assistant. I have maintained my home across from Tigerlily's house since she bought it for me. I know he still lives, as I can feel a connection; I have not been released from his service. Frequently, Brownies will move on when their Masters die or Fade. I am still stuck. Therefore, he lives."

Tears coursed down Mara's face as she suddenly jumped up and pulled Dougie into a hug. *Why didn't Grandpa say he had proof?* Others had been watching and now came to her side. Ironwood with his wife, and even Brand the Bright.

✳✳✳✳

Harmony and her mother Laurel watched. Harmony sniffed, "She is unquestionably moody."

Laurel looked at her daughter with an arched brow. "You are a fine lass to be talking about moods! But yes, I do wonder what that was all about. Aerrvin said the Brownie lives across the street from her. She seems a dear, though, perhaps we should go sit with her."

281

The Queen led the way, and a petulant Harmony followed, looking about to see where Culain had gone off to. Harmony spied him talking with Gareth and Jaera. She knew Jaera was flirty, but only because she wished to gain Gareth's attention. Culain was safe then.

Brand sat next to Mara, and each seemed to beam a bit brighter; perhaps it was the darkness settling. Laurel thought she saw a resemblance in them. *Mara could be a twin to Tigerlily,* she realized with a sudden shock, *no wonder Brand appears to be so fond of her.* Laurel felt pity for poor Brand having lost all his daughters and now his wife and kingdom. *Let him find peace,* she thought.

"Mara, have you enjoyed the music? Isn't Balmoral's skill divine?" Laurel asked.

Mara had recovered, and Brand had dried her tears with a warm glow. She knew she was radiant, but it felt so good she didn't care. Smiling broadly she declared, "Yes it is. I have enjoyed this evening so much, I look forward to the real party too. I understand formality ends? Aerrvin referred to it as 'midnight madness.' Is it truly chaos, or can he maintain some sense of control?"

Laurel smiled, impressed with her future daughter-in-law's inquisitiveness. "Yes, it will become wild, but as a Royal Heir he will always have a modicum of control, as well as being the current homeowner, one can always expel them with a wish and a simple wave of the hand." Laurel demonstrated the wave without the wish.

Harmony added, "You will learn all these things by and by I am sure. Do you plan on attending the Academy in Ireland, France, or elsewhere?"

"I have not thought about it yet. I will seek wise counsel and get back to you." Mara smiled politely. "How long did you study?"

This was a touchy subject for Harmony; she realized she should not have brought it up. Slow spiraling sparks escaped as she tried to maintain control, she felt a need to add a little Silver to soothe her Yellow tendencies, hoping her mother would understand. Glowing brighter, she stopped most of the sparks and calmly replied, "I attended the Academy in Ireland for fifty years, then tried France for thirty. But I found I preferred Ireland's teachers better, so I returned and stayed another twenty years." She sniffed and then added, "Of course, I still study as the mood suits me, you know, or perhaps you don't, but we Fair Ones are ever pursuing knowledge."

Most serious students finish their formal schooling in eighty years. Harmony's temper prevented her from grasping concepts, more than her actual skill or mental ability; she hated to admit her failings, so she pretended it was her love of school that kept her there. None dared contradict, not even her mother.

The music settled to a sweet lullaby, and the dancing ceased as the guests all found seats. Most were gathered around Mara as Aerrvin directed more settees to be placed near hers.

"Welcome, friends," Aerrvin said as the lullaby ended and went on to echo the whispering wind. "I am so pleased all of you have chosen to attend my party. I will accept my gifts now; you may place them in the baskets provided."

Bronwyn set three large baskets in front of Aerrvin. A line of glowing Fairies appeared as they left the trees and greenery, some even arrived from inside. Mara assumed they had been in the garden room, perhaps they had been swimming. One by one they bowed and dropped a gem or precious metal into the baskets, sometimes minted, sometimes raw nuggets. More often than not, he received a feather, the soft downy ones being the predominant choice. When one basket was completely full, Bronwyn covered it to prevent them from blowing away. Aerrvin looked longingly at the basket, and Mara smiled, remembering lessons on plopping. It seemed only a moment, and the magical light parade ended.

Then the Brownies gently arrived and offered their own gifts, their numbers were smaller as most only sent a representative from their clans. They offered shoes and clothes, all in miniature, of course, they fit in the baskets easily. Some offered wooden carvings and jewels; Brownies are varied in their talents.

Next, the Elves invited to dinner as well as Mara's other attendants offered their gifts. Most were wrapped, requiring Aerrvin to open them. He waited until they sat down. Ironwood gave him a leather strap with a small, carved wooden medallion. Aerrvin tied it around his neck in thanks. The ornament was flat and rested below his suprasternal notch. Mara was curious to see what was carved on it.

Clay presented a particularly fine knife, gaining nods of approval from Jasper as his eyes gleamed with a desire to handle it. Aerrvin passed it around, allowing Jasper his wish. Hannah provided a belt and case, so when the knife returned, he strapped it on. Mara was beginning to see that it was tradition to put on the gifts offered during this portion. Obviously, he could not put on all of the Brownie gifts. It would be taxing even; especially if all nineteen dinner guests brought apparel. Fortunately, not all gifts were things to put on.

Morthe presented a book and the Fairy girls from his Ring each offered a massage before the night was done. Mara was not sure she liked that one, especially the way he smiled at them in thanks. Jaera kissed him soundly and promised to never leave him, and Gareth said he would present his song with Dougie and the others he had gathered for his band, after the main event. That left the royal party as well as Brand and Mara.

Mara wanted to be last, as she was sure hers was the most glorious, but all eyes turned to her, so she reached into the air and plucked out her gift from the entry table where she had left it. She walked over to Aerrvin, curtsied humbly, and offered the gift on her open palm. He took her hand and scooted over on his seat making room for her to join him. He stroked the silk ribbon, taking his time opening the gift.

"Hurry up already," Gareth called musically, "it's nearly time!"

Aerrvin lifted the lid and breathed in, in wonder. "Mara! This is a Dragon shed!" Slipping the bracelet on his wrist, he asked, "Where did you manage to find it? Hannah, you still have yours, yes?"

Hannah revealed arms covered in oily swirls. Aerrvin looked at Mara again, "Mara, you went before a Dragon? *And* returned on the same day?"

Mara smiled happily, pleased to see he liked it. "Yes, Aerrvin, I saw Hannah's and knew it would please you."

Suddenly he erupted, confusing Mara. "Don't ever do that again! Mara, you need to be careful. How could you endanger yourself that way…?"

Mara lost her cool, "Here I thought I was giving you a gift you would be pleased with. I had my Attendants with me, as well as Seamus. If Hannah could talk to a Dragon, then why couldn't I?"

Mara realized that her Attendants were now flanking her, as she stood before Aerrvin chastising him. But she was not yet spent. Mara had more to say even as she realized she was truly losing control. "You know, Aerrvin, I was afraid to meet Meriel especially when Hannah told me that her young were only forty years old. But how was I to know what was an acceptable gift for a prince? I would do anything for you, trust me. Besides, Meriel was delightful, she gave me three sheds, in fact, as well as granting a desire for Seamus and Clay—," remembering her mistake with the ring dampened her fury, she looked around to see everyone bowed on their knees, faces down, again.

She crumpled her face into a pout as she realized she had ruined Aerrvin's surprise as well as his Birth Day.

Aerrvin, for once, had not bowed but had kept his eyes on hers. He marveled in her beauty, but far more, he gloried in her Light, especially now that he wore the Dragon shed. Seeing her face turn to a pout, caused his compassion to swell.

"Mara—now, Sweet Pea, please don't cry! It's okay."

He took her in his arms and held her tight and then kissed her, not caring who saw, though he knew few dared to look. "Mara, you are blinding everyone again." His lips twitched against hers.

She blushed furiously as he laughingly collected the dust with his breeze. She tucked away two of the pockets of Light. *Everyone knows. Why should I hide it now?* she thought defiantly.

Aerrvin soothed, "That is better, Mara, maybe one more pocketful? I did not mean to yell at you, please forgive me. I was afraid for you, which was silly since you apparently returned triumphant. I will trust your Attendants to know how to care for you. I am, after all, a mere Fairy."

Mara did not seem to be able to respond, so Aerrvin went to his knees as well. He broke eye contact and bowed his head. "Please, Mara; I thank you for your gift. I will keep it with me always."

Seeing Aerrvin groveling snapped her out of whatever held her. "Aerrvin, all of you, please rise. I am so sorry. You know I am just a baby at this.

I *am* learning control, really, I am, but for some reason—I don't know. Brand, can you explain, please?"

Brand stood and with a respectful nod, faced the group and explained Mara's relationship as well as Ironwood's and their pending Quest to free Gwennara and possibly Brentwood. He dared not hope Arianna was there, so he did not mention her.

"Mara is to be crowned Queen of the Crystal Throne on the day of her Birth, even Midsummer's day. She will only be twenty-one, but having lived those years as a Human, she is nearly as wise as any Fair One at the age of One hundred-fifty." Then grinning broadly he said, "Now that the cat is out of the bag, let me welcome Aerrvin heartily to my family; it will be wonderful for all of us to continue the beautiful relationship Gwennara and I have built between Fairies and Elves. Ah, such joy! To have a second Fairy married to the Queen of all the Realms."

Brand glowed as bright as Mara did with three of her pockets loosened as he hugged Aerrvin and kindly shook hands with Jasper. He kissed Queen Laurel's hand, bowing slightly to Harmony, before taking his seat.

Aerrvin resumed his jaunty self, pretending nothing had occurred. "Well now, I guess I have time for a few more gifts before I present myself to the world. Harmony, Culain what do you have for me?"

Harmony was steaming inside, knowing that Aerrvin would be raised in rank above her. *'Tis not fair!* She knew her parents would continue to fawn all over him, and now Mara too. But Mara's Brightness had truly shaken her, and she could not even shoot a single spark. So with seeming grace and calm, she offered Aerrvin a gift with Culain by her side; they each bowed to Aerrvin.

"'Tis from both of us, it took us some time to create it, we hope you enjoy it." It was a blown glass sculpture on a carved wooden base. The glass flowed from purple to white with sparkles of silver and gold in tiny veins throughout.

"Harmony, Culain, thank you. It is beautiful. I know exactly where I want to put it, really, I thank you." Aerrvin beamed. "Brand, do you have an additional gift?" Aerrvin asked, hugging Mara about her shoulders, causing laughter.

"I do," Brand declared, standing once again. He pulled from the Light; a sword. "For your pending journey in our Quest. May it always protect you from the Dark."

Jasper rose next, "Son, had I known of your future plans I would have prepared a more suitable gift. Please accept this gift with my love and blessings of protection." He offered a gift encased in a silver box. Inside was a set of three throwing knives.

Aerrvin protested, "But, Father, these are your favorite throwing knives!"

"Aye, and you are my favorite son; please use them in good health!" He smiled but looked somber as he thought upon the dangers he felt were in store.

Finally, Queen Laurel ap Rose stood regally to confer upon her son his gift, only minutes remained before the time of his birth. She had sat there recalling the moment of glory when her newborn son had entered the world. A sweet little Purple, she knew he would bring her joy all the days of her life. And now he would be King of all the Realms! She was so proud of him. A tear slipped down her face as she caressed his.

"My dearest son, how I have gloried in your Light! Please accept my simple gift, it was chosen as was Mara's, meant purely to please."

She handed him a crocheted coverlet made from the softest spider web silk and crocheted in the most delicate manner. Aerrvin rubbed it on his cheek the same as he had as a baby and offered a delighted smile of gratitude and then hugged her. "Thank you, Mother, it is perfect, as always."

Balmoral's gift was his music, causing it to crescendo to a new height as the midnight hour drew near. Aerrvin moved the group as they followed him to stand on the terraced hill once again.

Everyone hung back with expectation, waiting for Aerrvin to reveal his Light. Mara had thought she had seen it all, but he had somehow managed to hold some back—because now as he unfurled his wings in that glorious mix of Purple, White, and Silver, they shot out sparks of Blue showers on the hill, and all around he shone with a glorious golden glow. Most of the guests did not know about the new acquisition of power, so now there were oohs and ahhs of delight. Then once again, since he was *The Prince,* they all bowed for one minute. Once past the moment of his birth, the music started up again with reckless abandon. The real party had begun.

27

Midnight Madness

Me watching You

as Sun settles abed

Glorification of her descent

shines within Your eyes

~ Mara Lilyana Jamis

May 23, 2009

Mara had hopes of spending more time with Aerrvin, but seeing as he was the Birthday Boy, everyone wanted to talk to him. It took an hour before he slipped away. Mara spent the time talking with Clay, Jasmine, and Daisy.

She even let Clay talk her into dancing the minuet. With someone to guide, a girl can do just about anything. "Clay, why are you so aloof? You are pleasant enough company."

Inhaling deeply before replying, he said, "I have things to think about and socializing interferes." His tone was smooth, controlled. "I enjoy my fellow Elves from time to time. Fairies really are too excitable for me. You must remember I am quite old, I partied well enough in my youth. You should go along now and have your fun. I need to make a circuit of the perimeter again, my lady." He bowed away graciously.

Harmony came by with a Green Fairy whom Mara did not know. "Dancing the minuet is fun, but I think it is about time we gave up the old people music and hear what Gareth has written. I had a rock band at my wedding in 1999, and it was a blast. What do you say, Mara, want to go find Gareth with me?"

Mara agreed. They walked about in search of Gareth or Aerrvin supposing they were together. Most of the properly small Fairies had adorned themselves to look like insects or flowers; others had shed most of their attire all together, but as far as Mara could tell all those who were Elven/Human sized had maintained their decorum. She thought she could probably handle it as long as she did not shrink down or the ones her size did not shed their clothes.

As though reading her mind, Harmony asked, "Do you mind if I change my attire to suit the new music?"

Mara replied, "You mean to suit rock? No, that's cool. Did you see those pictures I took of Gareth with his hair all done up?" Mara smiled at the memory, not only the hair but the kittens.

"You took those? Those were lovely pictures. Have you seen the kittens since they opened their eyes?"

Harmony transformed her beautiful gown into a pair of torn black leggings and a barely-there pink and black diagonal striped top made of a fluttery fabric that would move nicely when she danced. Mara thought, *talk about old style! Harmony is already behind the times in what should be cool. I could create a better style than that. Ummmm—I don't think I'm going to like Culain's get up either.*

Mara answered the questions about the kittens first. "No, I have been so busy this week I have not even been in the servant quarters, let alone the nest." Harmony raised her brows, but Mara could not decipher if it meant anything. "And pictures are my passion, I adore photography. I intended to set up my studio this summer before all this happened. Now, I don't really have any plans. I guess I will simply bend with the breeze."

Mara decided to wear her armor like a catsuit with a slick black raincoat belted over it, it had quarter sleeves and came mid-thigh, so she also chose thigh high shiny purple boots. Hating to do it but with a relief of pressure she hadn't felt until she did so, she let her hair down, maintaining the butterfly braids at her temples. Finally seeing Aerrvin, she waved him over. Gareth was with him, as well as Dougie.

"Okay, Birthday Boy, it's time to get this party rockin'! We are tired of the soft and sweet, and even the jigs. Make Gareth deliver his present." Mara pouted prettily.

Aerrvin smiled. He liked the look she chose; *competition is good! Though it does not take much to improve oneself above Harmony, she is utterly hopeless among Humans.*

"Hey, you heard her, Gareth, let's get things hoppin'!" Aerrvin's attire became tight leather pants which laced up, matched with a dark purple muscle shirt; he extended his Dragon shed into full armor as well. It was the first time Mara had seen it up close. The swirls were larger than the ones on Hannah's suit, let alone her own. He looked like a bad boy covered in tattoos, albeit moving ones.

With a whoop, Gareth gathered his band and soon had everyone assembled. He announced his first song as the one written for Aerrvin. It had a great beat and was danceable. Soon everyone was dancing and joining in on the chorus. They asked for an encore. Complying, he then went on to play current alternative rock, as well as mixing in old classics from the 60s through the 90s, but only if they were totally cool.

Soon after the modern music started, the older Elves and Fairies began to depart. Ironwood, Lorelei, and Brand said their goodbyes, and then Queen Laurel with Jasper announced their desire to go to their rooms.

"It was a pleasure to meet you. I look forward to seeing you again tomorrow." Mara hugged each of them goodnight and then she was hustled off by Aerrvin to party.

"The music has gotten quite loud, do you have a sound barrier over the yard?" Mara asked belatedly.

"Yes, otherwise the police would have arrived hours ago— it is nearly 3 a.m."

A slow song ended, and Dougie switched to a CD so the band could have a little fun too. Aerrvin asked, "Do you want to go swimming in the pool? I never asked, but you do like swimming, don't you?"

"Yes! I like swimming, I am half Water Sprite, remember?" Mara answered with a halfhearted slap.

"Great, because I have a water course which should be pretty fun, but you have to go mini-sized." He looked expectantly as she surveyed the pool. Fifty or so Fairies cavorted in the water, most seemed about as dressed as could be found on any beach, albeit Caribbean ones for partiers.

"Okay, but I don't know how to transform myself." As she answered, he shrunk her down along with himself. He lost the rocker dude look and was now a beach boy with long white board shorts. He turned his armor into a short-sleeved diving suit—even adding a zipper and logo on his chest.

"Whoa! I didn't think of that. How did you do it? Does the zipper work?" Mara asked pulling it down to check.

Aerrvin shrugged, "I figured I could treat it like any other fabric, and it works. Only not anyone could work the zipper, Dragon armor only comes off if the owner wants it off." He arched an eyebrow and headed to the shallow end of the pool with a grin.

Grabbing a surfboard, he headed to the corner, where a moderately sized device created waves; about twelve Fairies at a time could surf. Two left as the prince and future queen arrived. Mara had removed her boots but was still trying to decide what swimsuit to wear. She really wanted to see what it felt like swimming in a Sea Dragon's skin, but she felt self-conscious, with so many others around.

Aerrvin solved her dithering by putting board shorts on her too. So she moderated her shed to look like a scuba suit like Aerrvin's and grabbed a board. She had only gone surfing twice before, and it had been years earlier, so she fell a few times, but she swiftly caught the feel of it. It helped that the wave machine made perfect waves.

Aerrvin challenged her to beat him on the obstacle course; he had built two identical water courses for racing, and they were challenging. Mara lost the first time, but she believed it was because he knew the course, so she challenged him to a second, and she beat him by twenty seconds. After that, she let others try; no one beat her time. She deflected thoughts that it was due to her station.

Swimming in the bodysuit was like slicing through Jell-O with a hot knife. An initial resistance and buoyancy could be felt, but once beneath the surface, it was like flying through the air. Mara found she could hold her breath for twenty minutes before feeling a need to surface. Later, she learned that the properties of the skin act like gills, adding oxygen to her own body, thus allowing the longer underwater time. In truth, she could stay under longer, but her mental conditioning would not allow her to stay below the surface longer than that.

※※※※

Before dawn, Aerrvin invited Mara to go for a ride in his car to watch the sunrise.

Realizing she had lost the shorts in the thrill of swimming, she added a slip of a dress as she left with Aerrvin in his Viper.

"How about we go to Colorado? There is a peak where the sunrise is always perfect."

Aerrvin whisked the car to a ledge barely big enough for them to get out.

"Aerrvin this is tight! What if I fall?"

293

"Mara, you should know how to fly by now; you have done it in your Dreams."

"I know, but I thought that was by your power. You mean, I just need to desire it, and it is so?" Mara asked. "Not by asking the neighbor? I mean if I was falling, I might be too afraid to remember to ask, you know."

"Yes, I do, my father pushed me off a tree limb when I was only five years old," Aerrvin replied with a rich laugh. Mara grabbed his arm to prevent him from doing the same. "I did not need to ask, it is the same as walking, you desire to go forward, and your legs take you forward same as flying. Come along then, do it on your own." Aerrvin stepped off the ledge and beckoned Mara to follow.

She knew it was silly, she had flown all over with him for days, and then with Hannah when she went to Italy. But her faith had been in the other's power not her own. Taking a breath, she leaped and went nowhere except forward, as she desired. With joy, she chased Aerrvin higher until they could see the first rays of dawn. Then they returned to the ledge and found Aerrvin's favorite spot; it was not ideal for full-sized people, so they resized.

"Did I resize myself or did you?" Mara asked cuddling closer in the mossy hollow.

"You did that too. Mara, you are not as helpless as you think. Or is it that you are only as helpless as you think? Either way, by the Light, you can do amazing things. Relax, let your mind go and make it so. Still, I thought I told you, but maybe not, flying full-sized takes up a lot of energy. We are going to be hungry from all that flying."

They stopped talking to watch the sunrise. Mara chose to watch the light appear on Aerrvin's face instead. She marveled at his fine features as the sun revealed them with ever-changing angles defined. His golden hair hung silkily, resting with a little flip upon each shoulder. The joy in his eyes thrilled Mara beyond measure. *Ah, my golden Mr. Sunshine.*

With the full sun shining, Aerrvin produced two granola bars and a small carton of chocolate milk. Mara found she was indeed hungry and ate, happily snuggled up to Aerrvin. She enjoyed the distinct smoothness of the armor he wore, but at the same time, she felt like she was touching his flesh, the same with her own armor; she could feel it, yet not. It was rather titillating trying to understand what she was feeling.

Aerrvin created a nest of feathers from the air and gathered Mara to him. Caressing her bare shoulder covered with the Dragon skin, he thanked her for the gift. "You have not yet told me the story of your Quest. Do you have the time or do you need to be at school?"

"School? What is school? I completely forgot about school. No, it's Saturday. You scared me, there. No school!"

Mara spent the morning telling Aerrvin about her Quest while he enjoyed her Dragon-skin-covered body.

The morning sky went from deepest purple to pinks and orange and glorious yellow gold until finally, the sun was fully up, shining in a brilliant blue sky with receding clouds moving ever eastward.

"I should go home and shower. And I should probably call Jill. She will be worried whether I told her to, or not." Mara sighed, untangling her hair from Aerrvin's fingers. "Do you want to teach me how to draw a line of light to—what is it called? Transport?" Mara asked.

Aerrvin chuckled, stretching his back and shoulders. "We call it Traveling. It is similar to what you have already been doing, except you need to be able to tap into the Land of Dreams, and then not actually step in, but think of your destination. Somehow in a way we have not discovered this creates the bend of light which you see when looking at another person doing it. When I look, I see the location as it is; that way I am not stepping in on someone when I do not wish to. Try it."

"So I can't accidentally get lost, or stuck in anything—like a wall?" Mara asked.

"No, the light is not actually slicing through anything, it is only creating a portal if you will. Portals can only be fashioned to put you in a place you have been before. You can take others with you, but they must be within reach, yet they do not need to be touching. Usually, we as Fairies prefer to Travel by air anyway, so we often pop out of one place into the air above the place we wish to be. It takes far more practice say—to move a car and have it land safely on a tiny ledge." Aerrvin offered a crooked smile of mischief. "Go on, try to get into the car," he urged.

Mara thought about being in the driver's seat, but it would not appear, so she thought about the passenger's seat, and a window opened. She stepped through and found she was indeed sitting in the soft leather seat. Suddenly the car was on a highway.

Mara turned and said, "I did it!" to Aerrvin.

Only Aerrvin was not in the driver's seat, Morvayne was. "Yes, you did, my Buttercup."

A Quick Reference Guide to the Faire Realms

In Order of Power and Importance

(Not an exhaustive list.)

Dragons – Chose to serve neither good nor evil. Therefore, they are free to serve either on a whim and are consequently revered as capricious beings.

Elves – Serve good. The Queen of all the Realms is precisely that. She rules and judges all magical beings. Elves can transform into anything.

Goblins – Serve evil. Live below the surface of the earth and are cousins as well as enemies to Brownies, Gnomes, and Dwarves.

Brownies – Serve good. Live below the homes of Elves and Humans. They are a servant class but are revered for all the good they do.

Fairies – Serve good. Wings are not physical appendages, rather they are holographic in nature and represent the qualities of each particular Fairy.

Red = Poetic. Orange = Loyal and temperamental. Yellow = Studious and often perfectionistic. Green = Wild and carefree. Blue = Sincere and great strategists. Purple = Playful. Silver = Nobility. Gold = Royalty. White = Singular focus and a need to withdraw. Black = An absence of conscience, only two have ever been recorded. Other winged beings are all related to Fairies but rank lower, some of these are **Aeries, Sprites, Nyads,** and **Dryads.**

Mermaids – Serve good. Limited powers, but they can still transform.

Others who chose evil include: **Kraken, Trolls,** and **Ogres.**

Characters in Books One and Two

Mara Lilyana Jamis at twenty years old is soon to graduate as a photography major. She has been raised to deny that the mystical world exists and lives among mere Humans.

Aerrvin ap Rosewin is a Fairy Prince sent to America by his parents to prevent squabbling between him and his sister **Harmony,** who is to become the new Fairy Queen when her mother steps down from the Rose Crown. Aerrvin has been given the Americas to create his own Kingdom.

Bronwyn of Clan MacIntash is a Brownie Chronicler. He is married to **Button**, and their children are **Gingham, Seamus,** and **Calico.** Seamus is a Chronicler in training and more often than not accompanies Aerrvin on his travels and exploits. Brownies are a servant class serving either a location or an individual.

Jill Beckett is Mara's renter/roommate. Jill is a chef. She watches out for Mara like a big sister; they are best friends.

Amanda Powers is Mara's mother. She remarried when Mara was young and moved from Seattle to Sequim, Washington, where Mara's stepfather owns and operates an electronics store. She very strictly frowns upon the mention of, and belief in magic.

Rick Powers Mara's stepfather. Father of **Ricky Powers** Mara's eighteen-year-old step-brother, as well as the father of Mara's half-sisters **Sarah** and **Becky**.

Ironwood ap Jamis is a wealthy professor and Mara's grandfather whom she loves but rarely sees. Father of **Brentwood Jamis** Mara's father who was lost at sea.

Gareth ap Rosewin is Aerrvin's cousin and bodyguard, chief of security and most importantly Aerrvin's Nest Mate and best friend. Fairies prefer to sleep in nests, so those with whom they sleep and choose as lifelong companions are called *Nest Mates.*

Jaera the Green another Nest Mate and best friend of Gareth and Aerrvin. They had two other female Nest Mates, but they do not go to Seattle for the adventures which follow.

Laurel ap Rose Fairy Queen of the Rose crown and Aerrvin's mother.

Jasper ap Rosewin Consort to Queen Laurel and Aerrvin's father.

Pastor Mike is Mara's pastor and also psychologist to whom she turns when she fears she is going mad.

John and Sarianne are very minor characters who are the youth pastors at Mara's church.

Dougie of Clan Byrne is the geek neighbor who lives across the street from Mara and Jill.

Sylvie of Clan Dunkirk is a Brownie. Her family has served the house Mara lives in since it was built in the 1800s. Her parents are **Duncan** and **Juniper**.

Gwennara Wallace is the Elven Queen of all the Realms and mother of the three princesses **Daffodil, Tigerlily**, and **Arianna.**

Brand the Bright is a Fairy. More importantly Brand is King Consort to Queen Gwennara, and father of the three princesses.

Morthe is an Ogre friend of both Ironwood and Clay.

Balmoral is a famed musician among the Fairies and all the magical Realms; he resides in Tacoma, Washington, living quietly while tending a library for the Fair Ones. He is quite old for a Fairy, well over 900 years of age.

Lorelei is Ironwood's second wife; she's a very shy Elf and is a naturalist, with a preference for study over interaction.

Rowan is Lorelei's sister.

Johann and Sasha are husband and wife, they are Fairies, and are the parents of rare twins named **Berry** and **Bright**.

Meriel is a Sea Dragon with three young Dragons at home in her cave. Dragons are neutral as far as good and evil, so they are best approached with caution.

Mirri Sihee is Aerrvin's constant companion, she is an Aerie or Wind Sprite.

Morvayne ap Stewart has chosen to serve evil. As an Elf, he ranks higher than Fairies, Brownies etcetera. He has had a major upset in his life, causing him to hate and despise Humans. He desires to cleanse the of two-thirds of its Humanity.

He is confident that the remaining people will come to worship and adore him as the King of the world. He chose Mara as his bride long before she ever learned about him and the world of the Faire.

Clay of Glennferry is Mara's Personal Protector and Attendant. He is a Hold Master, meaning he requested his friends to pledge fealty to him, and in return, he offered them a home for life. Mara comes to depend on Clay, and he commits to serving her as long as she needs him. He is excessively pale and thin. The other five Attendants are —

Hannah Thistlewite: second in command of the Queen's guard. She has blonde, billowy hair and wears Dragon armor.

Daisy du Lac: best friend of Princess Arianna. She has red hair and a fiery attitude to match.

Jasmine ap Weaver: fairly reclusive, yet loving. She has dark brown nearly black hair and looks like Audrey Hepburn.

Ivan Andiluv: owns a spaceship inherited from his parents. He grew up in space and was too shy to start school at the traditional age of twenty-one, so he is slightly older than his companions. He has red hair and keeps it short, an oddity among Fair Ones.

Elwood (The Mighty) Kildare is Mara's final Attendant among her appointed six. He is large for an Elf; most Elves are slight, but Elwood is broad and well-muscled. He has dark brown hair and an affinity with trees and Dryads.

A Genealogy

Gwennara ap Wallace + Brand the Bright

/ | \

Daffodil ap Wallace   Tigerlily ap Wallace   Arianna ap Wallace

(+ Jacques Jamis M. 1888) | |

/ | | | |

Son   daughter   Goldenrod   adopted daughter   son

/   / | \

(Human daughters)   / | \

Lily   Silas   Ironwood

/ \

Irene   Brentwood + Amanda

/ | \   / \

Mary Lynne   Jaimie   \   Sylvan   **Mara Jamis**

(3 more unnamed daughters)

Aerrvin's Family

Laurel ap Rose + Jasper ap Rosewin

/ \

Aerrvin ap Rosewin   Harmony ap Rose + Culain the White

ABOUT THE AUTHOR

M. Kari Barr has been accused of being a Fairy in disguise. In truth, she is a lover of fantasy and books in general. As the mother of eight children and nearly as many grandchildren, Kari has an affinity for all things make-believe. Growing up with a storyteller for a mother adds dimension to her experience, as does living in a log home…on top of a hill…surrounded by trees…in the middle of miles, and miles of wheat fields. Says she, "Solitude is lovely."

Once Again ~ Tales of Destiny is her debut novel with imaginative interpretations of old myths, legends, and folklore. Several more books in the series will follow.

Visit her website intangience.net

All of the Books in the Tales of Destiny Series

Once Again

And Again

(Release date 2019)

Of Love and Loss

(Release date 2019)

Triumph

(Release date 2020)

Future Books in the Series

Clay and Arianna: A Prequel

Arthur and Lilyaura: The Conclusion

Other Books by M. Kari Barr

Thinktacular Thoughts

They Came From the Sea

Rain on Me ~ Poetic Frenzy

Arcadium Autum Emporium ~ Tales of the Gatekeeper